Black Ops veteran Leo J. Maloney delivers a high-level thriller that spans the globe, changes the game, and raises the threat level to all-out, worldwide destruction . . .

## THREAT LEVEL ALPHA

They strike without warning, in key locations around the world. In Russia, a Soviet-era storage facility is raided by terrorists. In the Phillipines, an important international conference is under siege. In the United States, Dan Morgan is stalked by Russian agents. And at Berkeley, Morgan's daughter is kidnapped with other students and taken to a remote laboratory. The attacks are neither coincidental nor random. They are part of a carefully orchestrated plan by a new and merciless organization. As Zeta Division struggles to make sense of the international chaos, Dan Morgan races to stop a deadly biochemical weapon—one that Morgan's daughter is being forced to help build . . .

D1367516

**Highest Praise for Leo J. Maloney and his thrillers**

## Arch Enemy

"Utterly compelling! This novel will grab you from the beginning and simply not let go. And Dan Morgan is one of the best heroes to come along in ages."
**—Jeffery Deaver**

## Twelve Hours

"Fine writing and real insider knowledge make this a must."
**—Lee Child**

## Black Skies

"Smart, savvy, and told with the pace and nuance that only a former spook could bring to the page, *Black Skies* is a tour de force novel of twenty-first-century espionage and a great geopolitical thriller. Maloney is the new master of the modern spy game, and this is first-rate storytelling."
**—Mark Sullivan**

"*Black Skies* is rough, tough, and entertaining. Leo J. Maloney has written a ripping story."
**—Meg Gardiner**

## Silent Assassin

"Leo Maloney has done it again. Real life often overshadows fiction and *Silent Assassin* is both: a terrifyingly thrilling story of a man on a clandestine mission to save us all from a madman hell bent on murder, written by a man who knows that world all too well."
**—Michele McPhee**

"From the bloody, ripped-from-the-headlines opening sequence, *Silent Assassin* grabs you and doesn't let go. *Silent Assassin* has everything a thriller reader wants—nasty villains, twists and turns, and a hero—Cobra—who just plain kicks ass."
**—Ben Coes**

"Dan Morgan, a former black ops agent, is called out of retirement and back into a secretive world of politics and deceit to stop a madman."
—*The Stoneham Independent*

### Termination Orders

"Leo J. Maloney is the new voice to be reckoned with. *Termination Orders* rings with the authenticity that can only come from an insider. This is one outstanding thriller!"
—**John Gilstrap**

"Taut, tense, and terrifying! You'll cross your fingers it's fiction—in this high-powered, action-packed thriller, Leo Maloney proves he clearly knows his stuff."
—**Hank Phillippi Ryan**

"A new must-read action thriller that features a double-crossing CIA and Congress, vengeful foreign agents, a corporate drug ring, the Taliban, and narco-terrorists...a you-are-there account of torture, assassination, and double-agents, where 'nothing is as it seems.'"
—**Jon Renaud**

"Leo J. Maloney is a real-life Jason Bourne."
—**Josh Zwylen**, *Wicked Local Stoneham*

"A masterly blend of Black Ops intrigue, cleverly interwoven with imaginative sequences of fiction. The reader must guess which accounts are real and which are merely storytelling."
—**Chris Treece**, *The Chris Treece Show*

"A deep-ops story presented in an epic style that takes fact mixed with a bit of fiction to create a spy thriller that takes the reader deep into secret spy missions."
—**CyHilterman**, *Best Sellers World*

"For fans of spy thrillers seeking a bit of realism mixed into their novels, *Termination Orders* will prove to be an excellent and recommended pick."
—*Midwest Book Reviews*

# Books by Leo J. Maloney

**The Dan Morgan Thriller Series**
TERMINATION ORDERS
SILENT ASSASSIN
BLACK SKIES
TWELVE HOURS*
ARCH ENEMY
FOR DUTY AND HONOR*
ROGUE COMMANDER
DARK TERRITORY*
THREAT LEVEL ALPHA
WAR OF SHADOWS
DEEP COVER

*e-novellas

# Threat Level Alpha

*A Dan Morgan Thriller*

## Leo J. Maloney

**LYRICAL UNDERGROUND**
Kensington Publishing Corp.
www.kensingtonbooks.com

LYRICAL UNDERGROUND BOOKS are published by
Kensington Publishing Corp.
119 West 40th Street
New York, NY 10018

All Kensington titles, imprints, and distributed lines are available at special quantity discounts for bulk purchases for sales promotion, premiums, fundraising, educational, or institutional use.

Special book excerpts or customized printings can also be created to fit specific needs. For details, write or phone the office of the Kensington Sales Manager: Kensington Publishing Corp., 119 West 40th Street, New York, NY 10018. Attn. Sales Department. Phone: 1-800-221-2647.
Lyrical Underground and Lyrical Underground logo Reg. US Pat. & TM Off.

First Electronic Edition: December 2018
ISBN-13: 978-1-5161-0331-7 (ebook)
ISBN-10: 1-5161-0331-9 (ebook)

First Print Edition: December 2018
ISBN-13: 978-1-5161-0332-4
ISBN-10: 1-5161-0332-7

Printed in the United States of America

*I would like to dedicate this book to all the brave men, women, and animals who serve in our Armed Forces and make so many sacrifices to keep us and our great country safe. I also want to recognize all the police officers, firefighters and other first responders. Thank you all for your service.*

# Prologue

Dan Morgan had just entered his home office when his phone beeped. The alert sound told him two things: it was Lincoln Shepard, and it was urgent.

Morgan didn't even open the text. Instead, he dialed Shep's number. If the news was what he thought it was, he'd be damned if he read it on the screen of his phone. The other man answered on the first ring and didn't make him wait for the news. "We've located the Package."

For a moment, Morgan did something he almost never did—he hesitated. Then he took a breath. "Have you confirmed that it's...authentic?"

"It looks like the real thing all right," Shep said. Morgan could hear the pride in his voice. "I'd have to see it in person for final confirmation."

"Was it in...?"

"Mexico," Shepard finished for him. "You were right. Turns out that if you're searching for something that isn't supposed to exist, it helps to know where to start. I'll send you the location. How soon can you be there?"

"I'm on my way," Dan said. He was already moving, taking the back staircase up to the master bedroom, where he grabbed a suitcase already packed with a few days' worth of clothes and essentials.

His wife Jenny came to his side. "I assume you'll be needing this," she said, holding his passport.

"I will," Dan said. "Honey, we found it..."

"Are you sure?" she asked.

"Yes."

"Are you telling Diana you are going after it?" Jenny asked.

"There's no time for approval. For now this is need-to-know. And she doesn't need to know, not yet."

Strictly speaking, that wasn't true. Diana Bloch ran Zeta Division, the secret, private intelligence organization that employed Morgan. For this operation, he would be diverting a number of Zeta resources: Shep's and his team's time, for one—and then there were the expenses involved.

"You just don't like to ask for permission," Jenny said. It was an observation, not a question. Dan didn't argue the point.

"We just can't wait. Any delay increases the risk that we'll lose it," Morgan said.

"It's been sitting wherever it is for, what? More than 40 years? And you don't want to waste time on a conversation, or, God forbid, a meeting..."

"You know me so well," Dan said, kissing her and heading out the door. "I'll be just a few days. Whatever happens, don't tell Alex. I'll tell her myself when the time is right."

Dan was long past worrying about Alex finding out that his job as a classic muscle car dealer was just a cover—that his real job was with Zeta Division, where he put his experience as a black ops agent with the CIA to work.

Alex had learned the truth more than two years ago. And, more to the point, she now worked for Zeta herself, so that jig was definitely up.

Nevertheless, for his entire adult life, Morgan's work had required him to keep secrets. These days he didn't have many that he kept from his daughter, or his wife, for that matter, but this is one he had to keep—at least for now.

Seven hours later, Morgan and Shepard pulled up to the site in a rental. They were less than an hour from dusk, but neither wanted to wait until tomorrow to see it for themselves.

Their contact met them at the front of the junkyard and introduced himself as Dave. He was a young American in maybe his early thirties, one of the contractors Zeta used to move important items into or out of the country.

The place had just closed, but after a brief conversation, the junkyard's proprietor unlocked the gate just as Dave directed a large, white truck inside.

Morgan was pleased; he didn't like the idea of waiting until tomorrow to move the Package. He would feel better when they had it in their possession and back in the States.

The led them into the junkyard. From inside, it seemed endless. There were long rows of old cars. Out of habit, Morgan found himself identifying the models and years of each vehicle and part. Mixed in with the cars were rusting helicopters and planes, as well as electronics and more than a few pieces of military hardware.

Morgan saw Shepard looking wide-eyed at some of the exotic pieces of equipment they passed. No doubt the younger man would have loved to get lost in this endless sea of technology, but to his credit, he stayed focused on their mission.

After ten minutes of walking, they turned into another row and there it was...

It sat almost completely inside what was essentially a hollowed-out bus. That was good; the roof of the bus had protected it from the elements. Forty-plus years' worth of rain had barely touched it.

Dave spoke first. "Um, *that* is why we're here?"

"That is exactly why we're here," Morgan replied.

"You called me and my crew out for this? I mean, it's just a car, and an old one." Morgan winced and saw Shepard do the same. "Even if it's worth a few bucks it can't be worth what you are paying me. And this was a rush," Dave continued.

Shepard gasped but Morgan just shook his head.

"Just load it up," Morgan said.

# Chapter 1

*Three Months Later*
*Over the Pacific Ocean*

The aircraft alarm beeped, and Dan Morgan checked the clock on the fuselage wall.

"That's our cue," he said, as he reached for his helmet.

"Copy that," Peter Conley replied.

Both men put on their helmets, which seemed like they belonged on a space suit—with a hardened top and a bubble of glass in front of the face for visibility. They were also surprisingly lightweight, with a roughly triangular aerodynamic shape that got smaller toward the back of the "head."

Morgan had watched Lincoln Shepard designing them in his lab. It was half a day's work that Shepard would never think about again, but Morgan suspected that it was probably better than anything else used in civilian or military high altitude jumps.

Once Morgan had fastened the helmet to his neck seal, he was breathing pure oxygen instead of the standard oxygen, nitrogen, and carbon dioxide mix in the plane's hold. It was supplied by hoses than ran from the wall of the plane to the back of their helmets.

The first few breaths made him lightheaded, but Dan Morgan adjusted to the pure oxygen. They would be on it for the next forty-five minutes. It would take that long for the nitrogen to be purged completely from their bloodstreams. Otherwise, when their plane hit the extreme low pressure of the stratosphere, any nitrogen in their blood would boil and the mission would be over before it began.

Though the helmet was cutting edge, their jumpsuits were standard high altitude jump gear. They offered some protection from the cold, but not enough. The safer and more comfortable option would have been to perform the jump with full pressure suits, but that would add weight and would make it much harder to reach the landing target. And more weight on their bodies meant fewer weapons and ammo strapped to them—which would cause other problems later. So Morgan and Conley had decided that the lower the weight in the air, the greater the chance of success on the ground. The important thing here was that they had a choice.

Diana Bloch had presented them with the mission objectives; the details were left up to them. When asking people to risk their lives, it was the only way to do business as far as Dan was concerned.

But that was not the way they did things at the CIA, which was one of the many reasons why Dan and that institution had parted ways.

The plane rocked from turbulence. Morgan and Conley were strapped into the jump seats that lined the sides of the fuselage. However, the NSA guy in a suit who was sitting behind a desk—and safely behind thick Plexiglas near the front of the plane—was nearly knocked off his seat in front of the computer monitor he was studying.

"You okay up there?" Morgan said.

He felt Conley's eyes on him. He didn't have to look to see his friend was giving him a dirty look that said—*leave the kid alone.*

"You might want to strap in," Morgan said helpfully.

"Um, I'm okay, Cobra," the young man said, using Morgan's code name. He was in maybe his mid-twenties and wore a suit, with his NSA badge clipped to his lapel.

"Next time make sure they give you a seat belt," Morgan said.

He felt Conley elbow him in the side and gave his friend an innocent look.

"Yes sir," the kid said. Morgan remembered his name: *Stevens.*

Morgan didn't have anything against the kid, except for the fact that he was sitting in heated, fully-pressurized comfort while Morgan and Conley froze their butts off in the jump section of the plane.

"It will get easier when we hit our altitude. Not enough air at 40,000 feet to make turbulence," Morgan said.

Of course, at that point things would get tricky for the agents. It would start to get really cold in the back of the plane. It was heated—sort of—but when the air got that thin, the heaters couldn't heat what wasn't there. And, still, that was nothing compared to what they would feel when they jumped out of a perfectly good aircraft.

At that point, Stevens would still be sitting in comfort while Morgan and Conley plummeted out of the plane, freezing their butts off even more.

Come to think of it, Morgan *did* have something against the kid.

The pilot increased their altitude gradually. Forty-five minutes later, as if on cue, the ride smoothed and Morgan knew they had hit the stratosphere.

Though the turbulence was gone, the plane banked frequently, which Morgan knew was necessary to avoid the line of sight of the Chinese satellites overhead.

"Approaching Tibetan airspace, sirs," Stevens said, still a little green around the gills from the recent maneuvers. "Ten minutes until our mark."

It was difficult to hear Stevens' voice through Morgan's helmet, especially since the sound had to travel from the speaker on the wall through the rapidly thinning atmosphere air in the cabin as they approached 40,000 feet.

They couldn't use helmet radios because any radio signals could, potentially, be "heard" by the Chinese. So there had been no transmissions from the aircraft for hours.

"Entering Tibetan airspace, sirs," Stevens said. Morgan gave him a nod. Well, as a practical matter, they were entering Chinese airspace, since the people of Tibet had no more control of their sky then they did over their land. They'd lost that control to the Chinese army in 1950.

However, that was not the reason Morgan and Conley were there today. Their mission was much more...targeted.

"I'm coordinating with our CIA and naval contacts. They will be ready for you on the other side," Stevens said.

Morgan felt his blood run cold and shot Conley a look. "You're kidding me," he said.

"Stevens, we may have a change of plans," he called out.

"Sir?" Stevens said.

"Morgan..." Conley began.

"We talked about this," Morgan cut in. "I don't work with the CIA. Ever. What part of that do you have trouble with?"

"There is no CIA *directly* involved," Conley said.

"What?"

Conley turned to Stevens. "What's their role here?"

"Logistics and support, Mr. Conley," the young man offered. "We're using their naval liaison," Stevens continued nervously, clearly not knowing what was going on.

"Indirect...paperwork mostly," Conley said. "Barely even errand boys on this one."

"What part of no—" Morgan began, his temper rising.

"The country needs this mission, Morgan. You know why we're here, you know it's true," Conley said evenly.

That stopped Morgan cold, as Conley knew it would.

"One day you're going to play that card and it's not going to work," Morgan said.

"Not in this lifetime and you know it," Conley said, the easy smile back on his face.

Morgan felt his anger slowly melting away.

"Stevens, why don't you tell your CIA contact to—"

"Morgan," Conley interrupted.

"Tell them to what? What's the message, sir?" Stevens asked.

"No message," Conley replied. "Don't make trouble for him. It's not the kid's fault," Conley said to Morgan.

"No, it's yours," Morgan shot back.

Conley checked the clock on the wall. "Almost time to go to work," Conley said.

"Opening the jump door in two minutes," Stevens called. "Good luck, sirs," he added.

Both men waited until they heard the click as the door started opening. The plane jolted as the opening changed its aerodynamics before leveling out.

Looking out at the open door, Morgan saw a nearly black sky. Beneath that, he could actually see the curvature of the Earth. Well, they were in the stratosphere. And the air pressure was closer to the vacuum of space than it was to standard air pressure at sea level.

He felt the additional chill. Though their protective jumpsuits were the best available—knowing Shepard, probably better—there was no getting around the fact that it was 70 degrees below zero out there.

He and Conley worked quickly. They disconnected their oxygen hoses from the fuselage of the plane and re-connected them to the small bottles of oxygen at their waists. Then they checked the line that tethered them together at the hip, and the smaller one that connected their helmets.

The helmet tether had been Morgan's contribution. Shepard and his engineers had struggled with a communications system for Morgan and Conley on their way down. Simple radio would have been best, but any signals risked being picked up by Chinese satellites, a particular concern given where they were going.

At Zeta headquarters, Morgan had watched the engineers squabble over how strong a signal would be safe for hours. The next day, he'd told Shepard he'd cracked their problem and tossed the young man two soup cans connected by a dozen feet of string.

Now he and his partner were depending on a variation of the same system to keep in touch during their fall to Earth.

Morgan took a few breaths and knew the pressure in their helmets was good; the low-oxygen, low-pressure atmosphere outside would have rendered them unconscious in less than thirty seconds if the helmets weren't working.

He and Conley made their way to the back of the plane and the jump platform. The digital clock above was counting down from sixty seconds.

Then forty seconds.

Morgan gazed out at the Earth and was struck by fact that it appeared as if they were literally jumping into space.

He shot Conley a look.

Ten seconds...

He kept his eyes forward, finishing the countdown in his head.

When he was a kid, he had briefly dreamed of becoming an astronaut. Well, now was his chance.

Two...

One...

Morgan and Conley jumped at the same time.

His first thought was that they were falling too fast. Morgan had been on jumps before, but not from anywhere near this height, and none of them had felt anything like this. The almost non-existent air pressure didn't provide the normal pushback, and the acceleration was startling. Yet they had to work quickly. Morgan maneuvered himself until he and Conley were both falling face down and he felt the tether at his hip pull tight.

Then he counted to three and spread his arms and legs open, engaging the lift areas of his wingsuit as Conley did the same. Almost immediately, their downward velocity was cut in half as they glided forward, the GPS units on their right wrists telling them which direction to go.

Together, the two men adjusted their position until their heading was correct.

The normal glide ratio for this sort of jump was 2:1, or two feet forward for every 1 foot down. Because of the distance to the landing site, they would have to do a little better, but Morgan trusted that the modifications Shepard had made in the suits would get them there.

Morgan gave his head a slight tug to the left, tightening the second tether that connected their helmets.

Conley's voice filled the air around him.

"How you doin' over there, Morgan?"

"Okay, but I'm thinking of complaining to the airline," he replied. "There really ought to be a meal on a flight that long."

"I hear you brother. Not even peanuts," Conley replied.

"And no movie."

"I was almost glad when they opened the door and kicked us out the back," Conley said, with a chuckle.

The ground still seemed a long way from them. "How do our numbers look?"

"Heading…airspeed…all solid," Conley said. "We've got a ways to go, but we should hit the target."

That was good. If they didn't hit their mark precisely, they would miss their even narrower time window. If they were even a mile or two off, they would lose precious time walking to the base. And that meant they would almost certainly run into the soon-to-be-visiting Chinese General and his honor guard.

There were fifty things that could go wrong on this mission if everything went according to plan. The last thing they needed was to face another couple of dozen heavily armed, highly trained, and dangerous troops.

After a couple of minutes in the air, Morgan realized the activity, adrenaline, and exhilaration of flight had almost made him forget the cold. Now that they were more than halfway down it was a bit warmer, or rather, less freezing—barely ten below zero.

By now they were close enough to the ground that Morgan could see mountains and hills. He checked his own heading and identified the mountains that ringed their landing site.

"I see it too," Conley said.

They dropped a little altitude and adjusted their course for approach.

"There," Morgan said, getting his first visual of the small space between the two mountains north of the objective.

"Approach is good. Altitude is good. Speed is right on the money," Conley said. "Thank you for flying—"

And then they dropped.

To Morgan it felt like a giant hand was pushing him down for several long seconds. Then the hand let up.

"What the…"

"Downdraft," Conley spat out.

They were losing altitude fast, too fast.

Less than two miles away, the pass loomed. It was straight ahead, the bottom of the pass just below their flight path. At this rate, if they were very careful and very lucky when they reached the mountains they would be just a couple of hundred feet below the lip of the pass—which meant they would hit the rocky face of the mountain at a couple of hundred miles an hour.

Morgan had been concerned that there were fifty things that could kill them on this mission.

Turns out it would only take one.

# Chapter 2

"Angling up," Morgan said.

"Just a little," Conley replied.

They could gain some altitude now, but it would cost them speed, which would cost them distance. In the long run, it would still cost them altitude as they lost momentum and started dropping out of the sky.

"Level out. That's a little better," Conley said.

"Better as in we'll make it? Or as in we'll almost make it but still hit the side of the mountain?"

"Could go either way," Conley said. "If we hit, it will be higher up the mountain at least."

"We need to work on our plan," Morgan said.

"We can abort if we do it in the next twenty seconds, but then we'll be walking home."

They had both understood from the beginning that there would be no extraction. They would have to get their own ride out, and that would happen only if they succeeded in their mission.

Morgan did a little math in his head. "Well, there's definitely a *chance* we'll make it."

"Exactly," Conley said.

"I'd hate to walk home," Morgan said.

"And I'm looking forward to our new ride," Conley said.

That was all the conversation they needed. It was decided. Morgan counted off in his head and then watched as they passed over their last chance to pull their chutes and end the mission early.

And then they dropped again. Not as fast or as far as before, but it was enough. At their current course and speed, they would slam into the mountain ahead of them in less than a minute.

He heard Conley muttering.

Morgan saw the ground rising up—not because they were falling but because the ground under them was now part of the mountain rising to meet them.

"Two thousand feet," Conley said.

Not enough.

"I have an idea," Conley continued. "Angle down, about thirty degrees."

That didn't make sense. That would get them to the side of the mountain quicker, but he didn't argue.

"Mark" Conley said.

Morgan angled himself downward.

They raced toward the ground.

"Pull up," Conley said.

They angled back up and then leveled off at twenty four hundred feet. Pretty good given that they were about 1,000 feet out.

But their speed was down and their 2-to-1 glide ratio was closer to 1.5.

They would never make the pass unless they hit an...

*Updraft.*

It forced them up as fast and as hard as that first downdraft, though not for as long.

But it was long enough to put them just over the bottom of the pass...maybe.

Morgan could see the mountain below them, almost close enough to touch. He kept his concentration and his focus forward. They'd either hit the rocks below...or miss them.

In three.

Two.

One.

Morgan and Conley shot out through the pass and into the open air, their altitude increasing as the mountain fell away from them.

There were five hundred feet between the two men and the ground. Then a thousand, then two.

Morgan let out his breath.

"Nice," Conley said. "Close enough for you?"

"Just right," Morgan said.

"Two o'clock," Conley said.

"I see it," Morgan replied.

What happened next was relatively easy. They kept their eyes on the landing site as they detached their hip tether.

"See you on the ground," Conley said.

Then they disconnected the helmet line, breaking their communications link, which was fine, since they didn't need it for this part.

Morgan watched his position and altitude.

Seven hundred feet.

Then six. Five hundred was the floor, the lowest they could go and still have a good jump—a jump they would walk away from.

Of course, that would only work if the chutes deployed. If the parachutes failed, they still had their reserves—which would open at almost precisely the same instant they hit the ground.

Morgan pulled his ripcord and felt the tug of the open chute. His peripheral vision told him that Conley's parachute had deployed as well.

The landing was softer than Morgan had anticipated. He kept to his feet and didn't have to roll, which was fine with him, given the weapons and other gear he was carrying.

A few seconds after he hit the ground, Conley came down a few yards away. By then Morgan had his mask off. "Glad you could make it," he said.

Pulling his own mask off, Conley said, "You made it down first, but I hit the bull's-eye."

Morgan saw that Conley was dead center in the circular clearing that was their landing target.

"So we're tied," Conley said. "And congratulations, we just set the world record for horizontal distance on a HALO jump from 40,000 feet. Of course, no one outside of Zeta will ever know."

Morgan grinned. That was the life they had chosen. "Now for the hard part."

The two men collected their jumpsuits, helmets, and masks and dropped them into a Mylar bag with one of Shepard's incendiaries. Morgan set the timer on the explosive for four hours. Whether they succeeded or failed, they had to make sure there would be no way to trace the operation back to Zeta, or the United States.

Morgan inventoried his weapons. Two of his Walther PPK pistols were holstered around his waist. He assembled his sniper rifle while Conley did the same. They also turned on the phones and ear comms that they had turned off during their descent.

A few minutes later, they were looking down on the Chinese military base. It was nestled inside a ring of mountains, the tops of which the two agents had barely cleared during their jump.

Conley recognized the layout from the satellite photos and the interactive computer walk-through that Shepard and O'Neal had created. The dominant feature was an airstrip that ran most of the length of the "valley" that held the base. At one end was the hangar that held their objective. At the other end there was a physical plant that held the generators and water pumps that fed the base, as well as offices and troop dormitories.

Fortunately, those dormitories would be mostly empty. The base had a small garrison of soldiers, whose main job was making sure that no locals wandered in.

"Impressive, for an installation that doesn't exist," Conley said.

Morgan agreed. "Of course, they are about to be taken down by agents who don't exist."

And if all went well, the Chinese would lose their prize new fighter jet that also didn't exist—at least not yet. According to official reports, the aircraft was not going to be ready for another two years. Intelligence suggested that this plane could rival the F-22. By itself, those two pieces of information weren't critical.

Misinformation about timelines for new military hardware was standard for most nations. And even if the plane was a match for the F-22, the Chinese couldn't hope to match the sheer number of fighters in the United States' arsenal.

No, the real reason they were there was because of the new weapons system that the plane contained. According to Diana Bloch, the new system was top secret and even if Zeta's contacts in the government knew what it was, they weren't saying.

But if all went well, the plane and any secrets it held would be in U.S. hands by the end of the day.

"Okay, we know the drill. Power first," Morgan said.

"Copy that," Conley said.

Their landing site had placed them almost directly behind the low building that held the generators.

However, their first stop would be the rear of the administrative offices a few hundred meters to their right. If they kept to the rocky base of the mountain behind them, they would be hard to spot. The agents took up position about 600 yards beyond the storage shed in the back of the building.

Intel said that it held office equipment and cleaning supplies. It was the least important location on the base. It was also their first stop.

Both men took position with their sniper rifles. Usually, Morgan didn't favor the .308—it was small caliber and low power. As a result, it was almost impossible to get a kill shot past 700 yards with the weapon; the rounds just didn't have the momentum. But the benefit for this mission was that the rifle was low in weight, and thus worked for the HALO jump. It was also perfect for this particular application.

Morgan and Conley took their positions and set up the rifles on their tripods. Morgan noted the wind and temperature, and did some quick calculations in his head. Then he adjusted the gun until one of the two small security cameras came up dead center in his scope.

He knew Conley was doing the same to the other camera.

"Ready?" he asked.

"Ready," Conley replied.

"On three," Morgan said.

"Two."

"One."

The agents fired together and Morgan was grateful for the .308's relatively quiet report.

Morgan watched through the scope as the security camera disintegrated.

"Got it," Conley said.

The agents grabbed their rifles and headed back to the power station.

Morgan knew that when the cameras went out, the base's few guards would investigate—though there wouldn't be any immediate alarms or any rush. When two cameras went out simultaneously in a non-sensitive area, their first thought would be equipment failure.

With luck, Morgan and Conley's next move would also be chalked up to equipment failure, at least for a short time. In unison, the agents each took a device from the webbing on their chests, and unfolded it to reveal a small drone with four propellers. Morgan hit a switch on the bottom of the drone and it sprang to life as Conley did the same.

When released, the drones took to the air, one in a random flight pattern behind the storage shed, while the other flew off to make mischief elsewhere on the base. Both would activate motion and heat sensors—telling the base security system that something or someone was moving around. Of course, video would show nothing and, once again base command would assume equipment malfunction.

"This may actually work," Morgan remarked.

"Clockwork so far, my friend," Conley replied. "Stealth. You don't always have to go in the front door, guns blazing."

Morgan grunted. It was true he often favored a more direct approached, but ultimately, he believed in doing whatever worked. In this case, sneaking around had worked out pretty well so far.

They were on the move, heading to the rear of the power station, where they used their sniper rifles to take out the video cameras and then simply walked up to the back door.

Morgan tried the door. It was unlocked.

Conley shrugged. "I guess they don't worry about unannounced guests."

"Not out here," Morgan replied.

The agents stepped inside. The room was filled with the hum of the generators in front of them. That was good; the noise would cover what they were about to do.

The primary and backup generators ran on natural gas. A larger base that wasn't top secret might have had a small nuclear reactor, but those were harder to hide.

There was nothing fancy or stealthy about what they did next. They took two of Shepard's incendiaries from their gear and placed them at two different points on each generator's natural gas supply lines and set the timers.

"Let's go find our ride," Conley said.

The door in front of them opened and two Chinese soldiers stepped into the generator room from the front of the building.

The soldiers were startled when they saw the Americans, but before either could react—or even reach for their sidearm—Conley called out something in Mandarin.

Whatever Conley said, the two soldiers turned their attention to the ceiling.

Instantly, Morgan and Conley were on the move. Morgan took three steps toward the soldier closest to him and threw himself into the air. The other man barely had time to look down from the ceiling to see Morgan hurtling toward him in a flying tackle.

The soldier went down pretty hard, hitting the ground with Morgan's weight on top of him. Yet the man stayed conscious and started flailing at Morgan. Twisting his body, Morgan positioned himself behind the solider and placed the man in a chokehold.

Still dazed, the soldier grabbed at Morgan's arm for perhaps a minute and then went still, unconscious. They were under orders not to kill the base personnel unless absolutely necessary. That order came from the very top of Zeta—from Mr. Smith himself, apparently.

Morgan saw that Conley had also laid out his soldier.

Normally, Morgan would not have liked to leave enemies around who could wake up and make trouble for them. But in this case, one way or the other, the mission would be over before these men woke up.

Morgan could hear voices from the front office area, even over the hum of the equipment. A quick look told him that there was no way to lock the door from this side. That made sense; there would be no reason to lock base personnel out.

That's when Dan reached into one of his pouches and pulled out four of his own favorite toys. They weren't as sophisticated as some of the ones Shepard designed, but they would do the job.

He heard Conley's chuckle as he took the rubber doorstops and placed two of them on each of the double doors, wedging the steel doors shut.

If anyone tried the door, it would buy the agents at least a few minutes—and that was all they needed.

"Less than five minutes," Conley said, checking his watch.

Morgan was up. Then he thought about the soldiers. The men weren't dead, but they would be close by when the incendiaries went off. Then, of course, the generators and their tanks would likely blow.

"Let's drag them outside," Morgan said.

Conley didn't argue. They took the soldiers outside and relieved them of their weapons.

Morgan checked his watch. Three minutes until the fireworks started.

They had to get away from the power station and in position for the next phase of the plan. With luck, they would be in the air in about fifteen minutes. And with no power, base command wouldn't even be able to report what had happened until they were long gone.

They kept to the foothills of the mountains as they ringed around, counter-clockwise, to the hangar.

"Do you hear that?" Conley asked.

"It's the hum from the…" Morgan said.

"I thought so too at first, but that's not the generators," Conley said.

Of course, they wouldn't be able to hear them this far outside the building. Certainly, they wouldn't be getting *louder.*

Whatever the sound was, it definitely wasn't good.

And Morgan was pretty sure he knew exactly what it was.

"Yep, there it is," Conley pointed.

The Chinese military troop transport was making its final approach on the airstrip. They would be down in minutes.

"Looks like the General's early," Morgan said.

"Not likely," Conley replied. "I'm sure he's exactly on time. They probably moved up the test flight." Checking his watch, he added, "By exactly two hours."

"How many men does he have in his honor guard?" Morgan said.

"About fifty. Then there's the aircraft crew," Conley said.

Morgan remembered something and checked his watch just as there was a thud from the power station, followed by a satisfying explosion. The flash reached maybe fifty feet in the sky.

"There goes their power, and communications," Conley said. "Of course, the transport will have long range communications."

They watched the transport sail over the pass that they had barely cleared in their wingsuits. The aircraft would be on the ground in minutes.

"I think we need a new plan," Morgan said.

# Chapter 3

The two agents watched as the military transport—which was the size of a commercial airliner—touched down.

"Maybe if we have a few dozen of Shepard's little helicopters we could confuse all of the soldiers individually," Morgan said.

"Or maybe if you had some more of your doorstops," Conley said.

"You know we can't abort," Morgan said.

Conley knew. It wasn't just about completing the mission. The base command and their new reinforcements now knew someone was here. Morgan and Conley couldn't just walk into the mountains—they'd be caught within hours.

There was still only one way out of here. They needed to get to their ride, and the faster the better.

"Do you think our plane is fueled?" Morgan said.

"Probably...Definitely. If they moved everything up it would have to be ready," Conley said.

"Can you handle the ground crew on your own?" Morgan asked.

"Course," Conley said. "What are you thinking?"

"Not sure," Morgan replied. "Just prep the plane and wait for my signal."

"So you have a plan?"

"Not exactly...I'm just going to look for a doorstop."

As Conley set out for the hangar, Morgan headed in the other direction. From behind him, Morgan heard Conley call out. "I'd make sure the doorstop is a big one."

"I'll see what I can do," Morgan replied.

He kept to the foothills as he watched the plane. It had landed and turned around. Now it was just sitting on the runway. Morgan knew why—the pass was the only way in or out of the small group of mountains. The transport was now positioned to take off and head straight for the pass.

It was safer for the plane and worked nicely for Morgan because it put a long runway between the base and the aircraft. Thus, there would be a healthy delay if base command wanted to use the plane's communications system to sound an alert to, say, scramble fighters at the closest airbase. To get any signal out, command would have to get to and use the aircraft's communications system.

If nothing else, that delay would give Morgan and Conley a few minutes' head start in the event that they actually got their own plane in the air.

By the time Morgan reached the hills behind the transport, a large group of soldiers had already filed out and was standing behind an older man in a general's uniform. He was talking to a small number of base personnel. Morgan watched as the entire group started to march together toward the base. There were no guards left outside the plane, which was one lucky break.

Even if there was crew left on the transport, with a bit more luck they wouldn't know he'd been there until he was gone. He stepped out of the foothills and approached the aircraft, then walked under the wing with purpose. He was out in the open, so there was no point in stealth now. In fact, creeping around would only call attention to him.

He made a point of examining the underside of the plane, as a member of the ground crew would do. He stopped at the wing's landing gear and then walked forward, along the fuselage.

He stopped again at the front landing gear and reached into a pouch on his side, confirming that he had two incendiaries left.

The problem was that he needed to save an incendiary for the fuel depot, but there were two tires in the front landing gear. A single explosive might take them both out, but maybe not.

And with even one tire, the plane could still get in the air. Even if it couldn't pursue them, getting airborne would increase its communications range.

So he needed to be sure that he'd taken both tires out—

Looking up into the plane, he smiled when he realized what he'd missed. He could ground the plane with a single device. Grabbing the incendiary, he set the timer for five minutes and tossed it into the fuselage through the opening for the landing gear.

Even if fire control put the fire out in record time, the plane would likely be out of commission—at least in the short term.

And the short term was all they needed.

Morgan gave up any pretense of belonging on the base. He sprinted for the fuel depot, following the hose that was already connected to the plane. He was relieved but not surprised. Protocol for the Chinese army required every available man to be there to greet the general at whatever reception or ceremony they had planned, so Morgan was able to work in peace.

The depot had four fuel tanks, large ones. He debated where to put the last incendiary. The tanks themselves were solid enough that they would likely shake off the blast, which was more flash than bang. His best chance was one of the relatively small pipes that connected the tanks.

He chose one of the pipes, and set the device for two minutes

Then he ran like hell.

The second incendiary would go off about two minutes after the one in the underside of the plane. He heard the device in the plane go off and didn't even turn around. He kept to the edge of the landing strip, keeping close to the rocky foothills.

His internal clock told him that there was about one minute left on the second timer. He had no idea how much fuel was in the tanks and how big any blast might be, or if he would even get more than one tank to blow.

But whatever happened, Morgan didn't want to be anywhere nearby when he found out.

\* \* \* \*

Conley moved fast but was careful to stay out of sight, keeping to the rear of the hangar, and keeping the foothills behind him. They provided a little cover and kept him partly out of sight.

He found a rear door and saw that it wasn't locked. Again, out here, in the middle of nowhere, what was the point of locking anything?

He took a good look inside. There was no one in sight. In fact, though the hangar was large enough for a transport even bigger than the one on the landing site, there was almost nothing there.

A single fighter sat in the center, gleaming in the morning light that poured in from the open doors. It was impressive, even more so than the reconnaissance photos and drawings he had seen.

Conley looked forward to stealing it and seeing what it could do.

There was even a ladder on wheels against the cockpit—as if the plane were ready and waiting for him.

Just to be sure, Conley crept up to the offices on the rear of the building. Empty.

*Bless the Chinese and their protocols,* he thought.

He sprinted for the plane. On the way, he saw stacks of what appeared to be one-meter drones of some sort. There were at least a few dozen of them.

He spared a second to wonder what they were for. Target practice, most likely. After all, the General had come today for a demonstration of the new weapon prototype. Well, Conley was determined to give him a demonstration—even if it wasn't the one he was expecting. He leapt into the cockpit and went right to work. The first thing he checked was the fuel tanks: they were full.

He could have the plane in the air in a couple of minutes. The only thing missing now was Morgan.

Looking up, Conley saw the nose of the troop carrier was billowing smoke, from both the underside of the plane where the front landing gear jutted out and the cockpit windows.

Well, that took care of their worry about base command using the plane's communications system.

Then there was a bright flash from just to the right of the plane. Then another. And another. And another.

And another.

He heard the loud report from each explosion. Each was impressive, reaching at least a hundred feet into the sky.

He guessed that Morgan had found his doorstop.

Then he received another surprise as the troop transport blew up in front of him. This sent a massive report, and Conley could actually feel the blast wave. The fireball was huge, and he could see pieces of the fuselage rain down from the sky. The plane must have had a fuel line running from the tanks when it blew.

Morgan had found his doorstop all right. And it was a pretty big one.

Conley could only hope his friend was far away when it blew, but he couldn't spare a second for worry. He had to run his pre-flight check on the plane.

Scanning the instruments, he was glad he had brushed up on his Mandarin. He recognized the controls and almost all of the instruments, enough to get them in the air. There were some Chinese characters that didn't make sense, and he assumed they were code names for something or other—most likely the new weapon system, whatever that was.

He had just started his pre-flight checks when he heard Morgan's voice. "Conley!"

He watched his friend sprinting toward the plane from the open front of the hangar.

"Hop in," Conley called out.

Morgan didn't seem any worse for wear as he approached the plane and raced up the ladder to slide into the co-pilot seat behind him.

"Impressive display," Conley said.

"Thanks," Morgan replied, catching his breath

"Any trouble getting out of there?" Conley asked.

"Nope," Morgan said.

Conley laughed; the smell of Morgan's singed hair told a different story.

"Can you get us in the air?" Morgan asked.

"Of course, we're fully fueled and ready. If we had time I would taxi to the other side of the runway so we could take off and have a straight shot into the pass. As it is, I'll take off toward your burning wreckage and swing us around."

"Can you get in the air and turn in time to avoid the mountains over there?" Morgan asked.

Under normal circumstances, on a plane he knew, Conley would say yes. But this was his first time in the cockpit of this plane. He didn't know what it could do, and had no experience in how it handled. He'd read the reports and the analysis, but the only way to know how an aircraft handled was to fly it.

And new planes were notoriously unpredictable. Thus, the most dangerous job in the Air Force was acting as a test pilot for a new aircraft. And that was after extensive briefings on the systems, and dozens of hours in a simulator.

However, they just hadn't known enough about this new jet to put together a simulation.

"Can you do it?" Morgan repeated.

"Probably," Conley replied.

"Probably?"

"Almost definitely."

"I guess that's as good as we get on this mission," Morgan said.

The mountains weren't Conley's greatest concern. Though the base didn't have anti-aircraft batteries, they would absolutely have shoulder fired surface-to-air missiles. The longer the two agents spent circling the base, the better the chance that someone on the ground would get lucky with a SAM.

Just then, Conley's ear comm beeped. He ignored it and powered up the jet.

"I'm getting it too," Morgan said. "It's a recorded message for us from Shepard. I'm on it."

* * * *

Morgan hit his ear comm as the prototype Chinese jet roared to life. The plane vibrated with power. *There really is nothing like a fighter,* he thought.

He heard Shepard's voice through his ear comm. "Gentlemen, I wanted to give you as much information as possible about the weapons system in the prototype jet. This information is highly classified and the CIA was unwilling to share the data. However, O'Neal was able to access the CIA system and retrieve the following."

"The plane is equipped with an offensive electromagnetic pulse device, operated by the co-pilot. The specs we've seen suggest that the EMP can be directed to target hostiles with variations on range and spread of the EMP field. It's an important piece of hardware. Needless to say, we'd love to get it in the lab."

"In the event that you would like to or might *need* to test the system, I've loaded the specs and some basic instructions that O'Neal and I pieced together. We made a lot of guesses but you should be able to get at least minimal functionality from the device."

Conley eased the fighter out of the hangar and brought it to the end of the runway. On the opposite end the fire was raging at what was left of the fuel depot and the wreckage of the troop transport—barely recognizable as a plane as flames still roared from its carcass.

He could see soldiers and a few vehicles scurrying around in the distance. However, there were no alarms, thanks to his and Conley's work at the power station.

Suddenly, the co-pilot headset hanging in front of him came to life. A voice was screaming in Mandarin.

"They've spotted us," Conley said, then shouted back in the same language.

"What did you tell them?"

"That we have new orders from Beijing. Headquarters has determined that base command is too incompetent to keep possession of this plane," Conley said, and Morgan could hear the humor in his voice.

"It's not a complete lie. So far I haven't been impressed by their security," Morgan said.

The plane lurched forward, accelerating down the runway. There was silence from the headset as they barreled ahead.

"We'll be up in a second," Conley said.

As they accelerated, the wreckage that Morgan had left seemed to race toward them.

The screaming in the headset got even louder. They were close enough to the fire and the soldiers around it that Morgan could make out their stunned expressions as the fighter shot toward them.

He was impressed that two of the soldiers drew their weapons and actually aimed at the approaching jet. Morgan didn't hear any impacts on the airframe, and then they were off the ground, racing right into the top of the flames from the transport.

And then they were through. Morgan saw that the mountains were now right in front of them—and unnervingly close. A proximity alert blared through the cockpit as Conley threw the jet into a sharp turn to the left and raised its nose. The maneuver tossed Morgan to the right as the plane shot up...and stalled.

Conley angled the nose down as they continued to turn. Now Morgan could feel their sudden descent stop. Then he felt a burst of power from the engine. Unfortunately, the plane was now pointed toward the ground, which was very close—and getting closer fast.

Conley pulled hard on the joystick and they dipped but straightened a good thirty feet from the ground, then angled up again, gaining altitude.

The alarms stopped.

"She's got some juice," Conley said.

Morgan grunted as he reached for his flight helmet. "Just get us out of here," Morgan said as they raced toward the pass and open sky.

Then he heard a ping, as something hit the plane. "That sounded like a bullet," he said. Looking around, he saw at least two-dozen Chinese soldiers pointing their sidearms at them. If this went on long enough, they might actually hit something vital.

Well, in less than a minute they would be far away from the base. And with no communications, the chances that one of the other bases could send pursuit aircraft before they reached the Indian Ocean was slim.

And then the proximity alert started clanging again.

"What the—?" Conley exclaimed.

"What's out there?" Morgan said. Then he saw them: dozens of black specs in a haphazard formation that blocked the entrance to the mountain pass.

"Drones. They were in the hangar. Base personnel must have launched them," Conley said, a note of respect in his voice.

Morgan understood. They had caught the Chinese completely by surprise, and even the General's extra troops weren't much help. And yet they had they somehow improvised a counter attack.

"Are they armed?" Morgan said.

"I don't think so," Conley said. "If I had to guess, they're for target practice."

"So let's shoot them down," Morgan said.

"No ammo. I guess they didn't get a chance to load her up," Conley said.

Or, the test flight didn't involve the aircraft's guns. "Can you fly through them?" Morgan said.

"No, a collision with something that size could take us out."

Of course—collisions with geese had taken down jetliners, Morgan remembered. And then he was being jerked around the cockpit again as Conley put the fighter into a sharp turn.

"I'll bring it around. It will cost us time, but I can circle until we get enough altitude to fly over one of these mountains."

And then another alarm beeped.

"Missile lock," Conley said.

"What?"

"Probably shoulder-fired. Hang on."

Dammit. The Chinese were really in the fight now.

As the alarm clanged, Conley pointed the fighter at the burning hulk of the troop transport.

Conley was coming in low…very low. They were so close to the ground that the soldiers in front of them abandoned their firing positions and scattered.

The alarm screamed louder, which Morgan knew meant the missile was gaining on them.

And then, a few hundred yards away from the burning wreck, Conley turned them sharply again, pivoting around and back toward the pass. Morgan turned to watch the missile hit the wreck and explode.

"We can't stay in here, circling around. It will just be a matter of time until they hit us with one of those missiles."

"I know, but…"

"I have an idea. Cut speed and head for the pass," Morgan said.

"But the drones," Conley said.

"Just do it. I'll take care of them."

Checking his phone, Morgan called up the specs for the EMP weapon. They were translated into English and very detailed. If he had half a day, he might be able to make sense of them.

But he had less than a minute.

He saw the targeting screen and rapped it with a fist in frustration. The screen flashed and Morgan realized it was a touch screen. It showed the drones. Using his finger, Morgan drew a circle around them.

A glowing line surrounded the drones on the screen.

The proximity alert sounded, warning them of the impending collision. And then the missile lock alarm sounded.

*Dammit.*

*How did you fire the damned thing? There were about a dozen different switches and dials...*

And a single red button.

"Morgan?" Conley said.

He pushed the button. Nothing happened inside the fighter and for a long second, nothing happened outside either.

And then—all at once—fifty or so drones dropped out of the sky, maybe two seconds before the fighter reached their position.

The proximity alarm went silent and then there was a flash behind them as one of the drones got in the way of the heat-seeking missile that was chasing them.

The cockpit alarms went silent...and then they were through the pass and in the open sky.

Morgan didn't look back. He was glad to leave the base behind them.

"Any sign of pursuit?" Morgan asked.

"No. And no chatter on the radio. I don't think anyone else knows we are in the air. If we stay low, we'll avoid their radar...Oh damn," he said.

"What now?"

"We've got a problem with fuel. Line must have been hit..."

"You've got to be kidding me..."

He heard Conley chuckle. "Okay, that time I *was* kidding. Plenty of fuel and open skies until the Indian Ocean. Enjoy the view. I'll put us down in about twenty-five minutes."

A few minutes later, his ear comm beeped and Shepard was on the line. "Congratulations, Morgan, Bloch says you are on schedule. I look forward to getting a look at that...new feature. In the meantime, I have something for you. It's the Package. It's ready."

Morgan let that sink in.

"Who knows?"

"Just me, O'Neal, and three from the team that worked on it," Shepard said.

"The specs we discussed?" Morgan said.

"Yes, plus some improvements. Morgan, it's...well. You need to see it for yourself," Shepard said.

"I'll be there in twenty-two hours."

The landing was a little rough. Since there was no hiding an aircraft carrier, they had to land on an improvised sea platform assembled from barges.

Conley maintained that the landing was a first of some kind but Morgan's mind was already focused on the news that Shepard had given him.

On the deck of the barge, Morgan told Conley that Shepard had called and his special project was finished.

"Understood. I can get her on her way," Conley said, gesturing to the plane. A team was already at work on the fighter, prepping it to be loaded onto a specially designed cargo container. "You head straight back."

Conley would ride with the plane as it was picked off the barge by a heavy lift helicopter, transferred to a civilian cargo plane, and then home. Thus, no leg of the trip could be tied to the U.S. government.

And if Morgan knew Diana Bloch and Shep, it would also mean that Shepard, O'Neal, and their team would have some *quality* time with the plane before they made delivery to the U.S. military.

"Thanks, I'll see you when you get back," Morgan said.

"It may be a while," Conley said. "I'll be hitting the beach first before I get home, and you'll be busy..."

A smaller chopper took Morgan directly to Mumbai, where he grabbed a flight home. When Morgan settled into his seat, he checked his watch; he had about fifteen hours before he reached Logan International. That would be perfect. He had some work to do before he got home, and then he'd need some sleep. Whatever happened, he wanted to be rested when he got there.

# Chapter 4

"Comrade, listen to this," Vlad said. "There is a war in Chechnya. On the road to Grozny there is a family. The mother-in-law is in front, then a few wives, then the children. Trailing behind all of them is the male head of the family.

"At the checkpoint, a Russian soldier asks him, 'Why do you walk behind all of the women? Doesn't your holy book tell you that the man goes first?' To that, the Chechen replies, 'My holy book says nothing about minefields. '"

"Very funny, Comrade," Pavel said.

"You know, Chechens are just Ukrainians who lived in Chernobyl," Vlad said, putting the bottle of vodka on the table.

Pavel smiled politely, but that wasn't enough for Vlad.

"You know, because of the radiation," Vlad explained.

"Yes, very good," Pavel said.

"A Chechen girl——" Vlad began.

"Here, have some more vodka," Pavel said, filling two shot glasses. Once the old soldier got started on Chechens, it would take some doing to get him talking about something else.

Vlad was as old as Pavel's own grandfather and had an endless store of anecdotes, many of them about the Chechens. Amazingly, most of the jokes went back decades, well into the Soviet era.

And yet for all of his bluster, Pavel had more than once seen Vlad playing soccer with groups of local Chechen children when he was off duty.

But his jokes…

In those anecdotes the Chechens were idiots or schemers or cowards. They would be offensive to Chechens, of course, but he had heard far worse in the barracks back in Moscow.

*That Chechen looks unusually peaceful, said one soldier.*

*That's because he's dead, said another.*

That was probably the kindest joke he had heard soldiers his own age tell about Chechens. Something had happened after the fall of the Soviet Union and the rise of the Chechen separatists. The jokes had gone from merely offensive to vicious.

Pavel had lost a couple of friends to Chechen terrorists and he knew a soldier who had lost some family to an attack in Moscow, but the jokes still made him uncomfortable. They just didn't seem funny to him, and even less so now that he and Vlad were stationed on the border of the Chechnya region in the shadow of the Caucasus Mountains.

So far from Moscow and home, near so many Chechen people who eyed their Russian army uniforms with clear hatred, Vlad's jokes didn't seem funny at all.

"First we eat, then *durak*," Vlad said, putting two bowls of his lamb and potato stew on the table.

Six months ago, Pavel had been impressed the first time he had tasted Vlad's stew. That whole first week, Pavel had enjoyed the food that tasted of home—unlike the odd dishes that the locals ate.

The second week Pavel had been less impressed. By the end of the first month, he had gently suggested that they could try some of the local dishes but Vlad had refused.

Now Pavel was resigned to his comrade's nightly stew. If Vlad cooked it without complaint, Pavel would eat it without complaint.

The base was quiet. Of course, it was quiet every night. The only noises were the sounds of the woods and the gentle hum of the generator. On the plus side, their living space was better than the barracks in Moscow. He and Vlad each had their own room, and there were empty rooms to spare.

The "base" had once housed a dozen soldiers who had watched over the warehouse in the small compound. Now it housed only Pavel and Vlad, and the warehouse stored old computers and electronics that were good for nothing but museum pieces. And then there were the spare parts for tanks that had gone out of service when Vlad was young.

And yet the two men guarded a place that should have been closed down twenty years ago.

Of course, Pavel had once spent a year manning a checkpoint on a road outside of St. Petersburg. It was a checkpoint that could be avoided easily by simply driving a short distance around it.

And yet Pavel had dutifully checked the papers of every car that came through—for the few drivers who thought it was too much trouble to drive around the checkpoint in bad weather.

That was the Soviet way, his commander had explained. And for many it was still the Russian way. 'You think things will change overnight?' the officer often said. 'What do you think this is, America?'

Now, sitting with Vlad in the armpit of nowhere, Pavel thought he had found the spot furthest from America in the world.

And yet there was plenty of vodka. And Vlad was usually an agreeable companion—devilishly good at durak. As the older man dealt the cards, Pavel studied his movements. Maybe in six more months of this duty, Pavel would uncover Vlad's secret.

"Simple durak to start," Vlad said.

Pavel knew the routine by heart. Always simple durak to start. Then as the hour got later and the vodka flowed it would be full durak, then crazy durak, and then (if the vodka held out), Albanian durak.

There were worse duties, Pavel thought as he studied his cards. Soon, Vlad would begin with his stories. After six months, Pavel still had not heard them all.

And then the lights went out.

Vlad cursed. It was his turn to tend to the generator. He grabbed a flashlight and headed outside. He hesitated at the door, studied Pavel, and warned, "Don't peek at the cards." Then he was out the door.

A few minutes later, the lights came back on. Then, at about the time he expected Vlad to shuffle back inside, he heard a distant *pop* sound.

That was odd. He'd catalogued each of the night sounds in this godforsaken place, and that was new.

He heard shouting. It was Vlad. Then there was another *pop* and another, followed by what Pavel recognized as automatic weapon fire.

Even as Pavel's brain was struggling to process this information, he was moving. He lurched across the kitchen to the radio station. They kept the radio on, but the temporary power outage meant it would take another minute to warm up.

There was more shouting. More single shots. *From Vlad's pistol,* Pavel realized, a cold pit forming in his stomach.

The light came on and Pavel spoke into the microphone. He gave his identification number and then said, "We are under attack. Automatic weapons fire…"

And then the lights went out again.

More shouting, another single shot. And then multiple blasts of automatic weapons. He recognized the sound: AK-47s.

Then silence.

*Vlad,* Pavel thought sadly.

Then he heard strange voices shouting in Chechen. *Fools,* he thought, *they must think we have real weapons here. They must think there is something to guard.*

Well, even if they prevailed, the joke would be on the Chechens. There was nothing in the warehouse but old junk.

And yet maybe they would not prevail. Perhaps they didn't know that Pavel was there. He drew his sidearm and got up from the radio console.

Yes, perhaps he could deal them a surprise or two. Just as they had surprised poor Vlad.

He switched off the safety on his pistol and calculated his chances of reaching his room, where he kept his extra ammunition. He'd have to wait. He couldn't risk it while he still heard the Chechens moving around the compound.

Maybe when they were all gathered in the warehouse.

What happened next happened fast: the door exploded inward and Pavel's pistol came alive in his hand, firing into the opening. However, there was no one there.

He held his fire, counting his remaining rounds in his head.

Without warning, two large figures threw themselves into the kitchen. Pavel aimed as he fired. He was glad to hear one of the men cry out, and then there were multiple flashes in front of him.

It took a second for him to register them as muzzle flashes. And another fraction of a second to register the sound of multiple reports. And only then did he register the burning sensation in his chest.

Pavel realized that he was on the ground, his chest on fire. He tried to fire his weapon but realized that it was no longer in his hand.

Then there were more figures in the room.

He tried to reach for his pistol but he wasn't sure if his hand was obeying his commands. Then the fire in his chest was gone and Pavel realized he was now cold.

He heard a weapon cock, and then a voice in Chechen-accented Russian said, "Don't bother, this one is finished."

\* \* \* \*

Alex rode her motorcycle into the garage at Zeta headquarters.

*More training,* she thought, shaking her head in frustration.

And to top it off, she had to break in a new hand-to-hand combat instructor. She had been training for months on weapons, martial arts, and explosives as well as general physical training in everything from swimming (with an emphasis on endurance) to running to rock climbing. There were also individual "seminars" on basic spy craft—tailing someone undetected as well as spotting a tail, using dead drops, navigating strange terrain without a GPS device, and even more prosaic but useful skills like pickpocketing and basic hacking.

Alex knew that her father had received his initial training in the CIA facility known as "The Farm." There, the curriculum had been formal.

However, at Zeta, the training was different. Challenging, yes. Exhausting, often. Yet it was anything but formal.

The fact was that Alex was the first "new" recruit in Zeta Division. All of the other agents were either ex-military or ex-CIA, or both. Alex, on the other hand, had basically joined out of high school.

And yet Alex had excelled in most of her training. That was part of the problem. Despite being the youngest agent, she was competitive with other agents in most areas and really shone in some, like marksmanship. And she had made real contributions to the Zeta Division in the last two years.

However, she had yet to receive her own undercover mission. And she had yet to work undercover.

Alex knew that she should be grateful to her father and Diana Bloch for the trust they had placed in her. And Diana had taken a great personal interest in her training, assigning staff to her seminars and reviewing her performance. But Alex was itching to get out of the classroom. She wanted to do more. And she knew she was ready.

First, however, she had to endure another one of Diana Bloch's endless training sessions.

"Hello Alex," she heard as she entered the gym.

Waiting for her on the practice mats was someone she recognized.

"Commander Schmitt," Alex said.

"You can call me Alicia. I'm retired and I don't think my rank means anything in this building," the woman said with a polite smile. "Nice to see you, how is your father?"

"Fine, he's on a mission right now," Alex said.

Alex guessed that Alicia Schmitt was somewhere between 35 and 40. A former naval commander, Alex and her father had run into Schmitt when she was still in the military.

"Diana recruited you?" Alex asked.

"Yes, and apparently my first duty is to evaluate your progress in hand-to-hand combat," Schmitt said.

Alex searched her memory for a few seconds and said, "I thought you were a pilot, that you flew fighters."

"I am. I also have some training in martial arts. Why don't we begin? I only have you for an hour. We can catch up later."

"I'll put on my sweats and—"Alex said.

"No, we'll begin now."

Alex shrugged and stepped onto the mats.

"Come at me and try to strike me," Schmitt said.

"Um, don't we bow first?"

"This isn't a dojo. And neither is the field," Schmitt said. "There, your opponents won't bow. They won't shake your hands after. They will simply try to kill you. It's not polite, but it's honest in its own way."

*Okay,* Alex said. *If that's how you want to play it.* She launched into a classic Krav Maga assault. She came in fast and brought up her left elbow as a feint. Her real attack came from her right knee.

What happened next happened almost too fast for Alex to follow. Schmitt sidestepped the elbow, and focused on the knee attack—as if she knew it was coming. Then, Schmitt was leaning into her and the next thing Alex knew she was on her back on the mat.

"Okay, why don't you try that again," Schmitt said.

This time, Alex decided not to do anything fancy. She simply charged, throwing a series of traditional punches, straight out of the boxing playbook.

This time, Schmitt seemed almost amused, and a moment later Alex was laid out on her back again.

"Again," Schmitt said.

Now Alex was angry and decided to wipe Schmitt's grin off her face. This time, she brought out the big guns. She flew at Schmitt, employed a karate attack, using a kata that had been her go-to move against tough sparing partners.

This time, Schmitt was forced to parry Alex's strikes. Keeping her on the defensive, Alex nearly landed a blow. She felt satisfaction at that.

And then she was once again on her back, looking at the ceiling.

Schmitt helped her up and said, "Okay, you've had some training. Now, let me see how you handle attacks."

For her first attack, Schmitt simply rushed Alex. It was a classic street fighting tactic and Alex was determined to meet it head on. She planted her right foot behind and kept her weight forward as she swung out with a hand blow.

She was face down on the mat.

And then again.

And again.

Her frustration level was high when she got up for the third time.

"Like I said, it's clear you have some training. And I see you fight like your father," Schmitt said.

"I'll take that as a compliment," Alex said, catching her breath. She was annoyed to see that Schmitt was breathing normally.

"I didn't mean it as a compliment. You father isn't a particularly disciplined fighter," Schmitt said.

"I think we both subscribe to the *whatever works* school of thought there," Alex shot back.

"Well, you can't afford to think like that. And you certainly can't afford to fight like that," Schmitt said. "After all, nothing you just did *worked*."

"Clearly, you have more training than me. I'll work harder," Alex said.

"That is part of your problem," Schmitt said, her face softening. "I'll call it your *Morgan problem*. This isn't something you can just power through. You can't afford to try harder than your opponent, you have to be smarter. Let me put it another way, you need to fight like a girl."

"What?! What does that have to do with anything?" Alex said, defensiveness coming up in her voice. "Every instructor I have had has said that gender has nothing to do with ability."

"Then every instructor you have had is full of crap. It's true that if you are built like a man, you can fight like one and your gender won't matter. But like most women, you are built nothing like a man." Schmitt studied her. "You are maybe 130 pounds, and strong for your size, but you are not built like a one hundred and seventy-five or two hundred pound man. Up until now, you've been told that size doesn't matter. Let me tell you something: size matters a great deal. In a fight between two people with the same level of skill and training, the larger fighter will win every time."

"I've seen smaller people take down much larger opponents," Alex said.

"And in every case, it was because the smaller fighter was smarter, had better training, and better sense of balance. Now look at me. I'm smaller than you. Can you guess how many fights I have lost in real combat situations?"

Alex sized Schmitt up. She was thin, lithe, with the body you'd expect from a fighter pilot, not a hand-to-hand combat expert. "Based on what you just did to me, I'd say not many."

"Close. I've lost exactly zero fights in the field," Schmitt said. "And do you know how you can tell?"

Alex knew where this was going. "Because you are still alive?"

"Exactly. Now when we were sparring you let me hit you, even leaned into a couple of blows to reduce their impact. Classic fighting techniques, but in the field, all that goes out the window. No matter how good you are, or how well trained, you don't want to let a two hundred and twenty pound trained killer land a blow on you. You *might* be able to shake it off, but if you can't, you won't have time to regret your choices."

"The key is that you never fight power with power, because most of the time in the field you'll be facing bigger and stronger opponents. That's why, for women like you and me, we're going to start with Judo. As far as I'm concerned, it's the best style for using a bigger opponent's size and power against him. Once you have the basics down, we can mix it up and put your other training to work."

"Okay, where do we start?" Alex said.

# Chapter 5

Valery Dobrynin returned to his small apartment with the newspaper. The news was old already—nothing he hadn't seen online except for some local reports. Yet buying and reading the paper had become part of his routine.

And for Dobrynin, routine was all. It had been that way for years now, even more so since he had helped that American and his daughter. Until then, he had been an irritant to the current administration of the KGB. Russia and the world had changed a great deal since he had been an active agent, and the new guard didn't trust old hands like him.

Yet he was too much trouble to kill. After all, he still had a few friends and a few tricks left. So they had let him be, choosing to see him as an embarrassing reminder of past sins.

However, that had all changed after an incident in Siberia. Dobrynin had done the right thing, and that had been a mistake. Now, he had angered people both in the army and at KGB headquarters.

That had forced him into hiding. He had assumed a new identity and moved into this one-room apartment. It was a small existence, far from the intrigue of his time at the KGB, but it kept him alive.

The one risk he took was staying in Leningrad—which he still could not bring himself to call it St. Petersburg as the young people did. Living here was no doubt foolish. If he were smart, he would be spending the rest of his days in a little dacha in the Urals, fishing each day for his dinner.

The only problem was that he hated fishing. The monotony of it drove him mad. And even if he was no longer part of the machinery that drove Mother Russia, in Leningrad he *felt* like part of it. There, he could still hear the great machine's hum.

Living there might shorten his life, but Dobrynin decided he was too old to become smart now.

The kettle whistled and he picked it up, but before he could pour the hot water, he heard a noise at his door.

Footsteps.

He reached for the PSM pistol he kept holstered at all times, and drew the weapon. He considered fetching the larger Tokarev he kept at his bedside but decided against it. In close quarters, the PSM would be fine.

He approached the door from the side and checked the peephole. There was no one there. That confirmed what he had thought—the sound he'd heard was footsteps walking away.

Opening the door, Dobrynin saw that indeed no one was there—or *still* there. However, there was a manila envelope at his feet.

Back inside, he opened the envelope and found a copy of a report that said Chechen separatists had raided a small storage facility in the Caucasus Mountains and his heart sank.

*Nothing is so bad that it can't get much worse,* his *babushka* had often said. And it had been true more times that Dobrynin could count.

The report said that two Red Army soldiers had been killed but nothing of value had been taken. However, he knew that wasn't true.

"Idiots," he said out loud. *Idiots for having it, and idiots for losing it,* he thought.

His instinct was to make a full report to KGB headquarters. The problem was that he would get nowhere near headquarters. And he knew nothing he said would be acted upon by the new administration—who had worked so hard to erase the past.

And even if they did listen, he doubted they would believe what he told them. Dobrynin hardly believed it, and he had been there when it was happening.

The Russian uttered a single word to himself, spitting it out simultaneously as a curse, a prayer, and a plan.

"Morgan…"

\* \* \* \*

Jenny greeted Dan Morgan with a hug, and the kind of kiss that they couldn't share when Alex was present but enjoyed more and more now that their daughter had moved into her own apartment.

"How was the mission?" Jenny asked.

Morgan shrugged. "A success."

She pulled away and gave him a quick once-over, apparently satisfied that he was all in one piece.

After years of secrecy, Jenny knew what Morgan did for a living, but that didn't mean she needed to know the kind of detail that would just worry her needlessly.

"And how is Peter?" Jenny said.

"Very good. He's on his way to a beach in Manila by now," Morgan said.

"I guess he deserves a vacation too," Jenny said.

"Not as much as you," Morgan said, kissing her again. He considered suggesting some alone time to Jenny before they left, but he had promised her this vacation and didn't want to start it by blowing their schedule.

"Do you need any help with the—" Jenny began.

Morgan waved his hand.

"It's all taken care of," he said.

"Do you want me to make any reservations?" she asked.

"I did it," Morgan said.

"What about—"

"I took care of everything. All you have to do is get in the car," he said smiling. He understood that, as with most things at home, Jenny took care of all of their travel plans: airline tickets, car rentals, dinner reservations, and even sitters for their German Shepherd Neika.

Because of the unpredictability of Dan's work, both his classic muscle car business and his real work for the CIA and then for Zeta Division, she had just taken on most of those duties. And that was why Morgan had wanted to give her one vacation in which she didn't have to think about anything. It was also, he realized, the first vacation longer than a long weekend that they had taken without Alex. Though he had made the plans with Jenny in mind, he realized that he was looking forward to this trip as well.

A few minutes later, Dan had loaded their bags into his car and pulled away, heading for Zeta Division headquarters.

"Just this one stop," he said.

Jenny squeezed his thigh. "It's fine, honey."

He pulled into the underground parking lot at headquarters. They really would be quick. He just wanted to check on his and Shepard's special project. It had been months since Mexico, and he had been determined to wait until it was finished to inspect it. Shepard was doing him a favor—multiple favors actually. He was not only personally overseeing the project, but he was keeping it quiet.

And that was pretty hard when you worked for an international spy agency.

Morgan was surprised when Diana Bloch greeted them personally.

"Morgan," she said, giving him a curt nod.

Then he saw something he had never see Bloch do before: she smiled broadly and warmly.

"Hi Jenny," she said. "How are you?"

"Just fine Diana, and you?"

Diana gestured in Morgan's direction. "Fine, but they keep me busy around here."

Jenny let out a knowing chuckle.

Morgan had to process what was going on here. First, Bloch had just smiled. And then had shared some kind of private joke with Jenny.

The world had just turned upside down. It was downright...unsettling.

Turning her attention to him, Bloch said. "Good work on your mission," she said. "Very good work."

Now he was getting *praise* from Bloch.

"And Shepard is very happy with the new tech you brought back. When he hands it over to our friends in government I think your country will owe you a debt."

Morgan simply said, "It was my job."

"Now I presume you are here to see the results of that *other* project you and Shepard have been working on," Bloch said.

Morgan made sure his face didn't betray his surprise.

"I wouldn't be much of a spymaster if I didn't know what was going on under my own roof," she said. Then she led the way to the elevator, "I'll join you."

The elevator stopped when it reached the lowest level of Zeta Division. 'The Basement' held O'Neal's computer servers and related tech, as well as Lincoln Shepard's various engineering labs and fabrication equipment.

It also held a special bay where Shepard worked on the vehicles used by Zeta agents. At the moment it held only a single car.

"1968 Mustang GT," Bloch said. "I always preferred the 1964s, if only for the styling."

Morgan disagreed. He had first taken notice of the Mustangs because of the 1968s. For his money, it was the best-looking of the Mustang fastbacks, but it was really the introduction of big block power to the Mustang line that appealed to Morgan. 390 cubic inches and 335 horsepower.

"It is a beautiful restoration though," Bloch said, turning her attention to Lincoln Shepard, who was staring at Bloch with his mouth open.

"It's okay, Shep," Morgan said.

"I presume it's for Alex's upcoming birthday?" Bloch asked.

"Yes," Jenny replied. "Dan is very excited for her."

"It is much nicer than my first car—an old Toyota. And also more valuable. At least it would be if it actually existed," Bloch said with a grin.

That was certainly true. This was one of two cars used in the 1968 film *Bullitt.* However, the one in front of him wasn't supposed to exist. This was the 'stunt' car that had done all of the real work in the chase sequence of the film—doing up to 110 miles an hour through the streets and hills of San Francisco.

The car used for close-ups was worth millions and currently resided in a private collection, whereas the "stunt" car was presumed destroyed after filming. And it would have been lost forever—and eventually actually destroyed by time—if Shep hadn't found it in a junkyard in the middle of nowhere in Mexico.

Now, it might as well as just rolled off the set of the film. It was the same rich hunter green. It also had the same stripped-down styling of the car in the film. Except this car appeared brand new, its paint gleaming in the shop bay's lights.

No, not brand new. Walking around the car, Morgan saw that Shep had kept the small dent on the driver's side door—a dent that Steve McQueen's car had gotten in the chase.

Morgan approved. This car was a veteran, not a show pony.

"I'll leave you to it," Bloch said. "See you soon, Jenny."

As Bloch left, Morgan and Shepard circled the car.

"Paint is a factory color match. Engine is original, of course, but with a little more power. It will now do zero to sixty in five seconds."

Morgan grinned his approval. That was quite a bit better than the car's factory specs of 7.8.

"And we did the suspension and handling upgrades you wanted." Then he turned to Jenny. "It also has all of the safety features we add to our field vehicles. Front and side airbags as well as collision avoidance sensors."

But what Morgan knew and Shep didn't want to say to Jenny was that those features included a reinforced frame, with armor in the door and body panels. And the glass would be bulletproof for anything less than high caliber, armor piercing rounds.

Shep leaned in to Morgan and said, "Of course, it has a full tactical package, with a few...new features."

Morgan knew that. This car would be Alex's daily driver, at least when she wasn't on her motorcycle. Alex was an agent and Morgan wanted her to have every advantage in the field.

"It is beautiful," Jenny said.

Morgan realized that it was, as he laid a hand on the right front fender.

"You know," Jenny continued. "Her birthday isn't for weeks. It might be a good idea to get it out on the road before that. What do you call it? A shake-down trip?"

"Better than sitting here for weeks," Shepard said.

Morgan couldn't deny that he would love to drive the car. Still, he'd intended it for Alex...

"That settles it. We'll bring it up and transfer the suitcases," Jenny said.

He didn't argue the point.

A few minutes later, they were on the road. Everything about the car seemed new, better than new in fact. The steering, the shifting, the raw power. He had no doubt that he was driving the highest performance '68 GT in the world.

The interior also seemed new. Fresh leather on the seats, new carpet, and even the familiar instrument panel seemed new. Looking closely, Dan could see which parts of the dash had movable panels, which would give Alex access to the tactical and defensive tech that Dan knew was now embedded in the car.

Morgan didn't explore those controls now, not with Jenny with him. His wife had taken her relatively new knowledge of his work fairly well. But this was their daughter's car, and highlighting the special equipment would only highlight the danger Alex would be in while she was working for Zeta.

And there was no reason for either of them to worry right now. Alex was still in training. And it was a beautiful day, the highway was pretty well open, and the car was a dream to drive.

Morgan checked the clock on the dash. At this rate, they would make Martha's Vineyard and their lunch reservation on time. He nudged the accelerator, and then nudged it again.

They might even be a little early...

# Chapter 6

Alex walked into Diana Bloch's office confidently—at least as confidently as she could muster.

Her father had often said, "If you don't feel brave, or sure of yourself, fake it. Most people can't tell the difference."

Though Alex had been to Bloch's office many times—for discussions about training or her general future with Zeta—this was the first time Alex had gone in there to ask Bloch for something specific.

Alex wanted a mission, her own mission as an undercover agent. True, she was younger than any of the other Zeta agents by several years, but she had already made significant contributions to the agency and its mission. She was confident about the progress of her training, particularly now with the new hand-to-hand combat skills she'd been developing with Alicia Schmitt.

Now she wanted something for herself. It was something she knew she was ready for, and something that would put her in a better position to contribute to Zeta's larger mission.

It all made perfect sense to Alex, but then why was she nervous now?

Stepping inside, Alex was surprised to see Karen O'Neal, Zeta's numbers analyst and computer expert, sitting in one of the two chairs facing Bloch's desk. Alex knew that before her time at Zeta, O'Neal had been a pretty high-level financial analyst, some sort of number cruncher. In many ways, she still was, but with a different mission now.

"Hello Alex, please sit down," Bloch said, indicating the empty seat next to O'Neal, who acknowledged her with an awkward nod.

"I know that you've been anxious to get assigned your first mission as a primary and I think we have something for you," Bloch continued.

*That was easy,* Alex thought, fighting to keep the surprise from her face. If she wasn't so pleased she would be more freaked out by Bloch's nearly supernatural ability to know what Alex had been thinking but had not discussed with anyone—not even her father.

"Karen has been working on new threat assessment software and it raised a red flag," Bloch went on.

O'Neal laughed quietly at that and Bloch shot her a quizzical look.

"Actually, the software doesn't use flags," O'Neal said simply.

Alex suppressed a grin. Alex knew she was smart, but normal smart. *O'Neal smart* was something else altogether. For someone who thought in high-level abstractions and could turn five conceptual corners before most people could count change, O'Neal could be oddly literal.

Alex didn't know for sure how old O'Neal was. Maybe late twenties? Maybe early thirties? The half-Vietnamese, half-Irish O'Neal was pretty, though in her jeans and collection of button-up blouses she looked like what she was, a brain who was more comfortable in front of a computer monitor than in a room full of people her own age.

And yet Alex knew that O'Neal was in a relationship with Lincoln Shepard, Zeta's other hacker and damned good general purpose engineer.

"The software identified a possible threat. How much do you know about what brought Karen to us?" Bloch said.

"I know she was a financial analyst on Wall Street. I know she got into some trouble over hacking and ended up here," Alex said.

"That's partly true. Karen developed a financial analysis scheme—"

"Algorithm," O'Neal corrected.

"An *algorithm* that was very effective but crossed certain legal lines," Bloch said.

"Actually, it was perfectly legal," O'Neal said.

"The SEC disagreed. Rather forcefully, as I recall," Bloch said. Then the director turned her attention to Alex. "At any rate, Karen has been working with Shepard to adapt her *algorithm* to identify security threats. Karen can explain it better than I."

"Yes I can," O'Neal said brightly.

Bloch said patiently, "Please do so."

Karen warmed to her subject. "My algorithm supplements traditional data analysis with the addition of metadata analysis."

Alex knew the term, at least as it applied to music. "That's the information attached to a song file. Artist, year, things like that," she said.

"Yes, but it applies to any digital file. It is data that provides information about other data. Most systems look for specific data points: large financial transactions, visits to extremist websites, or key words in telephone calls or emails. The current system is very good, but misses most of the terrorist activity it was designed to spot. The problem is that it only looks for the data and patterns it is programmed to find. It gets smarter all the time, but it is always behind.

"Our system is several orders of magnitude more complex because it combines traditional security data points with online shopping patterns, song choices, and a dozen other seemingly unrelated factors."

"How does that help?" Alex asked.

"We have no idea, but we don't need to know. The system looks at past patterns of metadata for, say, a public bombing. It examines every kind of data available from all of the parties involved."

"This system already helped us prevent the New York City subway bombing last month," Bloch said.

"But there wasn't a bombing last month," Alex replied.

"Exactly," Bloch said.

"We don't need to know why certain data and metadata patterns are there, just that they are."

"The tradeoff is that the system will sometime come up with a threat or a threat cluster that is…non-specific, especially if the threat is something we have never seen before. With bombs, there are certain ingredients that tip us off but with unorthodox threats it is more difficult. We may know something is coming but have no idea what it is. And that takes us to Berkeley."

"The college in California?" Alex asked.

Bloch tapped a remote on her desk. A large screen on the wall came to life with the image of a thirtysomething man in front of a lectern. It was a YouTube video whose title was "Dr. Apocalypse Addresses The Class."

"The Earth is an immensely complex organism and, unfortunately it has a disease—a very serious one that we call humanity," the man said. There was nervous laughter from the room, which Alex realized was a lecture hall.

"Pollution, global warming, nuclear waste, war…these are the symptoms of the disease. In that respect, humans are like a virus, a parasite that—if left untreated—will damage and then kill the host."

Proud of himself, the professor paused to let that sink in. "However, in this case the body—or the Earth—is not without defenses. It has bacteria and viruses that act as antibodies. And nature is getting better and better at defending itself. In the fourteenth century the Black Death wiped out about half of Europe and perhaps a third of the worlds' population. And that was with a disease that had a mortality rate of thirty to seventy five percent. Think about it, the world was almost rid of us once and for all. Imagine what a paradise it would be if the plague had succeeded?

"In 1918, Spanish influenza wiped out twenty-five million people in one year. On the one hand, it was very efficient in its transmission—it was in every state in the Union within a week. However, the relatively low mortality rate destined that particular antibody to failure.

"Now Ebola has a better than ninety percent mortality rate *and* is airborne. Yet the rate of transmission is still too low, and because of world health measures it's been limited to Africa. It's nearly the perfect disease, but it's not quite there…yet. But give nature time and the Earth will find itself a cure *for us*."

As he finished, Alex realized that her mouth was hanging open. And then the final surprise came. There was thunderous applause and the camera panned around the room, showing students in the lecture hall standing up.

"So, he's a crackpot and the standing ovation is creepy, but is this somehow a threat?" Alex asked.

"Not as far as we can tell, even though he's a biochemistry professor who has regular meetings with like-minded students in which they discuss their dream of creating a super virus."

"If there is no real threat, what are we talking about?" Alex asked.

"There is no threat that we can see," O'Neal added.

"The system says something's there, and we're going to investigate," Bloch said.

"Can't the police just arrest him and anyone in his little club?" Alex asked.

"Advocating for the death of every person on Earth is not really a crime. Now, even if they tried to create something in the university labs there is very little chance they would succeed, but at least then they could be charged under anti-terrorism law. I'd like you to go in and find out what is going on."

Alex kept her face as impassive as possible. She had wanted her own assignment as a mission primary. But this? This was investigating a nutty college professor and some student groupies—not exactly a lives-on-the-line situation. At best, they would be able to have a few of the idiots thrown in jail.

"I've chosen you because of your age and because the student group meeting with the professor is an offshoot of Americans for a Peaceful Society."

That got Alex's attention. She'd been a member of that group when she was still in high school, railing against what she thought was a corrupt, militaristic system. Back when she'd thought peace could be had if everyone just talked to one another. Back before she understood that bad guys were real, and surrendering to them might give you peace, but not a life worth living.

Back before she had grown up.

Alex could keep her face expressionless but she couldn't control the blood rushing to her cheeks, turning her complexion a bright red.

"Don't be embarrassed," Bloch said. "We all did stupid things when we were young. However, in your case, your youthful indulgences can help our cause. The real challenge for you will be to get back into that mindset, before you received your real education."

"That I can do. I'll just shut off most of my brain," Alex said.

# Chapter 7

"Honey, that was amazing, how did you get the reservation? They are booking six weeks in advance," Jenny said as they drove away from the restaurant.

"I told you I've been planning this," Morgan said casually. That was true. He had been planning to take Jenny on this long overdue getaway. It was the actual details that gave him trouble. Planning lunch six weeks ahead was insane, even if the seafood was pretty good.

Fortunately, he had a guy.

Apparently, after hacking the Chinese missile defense system, adding a reservation to an overpriced seafood shack was easy.

And it turned out most of the local restaurants were on the same system, so Morgan and Shepard were able to plot out the week during Morgan's plane ride back from India. As it turned out, working the hotel system was even easier.

Morgan was firm about the hotel. In the past, they had rented various beach houses and set up for extended periods. And every time, Jenny would make a great effort to make the new place like home. But on this trip Morgan was determined that there would be no grocery shopping, cooking, cleaning, or organizing. For the first time since their honeymoon, they were going to have a real vacation.

So he and Shepard had found a hotel that also had little cottages on the beach, so they could have some privacy without the work.

"Dan, you know there's a place I wanted to visit. It's on the way," Jenny said.

"Check-in is at—"

Then he stopped himself. He was still on mission time. After an assignment, he always had a brief adjustment period where he had to remind himself that schedules were not make-or-break—or life-and-death.

The relaxed work atmosphere was one of the reasons that he chose classic cars as his professional "cover." Though the stakes were sometimes high—at least in terms of the dollar value of the cars—there wasn't a great deal of pressure in the day-to-day aspects of the business.

He'd gotten plenty of that from years at the CIA and now at Zeta. And he always credited Jenny and Alex for helping him develop the ability to turn off that part of himself and become a husband and a father—to rejoin the 'real' world.

At least, it had worked for him. And he believed it helped him stay sharp in the field, even after almost twenty years as an operative. He had known men and women who had lived the mission, even when they weren't on one. They tended to have short careers. Either because they burned out, or because they got sloppy in the field and paid the price.

"Sure honey," Morgan said. "Where are we going?"

"I'll direct you," she said casually, reading from her phone.

Probably an antique store, he guessed. At heart, Morgan knew his wife was part treasure hunter, and it was close enough to his own interest in classic cars that he understood.

Of course, pride almost made him ask the name of the place. Besides the hotel and the restaurants, he'd plotted out a few antique stores, flea markets, and crafty gift shops. If the place was any good, he'd probably planned to hit it already.

Yet as they got close, Morgan didn't recognize the area as being near anything he had found online. "Turn right up ahead," Jenny said.

"But that's—"

"Just turn, Dear," she said gently.

He followed a sign that said, *Cape Cod Rod and Gun Club.*

Morgan appraised his wife, who kept her face casual, but he could see a twinkle in her eye.

"No questions, just park," she said. "You have your Walther?"

"Of course," he replied. He literally never left home without it. In the past, Jenny had given him some grief about carrying a gun when they went out. But since she'd found out about his real job—and faced a few of its dangers herself—she had not complained again.

This, however, was a whole other level.

While Morgan parked, Jenny reached into her bag and pulled out a something he recognized as a gun case.

She spun the combination with a practiced hand and pulled out something else he recognized: a Smith and Wesson Bodyguard .380. It was a small gun, easy to hide and good for close fighting.

He approved of the weapon, but what was it doing in his wife's hands?

Now she was laughing. "It's for me. I thought I should have something in case..."

Jenny didn't need to finish that. More than once, his intelligence work had put Jenny in danger. Or rather, *he* had put Jenny in danger.

"Alex helped me pick it out," Jenny said, with some pride—as if she and their daughter had gone shopping for a party dress.

Maybe if they had been a normal family, Morgan would have been upset, or concerned, or uncomfortable. But after everything their family had been through he was just...relieved. Jenny would be safer now, better equipped to handle whatever came.

And the image of the two women in his life clucking over pistols made him smile.

"I guess we're here so I can teach you how to shoot, or at least make a start," Morgan said.

"That would be great. And I packed some extra rounds for your Walther," Jenny said.

At the desk, Jenny showed a certificate from a gun safety course and they were headed toward the back.

A few minutes later they were standing in one of the firing lanes (because, of course, Jenny had reserved one) and she was handing him the hearing and eye protection she had packed—then putting on her own.

Jenny loaded her own weapon with the same meticulous care she took with everything she did. Only then, did she look up and him.

"Do you mind if I go first?" Jenny said.

Morgan let her take the center of the lane. He noted that she planted her feet just a hair wider than shoulder width. Then she placed her right foot (her firing side foot) even with the instep of her left foot.

It wasn't the beginner's Isosceles stance, or the Weaver, which was favored by law enforcement. It was the Fighting stance used by military and special ops. Jenny executed it perfectly, flexing her knees and lifting the weapon up to her head, which she kept level.

Jenny emptied the pistol's six round magazine into the target, which was a respectable twenty yards away. Morgan knew that she had done well. Jenny pushed the button on the side of the lane and the target raced forward.

It was a standard black silhouette in the shape of a bear on a white background. There were no hits in the bull's-eye on the bear's head, but he saw that all of the shots were center mass.

Jenny glowed with pride. "What do you think?"

"I think that bear is a goner."

"I've been practicing," she said.

"I noticed," he replied.

"Why don't you try, then we'll take the target out a bit farther. And later I've rented us two Uzis. I've never tried one of those."

Morgan realized that this was going to be an interesting trip.

\* \* \* \*

After her latest workout with Schmitt, Alex felt pretty good. She applied herself and trained like crazy to learn what Schmitt had to teach her.

As a result, Alex had taken her instructor down twice in their hour together. It was nothing compared to the number of times Schmitt had put her on the mat, but it was progress.

Even Alicia Schmitt was pleased, and she wasn't easily impressed. The commander had multiple black belts, but Alex was confident that in a year or two she might be able to give her instructor a real run for her money.

As it was, Alex was almost as good a marksman as her dad, at least with a handgun. She knew it was just a matter of time before she caught up with him and maybe even surpassed him.

That was a sobering thought. Growing up, she had definitely been a daddy's girl. And then there had a brief period of estrangement in her later teen years. It had started when she had joined Americans for a Peaceful Society. She had felt her father's disapproval then, and that had made her identify with the group even more.

Things had only gotten worse when she learned what her father really did for a living. Then, for a brief period, he had literally become the enemy—the embodiment of the arrogant military powers she and the APS believed were the true threats to world peace.

Though it pained her to admit it now, she had come close to hating her father then. He represented the opposite of everything she had thought she believed in. The only problem was that just about everything she'd believed in was wrong. Those beliefs were fairy tales she'd told herself about all people and all nations being basically good. She still believed that about all people—or at least most people—but less so about all nations.

Like people, governments could be corrupted by ideology, or greed, or—there was no other way to put it—evil. Once she'd understood that both individuals and groups could be evil, the world actually got harder.

In a fight between the truly good and the truly bad, you always had to make a choice. You couldn't sit on the sidelines and endlessly collect information, rationalize behavior, and speculate about motivations.

It a world of good guys and bad guys, you had to choose; you had to take a stand. As an agent you had to do it with too little information and too little time. You had to just *know*.

The way her father just *knew* what was worth fighting for and what to do in almost any tough situation. When she was in the APS she didn't know any of that yet. Of course that was still high school and seemed like a lifetime ago.

However, in reality, it was barely two years ago. Thinking back, Alex could hardly recognize that girl. And yet if Alex hadn't gotten involved in her father's business, Alex would still *be* that person. She'd likely still be a member of the APS and starting her third year of college.

She would be railing against the military and people like her father while remaining blissfully unaware of the real threats that were out there. She'd still be fighting imaginary monsters while the real ones were crouched in the darkness.

Alex definitely didn't miss that person. She definitely didn't miss being her, and yet she'd have to be, at least for the duration of this mission.

"Hello Alex," Lily Randall said, as she entered the small briefing room.

"Hi Lily," she replied automatically.

Alex liked Lily. She had given Alex some of her earliest weapons and hand-to-hand training at Zeta. Before joining Zeta, Lily had been an agent for MI5, the British intelligence agency. She was also the only female agent who worked primarily as an undercover operative, which was why she was giving Alex this last bit of training.

There were other women in the office, like Spartan, but she was a tactical agent and, as far as Alex knew, had never done undercover work. Alex, like her father, wanted to be able to do both, and do them at a very high level.

"Diana tells me this will be your first undercover assignment," Lily said.

"Yes, if you can even call it that," Alex said.

"What do you mean?"

"Well, I'm basically going as myself. I'm not even changing my name," Alex said.

"Smart," Lily said. "The fewer things you change about yourself, the less likely you are to get caught."

"That much I learned from my father," Alex said.

"What else did he teach you?" Lily asked, with interest.

"That when I'm undercover, the fewer details I have to keep straight, the less the chance that I'll be killed or captured," Alex said.

"Good advice," Lily concurred.

"But I'm not really worried about the killed and captured part. I mean, I'll be infiltrating a bunch of college kids who are either pacifists or environmentalists, or both. I'm not worried about the physical danger."

"Maybe, but what about mission failure? Because if you're caught, you won't be killed or taken to a dank prison somewhere, but you will fail in your mission, which is to collect intelligence about the group and their work. You can't do that effectively if everyone suspects or knows you aren't on the team. And I wouldn't be so quick to discount physical danger. The only guarantee on any undercover mission is that there will be surprises."

Lily gave Alex a minute to consider that. Alex knew that Lily had been captured and injured on a recent mission. And while Lily seemed normal now—though normal for her was drop-dead gorgeous—Alex knew she had not been in the field since.

"Never take your assignment lightly. Assume lives are always on the line, yours or someone else's, or both. I've seen your mission parameters and I know that the Americans for a Peaceful Society are likely crackpots, but they are working with someone who is a leading biochemist and whose stated goal is the elimination of all human life on earth. And even if we judge the risk of Spellman and his club succeeding to be low, I'd say the failure cost would be pretty high. Wouldn't you?"

Alex felt blood rushing to her treacherous cheeks. "You're right, I'm embarrassed that I dismissed them…"

"Don't be. This is one of the first steps in your education as an agent," Lily said.

"I understand," Alex said, "but why does my education lately make me feel like an idiot?" Alex asked.

"That's because you are doing it right," Lily said, smiling. "Now tell me what approach you are planning to take as you go undercover as Alex Morgan, college student."

"Approach? I was just going to be myself," Alex said, suddenly unsure.

"Okay, tell me how you feel about Professor Spellman and the student profiles you've seen?"

"Well, they're morons," Alex said. Even as the words left her mouth, she realized what was wrong. "Which, I now see might not be the right attitude to go in with if I want them to accept me."

"See, you are learning already," Lily said. "I know you were a member of the APS. At the time, I'm sure you were naïve and sincere in your beliefs. Assume they are too. And remember, even though they may be crackpots who fantasize about the end of the world, that doesn't mean they are stupid. These are biochemistry students, some of them on doctorate tracks. And the professor himself was on the short list for a Nobel Prize or two. Keep that in mind and you'll be fine."

Lily stopped to appraise Alex.

"Just a few more things before I clear you. And then we have to go shopping," Lily said.

"Shopping?" Alex said.

"Yes, you're going to college. We need to outfit your dorm room, make sure you have appropriate clothes. We're building you a character—you're going to need some props and a costume."

That made Alex smile, which was followed by a pang. She knew her father was pleased when she had decided to go into his business, and proud that she was doing something important.

However, she also knew her mother had been disappointed. When Alex had been in high school, Jenny Morgan had been looking forward to getting her off to college. There had been SAT prep classes and discussions about boys, and warnings about drinking too much.

Alex also knew that her mom had seen her friends send their children off to school, buying them clothes, setting up their dorm rooms.

Now Alex would be doing all of that in an afternoon with Lily. Well, Alex decided she would have to tell her mother all about it when the mission was over.

"Yes, let's go shopping," she said.

# Chapter 8

"See you later, Amado," Conley said.

The security guard smiled broadly at Conley as he left the hotel café. "Have a good morning, Mr. Conley," Amado replied, smiling even as he spoke. There were two things Amado was never without: a big grin on his face and an oversized pistol grip shotgun on his hip.

That was the Philippines for you. Possibly the friendliest and most heavily armed people Conley had ever encountered. There were armed security everywhere—literally everywhere. Gas stations, convenience stores, and burger joints all not only had security, but *armed* security. And pistol grip shotguns were the usual weapon of choice.

These guards kept an eye on everyone and did things like check bags as you entered a store. However, they also helped people carry packages, reached items from the high shelves for customers, and cleaned the tables at coffee shops. Conley had even seen armed security men scooping ice cream for children when an ice cream parlor was busy.

There was something sweet about it. Of course, with that many armed people in a city like Manila, there were occasional accidents. Training for these private security guards varied wildly, and every year there were a few accidental weapons discharges.

But Conley suspected that had never happened to Amado, whom Conley pegged as retired military, now content to keep watch on the hotel café.

The security in Manila was a response to the ever-present threat of robbery and kidnappings, and recently it was because the terrorist activity in the south had made its way up to Manila and the larger cities.

The Moro Islamic Liberation Front had gotten bolder in recent years, with strikes in Manila as recently as six months ago. Their acronym—MILF—always made Conley chuckle, but they were a deadly serious threat.

Though usually Conley had breakfast on the beach, today he wanted to make a point of spending some time in the lobby of the hotel. This wasn't a mission exactly; it was more like a working vacation. With the Chinese delegation arriving this morning, this was the beginning of the *working* part.

Not that he had many actual responsibilities. In reality, he was simply doing Diana Bloch a favor by staying at the hotel where the Chinese economic team would be staying. The conference could possibly strengthen ties between China and the Philippines, which—naturally—could affect the relationship between the Philippines and the United States.

The Philippines had always had a complex relationship with the U.S. Traditionally, the two countries shared a strong economic and political relationship, but the current administration in Manila had made it a priority to make their country less dependent on the U.S. At the same time, the Filipino government was increasing economic and political ties to China—ties which had been steadily building for about twenty years.

It was all fascinating and was probably keeping rooms full of analysts at the CIA and State busy—but none of those questions were particularly interesting to Conley. The Philippines and the U.S. had maintained their close but complex relationship since the Philippines achieved independence in 1946. Filipino administrations would sometimes flirt with China and get the State Department scurrying, but the reality was that the U.S. was the Philippines' strongest ally.

Rather than focusing on the always-changing diplomatic situation, Conley was there to assess the current local security situation, at least for the conference. The fact was that any international conference would be a natural target for terrorists.

On the streets there were some more of the Filipino police and the so-called 'Tourist Police,' who with their blue slacks and blue shirts were often mistaken for regular police. They even had virtually the same powers to keep the peace and make arrests. Their biggest defining characteristic was the assault rifle each tourist policeman had slung on his or her back. Many, if not most, were ex-military. And they clearly had much more training than their private security counterparts, or even the regular police. Conley was also there as part of a test of Karen O'Neal's new threat assessment software. He liked the idea of her project, but even if the idea was solid, optimizing the software to run it would take some doing, and probably quite a bit of trial and error.

Case in point: he was in Manila keeping an eye on an international conference that O'Neal's system had tagged as a security threat when there was none of the traditional online and telecommunications chatter that *always* proceeded a major terrorist attack. So either Karen's system saw something that all the traditional software had missed, or Karen's new project needed some work.

The problem with current threat assessment tools was that they were painfully non-specific. They showed an increased threat to a country, or a region, or possibly a city. That could be helpful, but hardly told authorities where to deploy their resources.

O'Neal's software had pinpointed the conference and the hotel specifically. Of course, they were logical targets, but in the absence of the usual online chatter and other signs, Conley—along with Diana Bloch—was not particularly concerned.

Still, it might help O'Neal and Shepard calibrate the software, which would make it useful in the long term.

Conley checked his watch. Based on the Chinese delegation's arrival time, they were due to be arriving at the hotel shortly. Positioning himself so he had a view of virtually the entire lobby, Conley lifted his Wall Street Journal and began to read.

Just a few minutes later, he saw movement outside and watched as proper Filipino soldiers took up positions in the front of the hotel. They were professional, focused, and didn't interact with the public in the way that even the heavily armed tourist police did. He counted at least a dozen soldiers and expected that they would be there for the duration of the conference.

Then there was movement behind him and he saw the hotel manager and two other staff members hurry toward the door.

Limousines and black SUVs pulled up. They were all American makes. Conley thought that Dan Morgan would approve.

The Chinese delegation was large, twenty people in dark business suits, flanked by eight Chinese soldiers wearing sidearms.

Four of the soldiers entered first, followed by the clear leader of the group. Conley was surprised to see that he recognized the man: it was Cheng Quan, the Chinese Minister of Finance himself. That was impressive. It showed that the Chinese government took this conference very seriously.

Conley imagined rooms full of analysts at the CIA and State jumping in their chairs all at once. Then again, that might have been the point of sending Quan—misdirection. Perhaps the Chinese were signaling that the conference was of supreme importance in order to divert the United States' attention from something else.

It was an interesting question, and he had more patience for those sorts of problems than Morgan, but there was no doubt that Morgan had rubbed off on him. Conley preferred a clear mission, with a clear set of challenges and objectives, to the endless game of feint and counter-feint that made up the bulk of international intelligence work.

For now, he had a simple mission, and he suspected it would be an easy one. Even if there were a significant terrorist attack, the combination of private security, police, and military from two countries would almost certainly be able to handle it.

Thus, it was time to focus on the vacation part of his working vacation. However, before he could fully formulate that thought, something caught his eye. No, not something—*someone.*

Standing to the left of Minister Quan was a Chinese woman in a no-nonsense business suit. She had the minister's attention and was leading him to the hotel manager. Clearly, she was one of his top aides, and she obviously commanded respect from the rest of the minister's entourage.

That was something. For all of its pretense of communist egalitarianism, China still had a deeply patriarchal culture, and still seemed—from a Western point of view—fairly chauvinist. But this aide certainly commanded the men's attention—including Conley's. She was in her early to mid, thirties. And she carried herself with the kind of confidence that was only born of extreme competence.

She was also beautiful—gorgeous actually. Her hair was past shoulder length and had a bit of a curl. It was light years from the short bob "liberation" hairstyle that most women in China had adopted in the 1950s, and which was still favored by women who wanted to get anywhere in the Communist party or in high-level Chinese business.

Conley didn't care for that bob, simply because it was intended to erase one of the differences between men and women. Obviously, the woman he was watching shared his view. That made her, he decided, a bit of a rebel.

She turned away from the minister, who was bowing to the hotel manager, and directly at Conley. She locked eyes with him and he realized that he'd been staring—like a smitten tourist.

Well, that was his cover, the tourist part anyway.

She held his gaze for longer than he would have expected. Her expression didn't change except for a slight tilt of her head and the raising of one eyebrow. Then she was back to work, leading the minister through the lobby.

Well, even if the work part of his vacation was uneventful, the vacation part was certainly looking up.

* * * *

"You've been cleared by all of your instructors. Do you have any concerns about the mission or your preparation for it?" Diana Bloch asked.

This was it. Alex had wanted it, she'd trained for it, and she thought she was ready for it.

All she had to do was agree that she was ready.

"I'm comfortable with the cover, the social aspects, the infiltration plan. However, I do have some concerns about the course material," Alex said.

"The course material?" Bloch asked.

Alex had been an advanced high school student, with a number of college-level courses and college credits from her AP exams. She knew she could keep up in her literature and history classes. However the people she'd be going to class with and hopefully infiltrating were now studying high-level biology and chemistry.

Alex had studied both biology and chemistry in high school and had even taken AP Organic Chemistry. She was proud of scoring a 4 on the exam, but she was still at a significant disadvantage when dealing with people who were majoring in biochemistry.

Alex remembered enough from her time with Americans for a Peaceful Society that she knew she could talk the talk. Playing fangirl for a professor who was advocating for the death of every man, woman, and child on the planet would be tougher, but she had studied him and his group enough that she knew she could do it.

But what about late night bull sessions about the finer points of cloning vectors or viroid propagation?

Alex remembered her talk with Alicia Schmitt. *Just because they are crackpots, don't make the mistake of assuming they are stupid.*

"I share your concerns. This is why I've assigned Karen O'Neal to go undercover with you," Bloch said.

"In what capacity?" Alex asked, her tone sharper than she had intended.

"Professor Spellman finds himself suddenly short a teaching assistant. O'Neal is the replacement."

Alex directed her next question to O'Neal. "Do you have a background in biochemistry?"

"Not really, but I've had a week to study," O'Neal said flatly.

"And you've learned biochemistry in a week?"

"Not enough to teach a class myself, but more than enough to grade papers and help in the lab. I'll be a teaching assistant, not a professor," O'Neal said, shooting an apologetic look at Bloch. "To take over any of Spellman's classes, I'd need another few—" Bloch raised her hand and O'Neal didn't finish.

"That's fine, you'll be there to observe Professor Spellman, not replace him," Bloch said. Then the director turned her gaze to Alex. "What do you think?"

Alex was stunned on a few levels. First, this would not be a solo mission, as she and Bloch had discussed, which hit her right in her pride. Second, Bloch had obviously given O'Neal the assignment at least a week ago. And third, O'Neal had—with no prior training—learned enough in seven days to pose as a graduate teaching assistant to one of the top biochemistry professors in the country.

Alex always knew she was smart herself, but she was once again reminded that O'Neal was in a whole other ballpark.

With all of that swirling around in her head she couldn't moderate her answer and said simply, "I'm glad to have the help, especially with the science."

Something flashed across Bloch's face and then the director was unreadable again.

"And I presume you didn't tell me O'Neal would be joining me on the mission because you wanted to test my reaction to the news that I would not be the mission primary," Alex said.

Bloch raised an eyebrow. "The field is a changeable place, consider this your first lesson. And you are still mission primary. O'Neal will be there for support and help with the course material. The APS is your area of expertise. Your job is still to infiltrate and assess. If appropriate, you may decide to have O'Neal join you at the APS meetings or involve her in any contact you have with them or other radical elements."

If anything, Alex realized that this increased her responsibilities. Now Alex was responsible for not only the success of the mission but also the welfare of another agent.

"Of course, bear in mind that O'Neal is not a field agent. She is there for technical support to you and to help assess the threat level of the group and their activities. I expect *you* to keep O'Neal out of danger," Bloch said.

"Understood," Alex replied.

Bloch stood up, signaling that the meeting was over. For Alex, it had been a roller coaster. In the end, Alex wasn't sure if Bloch was testing her or teaching her. Probably both, she realized.

"Good luck on your mission, agents," Bloch said.

O'Neal and Alex walked out together to find Shepard in the hallway, wearing his signature jeans and t-shirt. He didn't even glance at Alex; he only had eyes for O'Neal.

"Mom give you the talk before sending you off to school?" Shepard asked.

O'Neal shrugged awkwardly. "Something like that."

Alex was put off for a minute. She'd never heard anyone refer to Bloch as 'Mom' and realized it must be a private joke between them. That made sense; they were, after all, in a relationship.

But that by itself was odd. As smart as O'Neal was, she was a bit awkward socially, often unsure of what to say or do. Though brilliant in their fields and highly respected by everyone at Zeta, O'Neal and Shepard were the organization's nerds.

Yet they were very comfortable together. It was cute, Alex decided.

"Van is loaded. I'll drive you two to the airport," Shepard said.

On the way, O'Neal and Shepard chatted casually, shifting effortlessly between high end computer programming, biochemistry, video games, and T.V. shows and movies—some of which Alex had never heard of.

Shepard walked them to the security line and said to Alex, "Good luck."

Then he turned to O'Neal, who leaned in and kissed him. It was instantly passionate and Alex felt like she was intruding on something private.

She realized that they weren't just in a relationship—they were in love.

Alex, of course, had dated in high school, but that had stopped when she had gotten involved with Zeta and started her training. As she progressed, she'd seen that she had less and less in common with people her own age. And yet she was significantly younger than the youngest agents at Zeta.

Watching O'Neal with Shepard, Alex realized that she herself had never had a serious boyfriend.

When they broke apart, O'Neal was silent and Alex was sure she saw tears forming in the young woman's eyes. Alex realized that O'Neal wasn't just ahead of her in biochemistry.

Alex shook off the thought. She wasn't on a mission to shop for a boyfriend. She was going on her first undercover assignment to develop the skills she would need to make a real difference in the future.

# Chapter 9

"Dan," Jenny called gently.

Morgan put down his book. Jenny was standing in front of him, her hands on her hips. She was still wearing her painting smock—actually one of his old dress shirts—with her shorts peeking out from under it.

She had her oils out and was working on a landscape—or more likely a seascape.

"Come on, Mister Morgan. Time to get going," Jenny said.

Morgan checked his mental list. "The vintage upholstery show isn't until tomorrow," he said.

"I have something planned for us this afternoon."

Morgan perked up. "I hope it's the same thing *I* have planned for us."

Jenny put on her oversized sunglasses as she took off the smock. "I doubt it. This requires going out."

"Then it's definitely not the same thing," he grumbled as he got up from the Adirondack chair.

"What's the plan?" he asked.

"A surprise," she said. "I'll drive."

In the car he asked, "Have you been secretly practicing for this one too?"

"As a matter of fact I have," she said.

"More at the shooting range?" he asked as they pulled out of the driveway.

"Something new," she replied.

That was interesting.

"Rock climbing?"

"Nope," she said.

"Scuba diving?"

"Not even close," she said.

"Laser tag?"

"Closer, but no."

A few minutes later they pulled into a parking lot and Morgan saw what she had in mind.

"Why would you practice this? You always beat me," he said.

"Yes, but I really wanted to make it embarrassing this time," she said lightly. "Care to make a wager, Mr. Morgan?"

"Usual terms?" he asked.

"Of course," she said. "Unless you'd like to chicken out. I know the windmill scares you."

"Not the windmill, it's the anthills that get me. Every time," he said as they paid and collected their balls and putters.

Jenny won, of course, but it was close enough that Morgan hadn't shamed himself too badly.

As they left, she threw her arms around him and gave him a kiss. The game, the kiss—both took him back to their early days. Miniature golf had been one of their first dates.

"Come on, I want to collect my winnings," she said.

Morgan grinned. Those were the terms. The winner got to choose what they did next. Of course, in the unlikely event that he had won, he would have chosen the same thing.

That's what he liked about making bets with Jenny. No matter who won, the results were always the same.

As they headed for home Morgan caught a glimpse of a black, late-model Cadillac. He realized three things at once about the car. First, black Cadillacs were rare in Cape Cod, where the people there for summer vacation favored Mercedes and BMWs, and the locals drove Fords and Chevys. Second, the car had a New York License plate—not unusual by itself since a fair number of the visitors here were from New York. And third, this was the second time in three days he had seen the vehicle.

The last one was the detail that stuck with him. He was willing to bet it was the only car of its kind in Cape Cod. And yet he had seen it twice—both times, he realized, in his rear view mirror.

It was probably nothing, he reckoned. He had just come from a mission and while he was better than most at leaving his work at work, it still sometimes took him a few days to shake off his active duty reflexes.

As they approached their cottage, Morgan felt the twinge already fading. "I hope you're ready to pay up, Mr. Morgan," Jenny said.

"Always," Morgan said.

* * * *

Over the years, Conley had had his problems with the Chinese government, both politically and professionally. However, he would give them two things: First, they had gotten to be pretty good engineers. He still wished he'd been able to log a few more hours on their new fighter. It really was an impressive machine.

And secondly, they worked hard. Certainly, this group did. Minister Cheng Quan and his group had maintained a grueling schedule. A minimum of ten hours of meetings, presentations, and workshops. There were long lunches and breaks, but for Chinese officials at this level, the difference between work and rest wasn't as clear as it was in the West. Virtually all lunches were working lunches, either with their Filipino counterparts or with internal meetings for the team.

Conley's Mandarin was good enough that he'd been able to roughly follow the few conversations he had overheard. Of course, he hadn't been able to learn anything useful. Diplomacy was complex enough to make the sort of intelligence work he and Morgan did look simple. And economic diplomacy was the most complicated of all. Trade agreements had relatively long terms, and small details could have long and costly repercussions, both financial and political.

Conley watched as Minister Quan, his delegation, and the Filipino team emerged from the back room of the restaurant. It was only nine in the evening, early for the end of the day for this group. However, he knew it wasn't really the end.

The minister and two of his aides said goodnight to the rest of his delegation, including the woman who had caught his eye on the first day. He'd since learned that her name was Danhong Guo.

He'd been able to learn that much on the Internet. However, the dossier that Bloch had provided had been much more informative. Ms. Guo was thirty-four and had graduated from Fudan University in Shanghai with degrees in both finance and computer science. After college she also earned a number of technical computer certifications. And then she had worked for the Chinese government for most of her professional life, almost all of it in the Ministry of Finance.

There was nothing unusual in her background, except for the fact that she wasn't a member of the Communist party. However, given her work schedule and career trajectory Conley suspected that had more to do with time than anything else. She excelled at everything she did and he suspected that she would have little interest in membership in any organization to which she could not give her all.

Bloch had been mildly surprised when he had asked for the dossier on the delegation but had accepted Conley's explanation that he was curious and simply wanted more info to assess security.

That was true, at least partly. The fact was that he found her very interesting—an interest that was only compounded when he read her bio.

Conley watched as Ms. Guo and the lower-level Chinese delegates said goodnight to Minister Quan and his top three male aides.

From the dossier, Conley knew that Guo outranked one of them and was more valuable than the other two. However, Quan, his top male aides, and their Filipino counterparts would be exploring the nightlife—some of which would be unseemly, and none of which, he knew, would be interesting to a woman.

So much the better. Perhaps Guo would take the opportunity to explore the hotel bar and other amenities and he could meet her there. He was disappointed to watch as she promptly disappeared into the elevator.

Well, he was still at a hotel on the beach in Manila. There were worse places to be. He knew that for a fact, because he and Morgan had been in quite a few worse places.

He opted for a drink at the outdoor bar that was literally right on the beach. It was filling up, but he found a table facing the water. He was barely halfway into his drink when he heard a voice behind him say, "Do you mind if I join you?"

It was a woman who spoke English with a very mild Chinese accent. Before he turned, he knew it was Danhong Guo.

When he turned, he saw she had changed remarkably quickly into a very nice flower print dress that showed off her athletic figure. He also noticed she was wearing perfume. He didn't recognize the scent but she smelled good.

He managed to keep his surprise at seeing her off his face as he stood and said, "Of course."

"I hope I'm not disturbing you," she said as she took the seat next to him. "But you have the last table with this view." She gestured to the waves rolling into the shore.

"Not at all, I'm glad for the company." He noted that her hands were empty. "Can I get you a drink?"

"A cosmopolitan," she said without hesitation. He liked that. No pretense. No worry that it would seem unsophisticated. The fact was that she was dressed as a tourist, and the Cosmo fit that image.

He returned and handed her the drink. She thanked him and made surprisingly long eye contact. That was a bit unusual for a mainland Chinese woman, but she was anything but ordinary. Despite all of their political slogans about equality, the Chinese leaders were still remarkably sexist. She would have had to forgo a lot of her assigned gender role to get noticed and rise as fast as she did in the government.

"You like the ocean?" he asked.

"Yes, I grew up inland but went to school in Shanghai, and I work in Beijing," she said. Both places, he knew, were on the shore. "School was demanding, and so is my work. To have a night free and this view. It feels like a…treat."

"You are with the Chinese delegation?" he said.

"I am. And you are just visiting? A vacation?"

"A vacation. Really more of a sabbatical. I teach at the University of Texas. I'm taking a year to rest and write," Conley said.

"Interesting. What do you teach?" she asked.

"Native American languages. I specialize in the Southwestern dialects," he said. It was his cover, at least one of them. Dan Morgan often told him he looked like a college professor. And obscure languages were a safe cover since so few people spoke them.

"That is interesting. I have never met anyone with that specialty," she said politely.

That was the point. He wasn't exactly fluent in Sioux or any of the other related languages, but he knew enough to fake it, and certainly enough to convince most people.

Conley realized that he was staring at her. "It's important to enjoy your work, I think," he said.

"I agree," she said.

"And yet, a break is always welcome," he said.

"Yes, most welcome."

"Would you like to dance?" he said.

She took his arm and they moved to the small dance floor. She moved gracefully to the American pop music. That was a bit of a surprise. According to her bio, this was her first trip outside of China.

Conley decided there was more to Ms. Guo than was covered in her bio—and more than he would have thought watching her interact with her colleagues.

When a slow song started she allowed him to take her hand and put the other hand on her waist. The distance between them was respectable but close enough for him to learn she didn't just look, but *felt* athletic.

He decided there was indeed much more to her than he had thought, and he hoped he would have enough time to find out exactly how much more.

When the song ended she said, "Would you like to take a walk?"

A few minutes later they were walking on the beach. They chatted amiably, avoiding her work—or economics, or politics, or anything that might spoil the mood.

Too soon she said, "I should get back to my room."

"Do you have to work tomorrow?" he asked.

"No, but I was going to see some of Manila. I'm fascinated by this place," she said.

"Perhaps we could explore it together," he said.

"I would like that very much," she said.

Conley walked her to her door and decided against trying to kiss her. He would see her tomorrow. Even vacation romances had rules and he didn't want to rush it.

# Chapter 10

"You don't have to do this, Dan," Jenny said, seriously.

"I want to," Morgan said.

"For a spy, you are a terrible liar."

"No, I really want to do this. If you can learn to shoot, I can do this," Morgan replied. "Plus, it will go faster if I help you."

"Of course it will, dear," she said, patting his arm.

A few minutes later they were in the Mustang and on their way.

It wasn't just shooting that Jenny had learned. He realized that she knew quite a bit about his car business. And she'd been to her share of car shows and auctions.

Over the years Morgan had picked up some of the jargon from her interior design work. And he'd seen thousands of design drawings, paint color charts, and fabric swatches.

Today, however, would be his first vintage upholstery show. He decided it wouldn't be too bad. And Jenny had given him a folder of vintage ads and a few swatches to try to match.

So he had an objective, of sorts. Well, he'd done worse work for bosses he liked much less than Jenny.

He broke the rows of tables and booths into a mental grid and started searching. Fifteen minutes later he had found precisely nothing on his list and Jenny showed up with half a dozen bales of fabric for him to bring to the car.

Well, fair enough, this was her world. He lugged the upholstery back to the Mustang and dropped it into the trunk. On the way back to the show, he saw a young man in a tracksuit looking at fabric on a table. The man was maybe twenty-eight, with the scruffy beginnings of a beard.

He could not have been more out of place in a show full of people of various ages wearing neat but casual summer attire. This man was wearing probably the only tracksuit in Cape Cod and he stuck out like a...black Cadillac with New York plates.

The sight of the man nearly stopped him dead in his tracks. Only his training and years of experience kept him from showing what he was feeling. He continued walking casually into the show, resisting the urge to run, grab Jenny, and get the hell out of there.

The man was Russian mob, probably out of Brighton Beach. He was too young to be ex-KGB, which meant he wasn't very important. Still, he was there and Morgan knew that he had been following them.

That part made him angry. There were rules in this business; families were kept out of it.

Morgan didn't trouble himself with who might be after him. There was a long list of Russian agents and criminal figures whom he had crossed over the years—though most of them were dead now.

He would figure out the *who* later, once he had Jenny safe. He kept the Russian in his peripheral vision. The man was constantly checking his phone, as if he were keeping in touch with someone. Of course, there would be at least two men assigned to follow him, and to do what? Kill him in the open? Bring him in?

He wasn't in the mood for either of those options.

Morgan headed deeper into the show and then worked his way to the right. For what he was planning, he would need a bit of privacy. He picked a booth on the end of an aisle, where the seller had stepped out. He made a point of dallying over the fabrics, comparing them to the swatches and ads in his folder.

He studied a bale of fabric. It was a reddish and gold velour checker pattern with metallic threads running through the gold squares. A lurex, it was called. The label pinned to the fabric said: *Herman Miller, mid-century.* That was nonsense, he thought; any idiot knew that Herman Miller geometrics were almost exclusively wools.

That thought amused him. Jenny's work *had* rubbed off on him.

Looking up, Morgan gave the Russian plenty to time to reach him. When he caught the man in his peripheral vision again, Morgan moved through the back of the booth into the empty field behind it.

He brushed his hand against his Walther that sat in the holster under his loose short-sleeved shirt. Without looking he flipped the safety but didn't draw the weapon. He'd use it if he had to, but he would rather not. A gunfight would be loud, messy, and hard to explain.

A few seconds later the Russian peeked his head from the rear of the booth to look for Morgan.

Morgan made it easy for him and stepped into the man's line of sight. Grabbing the Russian by the tracksuit, he pulled with his left hand as he aimed a punch with his right fist squarely at the man's nose. He made good contact and heard the nose break. The Russian's hands went to his face.

But Morgan was already spinning him around and had him in a chokehold before he could reach his now freely bleeding nose. By the time the Russian realized that he couldn't breathe, he was nearly unconscious. And before he could struggle much, he was out.

Morgan put the man down and relieved him of his gun, which he'd kept in the pocket of his tracksuit top. *Amateurs,* he thought as he pulled out the weapon.

When he saw the cheap .38 the Russian was carrying, he was genuinely disgusted. It didn't look like it had been cleaned in…well, ever. And he strongly suspected that it had never been fired.

Then Morgan took the man's cell phone and turned it off so it couldn't be tracked, left the man where he lay, and waited. Fortunately, he didn't have to wait long. Another Russian in another tracksuit peeked his head through the simple black curtain that defined the back of the booth.

Less than two minutes later, a second Russian lay unconscious next to his comrade. Another .38. Clearly, these two knuckleheads shopped for their weapons and tracksuits together. They were young, poorly trained, and poorly armed. It was downright insulting.

He didn't expect the Russian mafia to be the KGB, but this was too much. Even their muscle used to be smarter than this. He turned off the second Russian's phone, put it with the other one, and placed the two guns inside his folder of swatches.

Then he rushed to find Jenny. It took him nearly three long minutes to catch sight of her and another minute to reach her. He called out to her, keeping his voice casual.

Even so, her head shot up and her eyes trained on the blood on his right arm.

"You're bleeding," she said.

"Not my blood," he replied. Then he saw that he would have to offer her some sort of explanation. "A guy had a bloody nose."

He gently but firmly took her elbow. "Something has come up, dear; we need to leave right now."

Jenny fell into step and the two walked with purpose toward the exit. The men would be out for anywhere from ten to thirty minutes. When they woke it would take them a few minutes to sort themselves out and start moving again. Morgan wanted himself and Jenny to be well on their way when that happened.

"I ran into some men. I'll explain when we get to the car," Morgan said.

He made one extra stop in the parking lot first. It didn't take long to find the black Cadillac with New York plates. He pulled his ankle knife and jabbed it into the sidewalls of each of the four tires. Even if the two Russians did wake up soon, they wouldn't be going anywhere in that car, at least for a couple of hours.

He felt better when they were in the Mustang and it roared to life. He pulled out and onto the street, keeping to the speed limit but watching all around him. There was no sign that anyone was following them. And his senses were mission-sharp, so that meant that, for the moment at least, no one *was* following them.

"I ran into some low-level Russian mobsters. They were tailing me at the show and they have been following us for two days," Morgan said.

"Do you know why?" Jenny asked.

"No idea. And I have no idea who they are or who they work for," he said.

"Are we safe?"

"For now, but I don't think we should go back to the cottage. I think we should head for Zeta headquarters until we know more."

Morgan put his phone on speaker and called Diana Bloch's direct line.

"Bloch. What is it, Morgan?" she said.

"I had just an issue with two Russian freelancers. I was their target but I don't know why or anything about their affiliation."

"Is Jenny with you?"

"Yes, we're on the road."

"I can direct you to a safe house in the area until we can get a Tach team out to pick you up," Bloch said.

"Not necessary. The freelancers won't be following me and there's no sign of pursuit. I'd just as soon come into Zeta. I have their phones for Shepard to play with."

"Your call. Will we need a cleanup crew?" Bloch asked.

Her tone was matter-of-fact, but in their business, cleanup crews were real multi-taskers. They would literally clean up the scene of an incident, remove bodies, and smooth things over with local authorities as needed.

"Not necessary. They'll each wake up with a headache and take care of themselves."

"I'd still feel better if we had you both somewhere safe," Bloch said.

Morgan turned the Mustang onto the highway. He decided that he wouldn't worry too much about the speed limit. For one thing, they were in a rush. And secondly, thanks to Shepard, no radar gun in the world would be able to get an accurate reading of this car at any speed.

"We are. Shepard has really outdone himself with this car. If find any trouble, I'm sure we can outrun it."

\* \* \* \*

"How are you settling in?" said a voice behind Alex as she entered her dorm room.

She turned to see a tall, neatly dressed student standing in the hallway.

"Um, fine," she said.

"I'm sorry, I'm Jason, Jason Fitzpatrick. I'm the RA on this floor, which means you have me to thank for the name tag on your door," he said, extending his hand.

Alex shook it and examined the tag. It looked like an old-fashioned hardcover book with her name on the cover.

"Nice work, better than the Hello Kitty ones downstairs," she said.

"Well, we are the third floor, I like to think we hold ourselves to a higher standard," he said, flashing her a quick smile.

He peeked into her room. She had decorated it fairly simply. Photos of her parents, a collage of pictures of her friends from high school, an interesting poster of a double helix, and a fairly large yellow sign with a hazardous waste symbol on it that read: *Warning, Biochemistry Major.*

"Bio-chem, that's serious," he said.

"We live in serious times," she said.

"You're a transfer right? How are you settling in? I am the RA so if you need anything or have any issues you want to discuss, my room is in the middle of the hall: it's 312."

"I'm fine, just trying to process..."

"Say no more, I know today was the last day of orientation for new students. How was it for you?" he asked, looking at her earnestly.

Alex wasn't sure how to answer that. The last few days had been *unusual.* However, she imagined that it would have been more normal to the Alex Morgan character who was her cover. On the other hand, that Alex was a bio-chem major and—as Jason had pointed out—that was pretty serious.

"Today was gender," she said.

"When I had orientation two years ago gender was just a single workshop. Now it's a whole day," he said.

"Well, apparently it's gotten complicated. And at the end there was a lively discussion about how many genders there are," she said.

He nodded knowingly. "An age-old question. Did you pick one? There's no rush you know, you just got here."

"I think I'm going to stick with 'girl'. It's worked out for me so far; I figure, why change now?"

Jason let out an involuntary chuckle. Then he gave her a quick glance and said, "Well, you picked a good one. It definitely suits you."

Before she could react, his face shifted and he actually blushed. "Oh my God, I can't believe I said that. That was inappropriate—and I'm the RA."

To that, Alex let out her own involuntary laugh. "Not a problem, I'm pretty hard to offend."

Of course, she understood why he had seemed genuinely worried. Yesterday's "seminars" were on microaggressions and harassment.

The good humor returned to his face. "I'm glad. Just as well though, because if anyone gives you any trouble you're supposed to report the incident to your RA."

"I will remember that if someone manages to offend me," she said.

"Look, just a reminder that we're having a floor meeting in the lounge tonight. I hope you can make it."

"What time? I have another meeting at eight," she said.

"Nine, and for a half-hour tops. Just going over a few rules, procedures, and some activities for the floor."

"I'll definitely be there," she said as she turned into her room. Before she could close the door, she saw Karen O'Neal walking down the hallway. "Hi, Karen," she said.

Then she turned to Jason. "This is Jason. Jason, this is my friend Karen, she's also bio-chem. She's actually a grad student, a TA in the department."

"Nice to meet you," Jason said to Karen. Alex noticed that he didn't shake her hand. "How do you know our Alex?" he asked.

"We are old friends from home," Karen said evenly.

"You could say that Karen is one of the reasons I'm here," Alex said.

Jason turned his attention back to Alex, as if Karen wasn't there. "So we'll see you at nine?" he asked.

"See you then," she said, ushering Karen into her room.

# Chapter 11

"Ms. Guo," Conley said when she showed up in the lobby promptly at eight.

"Mr. Conley," she said, nodding, a Western adaptation of the traditional Chinese bow.

"Please call me Peter," he said.

"Very well, Peter. Then you must call me Danhong. What do you have planned for us today?" she said.

"A tour. Museums, a few other places of interest. I've been to Manila a few times but I seem to have missed most of the sights. And I know you have already seen the beach," he said.

"That sounds wonderful. Will there be a bus?"

He shook his head as Amado approached. "Mr. Peter," the older man said.

"Amado, this is Danhong Guo, she is with our friends from China."

Amado bowed and fired off a quick greeting in what seemed like perfect Mandarin. She replied in kind.

Conley had sorted out an itinerary with Amado, who was happy to have the extra work as their guide. He knew the city well, and he was able to borrow one of the hotel's smaller vans.

Conley had considered getting them tickets on one of the popular tour buses but he wanted something less noisy and more private. It was Saturday; they only had two days to spend together before the workweek started in earnest and Conley was determined to make them count.

The streets were quiet, much more so than during the week. There were fewer people rushing back and forth, and there were no protestors. That was new.

There had been a number of protests during the last week, mostly demonstrating against the current Filipino administration over charges of corruption and a laundry list of other misdeeds. Since the Chinese delegation had arrived, there had also been a number of anti-capitalism protests.

Over the administration's work with the *Chinese* economic delegation. The irony of that was pretty rich and Morgan would have enjoyed it. The protests were rowdy, but not usually dangerous. The protest culture had a history in this country. Or, more accurately, the protest *business* did. The reality was that many—if not most—protestors were paid by various interest groups. The system seemed odd but it wasn't without its benefits. The rich, the middle class, and the poor lived remarkably close together in Manila. And for a number of the poor, their wages from protesting were often a significant source of their income. And because they were professional protestors—with often little or no connection to the cause they were demonstrating about—they were usually well-behaved. In these protests, violence always came from the true believers. The professional protestors didn't engage in it because violence threatened their livelihood, and their neighborhood.

Before lunch, they visited a contemporary art museum, as well as a toy museum and a "museum" that exclusively featured optical illusions. He was pleased to see that Danhong, like him, had an interest in almost everything. Conley was also surprised that she thoroughly enjoyed the illusions and had suggested the toy museum herself.

Though still reserved by American standards, her appreciation of the toys and the life-sized toy replicas was almost childlike. Well, China was a serious place. And she was in government, perhaps the most serious corner of that world. And she was a woman in a profession and a culture was still overwhelmingly dominated by men.

Amado recommended a small place frequented by locals for lunch but refused to join them, and Conley didn't push the issue very hard. He was glad to have her alone.

In the afternoon, on Amado's recommendation, they visited the Quiapo Church. "It is my church," Amado said proudly and accompanied them inside. It was beautiful. Most of the actual structure dated back to the nineteenth century. Given the assortment of people milling about, it was also clearly a popular tourist destination.

However, the real attraction, he knew, had to do with the history of the site, which had held a church since the sixteenth century. Fire, war, and earthquakes had taken their toll on the churches built there, but they had always been rebuilt.

And there was a statue inside that was said to have miraculous powers.

Danhong was very quiet in the church, which he initially chalked up to Chinese reserve and her generally respectful nature. But the quiet lasted until they reached the van.

Conley almost asked her if something was wrong but didn't want to pry. She broke the silence. "My parents were religious, but they are gone now."

"I'm sorry," he said.

"Thank you," she said. Then she seemed to visibly shake off the cloud that had settled on her. "Do you have plans for us for dinner?"

"I was thinking to head back to the hotel for dinner at the bar where we met. It's not fancy but it is on the beach," he said.

"Perfect," she replied, almost before he had finished.

When they arrived at the bar, Conley said, "Would you like a cosmopolitan, Dani?" Then he caught himself. "I'm sorry. Is it okay if I call you that?"

Conley knew that the rules for diminutives of Chinese names were complicated. And the actual diminutives were almost always as long or longer than the original names.

"No one has ever called me that before, but I like it. *Dani.* It is very *American,*" she said.

Dinner was like the day, pleasant and relaxed. He was surprised by how comfortable he was around Dani. It was especially surprising given how different their backgrounds and cultures were.

He wasn't like Dan Morgan, a one-woman man—a family man. Then again, no one else he knew in their end of their business had managed the life that Morgan had created for himself.

But Conley knew that a woman like Dani could change his mind. Perhaps if he'd met her earlier...

"Would you like to dance?" he asked.

She was already standing up as she answered yes.

The next song was a slow one, and Conley was glad that his generous tip to the bartender hadn't been wasted.

They danced more closely this time and Conley liked feeling her weight against him. The next song was also slow and they danced closer still. He realized that he had been wrong about one thing the night before: Dani didn't just smell good, she smelled *wonderful.*

In the middle of the song she lifted her head to look at him and then they were kissing.

The next song was faster and they reluctantly parted. "Thank you, that was very nice."

It *was* nice; the day, the dinner, the dancing—all of it. But he didn't want it to be over.

"I am free tomorrow," she said.

"Then I hope you will spend it with me," he replied.

"I would like that," she said.

"I will walk you to your room."

"So soon? I thought, perhaps you might like…"

"Not at all," he said. "We could still…"

"Perhaps you could show me *your* room," she said evenly.

To that Conley only smiled. They headed back inside at a brisk walk. Frankly, it took a genuine effort for him not to break into a run.

\* \* \* \*

Morgan scanned the road. Route 6 was reasonably free from traffic, which was important for a couple of reasons. He still had fifty miles to cover before they crossed the Cape Cod Canal, which separated the peninsula from the mainland.

It wasn't that the bridges were much of a barrier—the canal was less than 500 feet across—but they were a bottleneck. And if you were trying to run someone down, they were an excellent choke point.

Morgan cursed himself for putting them both on a peninsula that was virtually an island. Then again, he wasn't on a mission. He was with *his wife. On vacation.*

Their first real vacation alone together since their honeymoon.

Once again he thought, *there were rules,* even in this business. *Families were off limits.*

This wasn't the first time Morgan's work had put his family in danger. It wasn't even the second time. But with his rising anger came a determination that it would be the *last* time—at least for whoever had sent the Russians.

When they were less than ten miles from the Bourne Bridge, the traffic started to slow. That was normal enough. Weekly summer rentals were usually from Saturday to Saturday. It was eleven o'clock now, which meant the weekly exodus from the island would last about another hour. To be fair, it could have been worse. It could have been Sunday traffic.

In less than a minute, the traffic went from slow to a crawl. Morgan growled.

It *was* worse.

"It's okay, traffic report says there's a car fire," Jenny said.

Morgan didn't like the sound of that. It was normal enough. In a given year, Morgan would see a car fire or two on the street, and he couldn't remember the last time he had seen one.

But the normal traffic and a reasonably normal fire were conspiring to keep him on Cape Cod, where he had just run into two idiots who had meant him harm. Those two things together barely rose to the level of a coincidence.

Yet if Morgan had learned one thing it was that there was no such thing as a coincidence on a mission. And as soon as he had seen those two punks at the fabric show, this had become a mission—to get his wife to safety.

They came to a complete stop.

"One lane is closed," Jenny said.

Morgan did some quick calculations in his head. Traffic this heavy, funneling to one lane with the added bonus of people slowing to gawk and even take pictures at the burning wreck meant that Morgan and Jenny would be exposed for exactly *too damn long.*

The Mustang was fast and had a few tricks up her sleeve, but most of that wouldn't be useful if they were stopped dead in traffic. The thought galled him. Besides the danger to himself and Jenny, for *this car* to be stuck in traffic—to be trapped—was unthinkable.

Another thing that pissed him off today.

Morgan made his decision. He put the car in reverse to a little distance between the Mustang and the car in front of them, and then pulled onto the shoulder. He could see the exit less than half a mile up ahead.

He decided to accept Bloch's offer of a safe house. He knew the local roads pretty well—very well, actually. If it was just him, he might have waited until whoever was running this operation got here and taught them a few things about the rules of the game…and basic manners.

But he had Jenny to think about and decided to play it smart. They would hole up until Bloch could get a Tach team to them—by helicopter if necessary.

He'd let the team do some of the work. He was on vacation, after all.

Up ahead, Morgan saw a flash of black—two flashes, actually.

Two large black SUVs were barreling toward them. Cadillac Escalades. It was too far to see the plates, but he had no doubt they were from New York.

The coincidence meter in his head shook and then exploded.

Morgan cursed himself again. He had been lulled by the sheer incompetence of the two Russians he'd encountered earlier. Their mission had likely only been reconnaissance.

Two cars ahead of him had gotten tired of the traffic and were making for the exit on the shoulder. Morgan veered to the right and passed them on the grass. Then he was back on the shoulder and flying toward the exit.

His peripheral vision told him the SUVs had turned onto the median and were crossing it to get to them. Well, the traffic jam they had created with the burning car would work against them now. It would take them some time to get across the clogged westbound lane, and the local roads Morgan would soon hit were reasonably clear.

Finally. This was the kind of work the Mustang was built for. But the fact was that reinforcements had come up from Brighton Beach, they were driving a better class of Cadillac than the two morons, and Morgan had no doubt they had brought the big guns.

\* \* \* \*

Conley woke to see that Dani had gone. He understood.

The men in her delegation would be out most—if not all—of the night. But if she wasn't in her own room in the morning they would notice and would count it against her. It wasn't fair, but he knew it was so. He checked the clock, just past six. He would see her again in less than three hours.

He was in the lobby a full fifteen minutes before nine, but Dani was already there, chatting with Amado.

"Mr. Peter," Amado said.

"Good morning Amado, good morning Dani," Conley said, nodding to both of them. That was as intimate a greeting as he dared give her in the lobby. This was, after all, a working trip for her, and other delegates could be around.

"Peter," she said, returning the nod.

Conley had told her to dress for adventure and she had worn denim shorts, tennis shoes, and a short-sleeved button top.

She looked fresh and, well, *amazing.*

Despite his attempt at reserve for sake of her career, Conley realized that he was grinning like a fool.

"If you are ready," he said, and they headed to Amado's van.

They had breakfast in another spot that Amado recommended, and then it was a short drive to the bay where their guide introduced them to his friend who had a small boat—a long one with traditional pontoons on each side.

Conley had wanted to keep their destination a surprise for as long as possible, and was pleased when she got into the boat without hesitation. With an expression of almost childlike excitement, she asked, "Where are we going?"

Peter waited until they were on the water a few minutes when he pointed to an island up ahead, one that looked a bit like a mountain with its top sheared off.

"Is that a—" she began.

"Yes, Taal is a volcano," Peter said.

"Is it active?"

"Of course," he said.

"And we'll see it up close?" She was clearly excited.

A few minutes later their captain was guiding the small craft to the beach, through surf so rough that it had Conley holding tightly to his seat.

Dani, however, took the trip in stride and was the first to jump off the boat. She put on the surgical mask that would protect her from the volcanic ash without hesitation.

On their hike to the rim, she was very interested in the occasional volcanic vent holes they came across, which gave off white smoke and heat. She was also undaunted by the over ninety-five-degree heat and very high humidity.

At the rim she gazed down at the mouth of the volcano; inside which was a large volcanic lake. It was impressive, and Conley had seen his share of natural and man-made wonders.

When they got back to the mainland it was late afternoon.

"Would you like to go back to your room to clean up before dinner?" he asked. He liked that it was understood that they would have dinner together. It was Sunday and her grueling work schedule would start up early enough tomorrow morning. Until then, he was determined that they make the most of it.

"Or I could clean up in your room?" she asked casually.

Peter liked that idea. He liked it very much.

They didn't get around to ordering room service until almost nine.

As they sat in their robes and ate, she became uncharacteristically uncomfortable and quiet.

He could see that she had something to say, something that was difficult for her. That surprised him. As far as he'd seen so far, she wasn't afraid of anything.

"I have really enjoyed our time together," she said.

"As have I," he replied, and saw there was more she wanted to say. He could guess what. She was initiating her version of "the talk." They were caught up in a vacation romance, perhaps the most impermanent of all new romances.

The fact was that he was American and she held a relatively high rank in the Chinese Ministry of Finance and would have little or no opportunities to travel after the conference was finished.

Very likely, after tonight, they would never see each other again. Clearly, she felt the need to say it, though Peter would have been content to avoid the issue for a bit longer.

"It's okay," he began.

"I need your help with something, a favor," she said, her face strained and uncomfortable.

That was a surprise. Now Conley was interested. "Don't worry. The answer is yes. Just tell me what it is."

"I want to leave my country, to come to America. I want to defect," she said in a burst. Then she collected herself. "I told you that my parents were religious. They were Christian, probably only moderately religious by American standards but they belonged to a church that wasn't one of the three state-sanctioned ones and that made them criminals in China. When I was eight, they were arrested for refusing to "conform their religious beliefs to the requirements of the Socialist state."

Conley knew there were many tales like Dani's in China, especially twenty-some years ago. Even today, he knew that for all of the lessening of economic control, social control had been slower to loosen. And control over religion had been slowest of all.

"Did you find out what happened to them?" he asked.

"Yes, I was informed that they died in custody when I was in college," she said.

"I'm very sorry, Dani," he said.

"Will you help me get out? For them? For me? I just want to leave. I have no family they can retaliate against—they have seen to that." She hesitated and said, "I do need your help, but I don't want you to think that my interest in you—"

"Shhhh…" Peter said. "I know someone in the American consulate here. He's a good man. We can make arrangements and have you on American soil before you know it."

Conley did some calculations in his head. If they moved her at night, a military transport could have her in Hawaii before she was missed in the morning.

It wouldn't even be difficult. Diana Bloch could arrange it in minutes. As a high-ranking member of the Ministry of Finance, Dani was a very valuable asset.

She squeezed him tightly. "Thank you, Peter. Thank you."

Peter realized that he had flipped a switch in his head and was already thinking like an agent. But that was not what Dani needed right now. She was about to leave everything she knew. And she had come to him.

There was more going on here than she was telling him, he was certain. It couldn't be an accident that she had come to him, an experienced agent, when she needed help defecting.

And yet he sensed that their time together had been real, or real enough. And to be fair, he had not exactly told her the truth about himself. Was she also intelligence?

If so, where did that leave them? Could a relationship be built on such a foundation? He decided they would have plenty of time to talk about those issues when she was safely out of the country.

For now, Conley simply returned her embrace. This moment between them was real, he was sure of it. He also understood it was what she needed—*all* that she needed right now.

And he found that he was happy to give it.

# Chapter 12

"Do you have a plan for tonight?" O'Neal asked Alex earnestly. Though she realized that *earnestly* was a pretty good description for the way that Karen O'Neal said everything.

"This is just a getting to know everyone meeting, a welcoming of new members," Alex said.

"I understand you are not, technically, a *new* member," O'Neal said.

Alex had to work not to wince at that. Yes, when she was young and foolish she had been a member of Americans for a Peaceful Society, but that had been high school and now seemed like it was decades ago and light years away.

"Well, not of this chapter, so I may have a little credibility with these people but I'm practically a new member. Look, Karen, a lot of what you are going to hear is going to sound silly. Working at Zeta you've seen too much about how the world works. These kids don't have the benefit of your experience, or even mine. They think we—the West, the United States—can solve all of the world's problems if we just stop using our military and making trouble."

"That is reductive and short-sighted," O'Neal said.

"Exactly, but that doesn't mean they don't believe it strongly. And they need to think we believe it just as strongly," she said.

"I see," O'Neal said, but Alex wasn't sure. Karen was a high-level math genius and, technically, an intelligence analyst. But she wasn't a field agent, with even less training in that area than Alex herself.

And while Bloch would not have sent her on this mission with Alex if she didn't have faith in O'Neal, Alex wondered if the older woman could lie convincingly, let along play a part for which she would have to shut off the analytical part of her brain.

"Remember, you are an old friend of mine. Let me do the talking until you feel comfortable. This could take a while. We'll want them to trust us. Then we will try to wrangle an introduction to the group in the bio department that works with Professor Spellman. The only question is how long we have before the threat your software identified materializes."

"Strictly speaking, the software identified a potential threat only, though a serious one. There is no time-frame indicated, that's not how the system works. With luck, our mission here will help me optimize the underlying algorithm."

Alex tried to hide her frustration. The mission was a fishing expedition as it was. Alex had made peace with that, with the understanding that she would develop important skills for undercover work. But would she and Karen be here for a week? A month? A whole semester?

She checked her watch. It was time to go. She put on a tight smile and said, "Let's get started."

They headed out to the door. Alex pulled out a campus map as they walked down the hallway.

"You can put that away. I know where the meeting is," Karen said.

Alex kept scanning the map. "You sure? It's a big campus."

"I memorized the campus map last night," Karen said.

"Of course you did," Alex said, smiling. "Lead the way."

Ten minutes later they were at the lounge in another dorm. There was a hand-made sign on the door that said: *Americans for a Peaceful Society, Meeting Tonight.*

They stepped through the door and it was pandemonium inside. There were maybe forty people there, loudly chatting. The group was split fifty-fifty between men and women—assuming you went with the traditional definitions of gender.

The group was different from the mostly clean-cut, earnest high school students in her old chapter of the APS. At least half of the guys had beards, varying from traditional goatees to full mountain man. A lot of the girls had short hair and, from what she could see, quite a few piercings.

She saw that the guys had piercings too. They usually didn't have as many, but they tended to be more extreme. Two of the guys she saw had large circular holes in their ear lobes with rings so large that a quarter could pass through them.

Most of the kids were dressed in jeans and t-shirts. Quite a few Che Guevara tees, a number of rainbow tops, and others with angry slogans whose key words were "oppression," or "resistance," or "justice."

The one that made the least sense to her was the t-shirt that had an upside-down image of the globe and said: *Cartographers for Social Justice!*

One of the guys in the back started speaking. When the crowd didn't quiet down, he started yelling. Finally, people hushed enough so Alex could hear him.

He started talking about his "journey" and a number of things he was angry about, from poverty to the state of the environment. None of the things he mentioned—she noticed—had anything to do with peace, or even with war for that matter.

When he was (finally) finished, someone else started speaking. She talked about fracking, which she maintained perpetuated the system that gave us nuclear bombs and white supremacy. To her credit, at least nuclear weapons bore some relation to war and peace.

This went on for a while. As far as Alex could tell no one was in charge. When there was a brief lull, Alex started talking.

"I get it. I get that you are angry," she said, in a tone that was loud and firm. She realized that she had inadvertently borrowed that tone from her mother. Surprisingly, it worked and the crowd quieted.

"We are ALL angry. We are angry at poverty. We are angry at injustice. We are angry at inequality. We are just angry," she added. She realized that she now had their complete attention. Moreover, for the first time since she and Karen had arrived, all other conversation had stopped.

"But we know where all of those things come from, where all the trouble we face starts…"

She let that hang in the air to sink in. The guy with the giant holes in his ear lobes said, "Where?"

It took a physical effort for her stop herself from sighing. Did these people even know why they were here? Had they even read the sign on the door outside?

"Because the world, and this country, is not committed to the one thing that will solve all of these problems: peace. Instead, we have a system that perpetuates war. That's the real disease, and human beings are the carriers," she said, raising her voice at the end in conclusion.

Someone started applauding. Most of the room soon followed. When it died down she said, "My name is Alex and this is my friend Karen. We're both bio-chem majors and we are not leaving this school until we make a difference."

They were surrounded by students. Some of them had questions, but most of them just wanted to talk about their own pet issues—most of which had nothing to do with peace, or war, or things that had any relationship to the real world.

When they were alone, Karen said, "That was…impressive. They really responded to you."

Alex shrugged, "They're hungry for leadership, but that's not why we're here. I just wanted to get us noticed."

"Why did you tell them our major? No one else did," Karen said.

"Excuse me," someone said behind them. Alex turned to see a tall girl with blond hair whom Alex would have pegged for a cheerleader. "Hi, I'm Margaret. I really liked what you said—about making a difference," she said. Then she scanned the room and added, "Frankly, I don't think most of these people know *what* they want. Look, I'm in bio-chem too." Then she lowered her voice. "We have another group. It's kind of informal but we're all from the biology and bio-chem departments."

Alex followed along with interest.

"Have you heard of Professor Spellman?" she asked.

Alex flashed her eyes and said, "Of course, you could say he's the reason we're here. We heard his…"

"The speech? You heard the speech?" Margaret asked.

"I thought maybe you had when you talked about people being the disease," she said. That wasn't exactly what Alex had said, but she wasn't going to correct Margaret now.

"So Professor Spellman has this group that meets tomorrow," Margaret went on. "Like you, we want to really make a difference before we graduate. Anyway, there's a meeting tomorrow after lunch. The professor has some surprise planned, some sort of special guest."

"We'll be there," Alex said.

"Give me your number, I'll text you the details," Margaret said.

A few moments later they were in the hallway and headed outside. "That is why you told them our department," Karen said.

"Yes."

"And now we've been recruited into Professor Spellman's…"

"End of the World Club," Alex said.

Outside they said good-bye and Alex headed back to her dorm. Maybe she really could do this job. Not bad for her first day undercover.

And it wasn't even nine o'clock.

Nine o'clock…

Ouch, she'd told Jason she'd be at the floor meeting. She started rushing toward the dorm. Of course, it was just a floor meeting—not exactly essential to her mission. Yet it had seemed important to Jason. And part of her mission was to fit in. Taking part in normal activities would certainly help with that.

It was two minutes to nine. She wouldn't make it in time. Well, if she hurried, she would only be a few minutes late.

Alex knew there was something wrong as she approached the lounge at the end of the hallway. It was silent.

Alex stepped into the lounge. There was a *Welcome to the 3rd Floor!* hand-made sign on the wall. There were couches set in front of the fairly large flat-screen TV and a few café tables here and there.

And yet all of the seats and couches were empty.

Alex checked her phone. It was 9:06. Had she missed the meeting?

Then one of the couches moved.

Not, not the couch, the figure slumped on a couch that was facing away from Alex. A head turned and she saw Jason looking at her. His eyes lit up and he jumped to his feet.

"Alex, you made it," he said.

She scanned the room and said, "I thought I was late and missed it. Am I early?"

"Aren't you adorable? I think you are the whole meeting, I mean, besides me."

She saw bowls of chips and bottles of soda spread throughout the room. And then she saw a platter of Oreo cookies shaped into a rough pyramid.

"Was I the only one invited?" she asked.

"What do you mean?"

"Well, was this an elaborate ruse go get me alone for…I don't know, murder, or something?"

He shot her a nervous grin.

"No, I mean. I wouldn't…Actually, the school frowns on that sort of thing," he said.

"Don't get me wrong, it's a chance I'm willing to take. You do have Oreos," she said, returning his smile.

He said, "People are busy, and floor spirit isn't exactly a priority."

"Yes, but I'd expected more. We are the 3rd floor, we should hold ourselves to a higher standard," she said.

Alex remembered the talk her mother had given her when she started going to parties in middle school. "When you accept an invitation, you're also accepting a responsibility. Being a good guest is more than just having fun, it's about helping the host make sure everyone has fun."

Alex saw that she had a lot of responsibility here.

"That's just more food and more floor spirit for us."

With that, she headed over to the Oreo pyramid. She noticed that there was something odd about the Oreos.

"They're orange," she said.

"Well, yeah. For Halloween," he said.

"Isn't it a little early for Halloween?" Alex asked. Then she noticed that he had changed. He was wearing a white t-shirt with a black bird on it, a raven. Underneath, it said *Nevermore.*

Well, fair enough. When you went to a party—or a meeting—why not wear something that told people a little bit about who you were? Certainly, the people at the Students for a Peaceful Society meetup had done it. And their t-shirts were mostly angry.

"Well, you can get the orange ones early if you know where to shop," he said.

That answered the question of how he got the orange cookies, but not the why. She decided to let it go. She realized that she couldn't decide if he was weird or cute.

"Let me just put some of this away, he said. I can save it for the Halloween party. By the way, signup for the haunted dorm is right over there."

Not knowing what else to do, Alex put her name on the list. Hers, of course, was the *only* name on the list. She felt a pang of guilt when she realized that she might not still be at the school by the time the Halloween rolled around.

They packed up most of the food and carted it to his room—which was a surprise. So far the guys' rooms she had seen were either full-on frat-boy with posters of beer and girls, or decorated with movie or music stuff, or various political slogans.

His room had a lot of books and a full-sized cardboard standup of Edgar Allan Poe.

"Haven't seen many of those here," she said.

"Yeah, I'm a real rebel," he said with a grin. "How much time have you got? I can tell you how he changed everything that came after him. Then I can tell you about my senior thesis."

"Sure, why don't you tell me at the party," she said.

When they returned, Alex was not surprised to see that the lounge was empty. They had some left some chips and cookies, and soda—and Alex realized that her first college party was nothing like she had expected.

Judging by Jason, it was probably not a typical college party.

He did a quick monologue on Poe and it was actually pretty interesting. If nothing else, his enthusiasm counted for something. Then she realized that she had now met someone who fit in here even less that she did. Remarkably, it seemed to not bother him at all.

"So what was that other meeting you had earlier?" he asked.

"Americans for a Peaceful Society," she said without thinking.

She saw a flash of disappointment on his face. "Oh," was all he said.

She shrugged. "I was a member in high school. I was thinking of getting back in...but it's changed a lot."

*Why am I making excuses?* she thought. She was undercover at Berkeley to pass for a campus radical. She shouldn't care what one guy that she'd never met before thought of her choices. He was—to be blunt—at best, irrelevant, and at most, an asset.

Yet she did care. She didn't want him to think of her the way she thought of those angry, clueless kids at that meeting.

"We could watch a movie. I have a bunch of DVDs in my room," he said.

They decided on *Rosemary's Baby* and watched it on the lounge's big screen.

The film was great, and after it ended they just talked. He asked about home and told her about growing up in North Carolina. She talked about growing up in Boston. He was genuinely interested when she mentioned that her father was a classic car dealer. It had been a while since she'd had such nice time with a guy.

In high school there had been a few first dates, and a few more second and third dates. And then there had been Dylan. But she'd met him through APS and they'd spent most of their time discussing the organization or some outrage of the week.

This was different.

"Look, I had a really good time tonight. I'm glad you came to the party," he said. There it was again, the grin.

"Me too," she said, grinning back.

There was another silence, but this one wasn't awkward.

Then he was kissing her, and she was kissing him.

A few seconds later, he pulled away.

"I'm sorry, that was wrong," he said.

"No, actually it wasn't so bad. I mean, in terms of technique—"

"I mean I'm your RA, I shouldn't be putting the moves on you," he said.

That made her chuckle. "Listen, Jason, I don't think anything you've said or done tonight could be legitimately considered a move."

That made him laugh.

"You're just saying that to make me feel better. Even so—"

She interrupted him by kissing him. This time he didn't pull away.

When they separated, she studied him and thought: *cute.*

"What?" he replied and she realized that she had not just thought it; she'd said it out loud.

Clearly, she needed to practice her undercover skills.

"Before, I was trying to figure out if you were cute or weird. I'm going with cute," she said.

"I say it doesn't have to be a binary. Why not—"

Alex interrupted him again, even more firmly this time.

# Chapter 13

Morgan spared a quick look in his rear view mirror and saw one black SUV, then the other. They were too close. On the other hand, the Russians were driving standard-issue vehicles for high-level Russian mobsters—Cadillac Escalades. The cars were reasonably fast, but not as fast as the Mustang, and nowhere near as agile.

As if to prove his point, Morgan slipped around a minivan and pulled a hard right at nearly sixty. He'd have to get off of the residential streets if he wanted to maximize this car's advantages. Ironically, he needed a bit more traffic than there was on these sleepy summer cottage-lined roads. He needed enough other cars on the road to act as obstructions to the larger vehicles.

If he could stick the Russians behind a few cars at a traffic light, that would buy him enough time to lose them permanently. Checking the road map of the area he kept in his head, he pulled a left at high speed.

"Are they behind us?" Morgan called out.

"No. I can't see them," she said.

That was good. That meant that he would have enough time to get to the commercial district less than half a mile away. There would be some lunchtime summer traffic to tie the Russians up while he slipped away.

He was on a straightaway and got the car up to eighty. He was close now.

"Let me know if you see them," Morgan called out.

"Okay," Jenny replied, her voice tense but surprisingly calm.

Half a mile now.

"Dan, I see them," Jenny said.

"How far behind—"

And then *he* saw them, at the intersection less than quarter of a mile ahead of them. Two black SUVs. But it was impossible. They couldn't have gotten in front of him.

Unless it was two different cars. Four was bad. It meant a greater level of sophistication and coordination—and more resources. Who the hell wanted him this badly?

Morgan hit the brakes as he turned the car hard to the left. The maneuver threw the Mustang into a backwards skid. He said a quick thanks to Shepard for not putting anti-lock brakes into the car. Most government motor pools wouldn't release a car to an agent without the feature. But most federal motor pools were run by morons.

The new brakes were safer for most driving conditions and were good at preventing civilians from ending up in uncontrolled skids, but they made what Morgan was now doing impossible.

The Mustang had executed a full 180-degree spin and ended up facing the other way, while coming to a full stop from eighty-some miles per hour in record time. Morgan was also now in a perfect position to make a right turn onto an even smaller side street.

As he made the turn he saw two Escalades nearly on top of them. *Too close,* he thought. He had to get Jenny out of here, and fast.

Morgan opened up the Mustang again but he almost immediately saw the construction signs ahead.

*Damn,* he thought.

There weren't just signs; the road was completely blocked by heavy equipment. They were almost out of road—and options.

There was a single left up ahead. Morgan committed to it without hesitating, but even as he made the turn he saw the yellow *Dead End* sign.

Too late, he realized. He was already on the street, with less than a quarter mile of pavement ahead of him. But he wasn't done yet.

Morgan saw the steel barrier at the end of the street and cursed inwardly. He slowed down. Maybe he could drive around the barrier and—

Into the trees behind it.

*Damn. Damn,* he thought.

The car could handle a field, an unfinished road, almost anything.

But it couldn't drive through trees.

Morgan swung the car around again, in time to see the four black SUVs converging and making the turn onto the dead end.

*Our dead end,* Morgan thought.

"Dan," Jenny said.

"It's okay, honey. I will handle this," he said, having absolutely no idea how he was going to do that.

\* \* \* \*

"I hope this is going to be quick." Alex said.

"Why?" O'Neal replied, as they walked through the quad.

"What?" she replied.

"Why would you hope the meeting is quick? Making contact with this group is our mission. Therefore, the longer the contact, the better the…"

Alex waved O'Neal off. "I mean—" She hesitated for a minute. What *did* she mean? She meant that she wanted to get this part of the day over with so she could keep her lunch date with Jason.

Of course, she couldn't say any of that. It wasn't professional. It wasn't serious of her. And it definitely wasn't *on mission.*

And yet a couple of hours with Jason sounded a lot better than a long meeting with the kind of cranks she'd met at the APS get-together.

"What I meant was that I don't expect much from this meeting. It will be our first contact with potential radical elements at Berkeley. I suspect that establishing trust and getting any useful information will take multiple meetings over time. The quicker we're finished, the closer we are to real progress."

It sounded weak even to her own ears but O'Neal seemed to accept it. That made sense; numbers and high-level cognitive thinking were O'Neal's world. Alex was counting on her for that. On the other hand, O'Neal was counting on Alex to handle the human aspect of the mission.

*I've just told a white lie to my partner,* she said. *Not a great start to my career as an undercover operative.* She chided herself to keep focused. The fact was that they had been lucky to receive this invitation.

She wouldn't blow it because she'd been distracted by some… well, by anything.

They arrived at the lecture hall at exactly eleven-thirty and found it empty. Alex checked her watch. They were right on time; it's just that no one else was there.

Alex led the way to the front of the large hall. It was the kind of room used for introductory classes, where there were fifty or more students.

Alex took a seat and then Karen did the same. "We'll wait for a few minutes…" Alex began, but she heard footsteps before the words were out of her mouth.

A tall blond girl entered the room, followed by a guy with a scruffy beard and something in his ears. No, not *something*. Rather, he had large black hoops embedded into each ear lobe.

Then Alex remembered both of them. The girl was Margaret, who would have guessed was a cheerleader. She'd seen them last night at the APS meeting.

"Hi Alex, hi Karen. This is Avery," Margaret said. "Glad you could make it."

"Looks like we were the only ones who did," Karen said, nodding to Avery.

Margaret ignored the comment. "It was nice to meet you both at the APS meeting. What did you think of the APS crowd?"

Alex was sure Margaret was fishing, though she couldn't figure out what she was fishing for. She decided to play a hunch. "They were all over the place."

Margaret seemed amused. "What do you mean?"

To Alex's surprise, Karen spoke. "The group had no common set of concerns, not unifying interests, nothing that usually defines a group of that nature."

"Interesting," Margaret said, while the guy with the rings in his ears just stared at them.

"We saw one of Professor Spellman's lectures and we thought we could be part of something here," Alex said, tentatively. She watched Margaret carefully for her response.

"You mean the Dr. Apocalypse lecture?" Avery said.

Margaret shook her head. "Doctor *Spellman* hates that nickname."

Alex saw that it was time to stop dancing around the issue and move this meeting forward. "The name's unfair. He wasn't talking about the end of the world. He was talking about a new beginning," Alex said.

That got Avery's attention. "You think so?"

"It's not a matter of opinion. The planet has no future if people continue to do…what people do. If nature took humans out of the equation, the Earth would take a few years to recover and then it would begin to thrive. In a hundred years…"

"You'd have a real paradise," Margaret said.

"And all the problems that everyone in that APS meeting was talking about would just disappear. It's a good dream," Alex said.

"What if it wasn't a dream—or not *just* a dream?" she asked. Margaret was probing her, Alex realized.

"Well, hypothetically. If someone was going to help bring that about, I—I mean we—would love to be a part of it," Alex said.

"That possibility is what attracted us to Dr. Spellman. That and his work with bacteriophages," O'Neal said. Her tone was dead earnest.

"This is very serious. If you're not serious, we don't need you," Avery said emphatically.

"We're talking about saving the world, preserving it forever. We are very serious about that and we would do whatever was necessary to make that happen," Alex said. She could see that Avery was about to speak but waved him off. "And, yes, we all know what we're really talking about here."

Margaret broke out into her best cheerleader smile.

"Look, we had to be sure. We are very serious about Dr. Spellman's work." Then she turned to Avery. "*Our* work."

"And nobody likes a tourist," Alex said.

"I think you will fit in great," Margaret said.

"So this was a test?" Alex said.

"More like a compatibility questionnaire. We do have to be careful, we can't let just anyone into our organization."

"Does your organization have a name?" Karen asked.

"We call it 'The Club,'" Avery said.

"'The Club, ' really?" Alex said. "Kind of non-descript."

"Exactly!" Avery said. "You have to be careful what you call yourselves. The NSA has computers that search emails and web pages and even phone conversations, looking for keywords. But if they catch one of our messages and all it says is The Club..." He leaned in to them and added, "Keeps from raising any red flags."

"Very clever," Karen said. "I'm sure it will keep you from prying eyes."

"It has so far. And it's not like we're doing anything illegal. We're relatively new and we're in the pure research phase of our project," Margaret said, her smile blazing. "By the way, that's what we call our work, 'The Project.'"

"What happens now?" Alex asked.

"Now you come with us to the real meeting. It's in one of the labs. That's Dr. Spellman's idea. We're scientists, we belong in a lab, even when we're just talking about our work. Lecture halls are for transmitting information, but our labs are where we are going to change the world."

"It sounds great," Alex said.

"It is, but remember. This is a long-term project. If you've followed Dr. Spellman's work you know that he's brilliant. And even if we all help and contribute, Rome wasn't built in a day."

Alex had to stop herself from chuckling. Margaret and The Club were planning the deaths of every man, woman, and child on Earth and she was comparing their work to the building of Rome.

"We're right in here," Margaret said, pointing to the door ahead of them. "You're about to meet Dr. Spellman."

# Chapter 14

Morgan ran through a half-a-dozen scenarios in his head. There were four things he would try if he were with Conley. And two others he would risk if he were alone.

But he was with Jenny and all of those scenarios were simply too risky for her.

He had his Walther and this car had more than a few tactical surprises. However, they worked best when the car was moving. If it came to a firefight, the eight Russians in the four SUVs (which were no doubt armored themselves) could just pound the Mustang until it was destroyed.

He'd considered trying to ram his way out, but the Russians' vehicles would be too difficult to push through at the low speed he'd be able to make in the short distance between them. And while the Mustang had a number of advantages, the SUVs had size and mass on their sides.

In his years with the agency and with Zeta, Morgan had faced death more times than he could count. He'd made peace with the idea of his own death—not because he wanted to die, but because he knew that whatever happened to him, Jenny and Alex would be okay. And he'd worried about his partner on missions, but Conley was an agent who knew the risks of the job and was prepared for them like Morgan was himself.

There were a few times where his work had put Jenny in danger. During those times he wasn't at peace; he wasn't worried—*he was terrified.*

He only saw one option. He'd have to get out of the car and take the fight to the Russians. The Mustang would keep Jenny safe as long as she stayed inside, particularly if Morgan stayed in the fight long enough to draw the attention of the local police.

With luck, the Russians would be satisfied with taking him out and get out of dodge before the police arrived. Morgan opened the glove compartment and grabbed his two extra clips. That gave him a total of 21 rounds, 21 chances to surprise his new friends.

"What are you doing Dan?"

"I'm going to take care of this," he said.

"Honey, there are six men out there and I don't see how that is going to work if they're hostile. And since they just chased us across Cape Cod I'm going to guess they are not old friends."

On impulse, he kissed her quickly. "Jenny, you know me. This is what I do. I will go out there and do whatever I have to in order to keep you safe. But I can't do it if I have to worry about you. Right now I need you to stay in this car and keep it locked. Whatever happens, you should be okay."

"What about you Dan?" Jenny asked.

"I'll be fine, as long as—"

"Don't lie to me," she said.

"I'm not."

"Yes you are. And you are terrible at it. Now look me in the eye and promise me, *promise me,* that you will be all right," she said.

Morgan grinned at her. "I love you."

Jenny gave him a stricken look as he turned away and reached for the door handle. In their life together, Jenny had almost never seen him lose his temper. That had been a choice he had made. The fact was that there were sides of him he never wanted her to see. He'd made a promise to himself that she never would, and he had kept it—mostly. Now, whatever happened, he knew he was going to break it completely. The last thing his wife was going to see him do was to show a side of himself he had spent a lifetime trying to hide from her.

*Damn,* he thought. It couldn't be helped though. At least she would be safe. He only hoped that, in time, she would forgive him for what she was about to see.

Morgan stepped out of the car, keeping his attention focused on the SUVs. The six figures inside them didn't move, but he knew they were watching him closely.

He moved back carefully, keeping the car between him and the enemy, feeling time begin to slow as it did before a big fight, or an important one. He kept his Walther in his right hand and waited for the sound of an SUV door opening, the sound of the first gunshot. What he got instead was the sound of the Mustang door. He saw what happened with his peripheral vision, even though he brain rejected it.

Before he could even say *no*, Jenny was standing by his side, her own gun drawn and pointing at the black vehicles.

"Jenny," Morgan croaked.

"What can I tell you. I'm a real maverick. I just have trouble following orders. Must run in the family."

\* \* \* \*

Margaret led the way into the lab. Alex found she was actually excited. She was about to meet the figure who was ground zero for the radical movement within the biochemistry and molecular biology community at Berkeley.

On the one hand, it was easy to dismiss Spellman and his movement as crackpots. On the other hand, there was no denying that she had already been to her first APS meeting, then been recruited into the secret society, and now she and Karen were about to meet *Dr. Apocalypse* himself and learn about his plan to destroy the world.

*And it's just my second day of undercover work,* she thought, suppressing a grin.

Alex noted that the sign above the door read: *Macrolab*. She made a mental note to review the briefing material that Karen had prepared so she would know what that meant.

If her cover was going to hold she would have to get very serious about molecular and cellular biology. The lab itself was a large open room with a few small, glassed-off rooms on the outer walls.

She had expected tables full of beakers and bubbling liquids. And while there were some traditional beakers, Petri dishes, and lab equipment on the rows of lab tables, there were even more computers and devices that resembled washing machines or refrigerators or oversized printers.

Near the center of the room a group of about twenty students were facing Professor Spellman, whom she recognized from the video. It seemed like he was holding court and the students were all gazing at him raptly.

Spellman was good-looking in a generic sort of way but a bit soft, an impression that was completed by a weak chin. He wore slacks and a white shirt with the collar open and the sleeves rolled up. It was a uniform that said he was serious, professional, but ready to get to work. No, she realized—it wasn't a uniform, it was a costume. After all, it was a weekend. The only reason to dress like a professor was to establish his position of authority as the leader of The Club.

Alex noticed that Margaret visibly brightened when she saw him. He turned when they came in.

"Margaret, you've brought us some new members," he said. Alex noticed that his voice was nasal, not the booming or deep voice you would expect from someone nicknamed Dr. Apocalypse. All in all, Alex thought, he was a disappointment as a super villain.

Then, as an afterthought, he acknowledged Avery with a nod. "Avery." Turning his attention back to the newcomers, he stared at Alex and said, "You're the transfer student? From Drew?"

"I am," Alex said.

"Welcome," he said. "And you are my new lab assistant, Karen?"

"Yes," Karen said simply.

Dr. Spellman seemed to make eye contact with her for a long time. Then his eyes wandered a bit.

*Gross,* Alex thought. Then she saw with her peripheral vision that Margaret visibly tensed when that happened.

"I remember your introductory email. You requested a position and sent corrections on my paper on dissecting macromolecules," he said.

Margaret visibly gasped.

Karen replied, "I also suggested some improvements on your technique."

Alex thought Margaret might fall over but Dr. Spellman seemed pleased. "You were right, of course. I look forward to seeing what you can do in the lab."

"I'm better at the theory. I'm hoping to learn a lot in your lab," Karen said.

"I look forward to learning from each other," he said pleasantly.

Alex got the distinct impression that Spellman's interest in Karen wasn't just about her brain. It was weird. Though Alex knew, intellectually, that Karen was pretty and her half-Asian, half-Irish features made her exotic, to her she was just…Karen—one of the biggest brains Alex had ever met. Of course, Shepard liked her on more than one level.

And apparently so did Dr. Spellman.

And Alex wasn't the only one who noticed. She could practically feel Margaret seething.

*So Margaret is in love with the doctor,* Alex thought.

Again, gross. And made worse by the fact that both of them—and everyone else in the room as well—shared a fantasy about killing everyone on Earth.

If this was college, Alex decided, she hadn't missed anything.

"I'm glad you both could join us. Margaret tells me that you are very passionate about the issues that concern us as well," he said.

"I don't think anyone can afford to stand on the sidelines now. We want to do whatever we can to help," Alex offered.

"Glad to hear it. We're a new group—we've only been meeting formally for three semesters," he said, waving expansively.

"Have you made much progress?" Alex asked.

"Well, we're still brainstorming approaches and working out some theoretical paths."

They were well into their second year of meetings and they were still in the *early* planning stages? Alex knew what her father would think of them. As a death cult dedicated to the destruction of mankind, they didn't seem very serious.

Like Dr. Spellman himself, The Club was a disappointment—which was probably best for the human race.

The last thing the world needed was a competent and committed group with these goals.

"In addition, I teach a full load and have a department to run," he said. Then he gestured to the group. "And you are looking at a group of top students, who are committed to excelling in their field of study."

*Yes, nobody would want their work on the end of the world to affect their grades,* Alex thought. *That could make it hard for them to get a job later.*

The whole thing did make Alex feel better about the threat that this group might represent. Of course, they could still be dangerous—in the way that a toddler with a loaded gun could be dangerous.

"I want to welcome our two new members," Dr. Spellman said to the group. "As you know, we are a select bunch. Besides our shared concerns about the state of the world and its future, we all share a passion for biochemistry and molecular biology. The bad news is that our current level of industrialization and technology has allowed humans to threaten—for the first time in the planet's history—all life on Earth. The good news is that the science we study and the technology we master may also provide the ultimate solution to the problems we have caused. The very good news is that it might not be too late."

"I want to thank you all for being here and I want to pledge to each and every one of you that all of us are taking an important first step for the future of the planet. And to show my appreciation, I have a surprise for you."

"We have some people joining us today. There is a group—a private group of people who believe many of the same things we believe and run a bio-chem firm. They are from Eastern Europe, from the region of Chechnya. There, even though these people have faced persecution and oppression, they are still committed to saving the planet. I'm proud to say that we have formed our first partnership with a like-minded group. And for the first time, we can share knowledge and work together toward a common goal. This is our chance to be part of the change the world needs, perhaps the only change that matters. Together, we could make real progress in this journey that it feels like we just started."

Dr. Spellman gestured for the door and everyone's head turned.

And nothing happened.

Spellman checked his watch. "They should be here any time."

There was an awkward silence. It lasted for almost a minute and then the door opened. Two men walked in. They took long, purposeful strides as they approached the doctor, who extended his hand.

Neither man took it.

The men were in their late twenties to early thirties and they looked nothing like the biochemists or molecular biologists she had seen on campus, or in movies, or on T.V.

For one, they wore business suits that were dated and ill-fitting. And the men didn't seem comfortable in those clothes. They definitely appeared Eastern European, with dark hair and close-cropped beards.

Dr. Spellman was still holding out his right hand awkwardly. "In our culture, it is traditional to greet each other with a handshake."

The taller of the two men spoke first. "These are the students in your group?"

"Yes," Spellman said, putting his hand down. "This is our first meeting of the year. We are pleased—"

"And all of them have the skills to work on the project?"

"Um, yes. We are a diverse bunch. We represent many different—"

"The skills," the Chechen in charge interrupted. "They have the skills?'

Spellman was frustrated. "Yes, these people represent some of the best minds in the Berkeley biochemistry and molecular biology departments."

The man waved off the doctor and considered the group carefully. Then he scanned the room. "Your equipment here is good."

The professor didn't hide his pride. "This is a state-of-the-art facility. We have machines that—"

The man lifted his hand to shush the professor and Alex wasn't surprised to see him shut up.

Then Alex realized what was off about the Chechens. It wasn't that they didn't look like American scientists (of either the white button shirt or slacker chic variety), it was what they *did* look like.

They were ex-military. Or at least they carried themselves like men who had had some physical or combat training. Alex knew her dad had been in the service, if only briefly, as had most of the people at Zeta. And she had seen more than one military-trained operative in the field. Alex was suddenly on high alert. There was something wrong here. Besides her direct observation, her gut was telling her that these weren't good guys. And they weren't even the kind of soft, clueless bad guys that wanted to use their bio-chem skills to play at creating a superbug that would wipe out everybody.

As for Margaret, Avery, and the others, they were too stunned to even process what was happening in front of them. One look at Karen told Alex that her partner on this mission was feeling the same thing. And then Alex saw something that told her that not only was something wrong here, but something was *very* wrong.

Each of the two men had a bulge under their left arm, a bulge that was visible even under their ill-fitting suits.

"We were really hoping for more of an exchange of—" Spellman said, putting a bit of force behind his voice.

The man in charge raised a hand and said, "We have a facility to show you."

"Well, I'm sure we can arrange a time—"

"Now," the man said.

Spellman was desperately trying to regain control of a situation that was already hopeless. "I'm afraid that is not possible. I have a class in—"

"Now!" the man shouted, shocking Dr. Spellman silent. "All of you will come with us to our facility."

As the group began to grumble, Spellman made one last attempt to take charge of the room. He straightened up and said, "Sir, I'm afraid that—"

"Shut up!" the leader said, holding up his hand as a clear signal to Dr. Spellman.

Three things happened at once. First, Spellman stopped speaking. Second, Margaret gasped audibly. And third, Alex actually saw the large caliber handgun holstered against the Chechen's white shirt.

Still holding up his hand—which seemed to be invisibly reaching across the few feet between them to keep Spellman's mouth shut—the man pulled out a phone with his other hand, dialed, and barked something into the device.

Alex realized he wasn't just speaking to someone on the other end; he was giving him or her orders. Alex wasn't sure what was happening here, but she was sure it wasn't going to be good.

It was time to go.

What she needed was a Zeta Tach team to stop whatever this was until they could sort it all out. Since a team wasn't likely to appear, it was time to get out of there, file a report, and come up with a plan.

Alex examined the two doors on the opposite ends of the outer wall of the lab. The Chechens with the guns might not like it if they left, but she doubted they would draw their weapons and shoot the two women before they reached the door.

Alex wasn't armed but if it came to it, they could stay low, taking cover behind the lab tables as they worked their way outside. She started to get up when she saw three more men approach the glass doors from the outside.

At this distance she couldn't tell, but she had no doubt each of them had bulges under their ill-fitting suits.

# Chapter 15

"Morgan. There is no need for this. I just wish to speak to you. Please, toss out your gun and step away from the car," a Russian-accented voice said from inside one of SUVs.

The voice was familiar and Morgan struggled to place it as he considered his options. None of them were good.

Maybe if he played for time. They might get lucky.

"Why don't you throw out your guns and just get out of here?" Jenny's voice boomed out from next to him. "We're on *vacation!*" she added.

Morgan turned to his wife. He would have liked to tell her that he was handling this situation, but it wasn't as if he had done very well so far.

Jenny just shrugged.

Then she turned back to the Russians and said, "I'm going to count to—"

Morgan raised his hand and she stopped. For now this was a standoff. There was no reason to make it a firefight until it was absolutely necessary. If the Russians wanted him dead, they could have just started shooting. And if they really wanted to end this in a hurry, they could have just lobbed a few RPGs at them and been done with it.

No, they wanted something from Morgan. He could use that. Perhaps there was something he could trade for Jenny's life, or for a chance for her to escape.

That was the mission now. He'd realized that he'd given up on trying to work out a way for both of them to walk away, but he hadn't given up on getting her home without him. It was a trade he would make a hundred times. He'd certainly risked his life for much less than her.

"I was talking to the *other* Morgan," the same Russian voice said.

"What do you want?" Morgan called out. "But understand that you get nothing if I'm not absolutely certain that my wife will be safe."

"It is unfortunate that the woman is here. I do not want—"

"*The woman* has a name!" Jenny shouted. He wanted to tell her not to antagonize the Russians but realized there was no point. Things weren't going to get any worse for them.

"My apologies Mrs. Morgan," the Russian said. To Dan's surprise, the man sounded sincere.

Jenny shot her husband a look and raised an eyebrow. He knew as little about what was going on as she did.

Then he realized something else. She was scared but not terrified. And they weren't dead yet. He felt his own fear for her diminish a bit. Not much, but her presence calmed him. That was good; he was less likely to make a mistake now.

"*Mister* Morgan, I would like to talk to you," the Russian leader said. There it was again. That voice *was* familiar.

"You can make an appointment at my shop. I'm there most days eleven to four," Morgan called out. "Until then, I recommend you listen to my wife and pack it in."

At that Jenny actually smiled and Morgan realized something important: this would be all right. They were together and that made it all right—whatever happened.

"I'm going to come out. Please do not shoot me until we speak," the man said.

That was new. Where were the threats? Your wife first, then your dog, then you—or something like that. For a Russian gangster or KGB operative, this man was terrible at intimidation.

He watched the passenger door of one of the SUVs open and someone step out behind it.

"*Ne strelyai,*" the Russian called to his comrades. Morgan's Russian wasn't great but he understood *don't shoot.* Of course, he had rarely heard Russians he was facing down say that in the field.

"*Esli ne nado,*" the Russian continued. *Unless you have to.* Then, "*Vy mozhete udarit mashinu.*" *You might hit the car.*

"Worried about my car, are you?" Morgan said, glad just to keep the Russian talking.

"The Shelbys did put Mustang on the map," the Russian said. "It's a repaint, of course, but that is the best recreation of the Dark Highland Green that I have ever seen. It doesn't look like a color library job."

"It isn't. It's a custom mix—I've got a guy," Morgan replied.

"Dan," Jenny said insistently. "Really, they have guns pointed at us and you're talking cars."

"I'm buying us time," Morgan said with a shrug.

"Morgan, I'm going to put my gun down and step into the open. I would appreciate it if you didn't shoot me until you hear what I have to say."

"I won't shoot you, but I'm not the only one here," Morgan said.

"Mrs. Morgan, I do apologize for the interruption of your vacation," the Russian said.

This standoff wasn't going the way Morgan had expected. If this was Jenny's influence, he might just have to bring her on all of his missions.

"Take your jacket off and keep your hands in the air," Morgan said.

The man barked something Morgan couldn't hear in Russian and then said. "Okay, Morgan."

The Russian stepped out into the open. Morgan was glad to see that none of the SUV doors opened. The Russian's men wouldn't be covering him—that was something. It wasn't much of an edge, but Morgan and Jenny were so far behind that he would take whatever advantage he could get.

"Morgan, I cannot say that I am pleased to see you, but I do need your help," the Russian said.

No, not *the Russian*. This was a very specific Russian: Valery Dobrynin.

"*Yurievich* Dobrynin," Morgan said, unable to keep the surprise out of his voice.

\* \* \* \*

Alex put her hand out to tell Karen to stop but saw that it wasn't necessary. She also saw the armed men outside the doors. Both agents watched them step into the lab.

Now even the members of The Club could see them. Of course, the students around Alex had no idea what was going on, but—to be fair—neither did she. The only difference was that Alex and Karen understood one thing that would take the rest of them a while to process: they were all in immediate danger.

Alex also knew the men were Chechens. She assumed that because they had just taken a group of American college students hostage, they were also terrorists. Of course, there were problems with that theory.

For one, most Chechen terrorists were separatists, and while they had launched many attacks against Russia and Russian interests, a

Chechen terror group had never attacked America or even a Western European power before.

Whatever was happening here was new. However, that didn't mean the situation wasn't very, very dangerous.

As if to prove her point, the leader of the Chechens gave Dr. Spellman a shove.

"Now hold on. This is a meeting. And you are here only at our invitation. You are leaving me no choice—"

What happened next was inevitable.

The leader of the group reached into his suit jacket and pulled his gun. Before Spellman or anyone else could process that, the man's arm swung the gun around and hit the professor, hard, across the face with a loud crack in the now silent room.

Dr. Spellman went sprawling sideways and fell to the ground, clutching the side of his face. This time there weren't just gasps, there was a growing rumble of shouts from the group of students which was dwarfed by the single, loud scream that was coming from Margaret.

The Chechen leader appeared more annoyed than angry and lifted his gun to the ceiling, firing two shots.

That shocked the room—and even Margaret—into silence.

"Everyone, you will be coming with us. But before we go I want you all to take out your cell phones and watches and give them to that man." He pointed to one of his comrades who had a canvas bag in one hand and a gun in the other. As the terrorist approached the students, Alex could see that the safety was turned off on the gun.

She hoped none of the students balked. If they did, Alex had no doubt they would be shot.

But no one spoke as they all took out their phones. Alex did the same. She thought about trying to get a message out to Zeta, but there were too many gunmen watching the students and she couldn't chance it. As Karen gave up her phone, Alex was glad to see that her partner had concluded the same thing.

There might come a time when they could act, but that time simply wasn't now. Their captors were at the beginning of their operation, when they would be hyper alert. If they all lived long enough, that would hopefully change—especially since the men were only expecting to be dealing with docile college students.

Alex wasn't feeling very docile but knew she knew she had to bide her time.

The man collecting the phones took hers and a few others, and then headed over to one of the lab tables. The only sound in the room was his footsteps, Dr. Spellman's moans of pain, and some soft whimpers from the students.

"In a moment you will be escorted to our transportation. You will not speak."

There was a loud *crack* and Alex saw the terrorist who had taken their phones smashing one with a large hammer. Then another. Then another. When all of the phones and watches were in pieces—and now untraceable—the man collected the pieces and brushed them into the canvas bag.

Two of the terrorists dragged Dr. Spellman to his feet and Alex could see that the right side of his face was bleeding pretty freely under his hand. But he stood, and with a shell-shocked expression allowed himself to be led toward one of the outer doors.

"Follow," the leader shouted at them. Together, the students got up and headed after their professor.

\* \* \* \*

"Do you have a minute?" the message on her screen said.

Before Diana Bloch could respond, Shepard was knocking on her open door.

"Come in," she said, though she had the feeling that if she had hesitated, he would have entered anyway.

Shepard was wearing his usual uniform: jeans, t-shirt, and a hooded sweatshirt. But gone was his usual carefree expression. That look and one of intense concentration were the only ones he wore in public. This new demeanor said he was worried.

"Yes," she said.

"I haven't heard from Karen. Just wondering if you knew anything. Or if you've heard from her or Alex," he said. Shepard was trying—and failing—to make the request sound nonchalant.

"She isn't due to report in until tonight," Bloch said.

"Yes, but she missed our lunch," he said.

"Your what?"

He shuffled and then said, "When we're apart, we sometimes schedule these lunches, where we eat at the same time when we're on the phone."

Bloch knew they were seeing each other and it took some effort not to smile at that. Well, they were young.

"And she missed one?"

"Yes, but the real problem is that she didn't call or message me. That's never happened before," he said.

"She *is* undercover, Shepard," Bloch said.

"Of course, so I thought I would just check to see if you knew anything."

"Have you checked her GPS?"

"I can't ping it, or Alex's."

That, by itself, didn't signify an emergency. Zeta-issued phones would transmit their location even if they were turned off, thanks to modifications made by Shepard. But they still had limitations. If the young women were in a basement lab, or deep inside a large building, there might not be signal.

And the two women were on a mission, so they could very well be together and out of range. It was all perfectly logical, particularly when you factored in the nature of the mission. They were hardly in a hot zone. There was virtually no chance of physical danger from the mission itself—no more than either woman would face in daily life.

"Are you monitoring campus security?"

"We've been in their system since Karen's software flagged the campus. Once Alex and Karen arrived we started monitoring and recording all security camera footage."

"No indication of trouble?" Bloch said.

"Not really," Shepard said, embarrassed.

"I do understand that O'Neal missed your lunch date, but all we really have is that and the fact that their phones aren't showing on the system for…"

"About forty-five minutes," he said.

"And there are half a dozen reasons why that might be," Bloch said.

"Yes," he conceded.

"There's only one problem," Bloch said. "I don't like it, not one bit."

Shepard shot her a surprised look.

"Stay on it. Pull whomever you need. You have my authorization to hack into local law enforcement, traffic cams. Whatever you have to do. Assume we have a problem until you hear otherwise from Karen herself, or Alex. I'll make sure we have local resources in place and a Tach team ready to go if we need them. I wouldn't worry, Shepard, but I'd rather be safe."

Bloch watched Shepard stand there, dumfounded. He'd come in, embarrassed to say that he hadn't heard from his girlfriend, and now he'd just gotten an all-access pass to whatever resources he needed.

"Don't dawdle, Shepard," Bloch said.

The young man snapped to and practically sprinted out of her office.

She had learned a long time ago that it was better to be safe than sorry. As a practical matter, Bloch knew that there was no way to ensure absolute safety for her agents here or in the field.

But there was no rule that said she couldn't try.

# Chapter 16

"Okay, Dobrynin, what is it? Understand that we'll need to do this quickly," Morgan said. He gestured to Jenny who was standing right next to him. He noted that while she had lowered her gun, she hadn't put it away. "We have plans for the afternoon."

Dobrynin hesitated. "This may take some time. And perhaps we could speak privately."

"Anything you want to say to my husband, you can say in front of *the woman,*" Jenny said.

The Russian turned to Morgan for help but he just shrugged. Dobrynin then turned back to Jenny and said, "Mrs. Morgan, I am sorry for this interruption. I am also sorry for this…misunderstanding."

"You sent men after my husband," Jenny said.

"Just to watch him until I could get here. They were sloppy and your husband properly…chastised them. This is very important. It requires that Morgan and I speak. We used to work together and something has come up that is in our mutual interest to prevent."

"Dobrynin—" Morgan began.

"Wait, are you Valery Dobrynin?" Jenny asked.

That surprised Morgan.

"Yes I am," the Russian said.

"My husband has mentioned you," Jenny said.

"To be fair, we were *rivals* more than once," Dobrynin said.

"And you have helped him in the past," Jenny said.

"This is also true," the Russian said.

His wife shot him a look and he shrugged. The chances that Dobrynin was on the level were better than their chances if they decided to shoot it out with the Russian gang. The odds weren't *much* better, but any improvement was something.

"Have you eaten?" Jenny asked.

"What?" Dobrynin asked.

"Lunch. Have you and your men had lunch?"

Twenty minutes later Jenny and Morgan sat across a diner table from Dobrynin, while his five men sat at another table nearby. One of them had a bandage over what Morgan had no doubt was a broken nose.

"This is very serious, Cobra—I mean, Morgan," Dobrynin said, shooting Jenny a glance.

"It's all right, I know my husband's code name," Jenny offered.

The Russian continued. "In the late eighties the KGB and Soviet military had a germ warfare program."

"More than one," Morgan said.

"Yes, more than one. But this was a special program that dealt with only the most dangerous viruses and bacteria, ones that had the potential to create massive loss of life."

"You're referring to Project *Drakon*," Morgan said.

That startled Dobrynin. "You've heard of it? Few people who didn't work directly on the project heard more than whispers, or even know that name."

"East German records were made public after the wall fell. We picked up a lot of our best intelligence simply by asking for it," Morgan said.

"A chaotic time," the Russian agreed. "There was no control over information."

"We didn't get much on that one. Just that you had a project called Dragon that was shut down in 1989. Our analysts assumed it was a failure."

"If only that were true. It was shut down, but not because it was a failure. In the old stories, the stories from the villages, the Russian *drakon* breathes fire to repel foreign invaders. In this project, it was to be a weapon of last resort. In the event that the Soviet empire was lost to your nuclear bombs it would be released to destroy you. However, the dragon was too dangerous. If it was released even by accident, its fire would likely devour the world."

"You mean it would kill everyone? Everywhere?" Jenny asked, genuinely shocked.

The Russian nodded.

"I presume you destroyed it," Morgan said.

"Yes, even the most committed members of the Party did not want the great Soviet Experiment to be responsible for..."

"The end of the world," Jenny gasped.

"All samples were destroyed. The scientists who worked on the project were silenced. There was much discussion about what to do with the KGB agents who worked security for the project. The decision was split and a few of us are still alive."

"So what's the problem?" Morgan asked.

"All of samples of the virus were destroyed, and *most* of the data," Dobrynin said.

"*Most* means *not all,*" Morgan said.

"There was a storage facility in the Caucasus Mountains that had some old computer equipment, some old hard drives. My team thought we had destroyed everything, but the Party kept a backup. And then things got sloppy in the early nineties. I received a message a few days ago that there had been an attack."

"If your storage facility was in the Caucasus Mountains, that means Chechnya," Morgan said.

"Yes, Chechen terrorists hit the facility and killed the soldiers. They left all of the military hardware and spare parts. The only things they took were pieces of computer equipment," Dobrynin said.

"Can I assume that equipment was about twenty-five years old?" Morgan said, and the Russian nodded. "How bad is it?"

"If the data is intact, it would give them everything they need to re-create the virus. With the right people and equipment they could go into production immediately," Dobrynin said.

"Why would anyone, even terrorists, want a weapon that could kill everyone?" Jenny asked, aghast.

"It would be an effective threat. A group could hold the world for ransom, demand whatever they wanted," the Russian said.

"There are other groups who actually want to bring about the end of the world. In Iran there is a Shia sect that believes that if they cause enough chaos it will usher in the twelfth Imam, their messiah, to Earth," Morgan said.

The Russian shook his head. "This new way of doing things…"

"I know what you mean. We played hard, but there were rules," Morgan said.

"Yes, and the first rule was not to destroy—"

"Stop it!" Jenny said. It wasn't quite a shout—they were in public—but her tone stopped both men cold. "You're not talking about a game, something where one side wins for a while, then the other side wins. You're talking about the end of everything, the end of the world. And just to be clear, my daughter lives in the world! I live in the world! And my husband lives in the world! I want you to fix this and I want you to do it now."

"What can you give me?" Morgan asked.

"Photographs of the Chechens, some video. I have everything that was in the KGB file, but we lost track of the men when they entered the United States."

Morgan asked, "How long before they could re-create the virus?"

The Russian shrugged. "I have no idea. It took years to create even the small samples we had. Today, with modern equipment, who knows? It would also depend on the skills of the people involved. My job was security, not science."

"We'll have to bring this to my people. There is someone I need you to tell this story to."

"I will do whatever I can. I was part of it and bear some…responsibility," Dobrynin said. Then he turned to Jenny and added. "And I live in the world too."

Gesturing to the table of Russians, Morgan said, "You'll have to leave them."

"My cousin's boys and comrades. They have little loyalty to me. And this trip has already been more trouble than they bargained for," Dobrynin said.

Turning to Jenny, Morgan said, "We really should go straight in."

"Of course," she replied.

"It will be a little cramped in the back but you can ride with us," Morgan said.

Dobrynin stared out of the window, his gaze lingering on the Mustang. "It will be my pleasure."

\* \* \* \*

"What have you got, Shepard?" Bloch said into her phone.

"Nothing conclusive but…there is something going on there. I can…"

"I'm coming down," Bloch said.

Less than two minutes later she was peeking over Shepard's shoulder at his screen, which was flashing images and documents almost faster than she could follow.

Bloch could see that he had also put Spartan and the rest of the tactical personnel to work. They were all sitting at terminals. From what she could see they were manually reviewing many hours of security camera footage.

That was actually a clever idea. As tactical agents they didn't have much computer experience, but they were trained operatives. And part of their training required them to see what was really there, not what they expected to see. Their experience had trained them to see dangerous situations where most people saw nothing but everyday life.

"No word from Karen or Alex, and their phones haven't shown up on the grid, *any* grid for that matter," he said.

That was bad, it had been hours. Even if they didn't call in, neither Karen nor Alex would allow themselves to be electronically invisible for so long.

"So I started looking for other people on campus that might be..." Shepard paused, as if he was afraid to utter the word. "Missing," he said.

"Professor Spellman didn't show up for a doctor's appointment," Shepard said. "Once I saw that, I ran a check on email messages to any of his bio-chem students and about a dozen of them aren't where they are supposed to be. I mean, they have friends looking for them. Nothing conclusive, so I'm checking cell phones for all students in the bio-chem department. This will take a minute, I'm looking at recent calls, texts to and from... Wait," Shepard said, looking at the screen as if he couldn't understand what he was seeing.

"What is it, Shepard?"

"They're gone," he said flatly.

"Who? Who's gone?"

"Professor Spellman and twenty of his students. Their phones have disappeared. They don't show up on any system. No GPS signals. It's like all of their phones were turned off at once...or destroyed."

The room was silent as the Tach agents who were helping out stopped to listen. "Could be a classroom protocol, or if they're at a secret meeting," Bloch said, knowing how weak it sounded. It was possible, but not likely, especially if students were starting to be missed by their friends.

But, then again, if it *was* foul play someone would know something. This was twenty people we were talking about. That many college students didn't drop off the face of the Earth without leaving a trail—or making a splash.

"Local PD? Fire? Campus security?" she asked.

"Nothing. No flags anywhere," Shepard said, genuine nervousness creeping into his voice. "Except...there are a few security cameras out; a bunch, actually."

"Location?"

"All over, it's almost random, but there is a cluster near the biochemistry labs," he said.

That was it. Something was going on. Even if the students had all voluntarily turned off their phones and—somehow—her agents' location beacons weren't working, that wouldn't explain why security cameras would start going out, especially near the labs.

"When was the last time the campus lost this number of cameras at one time?" she asked.

"Never," he replied.

Bloch straightened up. That was it. She had two agents in trouble.

"Find them. Do whatever you need to but find them," she said. Then to the room, "Tach team personnel. Help Shepard with whatever he needs but be ready to ship out. I'll get us a command center out there."

Of course, that depended on where "out there" was and what they were dealing with. Had the radical professor and his merry band gone underground to fulfill their dream of killing everyone on the planet? Had they been kidnapped? Or was something else going on, something she hadn't thought of?"

If they had run or been kidnapped they wouldn't necessarily stay nearby. In fact, the further away they got from campus, the better.

As she left Shepard's section she called out, "Check the airports, run our missing people through facial recognition and look for any last minute charters or unscheduled flights at small airfields."

In the hallway, her phone buzzed. It was her assistant.

"I have Dan Morgan for you," the young man's voice said.

*Morgan,* she thought. She didn't want to talk to him when they still knew nothing. Morgan *the agent* was enough trouble; the last thing she wanted to do was set off Morgan *the father.* But she wouldn't keep this from him. If this situation turned into a mission—rescue or otherwise—she would need him.

"Bloch here," she said.

# Chapter 17

"I have an asset with a story to tell. And believe me you are going to want to hear it," Morgan said.

"An asset? Aren't you on vacation?"

"Yeah. We found this one on the beach," he replied.

"Can you sit on him?" Bloch said.

"No, time is critical," he said.

"Then bring him in, but Morgan, there's something you have to know first."

As Bloch briefed him, Morgan's heart hammered in his chest. "Morgan, remember the only thing we know for sure is that she hasn't checked in. This is Alex, and she's with Karen. They could simply be doing their jobs."

"But you don't know where they are," he said.

"No," she conceded.

"That sounds like missing to me," Morgan replied. He felt the burn of that hyper alertness that came with an important mission. This time it was mixed with something else, an extra layer of anger and a touch of fear.

This was Alex.

Unfortunately, he had nowhere to direct those feelings. So for now, he had to push all of that down. Whatever happened he couldn't let how he was feeling show. It wouldn't help to scare Jenny more than necessary.

"Jenny, there is a bit of a situation—"

"You're worried," Jenny said. It was a statement, not a question. "What has happened with Alex?"

"Nothing. She's on a mission, undercover, in a very safe environment. And she's with another agent, Karen O'Neal. HQ has lost contact and they are trying to re-establish it now."

"That's not true, or you're not telling me everything," Jenny said. She was remarkably calm, but there was an edge to her voice. Morgan knew he had to come clean.

"She is undercover at Berkeley as a student, investigating the possibility of a radical organization on campus. Zeta software showed it as a potential, future trouble spot. They are just there collecting information."

"Berkeley…" Jenny said thoughtfully. "What department at Berkeley?"

"Bio-chemistry," Morgan said.

"Isn't that where that Dr. Apocalypse teaches?" Jenny asked.

"Doctor who?" Dobrynin said.

"Some crazy professor who says that the only way to save the Earth is for a disease to wipe out people," Jenny said.

"How do you know about him?" Morgan said.

"His lecture went viral," Jenny said.

"And he's a *biochemistry* professor?" Dobrynin asked.

"Yes," Morgan said.

*"Bozhe moi,"* the Russian said.

Morgan didn't know what that term meant, but the Russian's tone told him enough.

Jenny turned to Dobrynin. "So the plans for a deadly virus get stolen by terrorists and then those terrorists show up in the U.S. Now Alex has gone missing while she's investigating people who say they want…Oh my God," Jenny said. She took a deep breath and then added, "You two are the professional spies here, but am I missing something?"

No one answered. All three of them were thinking the same thing. Of course, it could all be a coincidence. There was only one problem: Morgan knew that it wasn't.

"How long until we reach your headquarters?" Dobrynin asked.

Morgan did a quick calculation and said, "Half hour."

It was too long, but that couldn't be helped. No, that wasn't exactly true. They could get a head start on part of this.

He dialed the phone and put Bloch on speaker.

"Bloch here," she said.

"I'm in the car with a former KGB agent named Valery Dobrynin."

"I know the name, and a little about him," Bloch said.

"He ran security for a project in the 1980s…"

When the conversation was over, Morgan stepped on the gas. There was almost no traffic and it was time to find out how fast this car could go on the open road.

As it turned out, it could go pretty fast.

\* \* \* \*

The students were quiet except for some low sobbing and the occasional whimper. There had been no talking since the Chechen leader had backhanded two students for doing so. Margaret was sitting next to Spellman, who kept a wad of tissues to his face. The gash on his cheek seemed to have stopped bleeding. It would need stitches—quite a few of them—but Alex doubted that would happen any time soon.

She and Karen shared the occasional surreptitious look and hand motion, enough to say to each other that *now wasn't the time.* Alex didn't know if the time for them to act would ever come, but there had to be a better time than now, when they were trapped in close quarters with four gunmen.

Though it was only mid-afternoon, the light in the bus was dim. There were LED lights that ran the length of the walkway at the center of the bus. The terrorists had also insisted on keeping on all of the overhead lights above the seats. They clearly wanted to be able to keep an eye on their… what? Prisoners? Hostages? Slave laborers?

The students weren't allowed to speak or move, which meant they couldn't make plans to overpower their captors.

Normally, Alex's first thought would be to make a break for an emergency door or one of the windows to jump out when the bus slowed or stopped. The problem was that steel plate had been welded and bolted over the emergency doors as well as the two exit hatches in the ceiling. The Chechens had also covered all of the windows with some sort of sheet aluminum.

With time and makeshift tools, the windows would be her best shot at getting out of the bus, but Alex didn't think the armed terrorists would give her much time to jimmy or tear at the aluminum.

As a result, the only way out of the bus was up the center aisle, past the five men with guns, through the door to the driver's compartment, and then through the door outside.

Without emergency exits it would be tough for the students to get out of the bus if there was a crash. Of course, even so, a crash would be about the best outcome they could hope for, at least in the short term.

The only thing that kept the bus from total silence was the occasional mutterings of their captors. There was also, incongruously, music coming from the driver's compartment. She assumed it was Chechen. It was surprisingly upbeat, like Eastern European pop music. But the music was low enough that they could hear the outside world.

This told Alex something important. The terrorists preferred they did not see where they were going or how they were getting there, but in the end they didn't care that much. And that meant, of course, that the Chechens intended to kill them all.

Naturally, the terrorists wanted to make sure they didn't try to escape—and it appeared they were succeeding in that regard. However, the men didn't seem to care that the students had seen their faces and would be able to identify them after the Chechens were finished with them. Obviously, that was because for the passengers on this bus, there would be no *after*.

Or course, the terrorists assumed they were dealing with soft college students. They would underestimate Alex and Karen. It wouldn't be much of an advantage but it was something.

In a way knowing that their captors intended to kill them was another advantage. It freed Alex to consider options that would be too risky to try otherwise.

Yes, the students and Professor Spellman were probably sheep. But even sheep, when cornered, would fight. Alex knew she was no sheep, and she suspected Karen wasn't either.

Whatever happened, she would enjoy giving the Chechens a surprise or two.

She did her best to guess their speed (about sixty with a few patches of moderate traffic) and their time on the road (about an hour, though it was hard to be sure without a watch or a phone).

And then they hit traffic, stopping and starting for a few minutes.

She wondered how long it would be before they were missed. On Monday, Spellman wouldn't show up for classes, and neither would twenty students in the same major. Friends and roommates might start missing them tonight, if not this afternoon.

Would Jason miss her? They were supposed to have lunch. Would he make a report to someone? Unlikely. He would probably think she had stood him up. That upset her. She didn't want him to think that.

Especially if she didn't make it out.

Alex didn't finish the thought. She would have to get out of here to make sure she could apologize to him personally.

Girlfriends and boyfriends of the students would be the first to get antsy. They might even make a report to campus security. When that happened, Zeta would be on it immediately.

But even if there was a report by dinnertime, they could be 250 to 300 miles away. That would mean a search area that was as much as 2500 square miles in size. Even with all of Zeta's resources—both what they had, and what they could borrow or hack. And that nearly impossible search process would only start if Zeta got the message they had been taken.

Alex doubted she could count on any lucky breaks. She had to assume reasonable professionalism on the part of the terrorists. They would likely have taken precautions against security cameras.

Unfortunately for the students, the white bus they had been ushered onto was not only non-descript but identical to a number of other buses she had seen on campus, coming and going. That, she was sure, was not an accident.

Even if campus security caught the bus on camera leaving the university, it wouldn't send up any flares. No, she would have to assume they were on their own. They would have to escape, or get a message out. Failure was not an option.

If they failed, they all died.

Traffic stopped them cold and the Chechens began arguing.

That amused Alex. They hadn't counted on traffic.

Then there was noise from inside the driver's compartment. It was a knock. One of the guards opened the door to the compartment. Alex could see the driver dealing with someone outside. He was clearly annoyed as he tried to wave whoever it was off, but he or she kept knocking.

Who was it? The police?

Karen gave her a look. Maybe this magical mystery tour would be over before it began. If it were a policeman, and even if the Chechens somehow got away, there would be a report—a trail to follow.

One of the armed men called up to the driver, who yelled something back. And then the person outside just knocked harder.

Finally, the man she thought of as in charge—who had done all of the talking at the lab—called out and the driver reluctantly pulled on the lever that opened the door.

A male figure bounded up the stairs. "I'm looking for Alex Morgan, we were supposed to—"

It was Jason and he stopped talking when he saw the multiple guns pointed at him.

He scanned the bus until his eyes locked on hers. "Alex..." he said.

# Chapter 18

"I can have someone drive you home," Morgan said to Jenny as they pulled into the underground garage at Zeta.

"Dan, I'm not leaving until we know that Alex is safe," Jenny replied.

Morgan started to argue but saw his wife's expression and dropped it. A plain white van pulled in behind them. Two agents opened the side door and Dobrynin stepped out.

The van had met them on the way to take the Russian into HQ. Dobrynin had made the last leg of the trip in the van's darkened interior—thus keeping Zeta's location a secret.

Worldwide emergency or no, there were security protocols. Even though Dobrynin was his…Enemy? Rival? Friend?

None of those were quite right.

He turned to the agents and said, "Run the memory card he gave you over to Shepard. He knows it's coming."

One of the agents was off down the stairs. Morgan, Jenny, and their Russian guest headed straight for Bloch's office. She waved them in while talking on the phone.

"Jenny," Bloch said simply. She paused and then said, "We're doing everything we can."

"I know, Diane," Jenny replied.

"And we don't actually know anything. I'm going to assume that wherever she is, Alex has the situation in hand."

Morgan gestured to the Russian next to him and said, "This is my… *associate* Valery Dobrynin."

Bloch gave him a curt nod. "You have shown up in more than one of my reports. Now is there anything you can tell me that wasn't in the briefing you gave me by phone?"

"Just that the Chechens who hit our facility were very well-trained. I suspect that they will take precautions not to be found."

"Understood. And thank you for the information you provided. Perhaps we'll get luck with one of the credit cards or with a facial recognition hit on one of the photographs," she said.

"If they are sloppy enough to make a mistake," Morgan said. He didn't hold out much hope of that. It was easy enough to avoid large public places with facial recognition systems. And even if you had to use an airport or a train terminal it was possible to fool the system.

"What about finding the students?" Jenny said. "How can twenty kids and their professor just disappear?"

"Not easily," Diane admitted.

"Any sign they were moved off campus?" Morgan asked.

"No. Some of the cameras were out, but if that many people were moved we would have picked up a truck or a small convoy on traffic cameras. No unusual vehicles came or went," Bloch said.

"Are we sure they left or were taken off campus?" Dobrynin asked.

"Not at all," Bloch said.

"So they could be *on* campus?" Dobrynin said.

"We have a small army of local resources posing as safety inspectors scouring the school. It gets slightly easier if the group wants to be found, which is by no means a certainty."

"Alex and O'Neal would find a way to signal us or leave word somewhere," Morgan said.

"We're counting on that, but we have to assume there is at least a possibility that Spellman and his group are actively working with a foreign terrorist group to create a dangerous biological agent."

"If that's the case they will need a lab," Dobrynin said. "They won't stay in the school for long. And the Chechens will not want to risk themselves being recognized. They also will want to begin their project without delay. And the fact that they are in the U.S. tells me that they intend to deploy the agent or threaten to deploy it here, though I'm sure Mother Russia is also very high on their list."

"If I understand you correctly *everyone* is on their list," Bloch said.

"This is true," Dobrynin said.

"Well I have a list of my own. Where do we start?" Morgan asked.

"We're prepping the Tach team. We have quite a few volunteers, so the biggest problem we are going to have is finding people to stay behind to mind the store. For now Shepard is running the search from his area. If you have any ideas, talk to him. If not, he can always use another pair of eyes reviewing security or satellite footage."

Bloch turned to Jenny and said, "We can have someone take you—"

"I want to help," Jenny cut her off.

"You're with your husband then."

"I can also work," Dobrynin said. "Who is in charge of looking for the Chechen terrorists themselves?"

"No one yet, but the job is yours. Morgan, he's your responsibility," Bloch said, and they were off.

They took the stairs down to Shepard's level because it was marginally faster than the elevator. Morgan was the first to get to Shepard, who was in front of his computer station, which had racks of equipment and half a dozen monitors.

"Shepard," Morgan called out. The young man didn't turn away from the screen. "Shepard," he repeated, as they got closer.

When he turned their way, Morgan saw that Shepard didn't look so good. He'd obviously been at the computer for hours and he wore his worry on his face. Morgan knew that Shepard and O'Neal were seeing each other. Now she was missing on her first undercover mission.

Neither O'Neal nor Shepard was well suited for undercover work. Morgan was sure they had basic weapons and hand-to-hand training (Bloch would have insisted on that when they joined Zeta), but they were far more valuable at their computer stations.

Still, Karen was smart—possibly the smartest person at Zeta. That had to be an asset if they were in a tight spot. And she was with Alex, who was pretty smart herself and had the training and the heart of a field agent. Between them, they should be able to handle virtually any situation.

Based on that, he would have liked to tell Shepard not to worry. And he would have told him just that, if he thought it would do any good or if he was able to follow the same advice himself.

"What do we know?" Morgan said.

"Nothing above what Bloch probably told you. Twenty students and one Professor have disappeared. Their phones are off the grid, which means they have been turned off or destroyed. But there's no sign of foul play on campus and we have no idea how they were moved off campus—if they even were."

"They are not there," Dobrynin said.

"Bloch briefed me. You know the terrorists who may be involved?" Shepard said.

"I know something about them. I presume they have moved their assets by now. They are at or on the way to a lab to synthesize the biological agent. The facility will be remote and already stocked with equipment and supplies. If we can track their equipment, we can find the lab—and your people. It will be easier, of course, if they put the lab together recently. Harder, if they did it over time."

"We're compiling a list of lab supplies," Shepard said.

The Russian tapped his head. "I have the list. I need a computer and an operator with access to all of the relevant commercial databases."

"Some of that information may be flagged by Defense," Shepard said to Morgan.

"On Bloch's authorization," Morgan said.

A few minutes later Dobrynin was at a workstation with six screens and one of Shepard's people assisting him.

"What about us?" Jenny asked Shepard.

"I've got hundreds of hours of security footage from dozens of cameras around campus."

Soon Morgan and Jenny were side-by-side reviewing footage on computers in a cubicle.

Then had just begun when Alicia Schmitt walked in and said, "What can I do to help?"

Morgan heard Lily Randall's distinctly British lilt. "What can I do? Also, Scott told you to call him, he's ready to put his people on whatever you need."

In this case, Scott's 'people' was a group significantly bigger than the combined staff of Zeta. The Internet billionaire had resources in terms of technology and computers that rivaled anything Zeta and most medium-sized countries had.

In the constant buzz of noise and movement around him, Morgan realized something. Except for Conley—who was halfway around the world in Manila—just about everyone at Zeta was working the problem.

That had never happened before. Zeta was manned in shifts, with agents coming and going depending on their missions. For long periods, agents didn't see the inside of the office.

Certainly, there was the potential threat to the world. Everyone took that seriously, but this was something else. They were here for the two missing agents—who in the civilian world wouldn't even be missing long enough to rate a police report.

That was who these people were. That was what they did when two of their own *might* be in trouble.

Morgan's gut was screaming for him to get out and get moving. He needed a target; he needed a mission. He needed to do *something* to help his daughter, and Karen. He needed to take action.

But because they had no leads he did what he could—what everyone else in the room was doing. He scanned the screen in front of him looking for any scrap of information that might help.

# Chapter 19

"Hello, Amado," Conley said, as he left the café.

"Good morning Mr. Peter," Amado said with his familiar grin.

When Amado had first begun as his and Dani's tour guide, Conley had insisted that the man call just call him Peter.

"Of course, Mr. Peter," Amado had said, though Conley thought Amado might have been having fun with him.

Conley sat down in his usual place in the lobby and pulled out his newspaper. Less than fifteen minutes later the Chinese minister and his delegation—which, of course, included Dani—exited the café.

No one in the group spoke to Amado, and the security guard simply gave them his usual smile. Conley noted that Amado didn't speak to or even acknowledge Dani, despite that fact that he had spent two days showing her and Conley around Manila.

Without being spoken to, Amado had known that if Dani were too familiar with the hotel staff, it would be noticed by her people.

The man would make a good operative, Conley decided. Besides the military training that Conley had already assumed he had, Amado had an intuitive grasp of a complicated situation in which he had very little information.

Conley chuckled at the thought of recruiting Amado into Zeta. Pity he was nearly seventy. Even so, the man's good nature was infectious. They could use a little of that around Zeta.

Conley and Dani had agreed to keep to their normal routine for the week. She would continue her exhausting schedule with the minister while Conley made the arrangements for her defection.

They had four full days to develop a plan. Getting her to the American embassy would be easy, but Conley suspected that Bloch would want to go a different route.

As a high-value defector, Dani would be a great source of intel. And Diana Bloch would want to debrief her first so that Zeta collected some of that intel before Dani was transferred to the CIA.

Because that's how it worked. Assets were traded between organizations for favors, for advantage. And along the way assets were used and maximized—and when necessary, they were burned.

And that was the problem. Conley knew that once he made the call to Bloch, Dani would become an asset, not his...

What? Lover? Partner?

He settled on *friend* because he didn't have a term for what she was to him.

Morgan liked to joke that Conley had a woman in every city in the world. Of course, that was ridiculous.

In many cities he had two.

And yet something was different about Dani. Conley wasn't Dan Morgan, family man. Morgan had found a way to square the circle that eluded most operatives and agents in this business—a business that emptied people out, made them hard.

Morgan's family life had kept filling him back up so that never happened. And in the end, Morgan had done something Conley had rarely seen before. He had left the intelligence world behind for Jenny and Alex. Then, after years away, he had returned, but for Zeta, not the CIA.

No, Conley wasn't Morgan. He found his own ways to make peace with the life. Conley was not a family man and never would be. But if he ever were to go down that path, he couldn't help thinking that it would be with a woman like Dani.

And yet he was certain there was something—possibly quite a bit—she wasn't telling him. He and Morgan had a rule for coincidences on a mission: they didn't exist. He wasn't foolish enough to think that it was an accident that she had approached him thinking he was a civilian.

What did that make her—Intelligence? Maybe not an agent herself, but she likely had access to information. If she knew he was an agent that didn't mean that she wasn't sincere in her desire to defect. In fact, it showed that she was smart in how she was approaching it.

Of course, he was sensitive to the possibility of a trap, or a double-cross. He liked Dani, but he had been an agent for too long to fall into a honey trap. However, she hadn't asked him for information, or asked him to do anything other than help her defect.

Thus, his exposure was limited.

Once he got her out of the country there would be plenty of time to sort through possible agendas. But the simple fact was that though she had not been completely honest with him, he still believed that her desire to defect was sincere. In any case, they would soon find out.

Of course, her behavior raised questions about her sincerity in other areas. And while Conley didn't quite have Morgan's instinct for people, he knew something about women. And he believed Dani was sincere in her feelings for him, at least mostly. And the fact was that they had only known each other for a few days.

Rather than being hurt, Conley realized that he was intrigued. He had liked her very much and had found her very interesting. However, he suspected the real Dani was even more interesting.

Conley wouldn't let himself wait anymore. It was time to call Bloch and lay it all out. In a pinch, they could move a flipped asset overnight and even in hours. But the more time they had to make arrangements, the less danger there would be to Dani.

And Zeta wasn't the CIA. Conley didn't have the same problems with the agency that Morgan did, though he understood them. The CIA could be a cold place. There, everyone was an asset and everyone was expendable except the one protected class—the brass.

Bloch would see to it that Dani was protected, and Conley would make sure of it. Dani would trade what she knew for a new life in America. And what she knew would make America stronger and the world more dangerous for the kinds of people who had taken Dani's parents from her.

Yes, it was a trade, but it was a good one.

Conley kept Dani and the Chinese delegation in his peripheral vision as he checked his phone. Boston was exactly twelve hours behind Manila. So for Bloch it was nine O'clock at night—last night.

Well, there was a better than even chance that Bloch was still at Zeta. And even if she wasn't, they didn't exactly keep banker's hours in their business.

Conley tapped the phone. It barely rang and then Bloch was on the line.

"What is it Conley?"

"I have a situation here," Conley explained.

The conversation was brief, but still they were interrupted several times. Something was going on at Zeta, though Bloch maintained that it was nothing he had to worry about.

She listened carefully and told him he'd done good work considering he was on vacation. Dani would be a great asset, a literal treasure trove of intelligence. Bloch promised to make the necessary arrangements and told him to sit tight and to call her if there were any developments.

Conley watched as the minister, Dani, and the rest of the Chinese group finished their morning pleasantries in the lobby and then disappeared into the labyrinth of meeting rooms and conference halls that made up the lower levels of the hotel.

Conley did the only thing he could do. He waited. He would keep his routine, visiting the beach and some of the local sites while eating lunch and dinner at the hotel. On the outside, everything he did needed to appear normal.

Dani would do the same.

However, despite the external motion, he would be doing something remarkably difficult—he would be waiting. Waiting until he heard back from Bloch. Waiting until he had a time and place for Dani's extraction. Waiting until she was safe and out of the reach of the Chinese government.

Conley decided it was going to be a long week.

* * * *

"Don't shoot," Alex said as she stood up. It was a reflex and not a good one. Now all of the Chechens' eyes were pointed at her—as well as two of their guns.

Whatever she came up with next had better be good.

"He's my lab partner," she said, realizing that the only thing that would save Jason was if he was judged valuable to the terrorists' project. "We need him," she added.

"Alex, what is going on?" Jason said.

The terrorists started shouting at him in Chechen. The look of shock and incomprehension on his face was painful.

"Alex," he said as he lurched forward.

More shouting, a gun cocking.

"Jason, don't move," she said.

His life could end in seconds. In fact, it would unless she did something.

"We all want the same thing, but we need him to do it," she said.

Jason was frozen in his spot, his expression shifting from shock to fear. The terrorists were also still, waiting for a command. Finally, their leader barked something at the driver, who pulled the door shut. Then he approached Jason and held out his hand. "Give me your phone."

Jason pulled his phone out of his pocket and handed it to the Chechen, who dropped it on the floor and smashed it, repeatedly, under his heel.

Then the leader grabbed Jason and shoved him roughly down the aisle. The boy nearly fell and Alex had to restrain herself from getting up to grab him. Once again, he remained standing. Then he scanned for Alex and their eyes met.

The bus had two rows of two seats each and Alex was sitting next to Karen. However, the seat across the narrow aisle from Alex was free. She put out a hand to brush his as he took that seat.

Once he was sitting, he looked over at her and she touched her lips with a finger.

Everyone lurched, and then the bus was moving again, slowly through the traffic.

Jason was remarkably calm, despite the fact that he'd just been kidnapped by armed men and loaded onto a bus.

The bus had quieted. The light sobbing and whimpering had stopped, replaced with stunned silence. That was better for now. The Chechens were clearly determined to keep order. She suspected they would take extreme action to do it and didn't want to test them.

Alex kept eye contact with Jason. She told herself it was to keep him calm, but it helped center her as well.

He must have shown up for their date, and then gone to the site of her meeting to see if she was still there. Then what? Had he seen them getting onto the bus?

There was a slim chance that he had seen something and been nervous enough to call the police, but every passing moment that she didn't hear sirens told Alex that was less likely.

The bus kept lurching forward for a minute or two at low speed, then stopping. The pattern repeated over and over for the next half hour until the stops became shorter and shorter.

They didn't stop for a full five minutes and then began picking up speed. That meant that, for now at least, they were out of traffic.

Alex didn't know if that was the good news or the bad news.

\* \* \* \*

It had been a long day and that showed on the face of everyone in the conference room.

"How can so many people just disappear?" Jenny asked. Morgan was surprised at how normal it felt to have Jenny at that table, discussing an ongoing operation.

Shepard answered. "Honestly, we're no closer to knowing that than when we started." His face bore the same combination of exhaustion and worry that Jenny wore, and that Morgan knew showed on his own.

Bloch took the lead next. "The security footage we have shows nothing suspicious and our informal search of the campus hasn't turned up anything. We'll keep at it but it appears very unlikely that the group is anywhere on campus. We've also confirmed that the Professor's and all of the students' cars are still on campus. They didn't drive off separately, and we're reasonably certain that they weren't moved out in delivery trucks—since all major deliveries occurred in areas that still had working security cameras. That means we're left with two possibilities: One, they simply walked off campus, most likely separately. Second, they were moved via an underground tunnel or using some other method that we haven't figured out yet."

"It's been more than eight hours since they went off the grid. And there has been no word. No demands. Nothing. What does that tell us?" Jenny asked.

As a rule of thumb, in a kidnapping or hostage situation, the chance of recovery of the victims went down in a steep curve over time. And the odds of a good outcome decreased exponentially if the hostages were moved to a secondary location.

"We're throwing away the book on this one. None of our working theories include kidnapping for ransom or simple terrorism. Frankly, if it were either of those scenarios the situation would be very serious. We're assuming that Mr. Dobrynin is correct and that the group has been recruited or taken to participate in a specific project. If they were taken for their skills and are vital to that project then they will be safe for the duration of the operation. That gives our greatest assets—Alex and Karen—time to formulate and execute a plan to take action or get word to us."

"We do know one more thing," Shepard said. "Security footage and facial recognition has helped us rule out air or train travel, at least from local airports or stations. That means one way or another they are traveling by road and it's just a matter of time before we get a hit on a traffic stop or camera."

"They will be concerned about time, and will want to keep their travel simple. They also know law enforcement will be looking for them, at least eventually. I would guess they will get the students to a remote location within a single day's drive. Even stopping for gas puts them at risk of getting caught on a security camera. They will be confident because they will not suspect that anyone knows about the virus, so they will assume that the police will simply be looking for a group of radicals who went missing."

"Even if they don't stop for gas and haven't brought any extra tanks, that still gives them a range of at least two hundred miles and a search area that is thousands of square miles," Morgan said.

Shepard responded, "We have access to satellites that can read a license plate but we need to know where to look."

"Any leads on finding their lab?" Bloch said.

The Russian scowled. "This was a well-planned operation. If they had ordered their equipment all at once, it would be easy to find. However, they likely ordered it over time and shipped it to multiple locations."

Shepard stepped in, "But that just means it will take longer to find. Thanks to Mr. Dobrynin, we have a list of relevant equipment. We're tracking all sales of that equipment in the last two years. We can investigate each sale individually and track it. It's a big job but eventually, we'll find something we can use. The problem is that pretty much everything they need is readily available online. And most of the equipment isn't tracked by the government. We're using online retailers' own databases to analyze sales but there are a lot of them. It gets exponentially harder if sales were made over eBay or Craigslist"

This was bad, Morgan knew. They would be looking at thousands of orders. Tracing the transactions and shipping information would take thousands of man-hours, if not tens of thousands.

"It would be easier to track any DNA they bought online," Shepard said.

"You can buy DNA online?" Jenny asked.

"Nothing dangerous but it would give them a head start on some of the bigger pieces of the sequence. They can always sequence the virus from scratch but it takes longer," Shepard said.

"Let's hope they are in a hurry and got sloppy," Bloch said.

Morgan didn't like it. Counting on luck wasn't a plan.

He saw that Dobrynin felt the same way and was muttering under his breath. He heard something that sounded like...*koshmar.* Morgan was far from fluent in Russian but he had learned a bit from Natasha years ago. That one was new to him.

"No, not the lab equipment!" the Russian interjected. Everyone stopped and turned to him. "We can keep looking but by the time we trace their purchases their project will be complete. The pieces are just too common. But if the group is going to build the virus they will need safety protocols."

"Special equipment?" Bloch asked.

"Not exactly, but building what you would call a biosafety level 3 or 4 facility is complicated and expensive. Controls on the air conditioning system, high and low pressure areas. It's often easier to build a new building than to retrofit an old one for this kind of work. Ultimately, I doubt there are more than a dozen contractors who can build such a lab."

"I'll call the CDC and get a list," Shepard said.

Bloch addressed the rest of them. "I know this looks like a big job but we have cooperation from every possible government agency. We will throw people at this until we get a break, and we *will* get a break. If Mr. Dobrynin is right, the terrorists know people are looking for them, but the time frame for their project is built around a traditional search, using traditional resources."

"They don't know Zeta is looking for them—they don't even know we exist. And they don't know that two of our agents are watching their every move. This is what Zeta was created to do. This is what all of you were trained to do. Remember, the stakes here are higher than any problem you have ever faced. And if that wasn't enough, two of our own are in immediate danger," Bloch said.

It was a speech, designed to motivate them, to call on their sense of duty as well as their sense of loyalty to their fellow agents. In a way, Morgan knew he was being played, given a problem, and pointed at a target. The hell of it was, it had worked—partly because everything Bloch said was true, and partly because she was very, very good at her job.

"One more thing: even with all the help we are getting, this is likely to take some time. I can't have you doing this on coffee and attitude," Bloch said.

There was grumbling at the table.

Shepard was the first to speak, "We are on the—"

"You most of all, Shepard. We need you fresh. You're writing and tweaking programs—work that should take dozens of hours—on the fly. You can't do it without rest. It's official; this goes for everyone. If we get a break or lead, I need someone who has the cognitive function to pursue it. And when we have a mission, I need someone to in reasonable condition to complete it. That means as of midnight I'll be enforcing four-hour rest periods, taken in shifts. We have an international intelligence operation to run, and if our information is right, every man woman and child on the face of the earth is depending on us. We will not let them, or our two agents, down."

That was it. Meeting over. Morgan's eyes met Jenny's. He saw everything he was feeling: anger, worry, and determination. Jenny had been caught up in his work before, but this was the first time they had really worked together in his world. He realized that he was glad to have her. Everyone at Zeta and half a dozen government agencies would be fighting for the world, or their fellow agents. He was glad to have Jenny, with him, fighting for their daughter.

And if Bloch was right it was at least a fight. No, not a fight yet, but a race. And a race was something Morgan understood very well.

# Chapter 20

Alex guessed it was a couple of hours after they had picked up Jason that the bus moved off the highway and onto a road with occasional traffic lights.

By that time the Chechens had relaxed. They still didn't allow the students to speak, but they no longer screamed at every little sound, or every time someone shifted in their seats.

The gunmen passed out water bottles an hour or so into the trip. And then they allowed the students to use the small bathroom in the back of the bus when needed.

Their captors weren't exactly treating their hostages well, but they hadn't pistol-whipped anyone since Spellman so that was something. The Chechens needed the students, at least in the short term, but Alex had no illusions about how long that would last.

Escape had to be her and Karen's priority. They needed to get word to Zeta before the terrorists achieved their objective. Alex had a few ideas about what those plans might be.

When the Chechens had first turned up in class, they had talked to Spellman about a project and a facility. That meant the terrorists had a lab somewhere. Now they had a world-class biochemist and a group of students with varying degrees of knowledge and skill.

This was almost certainly a well-planned operation to create a bio-weapon. Alex had no idea how long such a project would take but she was certain that when it was finished the terrorists would have no use for a bunch of students who would go from an important asset to a serious liability.

Twenty-three liabilities. Twenty-four with Dr. Apocalypse.

Alex found her eyes drifting over to Jason. He was sitting quietly and looking up at the ceiling of the bus. He soon felt her eyes on him and met her gaze.

The first expression that registered on his face was concern. He scanned her and then his eyes found hers again. She smiled to reassure him.

He tilted his head forward to the front of the bus and rolled his eyes. He did it so quickly and casually that Alex actually laughed for a second.

Jason shrugged again.

Alex marveled that he was able to joke. He must have been scared but he was functional when so many of the other students wore vacant stares that shifted only when they broke into occasional whimpers.

Dr. Spellman's face had stopped bleeding and he appeared to be in shock. Next to him, Margaret was in about the same shape—though she would occasionally look over to check on him.

*She's in love with Dr. Apocalypse,* Alex realized. Were they seeing each other? Given that he led a club whose sole purpose was to wipe out all people, dating a student didn't seem like much of an offense. Yet the thought made him seem even smaller somehow.

Alex found she had little sympathy for the good doctor. Even if The Club was the equivalent of a fantasy football league, he had somehow made contact with actual terrorists. In a way it was like the plot of one of the horror films she'd seen with her dad—where a group of kids played at some satanic ritual and ended up raising a real demon.

Everyone in The Club was guilty of that to some extent. She and Karen were here because they knew there had been a threat brewing at Berkeley. And even though Alex hadn't taken the threat very seriously, she was trained for this sort of situation. She and Karen were part of Zeta and taking on people like these terrorists was their mission.

There was only one person who was completely innocent and didn't belong here at all—and she realized that he was still looking into her eyes. Jason was only on the bus because he was interested in her.

It wasn't exactly Alex's fault, but there was no denying that Jason wouldn't be here if she hadn't decided to mix her personal feelings with her mission. Now she realized that was both selfish and foolish. But what made Alex feel worst of all was that part of her was still glad that he was here, glad he was with her.

Now she just had to make sure she didn't get him killed.

\* \* \* \*

"Anything on the HAZMAT equipment?" Morgan asked Shepard, who was hunched over one of the keyboards at his workstation. Dobrynin was now working next to him.

"No," the young man said simply.

"Not yet?" he asked.

"Not ever," Shepard said, his voice flat. "We checked every contractor and every level 4 system built in the last two years. None of them are secret terrorist labs. Then we checked every level 3 facility, first in California and then in the entire country. It wasn't that hard; there aren't that many. They'd be crazy to make something so dangerous in a level 3 facility but we checked anyway. Nothing."

Morgan decided he didn't like the look in Dobrynin's eyes.

"What is it?"

*"Proklyatye* Chechens," the Russian muttered.

"What about them?" Morgan said.

"That means they are not bothering with *any* safety protocols," Shepard said.

"But what if they have an accident? They do intend to create a virus that could wipe out everyone," Morgan said.

"Not *if* they have an accident but *when,*" the Russian said. "They will be using students and that *proklyatiy* professor. And they will be working fast. They *will* have accidents, more than one probably."

"What happens then?" Morgan asked.

"If they succeed in creating the agent and someone gets infected they will have to immediately burn the body and anything that has been contaminated. If the world is lucky, it may even work."

Morgan let that sink it. Dobrynin continued, "This is why the Soviets gave up their program and destroyed all samples. Producing and storing the virus in any quantity would have risks, even if *all* safety protocols were followed."

Morgan had had more than his share of trouble with the Soviet Union but they hadn't been crazy. For one thing, they had seen that the destruction of the entire world was too big a risk to take to possess a weapon you could never use.

Even if Zeta assumed the terrorists didn't want to immediately deploy the virus and instead wanted it for blackmail, that wouldn't matter if it got out from the lab by accident.

The lab that Alex would likely be working inside.

There was no time, when before they'd thought they had weeks. Now they had a bomb that could go off any moment.

And no leads.

The Zeta team would keep checking security footage, satellite images, and traffic cameras, trying to track thousands of pieces of equipment—hoping that something would lead them to the location.

Morgan felt his stomach churning. The frustration was almost too much.

"What about the fire? If they have to burn one of their accidents, will the fire show up somewhere?" Morgan asked.

Shepard shrugged. "Sure, we would be able to see if on satellite, but do you know how many small fires there are in California this time of year?"

"No, how many?"

"A lot," the younger man said. "We'll track them, of course but…"

"*Koshmar*," Dobrynin muttered.

Is that what they were reduced to? Hoping that there would be an accident in the lab where the terrorists were creating the world-ending virus so they would have to burn an infected body?

*Alex is in that lab,* Morgan reminded himself.

There had to be a better way. There had to be something they could do, something *he* could do.

In the end, Morgan got himself and Jenny coffee and returned to his computer. Then he went through the campus security footage again, hoping that he would see something he had missed the first time…and the second time.

* * * *

Alex noted a change from local streets to what had to be a gravel road. They were only on that for a few minutes and then the bus came to a stop.

The Chechens had gone quiet. One of them—the leader who had spoken to the group at Berkeley—barked a few orders to the others and slipped up front with the driver.

Everyone was on edge and soon the students started muttering amongst themselves. One of the terrorists turned around and raised his gun, barking something in Chechen. Alex didn't understand the words but the meaning was clear: *Everyone shut up.*

For the first time since they had gotten on the bus, there were only four Chechens with guns in the passenger area. Alex was reasonably certain that if they got close enough, she could take one of them out and grab his weapon. But that would still leave three terrorists with guns. She wouldn't last long in an enclosed space in that scenario.

Alex knew she could count on Karen to try to help but she just didn't know what Karen could do. No doubt the woman had basic hand-to-hand and weapons training, but disarming a committed terrorist in a bus full of civilians was hardly beginner's work.

Alex had to do the hardest thing she had done since the Chechens showed up; she resisted the impulse to fight. It was the right move, she knew, but she couldn't help feeling that this might be the best opportunity she would ever have.

There were twenty-four lives at risk—and one of them was a hapless guy named Jason whose only mistake was trying to date her.

Alex's musings were cut short by the reappearance of the leader who spoke to the other men in Chechen. Then he turned to address the passengers.

"My name is Kattab. We have arrived at the facility. This is where you will stay and work until the project is completed. You will not leave the building during the project. You will cooperate at all times and you will follow all instructions given to you by me or by my men. If you do, you will be treated well. We have been watching your group for some time. We share some of the same goals but understand that we are not partners and we are not your friends. And also understand that this project is very important to my people and to our cause. You will do as you are told or you will die."

"Mister, um, Kattab," Dr. Spellman said, holding a t-shirt or something to his cheek. His voice was shaky but Alex was surprised to hear him speak at all. "It would help if we knew what your project was."

"A virus, doctor. You will synthesize a virus for us. It is a type you know well, but I doubt you have seen anything quite like it," Kattab said.

"What kind of virus?" Spellman asked.

"The kind you have dreamed of, doctor. I believe you called it a cure, a cure for humanity," Kattab said.

Alex would have liked to think that Kattab and his terrorist buddies were crazy, but he appeared deadly serious—not like a wild-eyed lunatic. She knew that was often the problem pop psychologists and even CIA analysts had with terrorists. It was very easy to dismiss them as 'insane.'

To be fair, terrorists often started with a crazy premise—like a desire to impose their dysfunctional ideology on the entire world despite the fact that the same ideology had often turned their old country into a place people would risk their lives to escape. But once they had made that leap, terrorists could be shockingly rational and methodical in their approach to their work. And the fact was that this was a very well-planned operation. They had kidnapped a real scientist and twenty-three assistants for him.

They had eluded capture for hours and they now had successfully moved their prisoners to a secret lab.

Alex had no idea how long it took to create a world-ending virus—she'd have to ask Karen when they could speak again. However, she wasn't going to dismiss anything Kattab had said. For now, she had a responsibility to act like this threat was real. Certainly, it was very real for the twenty of them.

The door opened and the group was ushered outside. Jason, she noted, slipped in front of Alex to put himself between their captors and her. It was sweet—misguided, but sweet. Karen slipped behind her as the group moved forward.

A moment later, they were outside in the early evening light. Scanning the area she saw they were in the desert. There was a large building in front of them but nothing else nearby. They were in a parking lot that was paved but the road they had just taken there was gravel.

In the distance behind the building she could see mountains. The Sierras? That meant Nevada, or maybe…

"We're in Lone Pine, California," Jason whispered behind her.

"What? How?" Alex said.

"Look at the sign," Jason said.

*Armagh Mining Co., Lone Pine, CA est. 1924,* the sign read.

If they were in the California desert, they were most likely southeast of San Francisco and Berkeley. That meant those mountains were definitely the Sierras, which put their location near the Nevada border.

The building was old, at least thirty or forty years. From the outside it resembled a warehouse. It was maybe three stories high and there were no windows except a row of small ones that ringed the top. There was a standard-sized door in the center of the building and large steel doors to its right—presumably for getting mining equipment and supplies in and out.

Alex saw there were no power lines running to the building but she could hear the hum of a generator. That was bad. It meant they were literally off the grid. If Zeta and anyone else were looking for a secret lab, they wouldn't see unusual power usage out here in what was obviously dead center of the middle of nowhere.

And that was bad in more ways than one. It meant there was a very small chance of someone stumbling on the lab and reporting anything suspicious. It also meant that even if Alex or Karen managed to get away on foot, there was nowhere to go—certainly no people or roads they could reach before they were caught.

*Okay then,* Alex thought. That simply meant that they had to take out all of the terrorists before they even tried an escape. Just one more item on their growing to-do list.

"Quiet," Kattab said as the students started muttering to each other. "Everyone inside."

Two of the Chechens led the way through the small door with the other four behind the group, guns pointed at their backs.

Alex, Karen, and Jason were inside in less than a minute.

The building must have been some sort of equipment storage space. However, it had been completely emptied out of whatever had been there before. Now, the roughly hundred-yard square building was a bigger version of the lab at Berkeley. Alex recognized most of the equipment, though some of it was bigger and older than what she'd seen at the school.

On the wall by the entrance there were offices that overlooked the open space though large windows. There were also closed doors that could have led to storerooms.

One of the distant corners held a kitchen area. Then there were rows of bunks on the far wall that ran almost to the other side. Between the bunks were lockers and some rough cabinetry.

Whatever happened, they would be living here until the project was complete. This was very well organized, very serious. The men had obviously done quite a bit of preparation, setting up an entire self-sufficient lab—complete with a dormitory—in the middle of nowhere.

They were preparing to succeed in whatever they had planned. The only thing that Alex and Karen had in their favor was their training and the fact that the terrorists would underestimate them.

Of course, that was only an advantage if they had an opportunity to act.

Alex was determined to find that opportunity, or make it. Eventually, one of their captors would let his guard down. If she could get her hands on a gun, she would have a good chance of ending their operation today.

"Excuse me," said a female voice from the front of the line. "Excuse me, Mr. Kattab," the voice said. It was Margaret and her voice sounded like she was making a great effort to maintain control of the situation. As usual, Avery was on one side of her, Dr. Spellman on the other. Like Margaret, Avery seemed to have recovered a bit. His half-vacant, half-scared expression was gone and he had started to get his usual glower back.

The Chechen turned to face Margaret, his face impassive. She took that as an invitation to continue.

"Look, Timothy told me about some of your conversations, about what you were offering," she said, turning to Dr. Spellman and nodding to him. Something about the way she looked at him confirmed to Alex that Margaret was in love with Spellman. Then she saw something very different flash in Avery's eyes. He was jealous.

Were Margaret and Avery dating before she started seeing Dr. Spellman? At least Avery's perpetual glower now made more sense.

"Offering?" Kattab said. His voice still seemed flat, with an edge of... what? Amusement? Anger?

"I know you have some information about a potential virus that we can all use. I mean, we do all have the same goal," she said, her voice getting more assured as she spoke.

"If we're on the same side, there is no reason for guns," she said. Then she gestured to Spellman. "Or violence. We should all be working together."

"You do not understand..." Kattab said.

"No, sir. I do not think *you* understand," Margaret snapped at him.

What happened next happened so fast that even Alex was surprised.

Kattab drew his pistol, pointed it at Margaret's chest, and pulled the trigger. The bullet caught her chest dead center and threw her backwards. She hit the ground hard, blood spreading out from the clearly fatal wound.

Avery screamed and went to her, while Spellman and the others watched in stunned silence.

Alex turned her eyes to Kattab, who was pointing the gun at the group. "You are dogs, and we do not work with dogs. We will tell you what to do. You will do what we tell you or you will die. Does anyone else have anything to say?"

# Chapter 21

"Morgan, I think I may have something," Shepard said.

Morgan and Dobrynin huddled around Shepard, who was studying his monitors intently. However, nothing in the myriad of open windows on the various screens made any sense to Morgan.

"It's not much, but another student seems to be missing. And it doesn't look like he's part of Spellman's group," Shepard said.

"What's the connection?" Morgan asked.

"He's on Alex's floor, a student named Jason Fitzpatrick. He's actually Alex's RA. I started expanding my email and text searches beyond the bio-chem department and included people in Alex's classes and students who lived in the same dorms as Alex or Karen. Same protocols, looking for people who have been missed by their friends or family. This Jason showed up and then I got a hit on his car. It turned up in a body shop in San Francisco. I cross-checked the body shop against law enforcement databases and it's tied to a number of stolen cars."

"It's a chop shop," Morgan said.

"Looks like," Shepard said.

"Could be that the kid just got his car stolen and he's on a bus back to school," Morgan said.

"That's what I thought at first, but then I saw that he had texted Alex in the morning about meeting up in the afternoon," Shepard said.

"Could still be that he had plans with Alex and then just got his car stolen or hijacked," Morgan said.

"Like I said, it isn't much," Shepard said.

It wasn't. In this case, a stolen car was easier to believe than the idea that someone who had nothing to with this radical group would somehow get caught up in an international terrorist operation. Occam's razor said that the simplest explanation for any turn of events was usually the correct one.

"Bloch can have local PD check out the car," Shepard said.

"No," Morgan said. He didn't want a well-meaning local cop who wasn't cleared for the real details of the operation to nose around looking for...what? Signs that the car might be tied up with a terrorist plot to end the world? Even local operatives familiar with intelligence work might miss something. The reality was that Morgan would only trust Zeta personnel for this task. And even then, it had to be someone who understood the stakes and the particulars of the case. It would also have to be someone who would be able to improvise if the situation got tactical.

"I'll go," Morgan said. "Brief Bloch, tell her I'm going to check it out and I'll need a jet standing by at Logan," he said.

"I'll go with you," Dobrynin said.

"What?" Morgan asked.

"I am no more good here. Mr. Shepard knows what I know about the project. I'm just a pair of eyes reviewing the same footage and data over and over. I need to do something," the Russian said.

*That* Morgan understood.

"Also..." the Russian began. "I was part of this project in the beginning. I was against it, but there were orders."

Well, it was true that Dobrynin was the most expendable member of the computer search team. This wasn't his country and he hadn't been an active agent in years. And it wouldn't hurt to have help if the situation got...tactical.

"Okay, but this might require some finesse," Morgan said.

To that Dobrynin let out a hearty laugh. "Then I had better go without you."

"I'll be making a special effort," Morgan said. It was true. More than anything, he wanted a target, something to smash through to get to his daughter and close this operation.

But this trip would be closer to investigative work than to a mission. They were looking for clues and connections, not targets for their rage.

"We'll leave in five minutes. There's something I have to do first," Morgan said.

He turned and walked to his wife's workstation. Jenny was glued to the screen, scanning images and documents almost as fast as Shepard did.

"Jenny," he said gently. "There's a lead in San Francisco. It's small but I'm going to check it out." Then he explained what they had.

"I'll go with you," she said.

"You'll do more good here. I don't expect to get much out of this but I'll be closer if you manage to find them," Morgan said.

It was true, mostly. Jenny would be more help here. She was better suited to this kind of data-driven search. Plus, she was the only one doing the job now who didn't have traditional military or intelligence training. That might mean she would see something the rest of them would miss.

"I have a feeling that the terrorists are in California, or at least nearby. I want to be there if something breaks," he said.

Morgan braced himself for an argument but she simply got up and hugged him. "Find her and bring her back."

Her voice caught at that and she squeezed him once, pulled away, and kissed him quickly.

Bloch, Shepard, and Dobrynin were waiting at the elevator when he got there.

Shepard, he noted again, didn't look good. Too much coffee and worry and not enough rest.

"Mr. Dobrynin tells me that you are prepared to use finesse on this one," Bloch said, the ghost of a grin on her lips.

"Desperate times," he replied.

Morgan waited for the lecture. He only hoped it would be quick.

"Do what you have to do," Bloch said simply.

Morgan tried to cover his surprise. "Go to the Zeta hangar at Logan, one of our jets is fueling now," Bloch said.

Morgan said his goodbyes and stepped into the elevator. He checked his watch; it was just after 10:00 p.m. They would be in the jet in less than an hour. Then there was the six-hour flight, and travel time to the body shop. They expected to arrive just before the body shop opened.

That was fine with Morgan; he was looking forward to his chat with the proprietors.

* * * *

Two of the Chechens had taken Margaret's body, after they had pried Avery off of her. Alex presumed they had gone to put her out back somewhere, perhaps to bury her.

Alex felt a ball of anger growing in her stomach. Margaret was clueless. But in a rational world she would have had a chance to grow out of her cluelessness. It didn't help that she'd had the misfortune of falling for her professor—who was a special brand of clueless. Of course, even that should have been something she grew out of—just an embarrassing period in her youth.

Unfortunately, that relationship had gotten her caught up in a squabble between a group of Chechen separatists and, apparently, the rest of the world. Alex felt the beginning of a dull anger at Kattab and his terrorist friends. They had already taken everything from a young woman. And they had taken something from Avery, she noted, who now looked like a zombie.

The Chechens ushered the students into the sleeping area and let each of them choose their own bunks.

Kattab and three other terrorists chatted normally, almost casually, and Alex understood something: shooting Margaret was a message to all of them. If she had died for simply talking too much, there was zero chance that the students would dare to speak back to them, let alone get any ideas about escape or overpowering their guards.

From this point forward, the hostages would be docile.

Of course, Alex didn't feel docile. Instead, she felt the ball of anger in her stomach only growing. She found herself sizing up each of their captors, looking for quirks, weaknesses, anything she could exploit in a fight. Part of it was her training. She knew there was a good chance she would prevail against any of the men if it came to a fight. And if she got her hands on a weapon she had a good shot at putting the Chechens down and getting most or all of the hostages out.

She resolved to keep her feelings under control. Properly channeled, anger could be an asset, though left unchecked it could be a serious liability. But curse or blessing, anger at injustice was built into the Morgan DNA.

The irony was she hadn't even particularly liked Margaret.

Alex grabbed a bed in front of one of the padlocked doors to the outside. Jason took a bunk next to hers. As he passed her, he put a hand gently on her shoulder. It was meant to comfort her, to tell her that everything was going to be all right. However, Alex knew that there was a very good chance that everything would not be all right.

Nevertheless, his hand on her shoulder undeniably made her feel better. Before he could pull his hand away, she put hers on top of his and turned to face him before they separated and sat on their own bunks.

Alex lay down in her own narrow bed. Karen took the bunk on the other side of her. The other woman acknowledged her with a nod and Alex saw something that surprised her: Karen was scared.

Of course, this was Karen, so to most people she would just look like her normal, serious self. However, Alex saw Karen's eyes darting around the large room. Alex also saw that as the older woman sat on the bed, she clutched the thin bedding in each hand and simply held it tightly through white knuckles.

For Karen, those two things were the equivalent of a normal person running around the room screaming. Alex understood the fear. Like everyone else in the room, she felt it herself.

But her growing anger dwarfed the fear. She lay back on the bunk staring up at the ceiling, doing her best to will the anger down. She would need it when the time came, but right now she needed her mind clear if she was going to find away to stop Kattab and his terrorist buddies. She also needed to rest. Whatever happened tomorrow, she wanted to be physically as well as mentally sharp.

Of course, once the time came to act, she planned to release that anger, and the soulless man who had gunned down a twenty-year-old girl to send them a message would be first on her list.

\* \* \* \*

Conley found that he was actually nervous. That almost never happened to him on a mission. This didn't make him particularly unique. Agents given to nervousness tended to leave the service in short order. Or they were taken out of the game by attrition—anxiety tended to have a real effect on agent mortality.

It was his nervousness that told him this wasn't a mission for him, not really. There was an asset: Dani. And there was an objective: get this asset safely to the U.S.

And the fact was that this was simpler than most defection operations he had run. Here, the defection was going to happen in a neutral, even friendly nation. There would be no mad dash through the defector's native land to get to the U.S. Embassy. And there would be no complications getting the asset out of the country.

This situation was relatively clean. They didn't have the cooperation of the Filipino government, but they were hardly in a hostile land. When it was all said and done, the Chinese government wouldn't be happy with the Filipinos, but that—he understood—would actually benefit the U.S.

He should have been at ease.

And yet there was that worry in the pit of his stomach, and he was forced to confront what it really was: Dani wasn't just an asset to him. And she wasn't just a vacation fling. The fact that, to Dani, Conley himself was likely an asset did not change his feelings at all.

Something had passed between them. It might not have been the whole story but it was real. And he would have to get her out of the country to find out just how real.

Damn, how did Morgan do it? How did he do the job, knowing that he had a family at home depending on him? And how had he handled the times when his work had put Jenny and Alex in danger?

Just one more day, he told himself.

Bloch had made the arrangements. Later in the day, a Zeta contact would deliver Dani's new American passport and papers to Conley. Then, tomorrow they would go directly to the airport where they would simply get on a commercial flight and head for Hawaii, where they would then take another commercial flight home.

Compared to his and Morgan's last mission to Tibet, this hardly even rated as work, and yet he couldn't shake the feeling that something would go wrong.

Conley felt naked without his Glock. He envied Morgan his Walther PPK. The weapon was small enough that it could be concealed even in the shorts and Hawaiian shirts that had been Conley's uniform for the last few days.

Checking his watch, Conley realized that it was time to keep his usual schedule. He signed the check and got up from the café. Amado greeted him with a smile.

"Good morning Mr. Peter," Amado said.

"Good morning Amado," Conley replied.

Then he took his paper and parked himself in the lobby as he'd done three times before. Like clockwork, Dani and the rest of the minister's delegation left the café and collected at the far end of the lobby.

It was remarkable how normal she appeared. She chatted informally (at least by Chinese standards) with the delegation and their Filipino handlers. Her body language was no different than it had been since she'd arrived.

Yet she was a day away from leaving her life, her work and her country behind.

Remarkable.

As per usual, the group moved down the hallway to the conference rooms and then disappeared. Conley decided he would maintain his normal routine: the beach, lunch at the beach bar, and then back to the beach. But first, he decided he'd grab his Glock from the room safe.

Maybe what he was feeling was just worry over someone who was important to him. Or maybe it was intuition, a warning from his subconscious. He never ignored those feelings on a mission and he wasn't going to start now.

# Chapter 22

Morgan sized up the building. Brothers Auto Body was apparently a big business. Four large steel doors covered most of the front of the building. They were still shut and padlocked.

Checking his watch, Morgan saw that it was nine o'clock. He didn't think much of the brothers' work ethic. Reading the sign, he saw they didn't open until ten.

They might as well have had a billboard out front advertising that they primarily dealt in stolen cars. A good body shop would be open by 7:30 or 8:00 at the latest so people could drop off and pick up their cars before work.

There was a double glass door that led to the office area, which was dark inside. Together, he and Dobrynin scanned the outside of the building. Cameras watched the doors, and if anyone missed those, a large sticker warned that the building was protected by an alarm.

A quick call to Shepard confirmed that the alarm was silent, but noted that the alarm did not flag the police or even the alarm company in the event of a breach. Instead, it reported any unauthorized entry to a nearby residence.

That wasn't surprising. Clearly the brothers didn't want the police crawling around their shop, even in the event of a break-in.

Morgan pulled out the small case from his jacket and chose a pick and tension wrench. The lock on the glass door was a simple pin and tumbler design, and he had it open in less than a minute.

He pulled the door open and held it for Dobrynin.

"They will be here soon," the Russian said.

"I'm counting on it," Morgan replied. Then, as an afterthought, he locked the door from the inside. It would confound the proprietors when they arrived.

The two men made their way into the shop area. There were about a dozen cars inside. Half of them were late model German: Mercedes and BMWs. That told Morgan what he needed to know. Four of the cars were already in pieces, their body panels laid out on the floor.

That made sense. Body panels on these cars were the most profitable and easiest to move parts, but it offended him to see good cars in pieces. And worse than that, the disassembly had been sloppy. The torch work was rough where the quarter panels had been cut and someone had bent the panel edges with a crowbar after removing the bolts.

The panels were usable but they would require too much filler to make clean repairs on whatever car they ended up attached to.

Morgan decided he was liking the brothers less and less.

They found the car they were looking for. The butchers in the shop hadn't gotten their hands on it yet. It was a less than one-year-old four-door Mercedes. Obviously the kid's parents' car.

Inside the car, Morgan found the key. That was strange.

According to Shepard, there was no sign that Jason Fitzpatrick had been involved with Spellman's doomsday club. In fact, he had no ties to any of the even mildly radical groups on campus.

Had the kid simply been carjacked the same day Dr. Apocalypse had disappeared with twenty students, including Alex? Morgan didn't take much stock in coincidences.

He checked his watch; ten minutes. The brothers were certainly taking their time. With Dobrynin, he investigated the rest of the shop.

There were two late model American cars getting crushed fenders repaired. On one, the fenders had just been replaced and the gap between the new fender and the rest of the car was a crime. The other car's replacement fender also had a gap—though not as bad—but the color match was a full shade off.

Morgan heard Dobrynin quietly muttering Russian curses. Morgan found the man behind two large sheets of plastic with two vintage cars. One was a white 1956 Thunderbird—white and in mint condition. The morons had already removed the front fenders and the hood.

The other car was a 1973 Corvette. It was a custom job, and very good one, cherry red with an oversized hood scoop. The car had been modified so that there wasn't a hood anymore. Instead, a single custom-molded front-end body panel—that included both fenders—opened on a hinge at the nose. The new "hood" was open to reveal the heavily modified and largely stainless steel engine compartment.

It was a very over-the-top mod and Morgan recognized the work. It was the kind of custom job that drove stock Corvette purists crazy, but it was still very impressive. The car could only have come from one shop in California. It was bad enough that it was stolen, but for it to be stolen by morons was too much.

Morgan checked his watch again; it had been fifteen minutes since they had arrived. He grabbed one of the shop benches from against the wall and gestured for Dobrynin to do the same. They dragged the benches to the open center of the shop floor, sat down, and waited.

And waited.

Ten minutes later they heard the outer door open, followed by voices and footsteps. Then the doors separating the office area from the shop floor opened and four men entered.

"Glad you could join us," Morgan said, making a show of checking his watch.

The two guys in the center were big, both over six feet and broad. One was Hispanic with a beard; the other was Asian with a shaved head. The two men flanking them were just muscle. Six-two or three, and even broader then their bosses. All four of them were somewhere in their late twenties to early thirties.

"What?" the bearded man said.

"Who are you guys?" the bald man added.

That was it. These must have been the proprietors, the 'brothers'.

"We're the guys who are going to ask you some questions," Morgan said.

"Are you cops?" the bearded brother said.

"If you're cops, you have to tell us." the bald brother added.

"No we don't," Morgan said. "We're not cops, but if we were, what makes you think we'd have to tell you?"

The brothers didn't know how to respond to that. Finally, the bald brother said, "We run a clean business."

"Clean? You keep shop hours like you want the police to pay attention to you. And your fillers look like they were done by kindergarteners trying out papier-mâché for the first time. No, there's nothing clean about your business, but that's not why we're here. We're here for information," Morgan said.

"I don't think you're going to find any information here, but I think you just found trouble, smartass," the bearded brother said.

The thugs were slowing fanning out to either side of Morgan and Dobrynin. Morgan kept an eye on them with his peripheral vision.

"You're locked in now," the bald brother said. "With us."

"First of all, your locks didn't keep us out, what makes you think they'll keep us in?" Morgan asked. He felt the beginning of the red mist of anger rising up from his gut. "And the biggest problem you have right now is that *you* are locked in here with *us.*"

The Brothers laughed at that, but the laughter was a little forced. They just didn't know what to make of the two men who had strolled into their shop.

"Boys, why don't you show these smartasses how we treat burglars," the bald brother said.

"We're not burglars. We broke in but we haven't taken anything. That makes us trespassers at best," Morgan said, the mist growing thicker. "This is your last chance—"

He never got to finish. The thug nearest him swung out with a heavy wrench. Morgan sidestepped the tool easily and it whooshed past him. The thug had put some shoulder into it and the weight of the wrench had pulled him around, giving Morgan a clear shot at the man's right kidney.

Morgan put some weight of his own into the punch and the large man dropped heavily to the floor, the pipe clanging down and skidding away. He heard a yelp behind him, followed by a quick scream. He turned to see Dobrynin's thug moaning on the ground and holding his forearm.

"Like I was saying, we want some information," Morgan said, turning back to the brothers.

The bald brother was pointing a .45 at them. It was a nice weapon, if a little flashy with its chrome finish. Like everything else in this shop, it was wasted on the brothers, Morgan thought as he watched the man hold his weapon sideways. His stance was crap. It would be amazing if the recoil didn't knock him on his ass if he managed to fire the weapon.

After the short burst of action Morgan felt his head clearing. The red mist receded a bit. He didn't want any more distractions. They had come for information.

"This is your last warning. Answer a few questions and we'll get out of your depressing excuse for a shop," he said.

"I don't think you realize what's happening, man," the bearded brother said.

"Comrade, why don't you give our friend here a warning," Morgan said, glancing over at Dobrynin.

"I've had it with you mother—"

The Asian brother was cut short by the small explosion from Dobrynin's weapon. Morgan didn't have to turn to see that it was the Russian's signature handgun, the Tokarev T-33.

The Brother shrieked in pain. Then he dropped the gun he had been holding and clutched his thigh as he fell to the ground.

"I meant a warning shot," Morgan said.

The Russian shrugged. "It was a warning shot. He'll live."

"Fair enough."

By now, the brothers had recovered a bit from the shock of actual gunfire. The Asian Brother was now holding his thigh where he'd been hit. The bullet had penetrated high and outside. As a warning shot, it was a pretty good one: through and through. He could always find some local quack to give him some antibiotics and sew him up.

The Hispanic Brother came out of his stupor and made a lurching motion for the chrome .45 on the floor. But by then Morgan's Walther was in his hands, pointed dead center at the man's chest.

"Don't," he said.

The man stopped.

"Would you like me to give him a warning?" Dobrynin asked.

"I don't think that will be necessary, will it?" Morgan asked. The bearded brother backed away from the gun.

The other brother was still moaning loudly and clutching his thigh.

"If you keep it down, we can all have a conversation and we'll be on our way," Morgan said.

"He shot me!" the bald man said.

"That's what happens when you point a gun at people who want to talk to you," Dobrynin said.

"Are you ready to talk now?" Morgan asked.

"I need an ambulance before I bleed to death," the Asian brother said.

"You're not going to bleed to death. My comrade here is a very good shot," Morgan said as he grabbed a blue work shirt from one of the nearby workbenches and tossed it to the man. "Sit up, apply some pressure, and stop complaining," Morgan said.

He saw that Dobrynin had ushered the two thugs to a corner of the room to keep an eye on them. Morgan waited as the bearded brother helped the other one sit up against one of the posts in the floor.

"What do you want to know?" the bearded man asked.

Now they were getting somewhere. Morgan pointed to Jason Fitzpatrick's Mercedes, "I need to know where that car came from. I need every detail about how and where you picked it up."

"One of our guys found it," he said.

"I need details," Morgan said, putting an edge to his voice.

"On Route 5 just outside of Modesto. He found it pointed south and running on the highway," the brother said.

"Running?" Morgan said.

"Yeah, but no one was in it. Some guy jumped out in traffic and left the car there."

"Abandoned the car? Your guy didn't toss him out, jack the car?" Morgan said.

"No, I swear. It was weird. The driver left the car running. It was just lucky," he said. The brother's eyes never left Morgan's gun.

"Not so lucky for your friend there," Morgan said.

"You can take the car," the bald brother added, stopping his moaning long enough to speak.

"If I need it I will and I don't need your permission," Morgan said, but he doubted a forensic team would turn up anything. He had a pretty good idea of what had happened to Jason Fitzpatrick.

"Can I go to the hospital now?" the bald brother said. He had gotten himself under control and was talking almost reasonably.

"I'll let you know," Morgan said. "I've got to make a call."

He walked to the office area where he called Bloch.

"How do we know Fitzpatrick isn't involved somehow?" she asked.

"It wouldn't make sense. If he went with the Chechens freely he wouldn't have left his car in the middle of a highway. I think he was set to meet Alex and saw whatever happened to her, followed her, and approached when they hit traffic. If he's still alive, he's involved now."

"It's possible. It fits the facts but there could be other explanations," she said.

"There could be, but that's what happened," Morgan said.

Bloch didn't argue. "We can have a local team look at the car," Bloch said.

It wouldn't hurt but Morgan had already found out what he needed to know. "We know when they were on the road and what direction they were going. Tell Shepard to focus his efforts Southbound on Route 5. I'd still assume a 250 to 300 mile range from Berkeley. It was still a large search area but considerably narrowed from their initial estimate.

Of course, they could have simply driven to a local airport—or even a private airfield—and flown anywhere from there. But Morgan didn't think so. The terrorists were on a deadline, and air travel meant flight plans, radar, and too many ways to attract attention.

He hung up and headed back to the shop floor.

"We'll be on our way soon," Morgan said.

By now the bald brother had gotten to a standing position and held himself up with some help from his partner.

"Good, I want you out of my shop," he said.

"I don't want to spend a second more than I have to in your crappy criminal enterprise. It will be a miracle if the cops don't shut you down in a week. This place is as depressing as your repairs. But you know what the real crime here is? You're disassembling a 1956 Thunderbird that's complete and all original. That's just not a crime against the automotive industry, it's bad business.

"We'll go in a minute but I'm not done with you yet. You're going to keep that Mercedes and none of your butchers will touch it. I may send some people to pick it up," Morgan said, raising his hand before either man could protest.

"Also, I want you to put the Thunderbird back together and leave it where you found it. If your guys can't handle the work, then I want you to send it out to a real shop. Then, I want you to take that Corvette and return it to Jerry's Custom Vettes. And I want you to give Jerry something for all the hassle you've caused him. Let's say two boxes of Cuban cigars—make them Montecristos, the number twos. You can just leave them on the front seat."

"Are you joking?" the bearded brother asked.

Morgan turned to Dobrynin, "Have you even known me to make a joke, of any kind?"

The Russian raised his eyebrows. "*Nyet.*"

You have until the end of the day tomorrow on the Vette. I'll give you until the end of the week on the Thunderbird. In the meantime, you'll hear from me about the Mercedes.

The two brothers and the two thugs stared at Morgan with dull incomprehension.

"Do you have any questions?" Morgan said.

The four men all shook their heads.

"Good, get hopping on the cars. And you'll want to get that leg checked. If it gets infected it might kill you…eventually."

# Chapter 23

Bloch saw that Shepard still appeared haunted, but he didn't look quite as desperate. Part of it was the lead that Morgan had just provided. Shepard had run off back to his workstation to follow up on the new search parameters.

Even if Morgan was completely off base there was a benefit to giving the team some hope, or at least a new direction to follow. It certainly beat checking the same data over and over again.

Shepard was also better after a few hours of sleep. Somehow. Jenny Morgan had talked him into it—after Bloch's own orders to get some rest had been ignored.

Bloch realized that she could use some sleep as well. She'd gotten a couple of hours but needed more. She had spent most of the night coordinating resources with the CIA, NSA, FBI, and Scott Renard's tech empire. Though a private company, Renard commanded more hackers, hardware, software, and network resources than most European countries.

And yet with all that at Zeta's disposal, the only real lead they had gotten had come from Dan Morgan and a former KGB agent—who was at least as much of a security risk as an asset—knocking heads at a small-time car ring.

Well, maybe that would turn into something. Now that Morgan had told them where to look, they might actually find something useful—before the terrorists intentionally or unintentionally released their virus.

Bloch decided she would get an hour of sleep on the couch in her office after she'd briefed Mr. Smith on what they'd learned so far. For that, she needed a cup of coffee.

In the mess, she'd found Jenny Morgan at the coffee machine.

"I think you should think about a little sleep yourself before you have another cup of coffee," Bloch said. Jenny obviously hadn't been taking her own advice on rest.

"I will, soon," Jenny said, in perhaps the least convincing tone Bloch had ever heard.

"When?" Bloch asked.

"There's just one thing bothering me," Jenny said.

"I assume it's the same thing that's been bothering half a dozen government agencies, hundreds of Federal Employees, and thousands of local law enforcement," Bloch said.

To that Jenny actually smiled. "Just one piece of it. I'm stuck on how they got the kids off the campus. Twenty students and one professor. And if they were kidnapped the kidnappers had to get on and off campus too. So that makes twenty five or more."

"Conventional wisdom says they used rented a truck with false I.D. and paid in cash." Bloch said.

"Yes, but all of the trucks that moved on and off campus have been accounted for, and all of them show up on one or more of the working security cameras. That leaves, what? The students left campus willingly, and separately, and then met up somewhere else later? Even if that were true and all of the students destroyed their phones at the same time, Alex would have found a way to contact us. And someone would have seen one or more of them as they left campus. They would have run into someone they knew or someone would have stepped in front of a security camera.

"That means they were together for their meeting and then all moved together. Yet according to everything we have seen that's impossible," Jenny said.

"This was a well-planned operation. They had time to think about how to do it and we have to assume they are at least as smart as—" Bloch began.

"But that's it. I don't think they are very smart. What have they done to show us their intelligence? They didn't develop the virus themselves. And even after they have stolen it they need a professor and some students to synthesize it. We have a lot of the best minds in the country trying to figure out their brilliant plan. What if it wasn't brilliant? What if we're overthinking it?" Jenny said.

"Okay, let's assume we are. What then?"

"We don't look for a brilliant trick, we look for something obvious," Jenny said. And then Bloch saw the flash on Jenny's face.

"What?" Bloch asked.

"Buses. They used buses, or more likely a bus. When Alex was a sophomore, I helped organize a school trip to Quebec. I was in charge of transportation and we hired buses, nice ones, not the yellow ones you and I rode on our trips. That's it, I'm sure of it."

"We checked out every vehicle that entered campus," Bloch said.

"All the ones we could see. Maybe we didn't see it or saw the bus and missed something," she said.

Jenny was certain, Bloch could see that much. It would be easy to dismiss her though. Mrs. Morgan was tired. She'd gone too long staring at the same screen with too much coffee and too little sleep.

But that didn't explain the certainty.

Bloch realized that she never would have made a dime betting against Dan Morgan's hunches. The least she could do was indulge this one.

Jenny grabbed Bloch's arm.

"Tell Shepard we're sure. If he knows that, he'll find it. That's our problem, we've been chasing down every possible combination. It's impossible to see anything when you're looking for everything. Tell him we're sure and he'll see it."

Bloch turned and was out the door.

Shepard's eyes flashed when she told him they were positive the Chechens had used one or more buses. He didn't ask questions; he just got right to work, as if Bloch had just given him the missing piece he was looking for.

That was the test of a good idea or explanation, she had always thought. It made things simpler, made the details fall into place. This one seemed to do that. If they were lucky, it would also be true.

For now, it had given Shepard and his group another boost.

Bloch headed back to her office; she saw a small cluster of agents huddled around a large monitor in the mess hall. And then she saw why. A picture of Dr. Spellman was on the screen, along with the headline "Dr. Apocalypse Missing, Along with 20 of his Minions."

The anchor explained that no one had seen the professor or twenty of his students for an entire day. Beyond that they didn't know very much. However, the report was followed by ten minutes of speculation.

One theory suggested Dr. Apocalypse and his students had formed a doomsday cult and had gone somewhere to commit suicide. This was based on the fact that there were unconfirmed reports that two or three of the members of Spellman's 'secret group' had previously tried to kill themselves. Another theory said they were secretly developing a bacterium that made biofuel. Of course, it didn't even occur to the analyst to ask why they would need to do this in secret. Still another expert suggested they were working on a plague of some kind to cleanse the earth of humanity. That, at least, was based on Spellman's viral lecture video.

However, no one in the press had yet connected the disappearance with Chechen terrorists. In fact, there was no indication that anyone in the press even knew about the terrorist attack that Dobrynin had reported to them.

The bottom line was that journalists were groping in the dark. To be fair, so was Zeta and half the Federal government.

The only advantages Zeta had so far were a disgraced former Russian intelligence officer and the combined hunches of Dan and Jenny Morgan. It didn't seem like much—certainly given the fact that the cost of failure could very well be the lives of every man, woman, and child on Earth.

But it was all they had.

\* \* \* \*

The shouting was gibberish to Alex but it's meaning was clear. *Get up you Infidel dogs!* Alex knew she was probably embellishing in her mind but she was sure about the *get up* part. The rest she inferred from the man's tone.

As Alex got up she saw that Karen was already up and watching her. The woman had clearly been awake for a while, though Alex wondered if she had slept at all. She assumed Karen O'Neal needed sleep but Alex had never seen her do it. Jason shook himself awake and said, "Hey."

For a civilian, Jason was holding it together pretty well. He hadn't moaned and cried through the night like some of them. He also hadn't retreated into himself, facing the world with a vacant stare like some of the others.

*Well, we are the third floor, we hold ourselves to a higher standard,* Alex thought.

She saw that Jason was looking at her quizzically. Then he grinned at her. She had thought his eyes were really something, but that grin was also very impressive.

The fact that he was still able to find some humor here and maintain who he was even in these circumstances told her that he was someone she definitely wanted to know when this was over.

*If we survive to see the end of it,* she reminded herself.

Well, that was one more reason to make sure they did survive, especially if their survival meant they had prevented these terrorists from getting a virus that could destroy everything.

Survival. One more thing for her to-do list.

The Chechens herded them off to the kitchen area and showed the students what they would be eating. The kitchen was stocked with exactly four types of food: breakfast cereal, milk, boxed macaroni and cheese, and ramen noodles. Doing some quick math in her head, Alex figured there was less than a month worth of food there.

Did that mean that the project would only take that long? Alex thought so. The terrorists could always restock the kitchen, but shopping would introduce an element of risk. And there was one thing that argued against the re-stocking idea: condensed milk.

There was a good supply of the cans in the cabinets. That told Alex that after the milk in the refrigerators expired, they would be using condensed milk for a week or two.

And then what?

Presumably, the project would be over, along with their usefulness to the Chechens. Alex had no illusions about what would happen then. Whatever the terrorists planned to do with the virus after Spellman and his students created it, they wouldn't live to see it.

Whatever happened, Alex had to make sure it never came to that. For one, Alex was in no rush to die. But secondly and most importantly, the kind of people who would cut down a twenty-year old girl so carelessly should never have power over anyone—let alone over the whole world.

Alex wasn't hungry but she forced herself to take some cereal, choosing one of the "healthy" brands she detested. The last thing she wanted was to be reminded of this place every time she sat down for breakfast.

Of course, she'd have to defeat the terrorists and get out of here for that to be an issue, but she liked the idea of thinking about the future. Certainly, it wouldn't do her any good to fret about the possibility of failure.

Alex chose one of the outer tables where the fewest people were gathering. The tables sat four each. Alex chose the seat looking directly out at the open lab. Karen sat next to her on one side and Jason on the other.

When no one else joined them Alex was grateful, that meant that she and Karen would have a little privacy. Of course, there was Jason to consider but one thing at a time...

There was only one Chechen guard nearby. If she could somehow silently coordinate all of the students to rush him at once—he would probably still be able to kill each of them before anyone got to him.

And even if one of them survived and got a hold of his gun there were five more armed men in the building. She'd have to wait for a better time, and a better plan that didn't involve group suicide.

The remaining terrorists were walking Dr. Spellman around the lab. He examined all of the equipment and discussed it with Kattab—and only him. Alex suspected that the Chechen leader was the only guard who spoke English. That made sense—if the others could communicate with the hostages, there was a greater chance of distractions.

And of course, if the captors and hostages started speaking there was always the chance of the guards sympathizing with their charges. Everyone knew about Stockholm syndrome in which, over time, hostages would develop a psychological alliance with their guards. Later, when they were freed, they sometimes still identified with their captors and even refused to cooperate with the authorities. However, Alex knew that the bond cut both ways. If the guards were expected to shoot any of the hostages, their leaders didn't want them to be friendly with the infidels. They couldn't take the risk of humanizing the students.

It was the same reason the staff didn't give names to animals at the pound: it made it harder to put them down when the time came.

As he walked with his captors, Alex noted how normal Dr. Spellman appeared. He was nervous, scared even, but he was functional. In contrast, Avery was sitting by himself and staring blankly at the table. It was sad but normal. Margaret had meant something to the boy and had died right in front of him. He wore his grief on his face as clearly as he still wore some of her blood on his neck.

Shock and grief were normal reactions.

Spellman had lost her too. And Alex strongly suspected that Margaret had been closer to Spellman at the end of her short life than she was to Avery. Alex realized that she didn't care much for Dr. Apocalypse; she didn't care much for him at all.

Alex saw that Spellman had a large bandage over one cheek. The bleeding seemed to have stopped but there was a large red spot in the bandage. He needed a couple of dozen stitches but he was functional and Alex had to admit that was a good thing for now. If the terrorists thought their project was making progress they would be less likely to start hurting their prisoners.

At the end of the tour, Spellman approached the assembled students and said in a surprisingly normal tone, "Our...hosts have agreed to let me speak to you to explain why we are here. They are in possession of the sequence and other information relating to a virus developed by the Soviet Union in the late 1980s.

"It came out of the Soviet work on bacteriophages, viruses that affect bacteria. As all of you know, most of my important work has been in this area," he said.

*Important work.* Alex marveled that, even now, he could be an arrogant jackass.

He continued. "And as most of you know, the Soviet Union's bacteriophage program was more advanced than anything in the United States at the time. A military project developed this phage for use as a weapon."

He paused, taking stock of the crowd. Up until now, he had gained confidence as he spoke, looking more and more like a professor giving a lecture. Now, he didn't know quite how to proceed.

A hand went up. To Alex's surprise it was Avery. "What does the virus do?"

"It reprograms bacteria in the human digestive tract to produce a modified form of the botulism toxin. It's a brilliantly designed virus. As you know, the paradox that most viruses face is that they can either be very deadly or very easy to transmit, but usually not both.

"This virus gets around the transmission problem because it doesn't attack the human body, it focuses on usually harmless bacteria that are inside every living person. The virus also increases the bacteria's resistance to antibiotics—ensuring that once symptoms begin to present, the host will be dead from the toxin before antibiotics would be effective in eliminating the digestive tract bacteria. Given the resistance factor, it's doubtful that gut bacteria could be eliminated from a given population. And even if it could, the long term effects of that would be fatal."

Another hand went up. "What would the fatality rate be for an infected person?"

Dr. Spellman swallowed once and then said, "Approaching one hundred percent. I suspect that if it were released in a population center with a reasonable amount of international travel, it would infect virtually all of the world's population within a year or two."

There was grumbling as that set in.

"Is there a cure?" another student asked.

That seemed to take Spellman by surprise. "No. Since the virus would affect bacteria, there is no way a cure or a vaccine could be administered. The release of this kind of pathogen would be akin to the kind of virus we have discussed in our meetings. The result would be to...eliminate humanity."

"Do they share our perspective on the environmental rationale for that sort of release? And do we have any guarantees that the virus will not harm animal life?" still another student asked.

"There is a possibility that the virus could affect primates and certain groups of mammals." There was more grumbling at that. Interestingly, even Spellman seemed to be growing impatient with the questions. "Our hosts have not chosen to share their motives with us but—and I want to be very clear about this—they are very insistent that we follow their instructions."

The professor let that hang in the air. Then he added, "They will not permit any obstacles to reaching their objective."

The grumbling ceased. Alex wondered at the students here. They had joined a club whose sole purpose was he elimination of all human life on earth. Then, when confronted with the possibility of actually fulfilling that goal, they wanted to know if there was a 'cure'. And then, when confronted with the idea that their work would destroy them, their families, and everyone they ever knew, they were primarily concerned about whether or not animals would be harmed and whether the terrorists were doing it all for the 'right' reasons.

"Because of the time-frame for this project, we need to work fast, but our procedures in the lab need to be impeccable. Typically, work of this kind would require significant HAZMAT safety equipment. Unfortunately, our facility here does not have such equipment so it is up to each one of us to ensure safety."

Safety? Alex wondered. How did you measure safety in a project whose purpose was to kill everyone? Certainly, releasing the virus accidentally early would kill them all a little sooner but the end result would be the same.

Of course, Alex assumed that the terrorists wanted the virus to hold the world hostage to some particular demands. If the Chechens released the virus in a closed environment—like an island—the danger of what they had would be obvious to even the most clueless world leaders. Of course, there was always the possibility that they really wanted to wipe everyone out. They wouldn't be the first religion or ideology to form a doomsday cult.

Alex knew they had to do something. Otherwise, the best-case scenario ended with the entire world held hostage to these murderous thugs. Unfortunately, these murderous thugs held all of the cards—and the guns.

"Today, we have some work to do to set up the lab. I'll need Karen O'Neal, Steve Dunaway, and Brianne Barker. Then we will divide you into groups. By the end of the day, we need to have our lab up and running, because tomorrow morning the real work begins."

Kattab leaned in to Dr. Spellman and spoke directly into his ear. The professor addressed the students once more. "Before we begin I need to remind you to obey our hosts. They expect full cooperation at all times and will not allow any trouble. I have been told to inform you that anyone who causes any problem whatsoever will end up like Margaret."

The professor spoke normally but Alex noticed that Avery winced as if he'd been struck at the mention of her name. Avery still wasn't all right, but he looked less like a zombie. That was something. With luck he'd live long enough to be back to his old, hostile self.

"I'll need my grad students," Spellman called out to the group.

As Karen got up, Alex grabbed her hand and said, "Be careful. We need time."

Karen said, "Of course. And I am always careful."

While Spellman conferred with Karen and the other two grad students, Alex noticed that there was a low hum of conversation throughout the room. That was something. Their captors were loosening up the rules, presumably because conversation and coordination would be needed to create the virus.

The gunmen could always shoot any student who spoke to anyone else, but they would soon run out of staff for their lab. Fortunately, this development would also allow Alex and Karen to coordinate their plan—whatever it turned out to be.

"I can't say that I think very much of your club," Jason said.

"My what?"

"Your apocalypse club or whatever you call it," Jason said evenly.

Alex grimaced. "I haven't really joined yet." She surveyed the lab and continued, "I'm not impressed by their initiation."

"I hear that. I also don't think much of their...gunman," Jason said. Then he added, "Look, I don't want you to worry. We'll get out of here. All we have to do is not get shot."

"Or expose ourselves to the world-ending virus we'll be making at gunpoint," Alex added.

"Right, that too—good safety tip. But I'm serious. We just have to last long enough for them to find us. There's too many of us. We'll be missed. The police are probably already looking for us. There's no way they'll get away with this."

Alex wasn't so sure. Certainly, the local authorities would be looking for them. And Zeta was definitely on it by now. That actually made Alex feel better, knowing that her father and the rest of the team would be looking for her.

However, she couldn't afford to relax and wait. Kattab and his terrorist friends had planned this carefully. The stakes were high for them.

She and Karen would have to act on their own.

"You don't look convinced," Jason said.

Alex merely snorted.

"I was just thinking." Jason was looking at her with earnest concern and she realized that even now that the Chechens allowed them to speak to one another, she and Karen wouldn't be able to make any meaningful plans when he was around.

Apparently, he wasn't going to let her out of his sight. He was sweet, but he was a civilian, and he was a problem. However, right now there wasn't much she could do about it. No, that wasn't true. There was one thing. It was desperate but her gut told her that it was the right move.

"Listen, Jason. I'm not a regular student. I mean, Karen and I are not regular students..."

# Chapter 24

As Morgan and Dobrynin left the diner, Morgan came to his decision. The instructions from Bloch were simple. Hold up somewhere nearby and wait for a break. He was mildly surprised when she didn't ask him to come back and rejoin the team at Zeta headquarters.

But then again she knew him too well.

Alex was in the area—maybe not close, but in the area, he could feel it. Bloch could send a Tach team here to wait with Morgan and Dobrynin, but Morgan would not leave California. That was probably a good idea. Even if they got a break, Boston was still six hours away, maybe five if the pilot cut a few corners and didn't care about how much fuel he or she used.

In an operation this complex six hours was an acceptable response time, but acceptable was a long way from optimal. And the stakes here were Alex and the world.

"I'm going to head south, but I can drop you at the airport first," Morgan said to the Russian.

Dobrynin got into the passenger seat and considered him. "South to find a place to wait?"

"Just south. I'll follow Route 5 and—" Morgan said.

"You're going to look for them?" Dobrynin asked. "By car?"

Morgan didn't say anything.

"Even if you're right and the *prokliatiye* Chechens didn't put them on a plane, that's still a search area of more than two hundred square miles. Do you know how many miles of road there are in an area that size?"

"No, how many?"

"I have no idea! But looking by car would take—"

"Less time than it would take sitting in a motel room doing nothing," Morgan said. Doing nothing was not an option, not when they had made some progress, and not when his gut was screaming at him to move. "You've done plenty. I appreciate it, I really do. I can drop you at the airport and…" *And what?* Dobrynin had burned more than one bridge in Russia. Morgan suspected that he had been living in hiding. Getting on a commercial flight to America would have put him on the radar of the KGB. Going back would be stupid, and Dobrynin was many things but stupid wasn't one of them.

Morgan couldn't worry about that now. The Russian was an adult, and an agent. He'd just ship Dobrynin back to Zeta and let Bloch sort him out.

"It would be foolish—"

"No one's asking you to come," Morgan said.

"It would be foolish to go in with only your *training pistol.* I have my Tokarev but you'll need a real gun if we stumble onto the Chechens."

"I'm fine with my Walther, but we could use some additional equipment," Morgan said.

"Something fully automatic," Dobrynin.

"And a sniper rifle. Some flash grenades, tear gas," Morgan mused.

"And body armor," Dobrynin added. "But this isn't Texas. You can't just walk into one of your Wal-Marts and fill a shopping cart. This is San Francisco."

"I know a guy," Morgan said.

\* \* \* \*

"I think we have something," Shepard's voice said through the phone.

Bloch was looking over Jenny Morgan's shoulder at her monitor. There were a dozen small windows open and all of them showed white buses entering or exiting the main entrance.

"All of these buses belong to the same company. They provide transportation for sports, cheerleading, the marching band, and various clubs," Jenny said.

"Yes, we checked out all the transportation and delivery companies. There wasn't a single vehicle big enough to transport that many people that wasn't supposed to be there," Bloch said.

"That's what we thought," Jenny said. "We compared the license plates of each vehicle and they match the company records. Each bus was supposed to be there on that day. But each bus was only supposed to be there only once."

"What do you mean?" Bloch asked.

Jenny pointed to the one of the windows on her screen. "At 9 a.m. this bus arrived to pick up the marching band. And the plates match the bus company records. The same bus leaves promptly at ten," she said pointing at another window which showed the bus exiting from the main entrance. "All of this is normal, but it doesn't explain why the same bus appears half an hour later, entering the school at a time when we know for a fact that the bus was twenty miles away."

Bloch examined the photo. The bus appeared the same as it did earlier, and the plate matched. Jenny pointed to another window. It showed the same bus leaving the main entrance at 12:30.

"A duplicate bus with duplicate plates?" Bloch asked.

"A duplicate bus, definitely," Shepard said. "But if it were me I would just switch the plates when the bus was parked somewhere. The bus company might not notice for months."

Shepard's phone beeped. He checked it and said, "That's a confirmation. The driver of the bus confirms that the plates are different, so somebody switched them. And we see the bus heading for the bio-chem building, but the cameras there were out because the terrorists didn't want us to see them loading the students."

Shepard pointed at another window. "Run this," he said.

Jenny clicked the mouse and the video ran. It showed the bus in profile driving past the camera. There was nothing strange that Bloch could see.

Then she ran another one. Still nothing unusual.

"Now look at the windows carefully," Shepard said.

She watched both videos again. This time she saw it. "The windows on the second bus are dark."

"Exactly. Even with the curtains drawn, you can see some light coming through from the other side. It makes sense; it's daytime. But the curtains on the second bus are completely dark inside as if the windows are covered," Shepard said.

"How do we find it?" Bloch said.

"I'm running every database. We've already gotten a few hits on red light cameras. And we know the bus was on Route 5 going south. If we're lucky, it will show up somewhere else," he said.

Possibly, Bloch thought. But if they were headed somewhere rural there might be no traffic cameras. These terrorists may not have been geniuses but they were careful, and you didn't have to be a genius to avoid cameras, especially if you knew the route you were taking.

"Keep looking. Pay particularly attention to out-of-service cameras on the way," she said.

Dan Morgan had limited the search area to a single haystack instead of a whole barn. And Jenny Morgan had given them something specific to look for.

All they needed now was one more small break. If the bus surfaced, they could find the lab and recover the hostages before the terrorists did any damage. The problem was that Bloch didn't like to count on luck; it just wasn't reliable enough.

She patted Shepard's shoulder and decided to count on her team instead.

"Keep at it. Call me the second you find anything," she said.

\* \* \* \*

"You're a...spy?" Jason asked.

"Not exactly a spy. I don't work for the government. My employer is more like a private international security agency, but we have a lot of former military and CIA working with us," Alex said.

"Were you tracking the terrorists?" he asked.

"No. I was sent undercover to infiltrate Dr. Spellman's group."

Jason held his hand up. "I've seen the Dr. Apocalypse video, and I thought he was just crazy."

"Us, too. This was my first undercover assignment, and I think they gave it to me because it was supposed to be a low priority and not very dangerous. But I guess the Chechen terrorists saw that video too," she said.

Jason was surprised but taking it fairly well. "I knew you were too good to be true. Is Alex even your real name?"

"Yes, I'm Alex Morgan and I'm twenty-one years old. I was chosen because I'm the right age and because when I was in High School I was a member of Americans for a Peaceful Society."

Jason absorbed this and he seemed...hurt.

They had been kidnapped by armed terrorists who had already killed one of them in cold blood. Now they would be forced to make a virus that could wipe out everyone. And yet Alex could see that something else was bothering him. Remarkably, she understood it completely.

"I like you. I didn't expect to meet anyone while I was here. It just happened," she said.

Jason grinned. "I'd hate to think my best first date in two semesters was just a cover for an international intelligence operation."

"Oh, it was, but that doesn't mean it wasn't real," she said, returning the grin.

"And if we get out of this we can get that lunch?"

"Of course, I really do live in Boston so we'll have some logistics to work out."

"Are you saying that because you mean it or because you're trying to motivate me to help you save the world?"

To that she almost laughed out loud.

"Can't it be both?" she asked, smiling.

"Fair enough."

Karen returned. "Alex, can I speak to you alone?" she said.

"It's okay. I told Jason why we're really here. Who we are," Alex said.

Karen raised an eyebrow at that.

"I'll do whatever I can to help," he said.

"Do you have any training? Skills?" Karen asked him.

"Um, I'm very good at library research," he said. Then, he added almost apologetically, "I'm an English major."

"Can you do anything else? Can you fight? Technical training?"

"No, nothing like that," he said.

Karen did not know how to respond to that, so she simply turned to Alex and said, "We don't have much time so I have to be quick. I have been put in charge of the microbe lab and I have had both of you assigned to me."

"Can you run the lab?" Alex asked.

"Of course," Karen said. "We'll be growing bacteria. It's not very challenging. It is also the simplest part of the process. Dr. Spellman gave it to me because he doesn't know me very well."

"Are you a biologist?" Jason asked.

"No," Karen said simply. Then, noting his obvious confusion, she added, "I'm a computer scientist, but I had some time before this assignment to study biochemistry."

"And you'll be running a bio lab with one student with absolutely no training in biology?"

"If it make you feel any better I don't have any training in biology," Alex said.

"So just to be clear, the three of us—"

"Don't worry, Karen studied up before we got here. Trust me, she can do this."

Jason shrugged and said, "Well if you've studied…"

Alex turned to Karen and said, "And you can help us keep from blowing our cover?"

"Of course, as I said we will be working on the simplest part of the lab. And you really don't know that much less than many of the undergraduate students here," Karen said simply.

"Great, for a minute I thought we were in trouble," Jason said.

Dr. Spellman called to Karen. "We'll talk more later. Right now, I have to assemble the rest of the microbe lab team and we need to set up our space."

Then she turned back to Jason, "Can you move equipment? Carry boxes?"

"That I can do," he said.

\* \* \* \*

Morgan pulled over when they got the call. He studied the photo of an apparently ordinary white bus. It was the same model used for some limousines and party buses—though this one was less flashy. It had enough seating to transport football players, or cheerleaders…or prisoners.

"At least now we know what we are looking for," Dobrynin said.

That was true. When they had started driving they were looking for a well-hidden secret lab—one that would no doubt be in a remote place and look completely innocuous.

Now they were looking for a well-hidden secret lab—with a big, white bus parked around back.

It wasn't much, but it was progress.

Morgan also felt better that they had swapped their rental for a large, black SUV and stocked it with a small arsenal. Besides the assault weapons and sniper rifles and other assorted gear, Morgan had picked up another Walther and another chest holster. Morgan's contact didn't have another Tokarev for Dobrynin, but the Russian had taken a liking to the chrome-plated .45 he'd confiscated from the car thieves in San Francisco.

So they were well armed and between them they had decades of training and experience. Now if only they could find their target, they might be able to do some good.

Morgan started the car and pulled back onto Route 5.

After a few minutes of silence the Russian asked, "What is the plan?"

"We'll drive Route 5. Look for anything suspicious. We know the range of the bus is about 250 miles," he said. That was one more small break they had received. This model bus was designed for 'school and church' trips, not long haul transportation.

Dobrynin simply grunted. The Russian had stopped arguing. Morgan knew that their chances of stumbling onto the terrorists were slim, but driving made him feel like he was actually *doing* something.

"How long?" Morgan asked.

"What?"

"How long to make the virus?" he asked.

"That would depend on the equipment—"

"We've established that the equipment isn't hard to get. Based on what they could buy or throw together, how long?" Morgan asked.

"With the professor and his grad students to run things and fifteen or so lab technicians: three weeks, maybe a month," Dobrynin said.

"A month to build a weapon that could kill everyone..." Morgan said.

"The real work was done thirty years ago. The *prokliatiye* Chechens are just forcing some children to follow a recipe. These terrorists build nothing, they create nothing."

"Did you ever think that maybe *you* shouldn't have created it?" Morgan said.

"Every day for thirty years," Dobrynin said. "It was a foolish risk to make it. At the time, even the KGB didn't even know what the objective was. We found out later and pushed to burn the project and all records. You have to understand what that took; Soviet pride was strong, and to give up a weapon that even the West didn't have, even America didn't have..."

"Except they didn't give it up, did they?" Morgan said.

*"Idioty,"* Dobrynin said, nodding. That was a Russian word Morgan knew.

Morgan had taken his share of orders from brass who didn't have to live with the consequences of their own decisions. And he'd watched friends die because some moron in charge had had a brilliant idea that was good for nothing other than getting people killed.

The problem was that this brilliant idea wouldn't just kill a few hapless soldiers—or agents—this brilliant idea wouldn't be nearly that selective.

# Chapter 25

Conley greeted Amado as he left the café. Then, like clockwork, he watched Dani and her group leave the café, stopping in the lobby to chat. The scene played out exactly as it had done before, but it was the last day of the conference and this was the last time the scene would play out. Then, at lunch, Conley would have a brief window to meet up with Dani. They would then get into a cab and drive to the airport. Her new passport was in his pocket. By this time tomorrow they would be in Boston, at Zeta headquarters.

Conley found that he couldn't relax. He kept waiting for the calm that came over him during an active mission but it would not come.

At first, he thought that might be because of his personal attachment to Dani. That was part of it, certainly. But as he watched her disappear into the conference area with the minister and his group, Conley realized that his nervousness was because of something far more tangible: noise.

Conley could hear the distant din of a protest outside. The sound was not unusual. He had heard it every day of the conference—though not on the weekends because the protestors took Saturday and Sunday off.

Typically, they didn't start until after ten and then built momentum during the day. Protests were timed to get maximum news coverage; the news crews preferred not to start too early, and the protest organizers were happy to accommodate them. It was all very civilized.

However, today there was yelling outside, then screaming.

That was *very* unusual, and *not* very civilized.

Then he heard something he'd never heard during the protests: gunfire. It was in the distance but there was no question that someone was firing an automatic weapon in short bursts.

As soon as the sound registered, Conley was on his feet. He was not surprised to see that Amado was on the radio, no doubt calling in to whomever he called for this sort of thing.

Conley's hand reached for the comforting weight of his Glock in its rear holster.

He wasn't worried yet. The gunfire was distant and there were dozens—if not scores—of armed police and private security between the gunfire and the hotel. And even if the trouble outside made its way to the hotel, Conley had his Glock and they all had Amado.

Conley watched the older man bark something into his radio. So far as he could tell, Conley and Amado were the only ones who had noticed what had happened outside.

Then it happened again. This time it was single shots, returned by automatic gunfire. Now there were more guns involved in this fight.

And they were closer.

More gunfire and returning gunfire—this time closer still.

Conley was on his feet.

The noise from outside grew louder as the protestors got closer to the hotel, but the gunfire stopped. That was something. Maybe the police had dealt with the problem.

Then he heard din from the protest that sounded like it was right outside the front doors of the hotel. It was louder than any of other protests so far and sounded…different. *It's angrier,* Conley realized. *Much angrier.*

There was a pause in the gunfire.

Then the sound of full auto returned by full auto. Then it stopped. Even the noise from the protest ceased…until it came back with a roar.

He could hear actual screams outside, followed by a rumble.

The rumble turned into a crashing sound and then the glass from the doors and windows at the main entrance of the hotel appeared to explode inward as two large trucks appeared from the right and left and headed toward each other in a low speed crash.

Conley understood when he saw that the trucks were garbage trucks—the closest thing to armored vehicles that you could find in the city. The trucks hit head-on at less than ten miles an hour and then came to a stop.

Even at that speed, the mass of each truck ensured that each one was now too damaged to move under its own power. As a result, the trucks formed a solid makeshift barricade.

These weren't protestors. Not paid ones, not even true believers in the cause of the day. These were terrorists—probably MILF, but certainly terrorists. If not MILF, they could be one of the groups who were keeping the government busy in Mainland China.

It was no accident that they had chosen to attack when the Chinese delegation was in the hotel—the high-ranking Chinese would make very newsworthy hostages, or victims if this turned into a massacre.

Whoever it was, Conley suspected they had chosen the last day of the conference for the same reason that Zeta had chosen it for the day of Dani's defection. Everyone would be tired, and their guard would be down after the bulk of the conference had passed without incident.

Two men who were dressed all in black kicked open the doors of the trucks and jumped onto the floor of the lobby. By now, people were screaming and scattering. That was good; the ones who got farthest away would have the best chance. The ones who got out of the hotel in the chaos would have the best chance of all.

*Dani,* was his only thought. He had to get her out before this turned into whatever the terrorists has planned.

Conley turned to race across the lobby and saw the two guards stationed at the front of the hotel raise their shotguns and fire at the first two terrorists to emerge from the garbage truck doors.

That was something, he realized. Maybe the guards would hold them off, or better yet, end this situation before it turned into a massacre. But Conley decided that he couldn't wait for that resolution to play out.

In any case, the crashing sounds and gunfire from deep inside the hotel told him that this wasn't the only entrance under attack. That sound, the garbage trucks, and the automatic weapons told Conley these people were serious and this attack was well-planned.

If that was the case, the smart money was on the terrorists to take the hotel. But until they did, there would be a brief window of opportunity for Conley to get Dani out. Once he'd done that, he would see what he could do about the terrorists if they were still here.

Conley heard more shotgun blasts and then returning automatic fire. He also saw Amado walking toward the doors with his shotgun drawn. Conley spared a look behind him and saw that the two hotel guards were down and terrorists were pouring out of the open doors of the garbage trucks. Each one of them carried either an AK-47 or Chinese military rifles.

He and Amado were badly outmanned and outgunned. They needed to get out of there now.

"Amado," he called out, running up to the man.

"Mr. Peter," Amado said. "You should go to your room."

"We both need to get out of here. Now!" Peter said. "We've lost the lobby, but not the hotel."

Amado sized up the situation.

"Can we get downstairs from there?" Peter said, pointing to the conference area.

"Yes," Amado said. "Follow me."

The older man sprinted across the remainder of the lobby. As Peter ran after him he heard bullets hitting the furniture behind them.

Amado was faster than Conley would have given him credit for. He added some speed himself, hoping he could keep up.

\* \* \* \*

By six o'clock Alex realized she was hungry. They hadn't eaten since the morning and had worked straight through. Karen had conferred with Dr. Spellman and Kattab, and then had taken charge of her portion of the lab.

Dr. Spellman and one of the grad students, a woman named Brienne, were in charge of the DNA lab. Karen explained that they would use their equipment to assemble the actual DNA of the virus, according to the information from some ancient hard drives that the terrorists had attached to the lab's computers.

Karen explained that the DNA was, by far, the most difficult part of the process. They were actually building a virus from scratch, and this part would require almost all of Dr. Spellman's attention.

The second section was the microbe lab, which was Karen's responsibility. This is where they would grow the bacteria that the virus would incubate in. As promised, Karen had made sure that Alex and Jason were on her staff, as well as three other students.

She spoke to the group but clearly directed her words to Karen and Jason. "The process is fairly simple. Once we have set up the lab, I will show you what to do and your jobs will soon become routine," Karen said.

Alex was relieved. She didn't want her cover as a bio-chem student blown. And now that she had gotten Jason involved, it was his cover too.

The third mini-lab was the harvesting lab, where they would separate the virus from the bacteria using centrifuges and other equipment. Karen explained that while not the most complicated part of the process, it was by far the most dangerous. Accidents with live virus could be catastrophic for anyone nearby, or in the lab…or in the world.

The lab didn't have any of the safety protocols or equipment to handle something so dangerous. All they had was a fire pit in the back, where they would burn any contaminated equipment, or people. A grad student named Steve was in charge of that portion of the lab. It also included a large freezer, which would hold the batches of stored viruses.

The day was spent moving equipment. Karen knew exactly how the microbe lab needed to be set up. That once again astonished Alex because Karen had virtually no training in biology. She had simply read up on the science and lab procedures so she could function as a graduate assistant to Dr. Spellman.

Karen spoke with authority and appeared confident. Even if she was faking it, Alex couldn't spot the difference.

First they chose a spot—Karen insisted on the place closest to one of the two utility sinks set against a wall. Then, they set up lab tables and racks of what appeared to be Petri dishes but Karen called "plates". Karen explained that these were where they would grow the bacteria.

There were also four microwaves and two pressure cookers. That was unnerving. Lab equipment was one thing, but seeing normal kitchen appliances in the terrorist lab unsettled her.

There were also four large incubators where the bacteria-rich solution would actually grow.

Most of the equipment was used, as if the Chechens had bought it at a series of garage sales. But Karen maintained that their lab had everything necessary to complete the project.

And, unfortunately, it was obvious that the other groups were also equipped well enough to complete their tasks.

*Is this all it takes to end the world?* Alex thought. *Some old equipment bought on Craigslist and less than two dozen kids?*

Every once in a while, Alex found herself getting lost in the work. She was able to concentrate on what she was doing and forget about why she was doing it.

Every hour or so, Dr. Spellman stopped by to check on their progress. After Margaret's death Avery had gotten a vacant look in his eyes. Spellman was different too, Alex realized.

He was slightly manic, as if he were in a hurry to get their work done. The first time he stopped by, he said, "Karen tells me that you are all working very hard and I want you to know that I appreciate it. Thanks to you, we'll have the lab up and running by the end of the day."

He said it as if it were perfectly normal. As if it were a good thing.

As if success in their task wasn't the beginning of the end of everything.

If he fell apart like Avery had, the work in the lab would come to a grinding halt. And if that happened the students would be of no use at all to the terrorists.

It appeared that denial helped Dr. Apocalypse cope with the fact that his little club that had made him the center of a lot of attention and allowed him to date college girls might be about to bring about the real apocalypse. That was fine with Alex. The longer he was functional, the longer Zeta had to find them and Alex and Karen had to get control of the situation.

After his brief visit, Spellman moved on to the purification section of the lab to observe and provide some more words of encouragement.

The day was long. They were allowed to drink from the large supply of bottled water but they didn't stop for lunch. However, by then she was sore enough that she didn't think about food any more. Karen impressed her as well. She was slightly built—even more so than Alex herself—but she more than pulled her weight when it came to physical labor. The other students, on the other hand, looked and acted like they had never worked with anything heavier than a computer mouse in their lives.

Some of them seemed to be intentionally slacking. Alex understood that sentiment. The slower they worked, the more they delayed the terrorist's plans. However, the armed Chechens constantly moved around and shouted at anyone who appeared to be moving too slowly.

Jason wasn't like the other students, she realized. Once he saw that they wouldn't be able to stall the terrorists, he did what Alex did and simply threw himself into his tasks. He took the lead in moving all of the heavy equipment and when that was done, moved on to help the other groups with the centrifuges, which were the largest and heaviest of all.

Alex realized that her father would have liked Jason. He liked people who got in and did hard work when it was required. She found herself hoping that Jason and her dad would meet and then pushed that thought aside.

It was a silly thought. For one, she and Jason had really just met themselves. And secondly, the chances of any of them surviving the week, let alone the month were slim. Instead, she inventoried the equipment that she thought they could turn into weapons. The microwaves and pressure cookers were obvious candidates. And probably the centrifuges. After all, they were heavy and operated at very high speeds. She'd have to talk to Karen about how they could be sabotaged and what sort of damage they could do.

There were also liquid chemicals and boxes of powders she didn't recognize that Alex hoped could be mixed to create explosives. Karen, she was sure, was already mentally cataloging those resources.

Alex found herself feeling something for the first time since the Chechens had herded them onto the bus: hope

They had a lab full of equipment, they had training, and they had the amazing contents of Karen's brain. In a few days perhaps they could arrange a surprise or two for the terrorists.

But first they would need to eat. As the day wore on Alex realized that she was hungry. Just before six, Spellman appeared again and inspected their progress. Alex saw that he had changed his bandage and the new one didn't have the ugly blood stain showing through. He should have looked better but he didn't. He was flushed and there was something forced about his speech.

"Very good work, all of you. I think in two or three hours, we'll be done," he said. Then he hesitated and added, "Our hosts have insisted that we finish before we eat again. I'm sorry about that but it really won't be long and it will be nice to stop for the day knowing that our lab will be ready to go tomorrow."

"We will be finished, doctor," Karen said, gesturing to the microbe area.

"Excellent, I want you all to know that when this project if finished you can each count on me for a recommendation," he said, leaving.

"Is he okay?" Jason asked when Karen and Alex were alone.

"He is functional but I think he has an infection from the wound on his face. He's running a low grade fever," Karen said.

"Can he do his job?" Alex asked.

"As far as I can tell his work setting up the lab has been flawless."

Alex understood. Spellman wasn't Avery but perhaps he was struggling with Margaret's death as well—in addition to the situation that he had brought on for his students. If focusing on the work kept him on his feet, that was fine with Alex.

Her stomach growled again. That was an incentive Alex understood and she picked up her pace.

Less than an hour later, she heard hushed voices and turned to see that one of the guys working on Spellman's team was sitting on the floor. In less than a minute everyone stopped what they were doing to look at him.

Now that it was silent she could hear him muttering to himself.

He was a normal student, wearing a t-shirt and jeans. He wasn't moving. He was just sitting on the floor, mumbling.

And crying.

He would stop speaking for a few seconds, let out a sob, and then continue muttering.

Dr. Spellman said something to him in a firm "professor" tone, and the boy turned his attention up.

"I want to go home!" he said clearly.

Three of the terrorists had come over by then. As soon as that happened Spellman and the others backed away from the boy on the floor.

One of the terrorists shoved him.

That made him look up and say, "I don't want to be here...I want to go home."

Alex didn't like this at all, she decided. She started taking purposeful strides toward the boy, with absolutely no idea what she would do when she got there.

However, before she had gotten two steps, Kattab shouted something from across the room and two of the terrorists grabbed the boy under each arm and started dragging him away.

"Wait!" Alex called out.

The third terrorist pointed his rifle directly at Alex and she froze in place. The other two men kept dragging the boy. He didn't resist but he did start shouting, "I want to go home...I want to go home..."

"Let me talk to—" Alex began.

"Quiet!" Kattab shouted from behind her.

Then the terrorists pulled the boy through the double doors leading outside. As soon as that happened he started screaming "I want to go home! I want to go home! I want to go home."

Then the three people were outside and the door shut behind them.

"I want to go—"

A single gunshot rang out, cutting the last scream short.

# Chapter 26

People were approaching them from the conference area and heading toward the lobby. Conley and Amado shouted for the hotel guests to turn around. Most of them were simply confused, until they heard the gunfire and screams coming from the direction of the lobby. They ran from the sound, deeper into the hotel.

More guests and a few hotel staff had fled the lobby and entered the hallway behind them. Conley heard the telltale signs of screams cut short by gunfire. Whoever they were, the terrorists were shooting everyone in their path.

And the only things between them and Dani's group were Conley and Amado. If they could stop the terrorists here, Dani would be safe and this whole thing could be over.

Looking to his right Conley saw double doors with a sign above that read: *Grand Ballroom.*

*Perfect,* he thought. As a rule, he hated large open rooms for firefights since there was no cover. On the other hand, they were great places for an ambush.

He pulled Amado into the alcove in front of the ballroom and said. "If you can find a position inside, I'll lead them into the room. Maybe we can stop them here," Conley said as he reached into his tourist disguise fanny pack to pull out a clip. He had worn it initially as a bit of a joke, but now he realized it was extremely useful.

"No, Mr. Peter. I will do this. You must get out of the hotel. It is not your job," Amado said.

"Amado, you protect the gift shop and café from shoplifters and people running out on their checks. This isn't *your* job," Conley said as he drew his Glock from its rear holster. "As it turns out, this is exactly what I do."

"What are you thinking?" Amado asked calmly.

"Is there an exit on the other side?" Conley asked, pointing across the room. Amado shook his head. "No but there is a store room."

"Good. Get there. I'll lead them in," Conley said. With barely a nod, Amado was running into the ballroom. His pistol-grip shotgun was still at his hip but his .45 was in his hand.

The gunfire had stopped in the hallway and when Conley peeked out from the alcove he saw why. At least a dozen guests and staff were lying dead on the floor. Behind them and heading toward Conley were six black-clad terrorists less than thirty feet away.

In a smooth motion, Conley aimed and fired a single shot, which caught the closest man in the chest. Before he fell, Conley had lined up another target and fired again, hitting another terrorist center mass.

By the time the first man hit the floor, the four remaining terrorists processed the fact that someone was shooting back at them and started firing blindly at Conley's position. Then, with amazing speed, they charged him.

Conley threw himself into the ballroom and raced across the open space toward a door on the opposite wall. His ears told him two things. First, his plan had worked and the surviving terrorists had followed him into the ballroom. And second, they were too close to him, and as a result he would never make it to the storeroom door before they were shooting at him from the ballroom entrance.

*This is why I hate gunfights in a ballroom!* Conley thought. He had time to consider whether he should simply turn to meet them head on when Amado leapt out of the store room and instantly got into a firing crouch.

"Down, Mr. Peter!" Amado shouted.

Conley didn't hesitate. He dove for the ground, just as he heard two shots whiz over his head. It wasn't a graceful dive and it left him on his stomach. As he twisted his body and brought his Glock around, he heard a series of shots from Amado's position.

Amazingly, three of the terrorists fell to the ground. One gunman was still standing. He had his rifle out and got off a single, poorly aimed shot before Conley fired his Glock and the top of the man's head sprayed blood behind him.

He had been aiming for the terrorist's chest, but he'd been firing from a prone position at a moving target. Ultimately, the headshot did the job and the man fell.

"Are you all right Mr. Peter?" Amado said from behind him.

"Yes, thanks to you Amado," Conley said.

The small, older man helped him up. It was quiet in the hallway and Conley hoped the attack was over. But he wasn't taking any chances. He approached the terrorists and grabbed one of the AK-47s. He also took clips from two other attackers, giving him four extra magazines.

Amado had chosen a Chinese assault rifle and was handling it professionally. "Were you in the military, Amado?" Conley asked.

"Yes," the man said simply, though Conley had no doubt there was much more of a story there.

The two men hurried out the door. The hallway was quiet and they raced forward. Less than a hundred yards later, they hit an intersection and turned right toward the conference area.

Conley had memorized Dani's itinerary and knew where she was supposed to be. If that had been the last of the terrorists, he would have her out of the hotel in minutes.

\* \* \* \*

It was nearly midnight by the time they were done setting up the lab. Alex, Karen, and the others in their group had finished work on the microbe section over an hour earlier and had gone on to assist the other groups with the molecular biology and harvesting areas.

Alex was exhausted but still glad to keep busy. The activity meant that every once in a while, sometimes for as long as a minute, she'd stop hearing "I want to go home" over and over again in her head.

To be fair, sometimes that loop was pre-empted by a visual of Margaret's shocked and frightened face as the bullet hit her chest.

All Alex wanted to do was lay down but she forced herself to sit at a table with Karen and Jason in the kitchen area. Some of the students had gone right to their cots. Others were eating cold cereal. The rest were either sitting silently at the other tables or talking quietly.

Almost as soon as they sat, Avery shuffled by, heading toward an empty table. Alex saw that he was still wearing a shirt that was mostly covered by Margaret's now-dried blood.

As soon as she had that thought, Jason was on his feet and approaching Avery. "Hey buddy, let's get you out of that."

Jason ushered Avery to the side and produced a surgical scrub top—of the kind they had sorted and put near the locker area when they set up the lab.

There were no laundry facilities but the terrorists had purchased a large number of surgical scrubs, the disposable kind used in hospitals.

Disposable like the bowls and spoons in the kitchen.

Disposable like the students who would staff the lab.

Maybe a quarter of the kids had opted for the scrubs. That made sense; they would be here for at least a little while, though perhaps not as long as the hostages hoped. In twenty-four hours the Chechens had killed two of the twenty-three people who had originally gotten on the bus.

Alex had permitted herself a bit of hope that with time and a little planning, maybe they could take out the terrorists and save all of the hostages. That seemed foolish now. Karen was not a field agent, and her brain was mostly valuable to the terrorists who needed her to help run their lab. Alex had been in a fight or two but she was still in training. Both she and Karen were in way over their heads.

And Dr. Spellman was holding it together, for now. But how long would that last, particularly if the infection and fever got worse?

One thing was certain: unless Alex and Karen did something fast, everyone who got on that bus from Berkeley would be dead before long. And then there was the problem of the world ending…

Maybe she and Karen could cobble together a plan if they had a week or two. Then they could make weapons and wait for the right moment. But it was far more likely that one or both of them would be shot by these vicious killers—or get infected by whatever super virus the students would be cooking up.

Watching Jason sit Avery in front of some food, Alex felt a low burn beginning in her stomach. It took her a minute to realize that it was anger.

Whatever happened, she needed to make sure that even if these monsters killed everyone in this warehouse, they didn't get to do that to anyone else.

Then Jason had made his way back to their table.

"How long will it take to produce the virus?" Alex asked Karen.

"Building the virus itself will only take a few days. However the whole process, growing it in quantity and purifying the result…three weeks, possibly four, depending on how much virus and bacteria they need for deployment."

"I don't know how much time we have, so we have to get right to it," Alex said. Looking at Karen, "I assume we can weaponize the pressure cookers and microwaves?"

Karen said, "The centrifuges can also be sabotaged. If we do it right, they would make an impressive display and do a lot of damage."

"Useful chemicals?" Alex asked.

"Nothing reactive, nothing explosive in the lab itself, but I will take a closer look at the cleaning supplies," Karen said. "Bear this in mind, Kattab is not an advanced bio-chemist but he must have studied somewhere. He has at least an undergraduate understanding of the science—and I suspect he was the one who supplied the lab with equipment and raw materials. He will be watching us. He'll know if we are delaying the work on the pathogen or engaging in something out of the ordinary. I think we will have to proceed carefully and take some time—"

"That's just it, I don't think we have time. We've seen that any of us could die at any moment. And because the stakes are so high, we have to assume we are the only ones who can stop these people from getting and using the virus—unless you can tell me the virus threat isn't real."

"It's real," Karen said. "The virus is ingenious. It affects bacteria normally found in the human digestive tract so there is no way to immunize against it. It turns normal E. coli bacteria into very efficient producers of a variant of the botulism toxin—one of the most powerful toxins on earth. The virus also encodes the host bacterium to be very resistant to antibiotics so that even if an infected person survived long enough to get treatment, there is virtually no chance it would be effective."

"How deadly is the virus?" Jason asked.

"Nearly one hundred percent," Karen said.

"How easily would it be transmitted?" Alex asked.

"Very easily. That is the remarkable thing about the pathogen. As Dr. Spellman explained, there is a commonly understood tradeoff in viruses. Usually, the more easily it is transmitted, the less deadly the virus and the more deadly, the harder it is to transmit. But this virus works around that trade-off because it is technically does not harm the bacteria it infects. The toxin the bacteria creates does not harm it directly—though the bacteria would eventually die when the host died. Additionally, this bacteria already exists in every person on Earth."

"What would happen if this virus got into the general population?" Jason asked.

"It would likely kill everyone, or nearly everyone, fairly quickly," Karen said.

"Define fairly quickly," Alex said.

"I'm not an epidemiologist," Karen said.

"You're also not a bio-chemist but you're running part of the lab here. Best guess," she said.

"If the virus was deployed at multiple locations in a medium-sized city with a moderate amount of international travel, no more than two years."

"Two years?" Jason asked.

"Two years to kill every person on earth. Less if they deploy in multiple cities at once," Karen said.

That took Alex aback. It could really happen. If they failed in this mission everyone could be dead. It wasn't theoretical, it wasn't a game, and it wasn't safely in the distant future. It could start in less than a month and then it would be all over for everyone in two years at most.

"Deep into that darkness peering..." Jason said. Alex had no idea what that meant but it summed up what she was feeling.

But were even these thugs crazy enough to do it? She realized that even if they weren't they could still do a lot of harm, either by accident or by design.

"The best case scenario is that these terrorists wouldn't deploy the virus but use it to make demands on the world. That would effectively give them power over everyone on earth. And we've seen what happened to people that the terrorists have in their power. Margaret and Philip could tell us if they were still alive."

"His name was Philip?" Jason said.

"Yes," Alex said. "Apparently no one knew him very well. He joined Dr. Spellman's little club at the end of last year." Alex had made a point of learning the boy's name. It made the whole thing worse in a way, but she didn't want to feel better right now.

She wanted to feel angry. She'd need that to do what she knew they had to do.

"We have to stop them," Alex said.

Alex noted that the others were looking at her for direction on how they were going to do that. She wished she knew.

"And I don't mean we have to stop them before long. Or before they finish their project. We have to stop them today, or tomorrow. We have to blow up their lab and take them out so there is no one left to try this again. That means we don't shoot for a safety margin. Our priority is taking out the terrorists, before this lab produces *any* complete virus. That means that we go at the first possible opportunity, and it goes without saying that we are expendable."

Alex studied at Jason. She and Karen were part of Zeta. They knew the risks—at least theoretically. Of course, Karen had never intended to become a field agent and Alex was still new at this. And yet they had gone into their work knowing what might happen.

But Jason had stumbled into this world simply because he'd tried to keep a date with Alex.

"It's a lot to ask, I know. You're not trained for this. When the time comes you should probably get under a lab table and stay there," Alex said.

Jason thought about that and said, "I have great faith in fools; self-confidence, my friends call it."

"What does that mean?" Karen asked.

"That means I'm in," Jason said. "My advanced literary research skills are at your disposal."

# Chapter 27

*What the hell was going on in Manila?* Bloch thought. And how did Conley get himself caught up in it? He was there only to observe. If she'd wanted trouble she would have sent Morgan.

That made three agents out of contact. Three agents that could be dead or die at any moment. Three agents she could do absolutely nothing to help.

The press was all over Manila. The incident had actually replaced the disappearance of Dr. Apocalypse and his students as the top story on all of the cable stations.

The problem was that the press didn't know anything except that there had been an attack on the hotel on the last day of the conference. Some reports said it was simply an active shooter situation. Others said that the terrorists had control of the hotel. And her sources at State and the CIA didn't know much more. The situation was too new and apparently no communications were getting out of the hotel. It appeared as if there were nothing she, or anyone else, could do about it.

*Except Conley,* she thought.

He would have been at the hotel, waiting to take his high-level defector to the airport. Maybe he would be able to achieve something from the inside of that mess.

Certainly, he couldn't do worse than the local police and military, who seemed to be wandering aimlessly around the perimeter of the hotel. For now, the terrorists were in control of the situation.

There was little anyone else could do except wait for their demands and hope for a break.

Bloch realized that this was the second time that O'Neal's software had predicted a major crisis. That was amazing. If only the software could follow up with some clue about what to do next.

* * * *

It was late and Morgan felt his eyes getting heavy. He also felt Dobrynin looking at him.

"I know," he said.

It was too dark to see anything, especially out here in the southern California desert.

They had been driving for the better part of a day and they hadn't found anything. Of course, that wasn't the point.

Morgan had no illusions about whether they would stumble onto the terrorists' lab but the driving quieted his mind a little. It also gave him something to do other than worry about his daughter.

And it kept him in the area that he still felt was the terrorists' destination. In fact, he was more certain than ever. For one, there was nothing out here. And the Chechens would want their secret lab to be as remote as possible.

Plus, the desert's dry air was marginally safer if you were working with a dangerous virus.

He pulled into the first motel he saw. He would need rest, if not sleep. He needed to be ready when Bloch called.

* * * *

Conley had memorized Dani's schedule and had no trouble finding the right conference room. There was no one inside. Yet it seemed like the group had just stepped out. There were nearly twenty chairs around a large table, miscellaneous papers in front of them. To the side there were smaller tables full of food and drink.

But there were no bodies, no blood. That was something.

Conley presumed the delegation had heard the commotion and gotten out of the room. Both the Chinese minister and his Filipino counterparts had security. Their first move would be to try to get their people out of the hotel. If there were no available exits, they would try to find a defensible position to hole up.

Conley pulled out his phone. No signal. Clearly, this wasn't going to be easy. He'd have to find Dani the old fashioned way. And he did know for a fact that the group hadn't tried to exit through the lobby.

"Is there another way out?" Conley asked Amado.

"This way, Mr. Peter," Amado said, leading him deeper through the hallway into the stretch of rooms the made up the conference area.

Conley heard a boom behind him. Then there was the sound of gunfire.

Conley had hoped that he and Amado had eliminated the terrorists and ended the problem. Clearly, it wasn't going to be that easy.

"There is an exit at the end of the—" Amado began but he stopped when he heard the gunfire up ahead.

*That would be the exit,* Conley thought. *Perfect.*

"Stairs?" Conley asked.

"This way," Amado said and let them to a heavy steel door next to an elevator.

Like ballrooms, elevators were on his list of things he hated to be inside during a firefight. You couldn't see what was coming and you could end up with the doors opening to a dozen of the enemy.

"Can we get to the basement?" Conley said.

Amado pointed and the gunfire sounded closer. They rushed into the door, saw that it was clear, and barreled down the stairs.

It was quiet on this level, except for the hum of air conditioning, water pumps, computers, and other equipment that ran the hotel. There were no sounds of people.

"There is a lower level; one that connects the towers," Amado said.

The hotel was really two twelve-story buildings, separated by a side street. They were connected by a glass skyway on the seventh floor—and apparently by a sub-basement.

That was promising. Maybe Dani and the rest of the minister's team had gotten out this way, made it to the other tower, and found their way outside.

Conley and Amado found stairs leading down and then they were in the sub-basement. Here, the ceiling was less than seven feet and Conley had to duck to miss lighting fixtures, water pipes, and electrical conduits.

Yes, with a little luck this would all be over soon.

Amado led him through a narrow hallway and then out into a slightly larger one. Then they were racing upstairs to the basement level. Again, there was no one there. Then they carefully walked up to the ground level.

Silence there too. Conley tried his cell phone. No signal. That was suspicious. This close to a window he should have gotten signal. Had the terrorists somehow managed to jam cell towers? Or taken the local ones out?

Neither option was pleasant to think about because both showed a level of planning and technical sophistication that was light-years ahead of most terror organizations. Terrorists were hard enough to deal with then they were thugs who attacked soft targets with guns and bombs. Terrorists who could plan large operations and pull off technical feats like this were a nightmare—the kind that would keep people like Bloch up at night.

They were in a hallway that led past an empty business center and a gym. Unfortunately, the gym wasn't completely empty. There were half a dozen bodies lying on and around the treadmills, stair climbers, and weights.

The terrorists had been here.

"Amado, get out if you can. I'll head upstairs and see if I can get across and find her," Conley said.

They moved carefully through the hallway, hugging a wall until they could see the open lobby area, where there were bodies scattered around on the floor.

*Damn,* Conley thought to himself. *Why did I think this might be easy?*

Inching closer, they saw that the glass doors on both sides of the lobby were blocked by trucks as well.

This was a very big and very well-planned operation. Someone didn't want the Chinese and Filipino governments to reach their economic accord. Or they just wanted to make headlines. Or they wanted to take hostages to further some agenda or other.

Whatever it was, the terrorists had killed a lot of people and would likely kill many more unless someone stopped them. But first things first. Right now, he had to find Dani.

Moving quietly, Conley and Amado stepped into the lobby. Conley scanned each of the bodies on the ground, afraid that he would see Dani among them. None of the delegates from either country were among the fallen.

Maybe that meant they had found somewhere safe to wait out the attack. Of course, if the terrorists maintained control of the hotel for any length of time, there would be no safe places.

And the terrorists had clearly taken both towers at the same time. He'd seen the ones in the east tower. Were there other attackers still here?

Conley got his answer when a man with an assault rifle slung across his shoulder rounded a corner and stepped right in front of him.

The man's face registered surprise. By the time he was able to fumble for his weapon, Conley's Glock was pointed at his chest and firing. The impact knocked him back to the floor.

Conley noticed that the man was Asian, but he appeared more Chinese, which set him apart from the attackers in the east tower, who were clearly

Filipino—and probably MILF. This man, apparently, was neither. And unlike the gunmen in the east tower, he wasn't wearing black but a green camouflage uniform.

Before Conley could even consider what that meant, he heard shouting and running. Then at least six more figures wearing similar green camo were racing across the lobby toward their position, guns out.

Then the guns were firing.

Conley returned fire and was pleased to see one of the men fall. Clearly, they were used to shooting unarmed civilians. Unarmed civilians *on vacation.*

As a result, it hadn't even occurred to the terrorists to take cover yet. Amado's weapon dropped another attacker as the remaining men (five now, by Conley's count) scattered, looking for cover.

From their covered positions, the gunmen kept up a steady stream of fire. Conley and Amado were forced to duck completely behind their cover. However, it was just a matter of time before the terrorists found a good angle on the two men.

Conley and Amado had to find a better position.

And then a bullet pinged over his head.

That was it. They had to get out of here, now!

"This way," Amado tugged at Conley and the two men sprinted toward the nearest solid cover—a recessed elevator bank. Before Conley could complain, bullets started flying over their heads.

They dashed inside. It was a two-elevator bank with a sign that said *Express to Skybridge* in Filipino and English.

The wall in front of him was solid and had a good four feet of cover. Conley's Glock was out and firing as Amado slapped the call button for the elevator. Conley considered switching to the AK-47, but to aim effectively he'd have to expose his shoulder and more of his body to enemy fire.

The elevator pinged and Amado called to him.

Conley stopped firing but didn't move. He waited a count of five and was rewarded when two of the terrorists left their cover and moved toward his position. Two shots later, the men went down.

Conley spun and dashed into the elevator, with Amado right behind him. The older man hit a button and then drew his shotgun pistol.

"Find Ms. Dani," Amado said.

"What are you going to do?" Conley said, not liking where this was going.

"My job, Mr. Peter," Amado said and then he slipped out the closing doors, shotgun in hand.

Conley dashed across the elevator to reach for the door open button, but the elevator was moving before he could hit it and it carried him upward.

Even if Conley could get back down after he reached the skybridge level, Amado's fight would likely be over—one way or the other—when he got there.

Unslinging his AK-47, Conley said a quiet thanks to his new friend and hoped Amado would make it. Then he resolved to follow the guard's instructions and find Dani.

The skybridge would take him back to the east tower, where he would have the best chance of finding her. The minister's security would most likely shelter the team in place.

With luck, the terrorists would have to go room to room to find them. They'd likely be starting at the bottom. Conley would start at the top and hope for the best. It wasn't much of a plan, but he and Morgan had worked with worse.

Half a minute later, the doors opened, and bullets rained into the elevator.

*This is why I hate elevators in a firefight,* Conley thought as his body hugged the elevator wall.

# Chapter 28

Alex couldn't bring herself to eat any cereal before the Chechens herded them into the sleeping area. Watching the boy getting dragged away and shot had been the end of her appetite.

"Go to sleep. We expect results in the lab tomorrow," Kattab shouted.

It sounded like a threat, but everything he said sounded like a threat—even more so a few hours after he had killed the second student in cold blood.

Karen was quiet, which was normal enough. But, remarkably, she was also nervous—which was as far from normal as anything on this mission.

Alex wondered if she was thinking about Shepard. That made sense. Was she more afraid of not seeing him again than of death? Alex thought so. She remembered watching Karen saying good-bye to Shepard and later talking to him on the phone. Alex realized what was odd about those images: Karen had resembled a smitten high school girl.

The funny thing was that Alex would have bet good money that Karen had never had that look while she was actually in high school. Alex knew she herself had never had that look.

Oddly, she had seen that look on her mother's face. And the reverse on her father's. It was at odd times, when they had been apart for a while, or when they laughed at a secret joke. Or for some reason Alex couldn't see.

Maybe that was what love did, make you look like a smitten high school kid.

Alex thought she would like to find out. However, she knew that didn't seem very likely.

Her primary mission was stopping the terrorists from getting any usable virus. Her secondary mission was to protect as many civilians as possible.

However, the best-case scenario involved explosions and gunfire. She had no illusions about whether or not there would be civilian casualties.

But it was neither necessary nor likely that she would survive, even if the operation was successful. If she did her job well, most of the gunfire would be directed at her.

Alex noted that a few of the students were talking quietly, some sitting together on their cots. The Chechens didn't seem to mind as long as the students didn't move around or try to leave the sleeping area.

Kattab, she realized, was gone—along with two of the others. They had disappeared behind one of the doors on the far wall of the warehouse floor.

Alex heard movement behind her. She turned just as Jason slipped onto the bed behind her.

"Hey," he whispered, keeping a respectful distance. "Want some company?"

"What about the guards?" she asked.

"What are they going to do, shoot me?"

"Yes!" she whispered as harshly as she could.

To this he laughed quietly.

She said, "You're crazy."

"I was never insane except upon occasions when my heart was touched," he said quietly.

Alex liked that but she wouldn't let herself think about what it meant.

"Look, Alex could we talk about something?"

"Okay," she said tentatively.

"Well, I…" he said. Clearly, whatever he was going to say was hard for him.

"What is it?"

"I don't want you to think I was following you. I mean, I was, but not in a creepy way," he said.

"What are you talking about?" she asked, genuinely confused.

"When you got on the bus," he said.

"Oh," she said. "Don't worry about it."

"I just don't want you to think I'm some kind of a crazy stalker," he said.

"That is what you're worried about? Now?"

He ignored the question. "I went to pick you up after your meeting and you were already getting into the bus. I got a weird feeling and decided to follow. I texted you, and then called you. When you didn't answer I told myself that maybe you'd forgotten our date and I thought I'd catch up with you and we could…reschedule. Then the bus got on the highway and I just kept going. I had a feeling that something might be wrong, but I didn't want to call the police because nothing really suspicious had happened. Then we all stopped for traffic and I thought I'd check it out."

"Really, don't worry about it. You know what's happening tomorrow, right?"

"That's why I wanted to talk about it. On the off chance we survive this whole thing, I didn't want to think I'd blown it with you."

There was something hopeful and sweet in worrying about things like that.

"Don't leave me hanging here. Say something," he said.

"I'm trying to figure out if you're weird or cute," she said.

"Well?"

"I'll let you know when this is over," she said.

Jason brought his hand down on her shoulder; she grasped it and used it to pull him closer to her—putting even less distance between them.

He brought his arm around her stomach and held her tightly with a touch that told her that everything was going to be fine. It was an illusion, she knew, but a good one and she was glad to have it.

Reality would come soon enough in the morning.

\* \* \* \*

Conley couldn't even guess how many shooters there were. At least a few, he guessed, as round after round slammed through the stainless steel rear wall of the elevator. He remembered another thing he hated about elevators.

There was a trap door leading to the roof of the elevator but it was nearly at the center of the car, so far from the cover of the partial wall on each side of the elevator doors that it might as well have been in the terrorists' laps.

There was only one way out and it was forward. Conley reached into his fanny pack and pulled out a fresh clip. It would help, but he had no illusions that it would be enough. The terrorists shooting at him had a direct line of fire and automatic weapons.

Conley decided to skip the frontal assault. Instead he hit the *close door* button. He could take the elevator back down to the ground level. Though there was a better than even chance that there would be more gunmen waiting for him, he could hit the stop button and scramble up and through the trap door on the ceiling of the car.

Once he was in the elevator shaft, he would have some options— certainly better ones than he had now. The door seemed to take forever to start closing—another thing he hated about elevators.

Was the *close door* button even connected to anything?

Finally, it moved a few inches, and stopped. This happened at exactly the same moment that the lights went out. The power outage was the first lucky break he'd gotten since he and Amado had run into the second group of terrorists in the lobby of the west tower.

For a second, the bullets stopped flying into the elevator car. Before that had fully registered, Conley had reached around with his Glock and fired two shots straight ahead, chest level, before he even checked the hallway.

He leaned his head out a split second later and fired as soon as he saw the targets: two men in green camo. One was already falling, hit by one of his blind shots. Conley put another round into the man as he fell. The second man was watching and had only started to swivel his head back to Conley when he took two rounds in the chest and fell backward.

It wasn't just luck that had saved Conley. Too often terrorists' training and experience was oriented towards shooting unarmed and unsuspecting people—like hotel guests. Most terrorists weren't used to enemies who shot back. And experience under fire taught you to react immediately to any changes in your situation. Well, these two would never learn that lesson.

He wondered how many innocent hotel guests they and their group had killed today. And then he thought of Amado, the friendly man who had clearly seen a few things in his time but greeted everyone he saw with a smile. He knew Amado had a wife, though the older man had never mentioned children. He was a good man; Conley had sensed that from the beginning.

Plus, he was able to hit multiple targets center mass in a chaotic, active-fire situation, and because of that he had saved Conley's life.

Conley hoped his friend had made it somehow. He left the elevator alcove and heard running footsteps.

*Damn,* he barely had time to think before he saw several men in green camo running down the hallway toward him. He had maybe a second before the bullets started flying again, but before that could happen he had turned the corner and sprinted for the skyway.

He flew through the hallway that seemed to hang in the air. It was maybe fifty yards, and took him only seconds to cross—though the trip seemed endless.

Counting himself lucky that the terrorists hadn't been able to get off any rounds when he was in the open, Conley threw himself to the side as soon as he hit the hallway of the east tower.

He rested against the wall and thought about just shooting at the terrorists as they charged through. There were at least six, and he doubted he would be able to get them all before one of them hit him.

The sound of their footsteps told Conley that they were in the skyway now and then Conley saw that his salvation was literally at his feet. He said a silent thanks to Dan Morgan as he reached down and pulled out the rubber doorstop that was holding one of the steel double doors open and against the corridor wall. He pushed it closed, jammed the doorstop in place, and then dashed across the small opening to repeat the operation on the other double door.

The doors were designed to shut this end of the skyway but they couldn't be locked from the outside—presumably to prevent anyone from getting stuck inside.

He heard shouting from inside the skyway and then he heard at least one body hurl itself against the doors, which barely budged. The great thing about the little rubber triangles was that the harder you pushed against them, the more they dug in—a lot like the man who had introduced them to Conley.

Maybe the six men in the skyway would eventually figure out how to get through, but Conley planned to be long gone by that time. He headed down the hallway where he could see the six gunmen through the window.

They were at the end of the skyway pounding on the door, enraged. Then one of them dropped to the floor. Conley couldn't figure out why. Then he saw a hole had been punched in the glass wall of the skyway.

Conley couldn't see the sharpshooter and neither, apparently, could the terrorists as they flailed around desperately. The fact was that they were surrounded on three sides by glass. They were literally sitting ducks.

By the time another terrorist fell, the remaining four were pointing their rifles in seemingly random directions. Then another went down, and another.

Conley had seen that these terrorists did poorly when fighting enemies who actually shot back. Turns out they did even worse against snipers.

The last two started moving and raced toward the far end of the skyway to escape through the only open doors. One of the terrorists only made it three strides before *he* fell. The other made it almost halfway across the skyway and then he went down.

Conley was pleased that the local authorities were in the game. Maybe there was some hope. If the minister's security could keep Dani and her group safe, Conley might be able to make it to them. With any luck, he'd have some backup from outside.

# Chapter 29

The rooms for the minister, Dani, and their colleagues were on the top floor. There was very little chance that they would be there, but it was a place to start.

Out of habit, he tried his phone again. Still no signal.

He was stuck on the fact that this operation involved more than one terror organization. He was almost certain that the terrorists he'd faced in the beginning were MILF, a separatist organization who wanted religious rule over some territory in the southern Philippines.

In China, most terror attacks were the work of Uyghur groups, and they had similar demands for an independent territory in western China.

The problem was that the Moro and the Uyghurs had never worked together. And they were not unique in this regard. Terror leaders almost never did—even when they shared a religion and had similar goals, as with these two.

That, however, was a problem for another day. Right now he had more immediate concerns. First, he had to get to Dani. Then he would deal with the terrorists.

Conley took the stairs, though with the power out he couldn't take the elevator even if he he'd wanted to. The stairwell was nearly dark, lit only by the dim red glow of the emergency lights.

It was also eerily silent, more so even than the rest of the hotel where guests were hiding in their rooms, staying quiet, and hoping for the best. Here, his footsteps echoed up and down the stairwell, announcing that he was there.

At every floor he would stop before he stepped onto a landing and listen for any sign of people above him. Each time he was greeted by silence and moved on.

Even moving relatively slowly and quietly, he was at the twelfth floor in less than ten minutes. He waited at the door to the hallway for nearly a full minute, listening for activity outside.

As soon as he opened the door he would be exposed.

*No guts no glory,* he thought as he pulled the door open and jumped into the hallway with his AK-47 leading the way.

No one was there.

The hallway was marginally better lit, simply because it had more emergency lights and exit signs that operated on battery power. There were also windows at the end of the hallway that let in some daylight.

Conley headed toward the light. Dani's room and all of the suites for the Chinese minister's delegation were at the end of the hall. The hallway was empty and quiet. He found her room open. In fact, all of the rooms assigned to the Minister's delegation were open.

They were also in disarray, as if they had been searched and abandoned. There were no shell casings, no bodies, and no blood. Obviously, the terrorists had not gotten what they had come for.

With no good options, Conley did the only thing he could do: he checked the rooms thoroughly himself and then moved on to the next locked room. He knocked and called out to Dani.

He was counting on the fact that even if she were with her colleagues she would respond to him. He certainly didn't have time to break down every door in the hotel. And he didn't want to scare whoever was hiding in the other rooms.

Moving down the corridor, he repeated the operation. Then he repeated it again.

This would take a while; each tower had hundreds of rooms. And, of course, there were still the terrorists to deal with.

He was only on his fifth room when he heard noise from far down the hallway, on the other side of the elevator bank that sat at the center of the tower. Looking down the corridor, he could see a small group of men dressed in black file out of the far stairwell. He stayed in the recessed space in front of a door and watched.

There was some commotion and he could see the terrorists handling something big that he couldn't quite make out. Then he heard them bang on the first room door on their end of the hallway.

He saw them swing the large item they had brought. It was a hand-held battering ram, the kind used by law enforcement. He watched the thing rear back twice and then disappear into the hotel room.

Then he watched the five or six men follow into the room. There was shouting. And then gunshots. More shouting and then more gunshots.

The group moved to the next room and started banging. Conley was on the move, even as he processed what was happening. While Conley was going door-to-door trying to save someone, they were going door-to-door killing people as they searched for the delegation.

For what? To use them as high-level hostages in a negotiation? To torture and kill them? Or to do both? And along the way were they going to murder hundreds or thousands of innocent people on vacation, or a business trip? Well, not if he could help it.

Conley, Amado, and the unnamed snipers outside had made sure the terrorists paid a high price for what they'd done so far. Conley was determined to stop them. Even if he failed he was prepared to make sure their price was quite a bit higher.

He had passed the elevator bank at the center of the tower when he heard the next set of gunshots, the next set of screams. Cursing under his breath, he poured on the speed so that a few seconds later he was able to take a position five doors down from the room.

By then the first terrorist was emerging into the hallway. Conley kept behind his cover and waited until a second terrorist appeared. Then the agent fired two quick shots, dropping both men. A third came running into the hallway and fell.

The remaining terrorists stayed in the room and Conley heard shouting from inside. They were definitely speaking Filipino. Conley recognized a few words but couldn't translate.

To his surprise, the terrorists went quiet. As usual, they weren't used to their prey shooting back. With any luck, they were huddled in fear in the hotel room. That image pleased him and then he remembered they were in there with the bodies of the hotel guests they had killed.

The anger returned. Conley decided he'd have to go after them. They would have the defender's advantage but they were also cowards. In either case, Conley was determined to make sure these particular gunmen didn't kill another innocent today.

Keeping the AK pointed at the door, Conley slowly moved from his cover into the hallway. There were two or three men inside the room and he knew he could take them even if they rushed out all at once.

Of course, it would be trickier if he had to storm into the room.

And then everything changed. The stairwell door at the end of the hallway opened and two terrorists ran out, rifles firing. Conley slammed himself back behind into the doorway as more bullets filled the air.

He realized that the terrorists in the hotel room had been shouting into their radios for backup—and backup had arrived. He chanced a look into the hall. Four men were there, guns pointed in his direction, as two others peeked out from the hotel room.

Conley slung his rifle and pulled out his Glock. He didn't have a lot of options now, and none of them were good. He reached out with his pistol and fired three rounds blindly into the hallway.

Then he reached back and grabbed the doorknob. To his surprise, it turned. Pushing the door open, he flung himself inside. Then he slammed the door shut. Out of habit, he locked it—though he knew the lock wouldn't hold for long. After all, they had their battering ram.

Now *he* had the defender's advantage, but he had no illusions about whether it would make much difference given their numbers.

Scanning the room, Conley saw there was no cover. Except for under the bed or in the closet, there was nowhere to hide in the room. There was a window that, at twelve stories up, was no use. Ultimately, there was nothing in his room he could use.

He heard the battering ram crack into the door for the first time. Nothing *inside* the room, he realized, as his eye settled on a door set against the wall, a door that led to a connecting room. Usually these doors were closed and locked. This one was partly open, which meant that the guests in this room had rented the other as well and had been using them both.

That was it. As the battering ram splintered door and frame behind him, Conley raced to the window, slid it upward, and threw open the curtains. Then he pivoted, vaulted over the bed and slipped through the connecting door. He pulled it mostly shut and then pushed open another door that opened into the second room.

From the empty room, he peered into the room he had just abandoned. Though the terrorists had smashed open the door, they waited to rush in. They peeked in and fired a few test shots into the wall and then the bed. Conley could see two of the men inching into the room. As he had hoped, their focus was on the open window.

Clearly, they suspected a trick and fired into the curtains. Then they strode up to the window and one of them stuck his head outside. That was when Conley fired. Two impacts to the terrorist's back threw him forward and out the window.

The gunman next to him turned in time to take another two shots to the chest. By now, the other terrorists had rushed in but Conley was already closing the connecting door on his side and turning the deadbolt.

He ran for the door to the hallway. He imagined the remaining terrorists were still puzzling over the open window and what happened to their friends. As he threw open the hotel room door he took a quick scan of the hallway and was already on the run as he heard the gunmen banging on the connecting doors.

It hadn't occurred to them to leave a man guarding the hallway. And they were still fussing with the connecting door, rather than simply using the door that led out to the hallway. Conley didn't want to hang around to see how fast they caught on.

He raced down the corridor, heading for the stairwell on the other side. He was just reaching the elevator bank—and the halfway point of his sprint—when he saw more black-clad terrorists filing out of the stairwell he was aiming for.

*Damn,* he thought, as he came to a dead stop. The terrorists in front of him had seen him by now and were raising their guns. He also heard shouts behind him, telling him that the geniuses had found their way out of the hotel room one way or another.

Conley didn't wait for the bullets to start flying; he dove back into the recessed area and partial cover of the main elevator bank. There were three elevators, set about four feet back from the hallway. That gave him pretty good cover from terrorists coming at him from any single direction.

And almost no cover if they were coming from both directions.

It was so bad that Conley found himself wishing the elevator had power. He wondered if he had time to try to pry the elevator doors open; he could take his chances in the elevator shaft.

Then he heard footsteps in the hallway.

Conley hugged the wall and peeked his head out to look into the corridor. A shot rang out from behind him and Conley pulled back. Damn, there was no way to fire in one direction without leaving himself open to gunfire from the other.

Everything seemed to slow outside.

Why hurry when they knew they had him? From this point forward they would be careful. Even if they had him cornered, they knew he could shoot back.

Conley realized that he had shifted his thinking. No longer was he working out ways to do as much damage to the terrorists as possible and move on. Now he was working out ways to do as much damage to them as he could before they cut him down.

Nothing about this trip had gone the way it was supposed to, even aside from the attack. From the moment he'd met Dani, he hadn't quite been himself. He had gotten involved in a way that he had not let himself do in a long time. And from the beginning of the attack, his first and primary thought had been of her—even though he understood that she wasn't quite what she had seemed. Though, to be fair, he had told her he was a Southwestern Native American language professor.

He realized that it was very likely that he would not have a chance to uncover all of her secrets, and to get to know the real woman.

From the start, he had acted out of emotion and every step since then had led him right here: with his back to an elevator door and heavily armed enemies closing in on both sides.

Remarkably, Conley didn't regret a second of the last week.

He wondered what Dan Morgan would think of his choices and realized that Morgan would understand very well. Conley's only regret now was that he wouldn't get to tell the story to his old friend.

Conley put a fresh magazine into his AK-47 and switched it to full auto. His hearing told him that there were more terrorists to his right than there were to his left. He made sure his Glock was securely tucked into his belt and prepared to do what good militaries had done from the beginning when they were heavily outnumbered: charge. In the Afghan war, a small band of British soldiers who were out of ammunition had fixed bayonets to their empty rifles and charged a nearly overwhelming force of Taliban…and won the day.

Well, Conley decided to give these terrorists one last surprise. There would only be a few in front of him and the ones behind would just as likely hit their own men as they shot at his back.

It wasn't much of a plan, but he and Morgan had worked with worse. Conley took a deep breath, let out a loud scream, and raced forward, aiming the AK as best he could and letting it rip. The thirty-two rounds were gone in seconds and Conley was pleased to see one of the three terrorists fall.

Then his Glock was in his hand as he continued. One of the gunmen peeked his head out and Conley was able to put a bullet into almost the exact center of his forehead.

As soon as he took the shot, Conley threw himself to the left side of the hallway. A split second later, he heard gunfire from his right. Without even turning his head, he aimed the Glock in that direction and started firing. By the time he'd fired the second time, his eye had found the target and he was able to put a bullet in the center of the terrorist's chest.

Conley heard gunfire behind him and was both pleased and surprised that he was still standing. He didn't risk turning around. Instead he found cover leaning into a recessed door.

He leaned out to take a look with one eye. The terrorists that were behind him were shooting, but not in his direction. They were fighting some group that had gotten behind them.

There was a hail of automatic gunfire and Conley saw three men fall. Two others turned and ran toward Conley's position. One made it maybe three steps before a bullet hit him from behind. The other caught a round from Conley's Glock.

And then the hallway went silent.

Conley leaned back into his cover and took a breath, once again vaguely surprised and pleased to be alive. He wondered who had just saved him. Or if the military or police who had provided the snipers that had saved his butt in the skyway had gotten into the building.

"Don't shoot. I'm an American. I'm going to come out slowly," he said.

"Peter," a voice called out. No, not *a* voice, *her* voice. *Dani?*

"Dani is that you?" he said, not even trying to keep the shock out of his own voice.

"You can come out Peter, it's clear," she said.

He had time to wonder if the minister's security detail had routed the terrorists as he stepped out into the hallway.

Black-clad bodies were laid out haphazardly up and down the hallway. Dani stood in the center, maybe twenty feet away.

She was alone.

He was angry that her security detail would leave her out in the open like that. If there were well-trained enough to take down this group, they should be doing a better job protecting her.

And then Conley noticed that she was holding a Chinese assault rifle. She was handling it like a professional, in precisely the way a deputy to the Chinese finance minister *would not.* She was wearing the same business suit and sensible shoes she had been wearing earlier but her body language, her expression...everything else about her was different.

In that instant, Conley understood something about Dani. She might have been a deputy to the Chinese finance minister but she was also an intelligence agent, and a very highly trained one.

"You have an interesting skill set for someone in your line of work," he said.

"I could say the same about you. Who knew that Southwestern Native American language studies was such a broad subject," she said.

"We can talk later, if we survive," Conley said.

Dani scanned him and asked, "Are you hurt?"

He shook his head.

She handed him a radio headset, like the ones the terrorists wore—like the one she now wore. "In case we get separated." Conley took it.

Then he grabbed her wrist and said, "Wait." He studied her, taking in the differences, the beginning of understanding forming in his brain.

She flashed him a smile and said. "Come on. We've got eleven more floors to clear if we're going to get out of here."

Dani turned and raced for the stairwell door, and Conley followed.

# Chapter 30

The beeping phone roused Bloch from her office couch. She shook herself awake and answered.

"I think I have something," Jenny Morgan said. "I think I may have found something."

A few minutes later, Bloch entered Shepard's domain, where Jenny was the only one there and awake, though she had been the one insisting that everyone get some periodic rest.

Bloch sat down in a chair in Jenny's workstation. On the screen were a series of windows that showed what Bloch instantly recognized as satellite thermal imagery.

"I've been helping Shepard create a search criteria for the controlled fires the terrorists will have to use if they have an accident in the lab," Jenny said.

The woman's voice was flat but Bloch detected something else there. Was it a note of concern? Worry? Panic? All of the above perhaps?

Whatever it was, it wasn't over the theoretical doom and gloom end-of-the-world scenario they were all fighting to prevent. It was over something much more immediate.

The fact was that Jenny and Dan Morgan's daughter was now a hostage in a secret terrorist lab, which was developing a super virus. And not only was an accident in such a lab possible, it was likely—if not inevitable, given the fact that the terrorists hadn't bothered with any of the normal safety protocols.

And worse yet, such an accident and the fire that the terrorists would set to contain it was the best hope they had at finding the lab. For now, that was their best-case scenario.

"I'm helping Shepard develop a baseline. It's the dry season in much of the search area, so there are quite a few brush fires, full-on wildfires, and, of course, the occasional building and house fires. In addition, there's private and local government incineration.

"The problem is that most of these are not immediately distinguishable from whatever the terrorists would use. Our experts say their best bet would be to dump anything or anyone affected by the virus into a hole and burn it for as long as they could."

"Wouldn't a controlled lab fire be hotter than, say, a brush fire?" Bloch asked.

"Not really, we're looking at 800 to 1200 degrees for most of what we're likely to see burning on the ground. That goes for everything from a barbecue to a fire at a municipal dump," Jenny said.

"So what are we even looking for?" Bloch said.

"We're not sure, we're just looking. But this is what I found," Jenny said, pointing to the screen.

The window showed a thermal image that appeared identical to every other thermal image in every other widow on the large screen—with the same pixelated yellow and red colors.

"It looks like all of the—"

"Look at the shape," Jenny said.

Then Bloch saw it. Amazing. Once she did, she couldn't believe it hadn't screamed itself out to her.

"The shape…" she said.

"It's a perfect rectangle. Looks like maybe ten feet by twenty feet," Jenny said.

"There were dozens of ground fires on the screen, each burning in odd shapes, with bulges and fingers jutting out randomly."

Of course, it was early for there to be an accident in the lab—her people had told her that it would take days to get any viable virus, let alone have an accident with one.

And yet the perfect rectangle bothered her. Nature could be messy and it could be beautiful, but it was almost never perfect.

"I'll get Shepard up, we'll have him look a little deeper. Then Bloch realized that she had a man nearby. Morgan had refused to come back to base, certain that they were on the right track with the search—and not wanting to be caught in transit if Zeta found the lab."

And it might pay to put the Tach team on alert. They needed to be ready to go at a moment's notice. No, not just alert.

It was time to move.

She needed to get her people in the air. Her gut told her that Morgan was right: the terrorists had set up their lab reasonably close to San Francisco. Even if this satellite image turned out to be a miss, the answer was probably still out there in the desert.

Once the decision was made, Bloch found that it felt good to be doing something—anything—rather than just waiting around for bad news.

Apparently the Morgans were having more of an effect on her than she realized.

* * * *

As soon as they were in the stairwell, Conley said, "Dani, stop."

She turned to look at him.

"The Minister? Your delegation?" he asked.

"They are safe—at least I think so. They were headed to some kind of safe room with the Filipino team. I presume they think I was just lost in the confusion." She paused. "The Minister doesn't know I'm Intelligence."

Conley understood. That was the problem for governments like China. No one trusted anyone else. And different groups wasted quite a lot resources watching each other.

"Then what are you doing up here?" he asked.

To that she smiled. This wasn't the practiced, meek smile of a female deputy minister. This was much more confident, and much sexier. "I was looking for you. I knew this is where you would come to look for me."

"I'm glad you came when you did," he said.

"Me too," she said, staring into his eyes.

He had liked her before, maybe more than just *liked* her. But she wasn't quite the same person he'd spent those few days and nights with. That Dani was in there, but someone else was as well.

And Conley *really* wanted to get to know that woman.

"Come on, we have eleven more floors to clear and then we can get out of here." She tapped the headset and the radio that was attached to her belt. "Of course, they make it pretty easy. They're on channel two; we'll use four to communicate with each other."

That was good. He would have taken one of their radios to monitor their communications, except he didn't speak Filipino. Of course, Dani did.

They headed down the stairs together. "The next group is on eight, but we'll sweep each floor just in case."

\* \* \* \*

Alex awoke to the sound of their captors shouting. She nearly fell off the small bed that she'd been sharing with Jason, recovered, and was on her feet in time to see all six terrorists pointing guns at the students.

Kattab addressed them as a group, "Thirty minutes. You begin in thirty minutes."

The students started stirring. Some were heading for the showers; others were changing into the blue scrubs.

Alex didn't want to bother with either. One way or another, she was determined that this would be her last day in the lab. Whatever happened, she would face it in her own clothes.

Karen and Jason stuck with her and the three of them sat at their table. 'Their' table, she thought wryly. She was glad that this would be the last day. She didn't want to develop any routines here. She didn't want any associations with this place that she would carry with her. Of course, for that to happen, she would have to survive these men and their plans.

Looking up at Jason, she realized that there was something she wanted to take away from this experience. She would have to get out of this; she owed him a date.

Karen insisted they eat something and they all took cereal.

"Each lab will be expected to get right to work. We will be preparing growth media for the bacteria, as well as culturing the bacteria itself. Dr. Spellman is expecting to have some active virus to infect our bacteria in a few days," Karen said. Then, before Alex could stop her, added, "But we will not allow that to happen."

"I want to move on the terrorists by the end of the day," Alex said. "We end this *today.*"

Alex gestured to Dr. Spellman, who was up and wandering around the lab. The side of his face was red around the bandages and he was sweating, though the temperature inside the lab was comfortable.

"He might not even last a few days," Alex said. "Not without antibiotics, and I doubt the Chechens will take him to a doctor."

"Once we have the complete genome and the live virus, the terrorists will view him as expendable," Karen said.

"Yes, but if he dies or is incapacitated before that, we're all expendable," Alex said.

In spite of his condition, Dr. Spellman moved with purpose, fiddling with the equipment and looking over the supplies—all the while wearing a white lab coat. It was almost like he knew he didn't have long and wanted to make sure his great project was finished.

Karen said, "Our goal for the microbe portion of the lab is modest. We will mix the media, which is simply adding water to a chemical powder. Then we will purify the media in the microwaves and pressure cookers. Most labs would have an autoclave system that would do the job. This setup is less efficient in terms of the project but it gives us more potential weapons."

"Can you make the pressure cookers and microwaves explode?" Alex asked.

"I will need a few things, some steel wool and cleaning supplies mostly, but yes."

"Can we set them all to go off at the same time?" Alex said.

Karen actually had to think about that. "The pressure cookers are all the same make, so that's fairly simple. However, the microwaves are different wattages so I'll have to adjust the time and ingredients for each but yes, within a minute or so."

"What about the centrifuges?"

Karen shrugged. "They are in the purification lab. If I can get over there, maybe, if I can get a few minutes with the machines."

"Okay, but first things first. We spend the morning developing the normal routines for the lab. Then, after lunch, we'll choose a time."

"Can we bring anyone else in?" Jason asked.

"Is there anyone we can trust? Not only trust to participate but trust to not give us away?"

Jason shook his head.

"We should be able to collect what we need in a few hours, even with our usual lab work. As for the final operation…"

"No one can help there," Alex said.

Kattab shouted for them to get up, and everyone complied. Alex noticed that Avery was looking a little better, maybe a little less vacant. He followed the instructions easily enough. Maybe he'd be okay.

Like the rest of them, Avery only had to last the day, and then this would be over. With luck, they would all walk out of here. Everything else, they could sort out when they were safe.

The only thing Alex needed was a plan. Blowing up some equipment was a start but Alex had to make sure that wasn't simply a temporary distraction. She'd have to make it count.

That meant disabling a guard and getting a hold of a gun and she had no idea how she was going to do that.

*Well, first things first*, she thought as she headed to their section of the lab with Karen, Jason, and their assigned team.

* * * *

Conley and Dani only met resistance on three floors. Every time they used the same technique: they each took a stairwell on opposite ends of the floor and worked their way toward the center.

Dani set their walkie-talkies to listen to the frequency the terrorists were using. Remarkably, despite the fact that they knew their fellow terrorists were getting picked off, it didn't occur to the rest of them that their communications had been compromised.

Well, that made Conley and Dani's job easier because the remaining groups regularly announced their positions. None of the groups had much fight in them, and none had given real trouble.

Conley wasn't exactly disappointed, but he was amazed that men of this low caliber had been able to take the hotel and kill so many people. He and Dani had seen dozens of bodies of unlucky quests and staff on their way downstairs. By the time this was done, there would be as many as a hundred casualties—and that was if he and Dani were successful.

If they weren't, he suspected all of the people in the hotel would be casualties, and that number would be in the thousands.

On the plus side, Conley was more and more optimistic that he and Dani would be successful.

"The last group is on the second floor," Dani said.

"How many?" Conley asked.

"I'm not sure, at least four. They are in the north end," she said. Then her brow furred. "Wait," she said, holding up a hand. "They're scared. They know something has happened to the other groups in the building." Then her face sank. "They have taken hostages, a family. They are waiting in the family's rooms, 220 and 222."

That complicated things.

He and Dani had taken the other groups in the hallways with no civilians around. This would be different.

If they charged into a room full of heavily armed terrorists, Conley wasn't sure they would win the fight. And he was certain that any civilians inside wouldn't survive.

"Difficult to remove them, but we can't bypass the floor," Dani said.

That was true as well. The final group and the leaders of the assault were in the lobby. Conley and Dani would have their hands full taking them on. It would be impossible if the terrorists from the second floor joined the fight. Dani and Conley would be caught between both sets of forces.

"I've got it," Conley said. "Come on."

Conley led her down the northern stairs. In a few seconds he found what he was looking for.

"What is that for?" Dani asked as he picked up the doorstop and jammed it into the bottom of the door.

"That will keep them stuck on that side of the door," he said. Then he led her back upstairs and down the Southern stairs and told her what he had in mind.

She liked the plan and helped him with the words and his pronunciation. It would help that he would be shouting, and doing his best impression of a panicked terrorist.

They made their way onto the second floor and took up a position a few doors down from 220 and 222.

Conley set his walkie-talkie to the terrorists' frequency and shouted, in Filipino, "Run! They are flooding each floor with poison gas. The lobby is safe!"

Nothing happened and Conley was worried that the terrorists didn't believe he was one of them

Then the door to 222 opened and four men in the black MILF uniforms ran out. They didn't even have their guns drawn.

Conley was relieved that they didn't try to take their hostages with them. *No, instead they left them to die in the poison gas,* Conley thought.

The men hit the stairwell door and found it stuck.

"Hey, tough guys," Conley said.

The terrorists had time to look in their direction before Dani and Conley opened fire. At this range, Conley was content to use his Glock, and he noted that Dani used her pistol as well. She took the two on the left and he the two on the right.

They headed back to the other stairwell. As they ran, Dani monitored the walkie-talkies.

# Chapter 31

Their part of the lab work was easy for Alex and Jason to learn, too easy. In fact, Alex found the whole process unnervingly simple.

She knew that Spellman and his team had the hardest job. They were using something called a PCR machine and a sequencer to build the virus itself. But even that process was under control.

*One week,* she thought.

Just a week or less to build the virus that could kill everyone. It seemed insane to her. And yet Karen had explained that it would only take that long because they were building the virus from scratch.

"It would be much faster if they bought the larger DNA segments on-line," Karen had explained. "Then they would just need us to create the unique segments and assemble the pieces. The virus would be ready in half the time, maybe less."

Ending the world should be harder. Much harder. And it should have been impossible for these two-bit killers. Yet, they had been able to set up a makeshift lab and staff it with students. And if no one stopped them, they would succeed.

Of course, someone would stop them. Alex would stop them. Karen would stop them. Jason too, she realized. Just three of them: a rookie agent, a math genius, and a Resident Advisor who studied literature.

If Alex failed to neutralize their captors, people would die. Even if she managed to somehow kill all of the terrorists, some of the hostages would likely die. It was impossible to avoid casualties in an operation like this using makeshift explosives and weapons against heavily armed men in an enclosed space.

Whatever happened, Alex was optimistic about their ability to disrupt the lab. By the end of the day, even if Alex failed to take out the terrorists, she would make sure they lost precious equipment—and some of their men.

A setback of even a few days or a week might give Zeta a chance to find them and shut them down.

Of course, if the attempt failed, Alex and Karen wouldn't be there when Zeta arrived. In fact, Alex doubted both she and Karen would survive the operation if it were a success.

Pushing those thoughts out of her head, Alex kept her mind on what she was doing.

She was mixing the glob they would use to grow the bacteria. It required simply mixing the nutrient powder with distilled water. Alex used a large stainless steel spoon to mix the two.

"You'll know you have the right consistency when it feels like Jell-O," Dr. Spellman said, appearing behind her. Alex couldn't help jumping a little.

He watched her stir the mixture for a minute and said, "That's it."

It did feel like Jell-O—brownish Jell-O—and smelled vaguely meaty.

"You're doing fine," he said, using what seemed to Alex like his supportive teacher voice.

She almost understood. He was retreating into what he knew and ignoring everything else—like the consequences of what they were doing.

She also saw that he really didn't look well. His bandage no longer had a red spot showing through. Now it had a yellowish spot and that meant the infection was pretty bad. Even if he got medical attention today, she doubted that his face would be the same.

"Keep up the good work," he said, and headed to the purification section of the lab.

Alex completed a batch, Karen came over to check on it, and then Alex poured the glob into a five-gallon container, sealed it, and placed it on the floor. Though they weren't handling anything dangerous, Karen insisted that the entire team wear lab coats and gloves, as well as surgical facemasks.

If nothing else, Alex realized that the coats and masks made it harder for the terrorists to tell them apart. The other teams started doing the same and Alex realized it was getting easier for her to move around the lab.

Jason was already doing that. Karen had made a fuss with Spellman and the other grad students over the sorry state of the lab and insisted on cleaning all of the equipment.

They had scoured the microwaves, the pressure cookers, the incubators, and even the centrifuges. The cleaning project allowed Karen and Jason to mix with the other groups. Alex also saw that they had moved all of the cleaning supplies to a central location in their section of the lab. Steel wool. Chemical cleaners. And even baking soda from the kitchen.

Meanwhile, Alex watched the guards carefully. There were always four armed men on the floor. The other two would disappear behind one of the locked doors to rest, or go outside, or do whatever terrorists did on their breaks.

The four Chechens on active guard duty would walk around randomly through the lab. For the first hour, they had carried their rifles in front of them.

It was very intimidating, especially given the fact that the gunmen had made it clear that they would not hesitate to shoot. However, while frightening for the students, the rifles were also apparently a bit heavy for the Chechens.

Alex knew that an AK with a full magazine weighed more than ten pounds. That was easy enough to wield for a few minutes at a time, but after a half hour of walking, Alex could see the men straining.

Then, one-by-one, they had given up and slung their rifles over their shoulders. Some tried holding their pistols out after that but by the end of the second hour they had all settled for keeping a menacing hand on the butt of their holstered guns.

That was all good news. By the end of the day their reaction times would be slowed. Of course, if there was trouble, the terrorists' first instinct would be to draw their sidearms, but they could do much less damage with a pistol then with an AK-47, particularly one set in full auto mode where it could fire thirty rounds in seconds.

Four men with pistols could still kill a lot of people quickly in an enclosed space, but there was cover behind equipment and lab tables. And in the first stage of the operation that she kept running in her head, there would only be three armed men after she took one out.

And one armed woman.

By the time the two guards who were on a break entered the lab she planned to be ready for them.

Alex kept mixing her growth media while the others set up the newly spotless beakers, large Petri dishes—*plates*, she heard Karen correcting her in her head—and various racks.

She also noted that Karen and Jason had one of the centrifuges partly disassembled for 'cleaning.' That was very promising and Alex assumed they were sorting out some sort of sabotage.

Alex would have preferred to be with them but it wasn't wise for the trio to be seen together too much. A number of the other students had tended to stay in pairs or small groups, but those groups weren't planning an assault.

Given how long their odds were, Alex couldn't take any chance of being noticed. They would have to meet during the lunch break to detail their final plan, though plan was a strong word for what Alex had in mind.

That was fine. She knew that no battle plan, no matter how well thought out, survived the first few seconds of contact with the actual enemy. In the end, they would have to wing it. However, before the fight started she would leave nothing to chance, so she kept an eye on Karen and Jason, as well as the guards.

Then when she finished another batch of growth medium she checked on Avery. He was engrossed in the task of setting up the Petri dishes on an expanding array of metal racks.

"How is it going?" she asked.

He didn't hear her the first time, or the second time

After the third time Avery turned to her and said, "What?"

"How is it going?" she repeated.

"Okay, we'll have plenty of cultures when we get some virus," he said. Then he studied the harvesting section of the lab, where Karen and Jason were still working on a centrifuge. "I think they will have trouble keeping up with us."

His tone was flat and his eyes weren't right. Avery wasn't okay, she realized. Of course, none of them were okay but he seemed especially detached—as if Margaret's death had unmoored him. Well, if Alex did her job he would live long enough to recover.

In the meantime, she had to make sure he didn't have a meltdown.

For now, he was functional, and that would have to be enough.

\* \* \* \*

"Morgan, we may have a location for you," Bloch's voice said through the comm. "Something for you to check out."

"What is it?" Morgan asked.

"It's not much, but we had an active burn pit. It's not under a state or local authority. Not a municipal site. But it checks out as the sort of thing the terrorist lab would need if they had an accident. Shepard says it's too close to the nearest building for a proper HAZMAT burn site. If that's our lab, Shepard says that any burn pit would have to be a minimum of half a mile away, but we're assuming the Chechens may be cutting some corners."

"How big is the pit?" Morgan asked.

"Twenty by thirty feet, big enough to incinerate any mistakes," she said.

"Would you say that it's big enough to hold twenty bodies?" Morgan asked.

Bloch didn't respond immediately. Clearly, that wasn't something she had considered.

"What do you mean?"

"I mean, that sounds like a pit big enough to hold twenty bodies—presuming they belonged to people you didn't need after they had served your purpose," Morgan said. He had seen a few mass graves in his time. They had always given him chills.

*And Alex is in that lab. And when their work is done, the terrorists won't need her or any of the students anymore,* he thought.

"We don't know this is it. We're still trying to check out the ownership, looking at delivery records. I'll send you the coordinates and you can look at it in person."

"By all means look into everything, but tell me one thing first: is there any earth moving equipment nearby?" Morgan said.

"What?"

"A backhoe, bulldozer, something you would use to fill in the pit if you were in a hurry, if you wanted to bury bodies," Morgan asked.

That time, he actually heard Bloch gasp.

"Wait, let me talk to Shepard," she said. Less than thirty seconds passed and then she came back on the line. "Yes, there's a backhoe, but I'm not sure that proves anything. It was likely used to dig the pit. This may turn out to be nothing."

"I know, but it's the best lead we have and you want me to check it out," Morgan said. "And next you're going to tell me not to do anything stupid when I get there."

"We can't take any chances. If that's an active lab, we don't know what they have in there. It hasn't been long but...we just don't know."

"So if I find anything you want me to wait for backup?"

"Of course."

"Fair enough, how long until you land?" he asked.

Bloch gasped. For the second time in the conversation, Morgan had surprised her.

"I can hear that you're in a plane. I presume it's a mobile command and you're on your way out here," he said.

"Yes," she said flatly. "I think you're right Morgan. I think they didn't stray far from San Francisco."

"Shepard is with you?" he asked.

"Yes, and a Tach team," she said. "We're a couple hours behind you."

Morgan saw the location come through on his phone. It was about a hundred and twenty miles away. On the desert roads they would be there in 90 minutes if they pushed it.

And Morgan intended to push it.

Even if this location didn't pan out, his gut told him they were on the right track. And more importantly, Bloch's gut was telling her the same thing…and that was unprecedented.

But first, he'd have to get Dobrynin out of bed. He considered leaving the Russian behind, but the man was committed to the mission—though for very different reasons than Morgan himself.

And at any rate, Morgan knew that if he did find something out there he could use Dobrynin's help and his skills. He wouldn't let pride or their troubled history get in the way of this mission—the stakes were simply too high.

"I'm on my way," Morgan said, closing the connection.

# Chapter 32

"How many do you think there are?" Conley whispered.

Dani listened to the headset and said, "Four."

That was it then. They had almost completely cleared the hotel, at least the east tower. And because of the incident at the skyway and the others they had taken out, there was at least a fair chance that these were the only terrorists left in the hotel.

They were close, but four armed men were still four armed men. Any assault was risky. He and Dani would have surprise on their side and she was good, but Conley wasn't going to take any unnecessary chances.

He told her what he was thinking.

"We've already used that," she said.

"Yes, but they don't know that and their friends can't tell them," he said.

They crept down past the lobby to the basement level. Then Conley headed for the tunnel that connected the towers. There, they took up defensive positions.

Once again, Dani coached him on the words and the pronunciation. When she was satisfied, he switched on his own headset and shouted into the microphone in Filipino, "Major assault from the roof! Many soldiers. The east tower is lost. We are coming down. Head for the basement, look for a tunnel!"

Then, for emphasis, Conley fired off a few rounds from his AK-47 right next to the mike and turned off the headset.

Then they waited.

It took a few minutes before they heard anything. Clearly, the remaining MILF gunmen were being cautious. Their operation had not gone as planned. They had suffered heavy losses and had no contact with their people—other than the message they had just received from Conley.

They were scared and that was good.

Conley heard footsteps. Then he heard one of the men call out in Filipino. Dani and Peter kept silent.

One of the black-clad terrorists peeked around the corner. Satisfied, the man waved behind him and stepped into the narrow passageway. Another terrorist stepped out and the two men walked together, leading with their rifles.

That was it. Just the two of them. Conley understood that there were two more waiting in the lobby. If they got the all clear from these two, the others would follow.

Conley waited until one of them activated his headset and finished speaking. Then Conley fired as Dani did the same. He took out the man on the left while she took out the one on the right.

As they stepped over bodies, Conley could hear frantic voices coming through the headset. *Let them sweat,* he thought.

How many lives had this group ended today? How many people had died in terror because of this bunch?

By now they knew their operation had been a failure. They hadn't gotten to the high-level officials they had wanted. And they had lost the hotel. Let them stew on that as they waited for what came next.

Though the terrorists had lost, this had hardly been a victory for Conley and Dani. Too many people had died for that to be true. And there were troubling elements of this operation.

As they headed up to the lobby, Conley said to Dani, "Better if we take them alive. Tell them to throw down their weapons and wait with their hands behind their heads in the center of the lobby."

Dani spoke into the headset.

She repeated whatever she'd said. No reply.

"Then I guess we do this the hard way," he said as they stepped onto the lobby floor.

Two shots rang out.

They came from behind the registration desk and were followed by two thuds as the terrorists fell to the floor. It could have been a trick, yet Conley was sure that it was not. It was over. The terrorists had killed themselves.

That was unfortunate. They would have had some value alive.

He and Dani approached the desk carefully and confirmed what they both knew. It really was over.

They headed to the café and put down their guns but kept them nearby.

There was nothing they could do but wait. Conley considered trying to find an exit but it was safer to wait until the authorities made their way inside.

Fortunately, they didn't have to wait long.

There was a loud screech and the sound of scraping metal. Then the garbage trucks that blocked the front doors and windows were dragged away. A few minutes later, soldiers poured into the lobby.

Conley reached into his pocket, pulled out Dani's passport, and handed it to her. They stayed behind cover and Conley called out, "We need help. We're Americans."

There was a beat and then and a voice replied in English, "Come out slowly, with your hands on your head."

Conley and Dani complied. By the time they were in the open there were dozens of soldiers in the lobby.

The officer in charge approached them and said, "Any survivors in the area?"

"I don't think so. We came from upstairs. Anyone who is left up there is in the guest rooms."

"Are you hurt?" the officer asked.

Conley and Dani shook their heads.

"Come. You can put your hands down. You're safe now. There's a holding area across the street," he said.

* * * *

Bloch looked over Shepard's shoulder. The satellite image was clear. Next to the rectangular pit was what appeared to be a small bulldozer. It was the kind of machine that would have been used to dig a pit that size.

Shepard was still trying to track down the company that now owned the place and then determine when the earth mover had been purchased. However, it was more than likely that Morgan would be there before he found those answers.

Bloch checked her watch and confirmed her math. Then she studied the satellite image again. There was something very unnerving about the backhoe posed in front of a mound of dirt just outside the pit—as if were standing ready to fill in the hole.

Everyone else on the private jet was sleeping or sitting quietly. However, Shepard was frantically at work in the computer area.

Like the aircraft itself, the workstation was impressive. Both belonged to Scott Renard, the billionaire gentleman friend of Lily Randall. It was part of the small fleet of private jets owned by his tech company.

This jet now carried a five-person Tach team that included both Lily Randall and Alicia Schmitt—who both had taken a personal interest in Alex Morgan. The very spacious aircraft—really a medium-sized passenger jet—also carried all of their gear as well as Bloch and Jenny Morgan.

Mrs. Morgan had insisted on coming, and Bloch knew better than to argue for long with a Morgan. Jenny had contributed quite a bit so far and, given the fact that her daughter was likely in the lab, it was hard to justify keeping her off the jet.

Surprisingly, Jenny was asleep in one of the plush, leather seats of the plane. Once they had gotten under way, she had actually been able to relax—or at least let herself pass out from lack of sleep.

Shepard, on the other hand, was working furiously, analyzing satellite images as he did five other things at once—including hacking into various secure databases to find out about their current target site. He was also conferring with Lily Randall while on the phone with Scott Renard's people to sort out helicopter and ground transport for the Tach team.

Though Renard was out of the country, he had been a huge help. Besides transport and support, he had also given them the run of one of his corporate offices outside of San Francisco to use as a command center. Bloch could have arranged all of those things with the CIA and the American military, but the bureaucracy and its attendant inertia would have cost them valuable time. Because of Renard they would be on the ground in San Francisco in less than two hours—in a private jet that Bloch knew was traveling suspiciously close to Mach 1.

And Bloch was glad for all of it.

The image of the mini bulldozer poised to fill in a pit that could very well soon hold twenty bodies if Morgan was right stuck in her mind. The end of the world was still a concern and a very real one. But it was theoretical. There was something about that pit that was all too real.

Initially, she had been concerned that Morgan would get there first. She had even considered waiting to tell him about the fire pit. He was more than likely to go in without backup and without a plan. He had certainly done it often enough before.

Yet for the first time since she had known him, Bloch was glad for that reckless nature. Someone had to stop the terrorists before they hurt their hostages and got what they were after.

If anyone could do it, it was Morgan.

\* \* \* \*

Conley noted that it wasn't long before hotel guests started showing up at the holding area, the lobby of a movie theater half a block away. That was good. Within fifteen minutes there were a dozen survivors around them. Ten minutes later there were fifty.

Some were shaken, some were shattered, but they were alive.

Conley was glad that he'd been able to help stop the terrorists. Of course, he hadn't done it alone. He was only alive because of a part-time security guard named Amado—a retiree who had had taken a job at the hotel to get out of the house for a few hours a day and to make some extra money for himself and his wife. There was also a sharp-eyed sniper or two who had helped on the skybridge. And, of course, Dani had taken down quite a few terrorists while also saving Conley's life. He wanted to talk to her about a number of things but he didn't want to risk it until they were far away from the scene. He just enjoyed sitting close to her in silence. They were playing the part of a man and wife who had just been through an ordeal.

Conley's phone beeped and he saw that cell service had been restored. Excellent. It would be time to get moving soon. He still had to get Dani out of the country. It might be a bit trickier now after a major terror attack, but this was, after all, part of what he did.

No one had come to talk to them yet, which was good. The police and soldiers outside were still clearing the hotel and collecting survivors. It was already getting chaotic in the movie theater and the survivors had started to wander away from the lobby.

The harried police told them to stay close but otherwise ignored them. That was Conley and Dani's cue. They shuffled away slowly, ambling into one of the auditoriums.

They wandered down the aisle and then slipped outside an exit door. The afternoon light greeted them. There was no one on the street and they simply walked away.

A policeman rushed past them and told them to stay away from the hotel as it was a "Dangerous Area." That was fine. Conley and Dani put a few blocks between themselves and the hotel, and then they hit a street that wasn't exactly bustling but had enough people that two more weren't unusual.

Conley saw that cell service had been restored and called Bloch, giving her a very brief rundown of what had happened. She was glad he was alive but kept her voice brusque and businesslike. She told him she had a contingency plan and would get them out on an American military transport. Then Bloch was in a hurry to get off the phone, telling him that a car would pick them up soon and giving him the address of a local coffee shop.

They found the place. It was tiny, but empty, which wasn't surprising given the activity just a few blocks away. They sat down with their coffee as a television on the wall showed a report on the attack.

He saw that there had been a bloody battle when the terrorists took the west tower as well as the east, and then the screen flashed a photo of a man Conley recognized. It was a picture of Amado in his uniform, smiling broadly.

"It's Amado," Dani said, with a slight gasp.

Underneath the photo a text crawl read, "Hotel security guard helps defeat terrorists and is injured in the attack. Hailed as a hero."

*They don't know the half of it, Amado,* Conley thought. A black sedan pulled up to the coffee shop. The diplomatic plates matched the ones Bloch had given him.

Conley got up and took Dani's hand. It was time; their ride was here.

# Chapter 33

There was some commotion in the molecular bio section of the lab. Kattab was there with another terrorist at his side as they talked to Dr. Spellman.

The man was clearly at home in his scrubs and lab coat, his assistants all wearing the same outfit. It was like a uniform and the whole scene seemed relatively normal—if you could ignore the fact that Spellman and his team were working at gunpoint to build a terrible weapon for monsters.

And worst of all, it was clear to Alex that they were making good progress. Karen had said that it would take a few days to make any useful quantity of the virus, but how long would it take them to get their very first samples? Two days?

The rest of the lab was running smoothly as well. All of the students were now wearing lab coats like Dr. Spellman. The microbe area was completely set up and clean. All of the equipment had been tested and they were stockpiling growth media.

The harvesting and purification section of the lab also seemed ready to go. The centrifuges, which appeared to Alex like big top-loading washing machines, had been cleaned and tested. Racks of one-gallon storage containers were ready to receive their deadly cargo. And the large freezer on the wall was ready to store them.

Until what? A refrigerated truck came to came to pick them up and delivered death to the rest of the world?

Well, whatever happened today, that would not come to pass. By the end of the day, this lab would be shut down. With luck, it would be in ruins. Even if things went badly, the terrorists wouldn't get any finished virus out of it for a few days or weeks. By then, maybe her father and Zeta would be able to find it and shut it down for good.

And yet her only regret now was that Jason deserved better than this. He had followed her into this mess and now he was in the same danger as all of them. Alex could take a page from her father's book and throw herself at that danger, but it might not be enough to save him, or Karen, or the surviving members of Dr. Apocalypse's sad little cult.

A better agent might be able to save them all and take out every terrorist. Alex had no illusions of being that agent. She could only do her best and hope that it would be enough to make sure the world didn't suffer for her failure.

Some of the other students were heating up water for macaroni and cheese and instant noodles. Like the odd routines they had developed after a very short time here, it was strangely normal. After all, they were college students and this was their regular diet.

Alex couldn't decide if it was a sign that they were completely clueless about what was really going on here, or if they were simply doing what people did in extreme circumstances: carrying on as normally as possible. *Just living.*

She decided it was both of those things.

Karen and Jason sat down with her at the table with their cereal. They were the only three people who knew that, one way or another, today was the last day in the lab, and they didn't pretend otherwise.

Alex got right to it. "I'm ready when you tell me everything is in place. I know the guards' routine, such as it is. Give me a little warning and I'll be close enough to one of them to take him down when it begins. Is everything in place on your end?"

"Yes," Karen said. "Jason has collected everything I need and I've mixed the compounds. When you give the word, we will place them in the microwaves and pressure cookers. He and I have also made some alterations to the two centrifuges. They will fail, somewhat spectacularly."

"Define spectacular," Alex said.

"I've compromised the O-rings around the rotor, added some steel wool to the shaft to create extra friction. I've also overloaded each unit and set it to run at an *unsafe* speed. Finally, I disabled the safety cutoff switch. Once the unit is activated, it will be impossible to shut off without unplugging it. And there will be very little time between the time the unit starts shaking and the rotor fails. The result will be explosive."

That was good. Even if one of the guards had the presence of mind to go for the shutoff, it would take time to realize something was wrong with that and try to cut power. By then, hopefully, it would be too late.

"What about the timing for the other units," Alex asked.

"I can adjust the microwaves to go in about five minutes, the pressure cookers will be about twenty minutes. The centrifuges are the trickiest. As I said, it won't be long once they start to shake but they may have to run for twenty to thirty minutes for that to happen," Karen replied.

"Great work just the same. This is an improvised operation, the key is to set things in motion and then I'll move when I think we have achieved maximum chaos," Alex said.

"What are you going to do?" Jason asked.

"I can take one of the guards, I'm sure of it. Once I have a weapon we all have a chance," she said.

"Maybe we could all just wait and see how much damage our sabotage does?" Jason said, obvious concern on his face.

"Jason, look, I've trained for this," she said.

He gestured around them and said, "How does anyone ever train for this?"

"Alex is proficient in a number of—"

"I can do this," Alex said, interrupting. "But it will be easier if I know you both are safe, so when it starts, get down and stay down. People are going to die. Even if we succeed, these men will start shooting. Please don't give them any extra targets."

"Okay," Jason said.

Then Karen did something unexpected. The older woman reached out and took Alex's hand. Alex saw that Karen and Jason were scared. Of course, she was scared too and she had no doubt that it showed on her face.

Her father had taught her that fear came before and after a fight. During the fight itself, things like fear and anger melted away, replaced by logical thinking, specific movements, and next steps.

Well, that was all the more reason to start the fight as soon as possible.

The trio finished their cereal and threw out their bowls as soon as Kattab announced it was time to get back to work. As they headed to the lab, she felt Jason's hand on her shoulder.

She turned to him as he was leaning down. "Just in case," he said.

Closing the distance between them she met his kiss. It was short and sweet. Then they broke apart and headed out. Alex made sure she went past the pressure cookers. She made a show of examining them, turning on each one. That was it, the fight had begun. There was no going back now.

She saw Karen switch on the centrifuges.

How long now? A half hour? Less?

Jason helped her mix growth media for a few minutes as the rest of the lab settled into its routine. Minutes passed.

The time was getting closer, she could feel it. She kept a careful eye on the nearest terrorist, judging his alertness, looking at the way the gun was slung on his back.

Even if she took him down, it would take too long to untangle the rifle. She'd have to go for his pistol and do what she could with that. Once she'd taken him out along with any other immediate threats she could go back for his rifle.

The handgun was a Colt .45. She knew the gun well and could find the safety in the dark. That would help. The hip holster was also simple, with extra straps or ties that would hold it down. She could pull the weapon free in a single motion.

Alex rehearsed all of the necessary movements in her head. Her father was right, the fear was gone.

Alex watched as Jason carried a tray with four specially prepared beakers to the bank of microwaves. Each beaker had some steel wool sitting in a chemical stew that Karen had put together. It would be more flash than bang but it would draw a lot of attention when the microwaves blew out.

They had stacked a ready supply of extra scrubs and lab coats nearby. With luck they would catch fire and—"

"What are you doing?" someone called out. Then louder, "*What are you doing with that?*"

It was Avery. He was looking at Jason loading the microwaves. To his credit, Jason ignored him and loaded the last two microwaves, switching them on. Now all of the units were running.

"Stop! Don't do that. You're not supposed to do that!"

By now Avery had reached Jason, and grabbed him firmly.

"It's okay buddy. It's all okay," Jason said calmly.

Then Alex saw that the guard she had been scoping had taken an interest in the commotion.

"Jason," she said, feeling helpless.

He turned his head to her calmly, shot her a quick smile, and started pulling Avery away from the microwaves.

The guard yelled something to them in Chechen and Avery shouted, "He put something in the microwave. He's going to ruin *everything!*" Then Avery turned back to Jason and screamed, "We have to do this! Margaret died for this!"

At the end of his rope, Jason gave Avery a good, hard shove backward and Avery fell, landing hard on the floor. By now, the other guards had taken notice and Kattab was making his way from across the lab.

They had barely begun and things had fallen apart already. This wasn't supposed to happen. One or more of the devices were supposed to go off and then Alex was going to capitalize on the confusion to get a gun. At that point, she would be able to take the terrorists out. At any rate, they would either be dealing with her, or with the explosions Karen had arranged. Now, two of them were focused on Jason.

The guard was yelling at Jason in Chechen and pointing to the microwave, and Jason was responding with an explanation she could not hear.

This was going to a bad place and Alex had to put a stop to it before it did. She strode over to the two men as the gunman leaned down toward one of the microwaves.

Jason tugged on the Chechen's shoulder with his left hand while he made a fist with his right and brought it around in an arc. It was a solid punch and caught the man square in the mouth. Not bad for an amateur, Alex thought, though it would have been even more effective if Jason had put a little more shoulder into it.

Still, the terrorist went down.

Alex was close and desperately tried to calculate whether she could get to the man before he drew his gun. Two more steps and she'd be able to dive for it.

And then a single shot rang out.

Jason grabbed his chest and Alex saw red spreading beneath his lab coat and scrubs. Then he went down.

It was bad. Not exactly center chest, and the bullet had probably missed his heart, but it had certainly hit a lung. It might be survivable if it happened near a hospital, but out here…

All of a sudden, Alex found she couldn't walk and fell to her knees. Someone was screaming, it was a woman's voice.

Then Alex realized the voice was hers.

* * * *

They were close, Morgan saw, less than a mile away.

As they got even closer he saw a road that branched off to the left. That was the way to the building on the satellite image. That road followed a gradual incline to the structure that was maybe a hundred feet below them.

Perhaps a tenth of a mile down the road was a shack. He couldn't see anyone there but there was smoke wafting up from the back of the small building. Next to the shack was a gate that blocked the road down to the facility.

"Someone is there," Morgan said, pointing to the structure.

"Stop the car," Dobrynin said. The Russian sniffed the air. "This is them, the Chechens."

"How can you tell? You can smell them?"

"Djepelgesh," he said. "It's Chechen. They are cooking it."

That was it then. This was the place. That meant the building down below held the lab, and Alex.

But between them and the lab was a shack with one or more terrorists who Morgan assumed were armed. If they were guarding the only entrance to such an important operation, they would be *heavily* armed.

"We could wait. Bloch and her Tach team will be here in—"

Morgan cut him off with the wave of a hand and listened. Sound was coming from the building. He heard shouting and a single gunshot down below, then more shouting.

He was driving before he realized he had made his decision. "We'll approach slowly. For all they know we are just stopping for directions."

A man stepped out of the shack dressed in black. He had a rifle slung across his back but he wasn't wielding it yet. The man held out his hand in a universal *stop* gesture.

Morgan kept moving, but more slowly. They needed to use the road. Finding another road down would take too long. And if they climbed down the incline they would be too easy to pick off either from above or below.

"He wants you to stop," Dobrynin.

"And I don't recognize his authority," Morgan said, adding a little speed.

Now the guard was pointing his rifle at them and waving them off. Morgan put on more speed as he saw another man stumble out of the shack.

The first bullet hit the front of the vehicle and Morgan had a decision to make. He could blow past the gate easily enough but that would leave hostiles behind him. And there might be more men or weapons inside the shed. Morgan and Dobrynin didn't have time to stop the SUV, take cover behind it, and clear the guards. He needed a faster solution.

A bullet slammed through the windshield, and then another. Morgan leaned down, seeing that Dobrynin was doing the same. Then he turned the wheel, aiming for the small building.

Seconds later, they were almost on top of the shed and the two guards were firing steadily into the SUV. It wasn't a Zeta vehicle and was not hardened against gunfire. It was just a rental and Morgan was fairly certain that he wouldn't be getting his deposit back.

Before he barreled into the shack, he saw a third guard in the doorway who almost made it out before the vehicle slammed into the structure.

The impact didn't stop the SUV but re-directed it hard to the right. They ended up in a skid and while turned sideways, the passenger side facing the two remaining guards.

Morgan didn't waste any time, he pushed open his door and threw himself out, shouting for Dobrynin to follow him, as gunfire peppered the side of the vehicle. The Russian dove after him and seemed to be in one piece.

The SUV was decent cover, particularly behind the engine block, but Morgan didn't have time for an extended firefight.

He hit the ground with his Walther out. He noted that Dobrynin was on the ground with him. From under the car, he pointed his Walther at the legs of the two terrorists who were now standing in the open. Dobrynin followed suit and then both men fired into the lower legs of the Chechens.

There were shouts as more than one of their shots found its target. One of the men fell, then the other. Then Morgan and Dobrynin emptied their clips into the terrorists, who went still.

As soon as that registered, Morgan was on his feet and slipping a fresh clip into his Walther. The vehicle was totaled. They would have to get to the lab on foot.

"Wait, we'll need weapons," Dobrynin said, gesturing at the SUV.

"Then I'll meet you there," Morgan said, as he headed down the mining road at a sprint. He heard the Russian shout "*koshmar*" and then race after him.

# Chapter 34

Someone was shouting at her to get up.

Alex turned and saw that it was Kattab and he had his gun pointed at her head from a few feet away.

"Now!" he screamed.

Alex knew she had to do something but her legs wouldn't obey her commands.

"Wait," another voice said and then Karen was standing between them. "I need her. We need her. We can't lose any more technicians."

Then Karen spun and grabbed Alex by the upper arm. The woman was stronger that Alex would have given her credit for, and Alex found herself getting pulled upwards.

"Alex we need you. If you don't get up this is all over," she said.

It was already all over for Jason. She didn't have to look to know he was already dead.

"The mission," Karen shouted into her ear.

Yes, over for him but not for the rest of them. Alex shook her head clear and was on her feet when Kattab shouted, "What is that?"

She scanned the microwaves, which were running but not doing anything unusual. Then she saw Kattab was pointing at the centrifuges, which were shaking like overloaded washing machines.

"They must be malfunctioning," Karen said.

Kattab shouted at one of other guards, who grabbed a student and dragged him along. The Chechen and the student stood in front of one of the centrifuges.

"What is it?" Kattab yelled over the noise of the machines, which were now rocking back and forth.

Alex realized she recognized the guy in the lab coat. He was one of Spellman's grad students, Steven something-or-other.

"Turn it off!" Kattab shouted. Then he yelled something in Chechen and the guard next to Steve shoved him toward the machine on the right.

The grad student slapped at the cutoff switch but the machine simply bucked harder. Then it shuddered once and, suddenly, the spinning steel rotor—which was about the size of a rotor on a car's wheel—tore through the front of the machine and caught Steven square in the chest.

The guard in front of the other centrifuge watched uncomprehendingly and turned to Kattab just as the machine came apart and sent its own rotor flying out. This metal disc was ejected from higher on the unit and screamed toward the Chechen's head.

The rotor nearly missed the man, but clipped the side of his head. The terrorist crumbled face first onto the floor and Alex could see he was dead before he hit the ground.

Nevertheless, she leapt toward the body and made a show of checking for a pulse with her left hand while her right reached around for his hip holster and drew his Colt.

In a single smooth movement she brought the gun around and pointed it at the first black-clad figure she saw. It was the terrorist that Jason had punched. Alex was pleased to see that he was bleeding from his mouth. From her sitting position, she managed to put two rounds into the man's chest, and he went down.

Instinctively, she rolled away as bullets tore in her direction, striking the body of the fallen terrorist. The nearest lab table and cover was still too far away so Alex continued her roll and brought herself up to a kneeling position as she scanned for Kattab.

He was pointing his AK-47 at her and ready to fire while she was still bringing her own weapon around. It would be close, she thought, but she wouldn't make it.

And then two microwaves to Kattab's left exploded. The doors flew apart and flames shot out, catching the terrorist's left side, from his hip to his face. He screamed and dropped his weapon. Then he crumbled to his knees, which was the only thing that saved him from the burst of the last two microwaves.

Somehow Karen appeared next to the man. She was on the floor and was able to get one hand on the butt of the AK, managing to slide the weapon in Alex's direction.

However, as Alex grabbed for the gun, she saw Kattab bringing his pistol around to fire at Karen. Alex was barely able to aim her own Colt and get off a shot before he did. Her bullet found its target.

"Stay down and find cover!" Alex shouted to Karen as she grabbed the AK and slid behind a lab table. There was one more terrorist on the lab floor. And by now she was sure the two Chechens on break were there as well. She heard the terrorist shouting in his own language as she called out, "Everyone get down!"

Then she heard one of the men let loose a spray of automatic gunfire and turned to see he was firing at the ceiling, issuing a warning to the students as he tried to gain some semblance of control.

Just then there was a loud *boom* as one of the pressure cookers went off. A few seconds later, the second one exploded.

She dispensed with caution, leaping to her feet and into a firing position. Aiming and firing with one motion, she put four shots into the air. Without even looking around, she dipped to a crouch and scrambled away from her previous position, heading for the molecular biology area.

Students were screaming but the final two terrorists weren't making any noise, so she wouldn't be able to find them by sound. She'd have to look. A shot rang out, then another. Students screamed and it sounded like at least one of them had been hit.

More shots. More screams.

Alex couldn't wait any more. She peeked out from around the machine she was using for cover, and could see only one of the terrorists. He'd taken cover behind an incubator. She had made a point of working with all of the machines in the microbe area when Karen had ordered that everything in their section be thoroughly "cleaned."

The incubators resembled large refrigerators, and she knew that—like a refrigerator—its sides and door were not very solid, just two thin layers of sheet aluminum with a bit of insulation between them. And since they were empty there was nothing inside them to stop a bullet.

Switching the AK to full auto, Alex sprayed the front of the incubator. There was a brief scream from behind it, but she didn't hear his body fall. She'd hit him but possibly not fatally.

She didn't have trouble finding the last remaining uninjured Chechen; he was standing against one of the far walls, shuffling to one side to try to get to an exit. Unfortunately, Alex didn't have a clear shot because he had surrounded himself with hostages. There were five students between Alex and the terrorist.

The black-clad man kept one hand on the student in front of him, which left him one hand to manage his rifle and keep it pointed forward. Alex recognized the student; it was Avery.

That made Alex laugh as the gunman shouted at her in Chechen. Did he really think he was safe hiding behind *Avery?* Alex was prepared to shoot right through him but decided that there was too much of a risk of hitting one of the other students.

The terrorist continued to shout gibberish at her. She didn't understand the language but she understood his meaning. He wanted her to put down her gun or he would start shooting hostages.

Putting down the gun would never happen, but she couldn't use it either.

There was, however, one thing she could do. She held her AK tightly with one hand and sprinted for the terrorist, screaming the whole way. The students scattered, now more afraid of the charging, armed Alex than they were of the Chechen.

She was glad to see fear in the terrorist's eyes and his sudden realization that he couldn't aim with Avery in front of him. The man tossed his now useless hostage aside and as he did Alex threw herself into a slide, bringing up her rifle.

Somehow, she managed to keep her AK pointed in the right direction as she slid to a stop while his bullets whizzed above her. Then she took final aim and fired. Alex completed the whole movement smoothly, as if she had practiced it a hundred times, though she knew its success had more to do with luck and adrenaline.

Unfortunately, luck had only gotten her so far, and the AK clicked empty.

There was a look of shock as the terrorist realized he was still alive, and then he gave a feral grin as he realized her gun was empty. He swung his own rifle down to take aim.

Alex reached for her Colt. The odds were heavily against her but she made the effort anyway. Just as she did so she saw the odds get worse. The Chechen she had injured was rising up from behind one of the lab tables. Even if the one getting a bead on her missed, this one would be able to finish the job.

When the inevitable shot rang out she winced, automatically bracing herself for the bullet, but it never came. Instead, remarkably, the top of the Chechen's head exploded.

Alex turned her head to see her father racing toward her, his gun still out. Just behind him was an older man who Alex thought she recognized. The other also had his pistol out and fired several shots in the direction of the last terrorist.

And then the gunfire stopped and Alex tried to clear her head. Somehow, her father had appeared out of nowhere and made a head shot while at a full run, from a hundred yards away.

\* \* \* \*

Morgan skidded to a stop and brought down his Walther. Alex was still lying on her back and twisting her head to look up at him.

"Are you hit?"

"Dad," she replied, confused.

"I'm here. Are you hurt?" He wanted to scoop her up but was afraid of hurting her further if she'd been shot. "Are you hit?" he repeated.

Alex spun around to her knees. "No."

And then he was on his knees and hugging her.

"You're really okay?" he asked. After where she had been for the last week it was almost too much to hope for.

"Yes," she said, grabbing him tightly.

"You did it Sweetie, you saved all these people," he said.

"No, not all of them," and then she buried her head in his shoulder and let out a single sob.

"You did great," he said as he brought them both up to a standing position. She turned to Dobrynin and said, "Are you..."

"He's with me," Morgan said. He turned to Dobrynin and said, "Scan for any hostiles."

The Russian took off.

"Are there any more?" he asked, pulling away to look her over. She was wearing a lab coat over her street clothes, but she really appeared to be okay.

"I don't think so. I think they are all dead. There were six of them and you got the last one," she said, wiping her eyes.

"Six?" he asked, scanning the room.

He counted five black-clad bodies.

Alex was clearly worried and scanned the lab herself. She studied a charred section of the warehouse and said, "Kattab."

Then she was racing over there, where there was a bloody smear on the floor but no body.

Alex followed the trail to a door in the far wall, a door that was just starting to close. Alex and Morgan got there before it did and burst inside.

A burned and battered man in black was hunched over a metal suitcase that lay on the ground.

"Kattab!" Alex called out as the man fell away from the suitcase, which she saw contained some sort of console.

"You'll never get out in time." He said, coughing up blood. "Now you will all die."

"You first," Alex said, drawing and firing her pistol in a single, smooth motion.

# Chapter 35

Morgan saw the cables leading out of the suitcase and knew what it meant.

"They've wired the lab," Alex said. It wasn't a question.

Morgan raced to the console.

"Can you disarm it?" she asked.

He scanned it. He might be able to, but not in the fifty-two seconds the digital display said they had left. Still, it was worth a try. They certainly didn't have any better options. As he examined the timer he tapped his ear comm.

"Bloch. The threat is neutralized but do not enter. The lab is wired. Repeat, do not enter." He scanned the room around him and saw leftover C-4. "Plastic explosives."

Forty seconds.

"Get out of there, Cobra!" Bloch shouted.

"No time. I'll try to disarm it," he said. But he didn't know where to begin. The simplest method would be to just start pulling on wires. Unfortunately, that would almost certainly set off the C-4.

Shepard's voice screamed into his earpiece. "Send me a picture. I'll talk you through it," he shouted.

Twenty-four seconds.

"There's no time. I'm sorry Shep," Morgan said.

He heard a guttural shout from Shepard and then the line went dead.

Nineteen seconds.

"Let's run for it Dad," Alex said, her eyes bright.

Morgan grinned. That was his girl.

At least they would both be on their feet. Morgan took his daughter's hand and they both ran out the door and onto the lab floor.

"Everyone get out," he bellowed.

By his calculations, they would be about halfway to the exit when the place blew. However when he guessed there was just under ten seconds left, there was great rumble and a crash.

*It's early,* Morgan thought.

But it wasn't the bomb. Something crashed through the far wall of the lab and then the lights went out.

*About now,* Morgan thought, when his internal clock told him that it was time.

Surprisingly, there wasn't a flash or a boom. Just darkness.

But not complete darkness. Emergency lights came on around the lab and there was a hole in the wall that let some light through the space where a Hummer had crashed through.

Shepard leapt out of the vehicle and scanned the floor, desperately calling for Karen O'Neal. She raced across the lab and then she was in his arms.

Remarkably, they were all still here. Whatever Shepard had done had worked.

The Tach team came in flashlights out. He heard Spartan telling everyone they were safe and to head for the front exit. Then Morgan saw his own personal angel, Jenny, walk straight for them, with Diana Bloch trailing behind her.

"Mom?" Alex asked. If possible, she seemed even more confused than when she first saw Morgan.

"We've been looking for you," Morgan said. "We've all been looking for you."

And then Alex was rushing for her mother, who pulled her into an embrace. Morgan was there a moment later, and then it was the three of them.

There were people moving around them, plenty of noise and activity, but it faded and for the next few minutes, for Morgan it seemed like they were the only three people in the world.

\* \* \* \*

Morgan was aware of people still moving around him. He could see Schmitt nearby, Spartan corralling the civilians, and Lily Randall keeping a close eye on Alex.

As soon as he could, he ushered Alex and Jenny outside, and after a short period of time Spartan brought the civilians out. They had identified a large amount of C-4 set all around the perimeter of the building. Though

Shepard had somehow foiled the immediate threat from this fail-safe system, there was still a tremendous amount of explosives in the building.

Spartan and the others kept everyone moving to put some distance between them and the lab. Four of the students were on stretchers, two of them alive and two in body bags.

Morgan noted that Dr. Apocalypse had survived. He had been tending one of the machines in the lab and had to be dragged away from it by two agents.

Soon additional support personnel showed up, and Morgan saw a couple of suits that told him the first Feds had arrived.

Bloch approached the Morgans who had stayed close to Shepard and Karen. "Everyone who was in the lab has been told to stay until they have been cleared by the CDC," she said.

O'Neal stepped forward. "But there is no danger of infection. No live virus was completed. There is no biological threat," she said.

"I understand but the CDC is insisting on a quarantine period," Bloch said.

Morgan took one look at his wife and daughter and said, "You can't be serious."

"I'm very serious, which is why I need all of you to get on that helicopter right now," Bloch said, pointing to a Renard copter that was sitting nearby.

The Morgans, Shepard, and O'Neal were flying over the desert. Morgan knew that their early departure would cause Diana Bloch no end of hassle and he appreciated the gesture, though, in reality, he understood that she'd done it more for Jenny and Alex than for him. Whatever the reason, he was glad to have his family together and eager to get them home.

The helicopter took them to a small, local airport where a Renard company private jet was fueled and waiting for them. Morgan noticed that his ear comm was out, and for that matter, so was his phone. He turned and spoke to Shepard for the first time since he'd seen the younger man come crashing through the side of the lab. "Shep, how did you do it?" he asked.

Shepard shrugged. "I pulled the prototype EMP weapon off the fighter you and Cougar recovered. We had it in the lab anyway and I thought it might come in handy.

"It will be a nice toy to have going forward," Morgan said.

"Of course, now that we both have it we'll all be working on countermeasures and hardening our circuitry, but it did the job today," Shepard said.

"True, but you did cut it pretty close, Shep."

To that Shepard smiled. It was the first one he'd seen on the younger man's face since the crisis started. "Well Morgan, you're not the only one who likes to make an entrance."

Morgan was finally able to relax. He saw Jenny and Alex huddled together, and Jenny was muttering to their daughter. Even Morgan could see that something had happened to Alex in the lab, something that wasn't just the operation, something that wasn't just the mission. She didn't have the shell-shocked look of someone who had been through something extreme. This was the look of grief.

She'd lost something, or more likely some*one,* in the desert.

The jet made suspiciously good time to Logan airport and then there was a car to take them back to their house.

Jenny prepared Alex's room while Alex washed off the last few days. She was tough, he knew that—she was, after all, a Morgan—but this would take some time.

He'd suffered a few personal losses on missions. They were harder than the professional setbacks or the physical ones and took longer to heal. Jenny was already helping and they would do what they could when Alex was ready to talk.

\* \* \* \*

Two days later, Peter Conley came in through the kitchen door while Morgan was having breakfast.

"I hear you've been busy," Conley said.

"You too," Morgan said. "Your vacation in Manila was all over the news. Remind me to explain to you the meaning of 'undercover.'"

"Strangely, your trip to the desert was not reported anywhere," Conley said.

"Like I said, undercover," Morgan said, smiling.

Somehow, the Feds had kept the truth under wraps. The official story of the kidnapping of the Berkeley students and their professor was that they had been taken by Chechen terrorists, whisked away to a secondary location, and held hostage.

According to the official report, they were rescued by a joint U.S.-Russian task force. Three of the students were killed and only two injured.

Some of that story was even true.

Morgan marveled that they could keep a secret that big. No doubt, the surviving students and their families had been sat down by men in suits and coached.

Amazingly, no one had talked about the virus yet.

Eventually someone would, of course, but by then they would be white noise on the conspiracy theory circuit.

The important thing was that the threat was neutralized and Bloch had assured them that all of the data on the Russian program had been completely destroyed.

But the truth was that three young people were dead. One of them had died during the battle with the terrorists. Morgan knew now that Alex had gotten close to that student, a boy who had died trying to help. The first two had died during the first forty-eight of the kidnapping, when the terrorists had shot two students for not following orders, or not following them fast enough.

Because of their own bloodthirsty nature and because they couldn't be bothered to bury the young people, the Chechens had used their biohazard fire pit to dispose of the first two bodies. If the terrorists had not done that, Morgan knew that Zeta might never have found the lab, or found it in time.

And then Morgan and Jenny would have likely lost Alex forever.

On the other hand, Alex and Karen had pretty thoroughly destroyed the terrorists' operation by the time Zeta arrived. Morgan had been able stop the terrorist who was trying to kill Alex but ultimately it had been Shepard who had saved every single person in the lab from death by C-4.

Conley disappeared into the den where he sat with Alex for about a half hour. When he emerged he was somber and said, "Bloch is waiting for us."

It was time for both of them to debrief the boss. Morgan had insisted that Alex's own debriefing would wait a few more days.

Karen had already provided most of the detail that Bloch had needed for her own report to Mr. Smith and rest of the Aegis Initiative, which supervised Zeta Division.

However, there were a number of questions that remained and Morgan would do his best to answer them.

"Morgan, I stopped by the shop on the way over here. Did you know you that a Russian has taken over your business? When I was there he was shouting into your office phone."

"Yeah, that's Dobrynin."

"I remember him."

"He was the one who brought us the original intelligence about the Soviet virus. Bloch didn't know what to do with him, so she made him my responsibility," Morgan said. "I was the one who brought him into Zeta headquarters. So I'll be babysitting for a while. On the plus side, he's very good at negotiating with suppliers."

"Right," Conley said.

"It's not safe for him to go back to Russia." Morgan added.

"Yes, I understand he has permanently pissed off the Russian brass," Conley replied. "Apparently failure to get along with your superiors is a terrible handicap."

Morgan ignored the comment. "Have you eaten?" he asked.

"No, but Bloch's waiting."

"Jenny always makes extra when she thinks you'll be stopping by."

"She made her eggs?"

"And hash browns," Morgan added.

Conley poured himself a cup of coffee, filled a plate, and sat at the table with Morgan.

# Epilogue

Two weeks later, Spartan showed up at Morgan's door. She was in civilian clothes and Morgan realized that it was the first time he'd seen her not wearing some sort of tactical gear or protective clothing.

"Bloch sent me to fetch you for the meeting," Spartan said.

"She doesn't think I can get there myself?" Morgan asked.

Spartan just stared at him, unblinking.

"Jenny, I'm going out," he called behind him.

He knew they would be early for the nine o'clock briefing but he decided not to argue with Spartan.

When they arrived at Zeta, he saw why she had brought him early. An attractive Asian woman in her early or mid-thirties was waiting in the lobby with Conley.

She extended her hand. "Hello, I'm Danhong Guo."

Morgan shook her hand and said, "I have heard quite a bit about you."

"And I you," she said, with only the smallest trace of an accent.

Morgan shot Conley a look. Peter seemed stiff. Not nervous exactly, but not quite himself. And he was watching Morgan and the woman carefully.

"You can call me Dani—Peter does," she said.

There was something going on here, Morgan realized. Conley mentioned that he had briefly gotten involved with the Chinese agent he'd met in Manila. But this was something else, or at least something he had never seen on Peter's face before.

"Are you finished with your debriefing?" he asked.

"Yes," she said.

"And she's been recruited. The CIA and State department were finished with her, and Bloch offered her a place at Zeta," Conley offered.

That was not a surprise. From what Morgan understood she was a highly capable agent and her background in the Chinese finance ministry made her invaluable. The big surprise was that State and the CIA had let her go without trying to recruit her themselves.

Well, he knew that Bloch could be very persuasive and Zeta had just saved the world from a deadly virus.

"We had better get inside," Conley said, gesturing to the interior door in a way that was a bit more formal that usual.

When they reached the war room, O'Neal, Randall, and Shepard were already there. Morgan took a seat next to Conley and Dani and noticed that the room was completely quiet.

Then Bloch came in and sat down at the head of the table. She was unusually reserved. If he didn't know better, Morgan would almost think she was nervous.

They sat in silence for nearly five minutes. Then Mr. Smith entered.

He was in his indeterminate sixties with thick but neatly combed white hair. He was athletic and slim, dressed in a very expensive business suit.

"Diana," he said to Bloch. Then Smith turned his attention to the table.

"I want to thank you all for your recent work. Manila was bad but it could have been a disaster. And the Berkeley situation could have been even worse," Smith said.

"That is an understatement," Morgan said.

"True. We had to invent a new threat level designation for it. But thanks to Zeta those situations were mitigated. However, we have seen a disturbing trend. Conley and Ms. Guo's reports and a further analysis of Manila showed cooperation between two terrorist groups that have never even communicated before. And the Chechen operation depended on knowledge of the original Soviet program that the Chechens should not have had. Moreover, the operation was several orders of magnitude more sophisticated than anything they have done before."

"Terrorists are getting smarter, but we have new tools like O'Neal's threat assessment software," Bloch said.

"Valuable indeed, and it may have literally saved the world, but our analysis shows that something else may be going on," Smith said. He paused for effect and then said, "Aegis suspects that these groups are receiving assistance—or more likely direction—from an outside organization."

"What?" Morgan said. "Who could possibly benefit from that sort of manipulation? For crying out loud, if the virus got out…"

"It would have killed every man, woman, and child on Earth," Smith said. "I can't tell you why, but I'm telling you what is happening. We've also seen evidence of similar activity in other terrorist groups and rogue states."

Morgan spoke next. "That would require an organization with the resources and reach of...Zeta."

"Precisely, but in a group committed to terror, destabilization of alliances, war, and chaos. As for the who and the why, I leave that for you to determine. Consider that your new assignment."

Mr. Smith gestured for Bloch to remain seated. "I will see myself out. You all have some work to do."

# War of Shadows

Don't miss the next exciting Dan Morgan thriller by Leo J. Maloney

Coming soon from Lyrical Underground, an imprint of Kensington Publishing Corp.

Keep reading to enjoy a sample excerpt…

# Chapter One

Dan Morgan's house exploded.

It was so sudden and devastating that Morgan's mind instantly reacted. The husband, father, and classic car dealer part of him went into shock. But the experienced, knowledgeable, veteran operative of the C.I.A. and now the clandestine organization Zeta went into overdrive.

He had just turned the corner at the end of the Andover, Massachusetts street where he lived, feeling the comforting purr of the green 1968 Mustang GT his team had presented him with during their last mission. Ironically, he had reluctantly just admitted to himself that he was the happiest he'd ever been…that is, since his wedding day and the day his daughter Alexandria had been born.

For once, everything appeared to be going great, both professionally and personally. Together with his team, and even his family, they had averted a biological apocalypse. The organization he worked for had never been so respected within the intelligence community, his superiors had come to fully appreciate his abilities, and even the skeletons in his closet had been cleared by his coming clean to his family about his previous double life. And now that the extremely capable young lady who was once his baby girl had moved out, he and his wife Jenny were even talking about having another child. Maybe adopting one from Asia or Africa.

The father and husband in him remembered that he couldn't wait to get home to her, the love of his life, when the unthinkable had happened. But the seasoned secret agent, to his growing rage, recognized the detonation.

It was what the experts called a "toothpick explosion"—where fuel and oxygen mix perfectly to render a house into a tearing, shattering, ripping, belching mass of glass, wood, concrete, brick, and metal shards in two blinks of an eye. The husband and father, teetering in shock, stomped on the brake, while the professional military and espionage operative dove to the seat, knowing what came next.

As the walls and windows of his once comfortable, happy home erupted in a million swipes of death's scythe, more oxygen rushed in to reignite the explosion's source. Sure enough, less than a second later, a *whomp* that was both a sound and pressure filled his ears, light blinded his eyes, and a fireball engulfed, then spewed, the house-shaped debris like a horde of maddened wasps.

In the milliseconds that took, Dan Morgan's eyes snapped back open. The husband and father inside him prayed that it might've been a gas leak accident. The intelligence operative inside him snarled, *bullshit*.

Both personas tromped on the accelerator, sending the Mustang screeching down the street, over the curb, across the lawn, and into the flaming hole where his front door had been.

"Jenny!" he bellowed, certain his voice carried over the detonation's dying roar. He had just been talking to her. With cellphones, she could've been anywhere, but he felt certain she had been talking from home. Even before the car stopped, half on the ruined porch, half in the burning maw that had been his front door, he was vaulting out of the car. "Jenny!"

The heat hit him like an angry monster's slap. He felt his eyebrows singe, but he didn't care. He charged through the conflagration, toward the stairs and the master bedroom. He opened his mouth to call out again, but the heat took that as an invitation and shoved itself down his throat like a hammering fist.

That stopped him. He stood, staring, at the wreckage of what had once been his beloved home. He couldn't recognize it. It looked like someone had shredded his life and sprinkled it onto a sizzling volcano crater.

Dan Morgan had witnessed many an explosion, seen many a dismembered corpse, and smelled many a barbequed victim of fire-bombing. You couldn't live the life he had lived in the military, the C.I.A., and now the Zeta organization, without having had such memories permanently branded in your brain.

But this wasn't some godforsaken hellhole he was infiltrating. This was his home, and if he stayed here he'd join whoever had been caught there when it happened.

"Jenny," he managed in a combination of a croak and a gasp as carbon monoxide stuffed his nostrils. He suddenly felt his flesh begin to crawl—not from fear, but from being baked. A combination of anger and remorse drove his spasming muscles.

*Don't be an idiot*, he heard himself bark inside his own head. *Hope is not your friend.*

Dan Morgan had gotten angry before. Too many times. But he could honestly admit that this was the first time he had gone blind with helpless rage.

He staggered blindly until he hit the car with his side. He looked around wildly as his fingers scrabbled for the door handle. He saw that his back porch door window was melting. The living room fireplace was a mound of flame. He heard his adjoining garage workshop collapsing as if Thor himself had just sledgehammered it.

The sweat and tears that managed to escape his eyes evaporated in less than a second as he fell back behind the driver's wheel, jammed it into reverse, and tromped on the accelerator. The now battered and bent classic car tore back onto the lawn as if yanked by a steel cable. He only went back far enough so the gas tank wouldn't explode and his clothes wouldn't immolate before jamming on the brakes again.

As horrifying as the last minute had been, the next few were even more surreal. Reeling from shock and exposure, he saw his horrified neighbors all around him like a small squad of concerned ghosts, as burning shreds of what had once been his sanctuary rained down around them like flaming confetti.

He sat there, staring down the shock that threatened to paralyze him. *Oh no*, he found himself thinking. *Not now. Don't have time for you now.* Somehow his agent's systematic brain recognized each on-looker...save one. Dan all but vaulted out of the car as his neighbors neared.

There was a small, shadowy figure near the bushes on the other side of the house, a figure hidden from him by the night's darkness, the flames' distorting heat waves, and some sort of black outfit, complete with visored helmet. Dan took a step toward it, a quiet prayer of "Alex" escaping his lips.

But as soon as he said it, he knew it wasn't his daughter. As he was about to take another step, he felt the hands and bodies of his neighbors close in on him. The shadowy figure disappeared behind the remains of the burning house.

Dan heard nothing the concerned citizens said, and felt nearly nothing they did to comfort and check him. Above their anxious, alarmed din, he heard a louder, commanding voice. It was his.

"Call 9-1-1," it demanded. "Now! Use your hoses to keep the fire from your roofs and walls. Steve...Steve Richards!" He had called his most trusted neighbor.

"Here, Dan," he heard the man say. "I have your dog, Neika. She staggered over seconds before it happened. I think she's drugged or something."

Dan's rage was about to engulf him again when he spotted an armored, tinted-glass SUV speeding by at the mouth of the street. He knew every vehicle owned by everyone for a mile around him. This was not one of them. And the dead giveaway was that its license plates were obscured.

"Take care of her, Steve," he seethed, already hurling himself back into his car. "See…see if they can find…"

But his wife and daughter's name was blotted out by the roar of his Mustang's engine as he reversed back across the already deeply shredded lawn. The neighbors scattered, mouths agape, as the GT squealed back onto the asphalt, did a smoking tire turn, and shot down the street as if fired from a cannon.

It was late, so the suburban streets were fairly clear, which made the sighting of the unknown vehicle easier. His catching the thing, however, was a different matter. Even from a distance, there was no mistaking it—especially from the mind of an agent whose cover was that of a classic car dealer. It was a black Grand Cherokee Trackhawk—all seven hundred and seven horsepower of it. From the shark-eye glint of its exterior and windshields, it was most likely bullet-proofed as well.

He narrowed his eyes and leaned forward. As if of its own accord, his left arm rolled down the window, letting the night air help wake him up. It also let in the sound of sirens approaching from the opposite direction. The father and husband part of him wished he could have stayed to help put out the fire and search the wreckage. The agent in him wanted to drive his Mustang down the Trackhawk's throat.

*What the hell had happened*, he thought, *and more importantly, why the hell had it happened?* His still addled mind tried to rifle through his personal list of enemies, then narrow it down to those who be so sadistic to literally bring it home to him, but he soon decided that was a waste of time. Both lists would be one and the same, and too numerous to whittle down. There was a far more pressing issue to attend to.

He found his smartphone in his right hand, not completely remembering that he had grabbed it. In the rear view mirror, he saw fire trucks pulling onto his street and the flickering shadows of his demolished home. When he looked back, his eyes searched the dashboard, remembering how his family had all but begged him to have voice-activated, hands-free communication in his car, but no, he had to be the classic car purist…

*His family. Had they been home when it happened?* Blinking furiously, Morgan's thumb stabbed the digital buttons, calling his wife's number again and again.

No answer. He remembered Lincoln Shepard, Zeta's resident communication whiz, telling him that no answer was worse than going to message. Going to message meant the phone still existed. No answer could mean the phone was destroyed...

The Mustang jumped, then shuddered, as the cars went from Route 42 to I-93. It took all the GT's five-liter V8 engine and nearly five hundred horsepower to keep up with the Trackhawk's teeth-shaking roar, even on the sparsely trafficked highway. Dan watched the speedometer rise—a hundred miles an hour, a hundred and ten, a hundred and twenty...

The Trackhawk seemed to wiggle its rear at him, doggedly staying a steady four car-lengths ahead. They stayed that way, mostly hugging the left lane, except for occasionally weaving around a speed limit idiot so closely that the state police would need a hair to measure how near they'd gotten to the slow-pokes.

A hundred and thirty...a hundred and forty...

*Maybe I'll luck out*, Dan thought. *Maybe there'll be a speed trap or radar surveillance to ensnare us both.* No such luck anywhere from Wilmington to Medford. *Maybe I should call the highway patrol myself,* Dan considered. But, although the smartphone was still in his hand, he had more important calls to make.

He called his daughter Alex, twice. That went to message. He called Shepard. That went to message. He called Cougar—his best friend and partner Peter Conley. That went to message. He called Lily Randall, he called Karen O'Neal, he even called the numbers he had for his boss Diana Bloch—something he almost never did. All went to message.

A hundred and fifty...a hundred and sixty...The speedometer trembled at the little red pin where the numbers ended. The Trackhawk was still, stubbornly, deridingly, four car lengths ahead.

"Idiot," Dan seethed, shoving the phone down on the seat beside him. Why bother with the phone when he always had the Zeta comm-link in his ear. It was so comfortable and ubiquitous that he had forgotten it in the literal heat of the moment. He pressed his right ear canal to instigate the connection. The resulting shriek deep in his head all but sent the car into the median.

He managed to regain control of the car in time to avoid a wreck, as well as wrench the tiny hearing aid from his auditory canal. It flew, like a dying bee, into the passenger seat's well, bouncing on the floor mat beneath the glove compartment.

*What the hell?* Dan returned his full attention to catching up to the Trackhawk, only to find that despite the Mustang's slowing and wavering, the SUV was still almost exactly four car lengths ahead. *You damn bastard.*

Morgan saw they were coming into Somerville. Then it would be Cambridge, and just beyond that, Boston. Neither of them could go a hundred and sixty there…not without committing vehicular homicide or suicide. But Dan could guess. Somehow, whoever was driving that SUV would stay four car lengths ahead. Whoever it was, they were that good— so good they could destroy his home, so good they could kill…kill his…

The father and husband inside him couldn't even bring himself to say it, to even think it. But the seasoned operative could.

*…they could have killed my wife…*

The Trackhawk took Dan by surprise by all but leaping off the highway onto an all-too-familiar exit ramp. The surprise only grew when the SUV started speeding down back streets in a route Dan knew very well.

His eyes widened as he realized the Trackhawk was moving as if the driver were a Zeta commuter. They were heading to the isolated parking garage that served as cover for the organization's underground headquarters.

Dan tried to catch up, but the '68 Mustang, as repaired and reconditioned as it was, just could not keep up…not after all the damage it had suffered at the house.

His fingers stabbed his phone's digital buttons as his foot tromped on the accelerator. He practically slammed the phone to his ear as his other hand grew white tight on the steering wheel. He was expecting Zeta's answering message so he could press a certain combination of numbers to get through, but that didn't happen.

The phone rang once…twice…a third time as both vehicles got closer and closer to the corporate complex that secretly housed Zeta headquarters. The closer they got, and the more times the phone rang, the more tense Dan became.

"Come on, come on, pick up, pick up!" he found himself seething, his words drowning out the ringtone. He took his eyes off the tail of the Trackhawk for a second to see if the phone was still connected.

In that second, he felt and heard the Trackhawk suddenly and sharply turn. When he looked up, its taunting tail was disappearing down an alleyway, leaving him a view of the entire parking garage that filled his whole windshield.

He heard a click on the other end of the phone.

"This is AZ27F," he snapped. "Code…"

He never got to finish his priority emergency message. The parking garage erupted like a volcano—a multi-tiered, billowing mushroom of flame engulfing the structure from its bowels to its crown.

The phone went dead.

# Acknowledgments

I want to give special thanks to my wife Lynn for all her help, patience, and encouragement over the years. I would not have been able to become a writer without her at my side.

I know many authors who have excellent editors, but I hit the jackpot when Michaela Hamilton became my editor. She is kind, sweet, and very generous with her time. I knew she was special the first time we met, and she has proven me right over the last five years. Based on her vast experience she has provided me with guidance that has contributed to my success. She has become very special to me and will always have a place in my heart.

I want to thank all the members of my very talented Kensington family and my literary agent Doug Grad, who all work so hard to make my books successful. I also want to recognize the excellent work by Mayur Gudka, who is my webmaster and social media consultant.

I am very privileged to have such great writing partners in Kevin Ryan, Steven Hartov, and Richard Meyers.

# About the Author

*Photo by Kippy Goldfarb, Carolle Photography*

**Leo J. Maloney** is the author of the acclaimed Dan Morgan thriller series, which includes *Termination Orders, Silent Assassin, Black Skies, Twelve Hours, Arch Enemy, For Duty and Honor, Rogue Commander,* and *Dark Territory.* He was born in Massachusetts, where he spent his childhood, and graduated from Northeastern University. He spent over thirty years in black ops, accepting highly secretive missions that would put him in the most dangerous hot spots in the world. Since leaving that career, he has had the opportunity to try his hand at acting in independent films and television commercials. He has seven movies to his credit, both as an actor and behind the camera as a producer, technical advisor, and assistant director. He is also an avid collector of classic and muscle cars. He lives in the Boston area and in Venice, Florida.

Visit him at www.leojmaloney.com or on Facebook or Twitter.

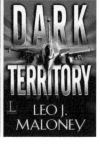

CPSIA information can be obtained
at www.ICGtesting.com
Printed in the USA
LVHW020557261218
601646LV00002BA/202/P

9 781516 103324